ALSO BY TATE JAMES

MADISON KATE
Hate
Liar
Fake
Kate

HADES
7th Circle
Anarchy
Club 22
Timber

ANARCHY

TATE JAMES

Bloom *books*

Published by Bloom Books, an imprint of Sourcebooks
P.O. Box 4410, Naperville, Illinois 60567-4410
(630) 961-3900
sourcebooks.com

Originally self-published in 2021 by Tate James

Cataloging-in-Publication data is on file with the Library of Congress

Printed and bound in the United States of America.
LSC 10 9 8 7 6 5 4 3 2 1

*To the kid in primary school who threw a moldy lemon
at me and laughed at my imaginary friends.
Look who's laughing now, asshole! Me and my
imaginary friends are making lemonade.
De-fucking-licious.*

CHAPTER 1
LUCAS

Blood fell onto the floor at my feet, a soft *splat* with each heavy drop rolling from my face. I hung loose in my chains, long since having given up wasting my energy trying to get free. The manacles around my wrists were metal, and for all my gymnastic skill, I was no Houdini.

At this stage of the game, my best and only option was to endure—grit my teeth, suffer through the pain, and maintain my bone-deep belief that it was only a matter of time before I was found. After all, I'd put my body through plenty of pain while training for a shot at the Olympics. I could handle this…right?

It was only a matter of time. She was too smart for this fucker. Too strong, too stubborn, too ruthless. He wouldn't be able to keep me here for much longer, and he knew it.

But that was part of the problem. He *knew* his time was limited, so he wasn't fucking around with long-winded villain soliloquies.

More's the pity. I badly could have done with a break, even if it meant listening to the complete bullshit of a raving madman. Years of dance and gymnastics had given me a small advantage over my pain, but nothing could have prepared me for this *literal torture*.

"You have no idea who you're messing with," I told my captor with a groan of agony as I tried to lift my head. I'd taken several hard blows, and who knew how long the split in my forehead had been bleeding. Everything hurt. Every damn inch of me. But I desperately pushed the pain aside in an attempt to keep my wits. I couldn't lose myself to fear and desperation, because that was undoubtedly what he wanted. He wanted to break me.

The hooded man in the corner of the room, his back to me as he heated a tool with a blowtorch, just gave a low, cruel chuckle. "What are you planning to do, stripper boy? Seduce me? Seems like that's your only talent."

I coughed a genuine laugh that hurt my bruised chest. "Not me, moron. *Hades*. She's gonna come for you. You're a fucking dead man."

He turned back to face me, shrugging his hood back to reveal a scarred face, partly covered with a leather eye patch, and a deranged smile. "You have no idea how right you are, pretty boy."

The metal brand in his hand glowed a hot orange, and he placed the blowtorch down on the counter. Apparently, it was hot enough to do the damage he was planning.

This was going to hurt *so much*. Tremors already shook my body as I eyed his weapon and swallowed heavily.

"Whatever you want to know, I'll never tell you." I forced the words from behind gritted teeth, the bravado weak even to my ears. It was a pointless statement. The asshole who'd initially taken me from Hayden's apartment—one of the security guards from 7th Circle for whom I'd stupidly opened the door—hadn't been even slightly interested in information. Just violence.

Up close, I found eye-patch dude roughly the same height as me, but a whole lot broader in the shoulders, where I was slim and toned. But that gave me no insight about what the hell was going on. Who the fuck *was* he? Who was he to Hayden?

He barked a slightly unhinged laugh. "You don't know anything useful anyway. No, pretty boy. I don't want you to tell me anything… *You're* the message to *her*. My Darling." With that, he pressed the brand tight against my chest, searing the flesh over my heart with blinding pain.

The scream that tore from my throat echoed through the small room, and I jerked against my bonds, frantically trying to pull away from the agony. But my torturer gave zero fucks, totally ignoring my cries. His one good eye remained impassive as he branded me.

It probably only took a second, but it felt like an eternity before he pulled the brand away and inspected his handiwork with a critical tilt to his mouth.

"You shouldn't have moved," he told me with an annoyed cluck of his tongue. "Now the lines won't be clean." He narrowed that one eye at his brand, then gave a sigh. "It'll have to do."

I was incapable of any snappy replies. I was incapable of anything but hanging from my bonds and groaning as the whole room swam. Cold sweat dripped down my bare back, and I had a sickening feeling I was about to pass out.

My tormentor's watch beeped an alarm, and he grunted an irritated sound. "Apparently our time is up already." He pulled a shimmery green butterfly knife from his pocket and flipped it open. Using the blade tip, he tilted my chin up so I was forced to meet his gaze. "That was quicker than expected. Then again, if anyone could do it, it's her." He looked…*proud*. Like this had all been some kind of game.

"Fuck you," I spat out.

He tilted his head to the side, like he was really considering that as a suggestion, then flashed me a grin and shook his head. "Nah, you're not my type, pretty boy." His watch beeped again, and his scarred eyebrow hitched. "That's my cue. Let my girl know I'm coming for her." He removed the knife from under my chin and trailed it in a line down my sternum, carefully, stopping just below the bone. Then he smirked again. "This is gonna hurt."

Then he stabbed me. As if branding me wasn't enough.

I must have passed out from the pain. That was the only way to explain how the eye-patched man disappeared from the room so damn fast. The deafening sound of gunfire had forced my eyes open, and the first thing I saw was the green butterfly blade still protruding from my chest.

Agony racked my body, and it took every ounce of control I possessed over my muscles to keep from moving. Any move, no matter how small, would only do more damage with that knife sticking out of me.

That thought immediately became irrelevant when the locked door and half the wall surrounding it exploded into the room like someone had thrown a grenade at it. The force of the blast made me jerk and twist in my chains, and I screamed again. My voice was already hoarse, but the intense pain in my chest still drew a sound out.

Blood ran down my stomach and soaked my trousers. My vision was hazy and dark, the room in front of me coming in and out of focus fast enough to make me motion sick. Yet somehow when she came into sight, she was crystal clear in my eyes.

"Hayden," I mumbled, relief washing over me in a dizzying wave. Not because she'd rescued me, simply that she was okay. When I'd first been taken, all I could think about was how they'd probably been targeting her. That someone wanted to *hurt* her. And I'd been glad it'd been me in her apartment instead. Call me a lovesick fool, but I'd happily take all the torture in the world to keep her safe.

My mama always said one day I'd meet someone and I'd *know*. She always believed in love at first sight, my ma, but not me. Nope. I was a cynic...or I had been until I laid eyes on Hayden and my whole world tilted upside down.

She strode into view outside the ruined mess of the doorway, pausing briefly over someone to fire three times into the fallen body. Then her laser-sharp gaze jerked up to meet my eyes.

A million emotions crashed through me all at once, and the fierce determination and cold fury painted across her face was like the most soothing balm for my injuries.

Zed was at her side, as always, and for once I was actually happy to see him. Even if he was head-over-heels in love with *my* girl. But there was no way in hell I was walking away from this mess. I'd be lucky if I even survived long enough to get medical attention...

Who will look after my mom if I die?

Hayden stepped through the blown-out doorway, but my vision was blacking out already. The pain was too much, the blood loss making me too weak.

Zed shouted something and there was a flurry of motion, but I'd lost the strength to hold my head up any longer.

"Lucas." Her rich, velvety voice reached my ears, and her soft hand cupped my cheek. She was so short I didn't even really need to lift my head to see her. "I've got you. You're going to be okay."

I wanted to agree, but no words would come out. I could do nothing but watch as her eyes darted to the knife protruding from my chest. Her jaw tightened as her whole body radiated tension, *fury*, but she didn't let it out. Instead, she just whispered reassurances while someone picked the locks on my wrist irons.

When the bonds clicked open, I dropped like a lead weight. But two sets of strong arms caught me before I hit the floor.

"Hang in there, kid," my boss, Zayden De Rosa, muttered from one side of me. "Don't fucking die on us now."

Whoever was on my other side just grunted a sound of agreement, and I wanted to laugh. I'd never imagined myself as the damsel in distress, but it seemed strangely *right* that Hayden had come to my rescue. She was flipping gender roles like nobody's business, and I was *here* for it.

"Ambulance is almost here," she barked to Zed. "Get him up to the south exit, and whatever you do, do *not* let him die. Clear?" Her tone brooked no argument, no matter how impossible her request.

"Where the fuck are you going?" Zed snapped as Hayden started down the corridor away from us. "Dare!"

She hesitated, spinning around just long enough to shoot him a hard glare. "Zed, I'm *trusting* you. Get Lucas to the hospital and don't take your fucking eyes off him."

Oh man. I *really* wanted to laugh at him for that, but for one thing, I was barely conscious. For another, I also wanted to know where the fuck she was going.

She didn't hang around to debate it, though, and took off again, completely ignoring the way Zed shouted after her.

"I've got this," the dude supporting my other side rumbled. He smoothly transferred my weight entirely onto Zed, then loped off after Hayden.

"Motherfucking shit-fuck cunt-licker," Zed cursed, but he didn't drop me to the floor to die like I half expected him to. Instead, he adjusted his grip on me, then started toward the exit. "If you fucking die now, kid, I'll personally take a trip to hell, resurrect your ass, and kill you all over again."

With that comforting statement, I passed right the fuck out.

CHAPTER 2
HADES

Heavy footsteps sounded down the corridor behind me, and I simmered with anger, knowing I'd been disobeyed but not altogether shocked by that fact.

"Fuck off, Cassiel," I snarled, not turning to look at him. "I gave you an order."

"No, you gave Zed an order," he replied, falling into step beside me. "If you thought either of us would let you run off after a goddamn ghost without backup, you were wrong."

His disobedience should have pissed me off, but I couldn't even muster the slightest irritation. In fact, I was almost glad for his company as I chased my dark past along a corridor beneath Anarchy that I'd never known existed.

Neither of us spoke again until we reached the end. There was only one way out, a narrow ladder up to an open hatch, and I took point. Both Cass and I had our guns at the ready, but we were met with nothing but disappointment.

The hatch opened into a grass-covered clearing in the woods behind Anarchy, with no immediate hints presenting themselves as to where Chase—if it had really been him—had gone.

A scream of frustration burned in my chest, and I clenched

my jaw tight enough to hurt in order to hold it in. Nothing could be gained from throwing a temper tantrum now. Nothing except possibly showing my hand to anyone within earshot—if there was anyone. So I ground my teeth together and swallowed the scream, the curses, the *rage*, then turned back to Cass, who'd followed me out of the hatch.

"There's nothing here," I said in a cold, detached voice and tucked my gun away to free my hands for the ladder. "Let's go."

"Hold up," he growled, grabbing my arm as I tried to brush past him.

I glared up at him but couldn't muster the energy to jerk my arm free. Partly because I was *exhausted*. It'd been over twenty-four hours since Lucas was taken and I hadn't slept a single minute as we'd tracked him down. Partly because I liked the warm strength of Cass's fingers circling my arm.

"What now?" I snapped.

His expression darkened as he peered down at me. It was close to midnight, and the faint sound of partying in Anarchy was the only sign of life around us. Otherwise, we were totally alone...or seemed to be. I knew better than to assume.

"Cass, if you have nothing helpful to say right now, get the fuck out of my way." I had zero patience left. None. I needed to get some of my guys up here to thoroughly search the area and figure out how someone could disappear so easily.

An unreadable expression crossed Cass's face, and he let out a frustrated sigh. He let go of my arm to scrub a hand over his face, but by no means did he move out of my way or even give me any indication that he intended to.

"None of this is your fault, Red," he rumbled after a moment's pause.

I cocked a brow and folded my arms under my breasts. "Of course it's fucking not," I replied caustically. "Last I checked, I didn't ask for my supposedly dead ex-fiancé to rise from his grave,

8

blow up my club, then kidnap and torture the guy I've been sleeping with."

Cass wasn't buying my bullshit, though. He just stared down at me, seeing right through my poker face to the bottomless depths of guilt washing through me. It *was* my fault that Lucas had been hurt. It was a direct attack on me, and he was collateral damage. There were no two ways about it. Had he never met me, he wouldn't currently be on his way to a hospital with a knife sticking out of his chest.

I didn't think for a second that he might die. It simply wasn't an option.

When Cass still said nothing more, I swallowed heavily and broke eye contact first. "He was holding him in the basement of *my own property*, Cass." The words were whispered so softly he might not even have heard me. "He was right under my fucking nose for twenty-seven hours. Now get the fuck out of my way so I can start to work out how in the *fuck* I never knew about these underground tunnels."

His dark brows dipped low. "You aren't going to the hospital to make sure he's alive?"

I scowled. "He's alive."

Yeah, stubborn denial was one of my favorite coping mechanisms. So what?

Cass just let out another long exhale, shaking his head. "Sometimes, Red, I don't know if you're the most stubborn, hard-headed woman I've ever met or—"

My temper flared hot, and I tilted my chin up. "Or *fucking* what, Cass?"

He met my gaze unflinchingly, though. "Or the most incredible," he murmured, his voice rough and low. "Or both."

That was so far from what I'd expected him to say that I was taken completely off guard when he pressed a hand to the small of my back to draw me close. Then he kissed me, and I was shocked enough to let it happen.

9

But my wits returned a second later, and I shoved away from his strangely intimate hold.

"Are you fucking kidding me right now?" I demanded with a bitter laugh.

He goddamn knew he was out of line if the frustrated set to his jaw was any indication. Or if he even possessed half a brain, he would know.

"I've already apologized," he ground out from clenched teeth. "When are you going to let me in? I *hate* the thought of you facing this threat alone, Red. Every time—"

"I'm not alone," I cut him off. "I have Zed. Just like I always have. And you *had* your chance, Cassiel. Hell, you've had more than one chance, and you blew them all. Suck it up and stop messing with my fucking head. I don't have the time or patience to be manipulated by your dick right now."

I didn't wait for his response. I wasn't in the mood to have him change my mind, and this sure as fuck wasn't the right time to reignite whatever microflame we'd had burning for all of three seconds. Lucas was in the hospital—hopefully—and Chase was potentially alive and gunning for me. Public sex with a man I frequently wanted to strangle wasn't ranking high on my list of priorities.

It only took a few seconds for him to follow me back down the ladder, pull the hatch shut behind him, and twist the locking wheel to prevent anyone from following us. Good to see he hadn't completely lost his sanity.

We strode back along the unfamiliar corridor in silence, the sounds of partying from Anarchy growing louder by the second. Mentally, I kicked myself again for not sealing off the supply rooms sooner. It'd been on my to-do list for ages; lots of them had structural damage and I didn't want to deal with the liability if anyone was hurt down here. But I never would have guessed that one of the rooms had a false wall leading to a section of tunnels and what seemed to be jail cells.

When we reached the room Lucas had been kept in, the one Zed had quite literally blown up to gain us entry into, I slowed down, then stepped inside and looked around.

Blood decorated the floor, some dark and dried and some still so fresh it was wet and glistening. Rusty manacles hung from the ceiling, the same ones that Cass had needed to pick to free Lucas, and I shuddered.

"Recognize this?" Cass asked, jerking me out of my violent daydream about what might've happened in this room. I blinked a couple of times to center myself once more, then turned to see what he was talking about.

In his hand, he held a long iron instrument, like a fire poker. But no, the end was flat with...

"Fuck me," I whispered, swallowing hard. "That sick fuck."

When we'd found Lucas, I'd been so focused on the knife protruding from his chest that I had barely paid any attention to the blistered, bleeding burn on his left pec. Now it made sense, though.

"Looks like this freak branded Stripper Boy with your personal symbol," Cass muttered, curling his lip in disgust as he eyed the brand.

I shook my head. "Don't call him that. I think if anything should earn him some respect from you, it's this."

Cass gave me a sharp look, then nodded slightly. "Fair point." He tossed the brand back on the floor, then gave me another hard look. "Come on. Your Wolves can deal with this mess."

"Excuse me?" I scowled at him.

His face was pure stubborn bullheadedness though. "You heard me. You've got plenty of employees that can handle a cleanup." His strong hand gripped my upper arm again as he led me out of the torture room and we stepped over a body. Chase—or whoever— must have hired help because we'd killed at least six unfamiliar faces on our way into the tunnels.

I was just about done with him playing alpha dog in my house. "Cassiel Saint—"

He whirled around on me, though, crowding me against the wall and bringing his lips down close to my ear. "No. You listen to me, Hayden Timber. I've stood back and watched you push people away and isolate yourself time and time again, making yourself utterly un-*fucking*-touchable. For fucking *years*. Now, in the short time you've been screwing Lucas, something has changed, and I for one don't want to see it change back. You care for him. You're going to the hospital and making sure he's alive. End of discussion."

His speech shocked me enough that I didn't protest when he started along the corridor once more, his hand still around my arm. He wasn't dragging me along, which was probably why I allowed it, and it seemed a whole lot like he just didn't want to let go for his own reasons.

We stopped briefly along the way so I could relay cleanup instructions to several of my security team, and I sent off a quick message for Alexi, my head of security, to meet me at my office in the morning. It hadn't escaped my notice that one of the men guarding Lucas's cell had been a Timberwolf. Had I not been in such a hurry to reach Lucas, I'd have made his death a *damn* painful one.

I didn't take kindly to traitors.

Cass led me straight over to his bike, bypassing my car, and jerked his head for me to get on behind him.

I hesitated, scowling, but he gave me that hard glare that was fast becoming my weakness.

"You're in no state to be driving, Red. Get on."

As much as I wanted to argue with him, he was right. The adrenaline of searching for Lucas, of finding him so hurt and nearly dead, was depleting fast. In its wake I had nothing but shaky exhaustion and dizziness. Not to mention the dull, persistent ache of my bruises and scrapes from the explosion of 7th Circle just a couple of days ago. Yeah, in fairness, I was a damn mess. So I huffed an annoyed sigh and climbed onto the back of Cass's bike.

"Hurry up and leave before anyone fucking sees this," I growled as I wrapped my arms around his waist. "The last thing I need is my Wolves thinking I've become your bitch."

Cass scoffed as he kicked over the engine and rolled us out of the parking lot. "No one would ever think that, trust me."

He was probably right; my reputation was too solid to be cracked with one trip on the back of a Reaper's motorcycle. But still, I remained tense and paranoid until we were well out of sight of Anarchy and all my Wolves. Only when we hit the dark, deserted streets of south Shadow Grove did I relax.

Cass must have sensed it, too, because he placed a huge hand over mine on his stomach. It was only a brief touch, a small tug to tell me to hold tighter, and then he returned his hand to the handlebars. Yet it clicked something in my brain, forcing me to see that he was—as he always was—looking after me.

The few minutes afterward that it took to get to the hospital gave me some time to wonder if maybe that had been the motivation behind his hot-and-cold bullshit. He was constantly looking out for my best interests, whether it was keeping an eye on Seph—something *way* outside his job description—or pushing me away from what *he* viewed as a toxic relationship. Like, say, with an older gang leader.

Then again, maybe he was just an indecisive fuckhead who couldn't decide if he liked me or not. Maybe I was giving him too much benefit of the doubt.

Only time would tell, though, because I sure as fuck wasn't putting myself on the line for him to reject again. No. Fucking. Way.

CHAPTER 3

Lucas had been taken into emergency surgery to remove the knife from his chest and repair the damage done, but we only waited a short time before the surgeon emerged to give an update.

"Mr. De Rosa?" the doctor asked Zed as he approached. He was still head to toe in blue scrubs but had taken his mask off and had it dangling from his hand. "You're Lucas's brother?"

I gave Zed a sharp look, and he shrugged. "Sure. What's the news?"

"Your brother is one lucky guy," the doctor said with a brow raise. "Somehow that knife slid perfectly between all the major blood vessels. It punctured his lung, but by leaving the blade in like you did, we were able to fix it up. So far, things are looking good for his recovery." He paused, frowning. "The brand on his chest will scar, though. He will need skin grafts if he wants to get rid of that mark."

There was no doubt in my mind that it had been no accident or miracle that the knife had been so perfectly placed. That wasn't a fluke; it'd been deliberate.

"We need to see the knife," I told the doctor in a flat voice that made his brows hitch. Then he gave my visibly displayed weapons a nervous look and nodded.

"Absolutely. I'll have my nurse bring it out." He shifted his attention back to Zed. "You will be able to see Lucas in about an hour when he's out of the recovery room."

"Thank you," Zed replied, and the doctor made a swift exit once more. I didn't blame him, either. The three of us—Zed, Cass, and I—made for an intimidating trio, even if he had no clue who we were. No doubt someone would fill him in, though.

When we were alone again—or as alone as anyone could be in a hospital waiting room—I cocked a brow at Zed. "His brother?"

Zed just shrugged again. "And legal guardian. Seemed like the easiest way to deal with paperwork. I doubt he has health insurance, and I didn't want to waste time with the whole *don't you know who I am* shit."

I just blinked at him a couple of times, then nodded dumbly. It actually made a lot of sense, but I sure as hell wouldn't have thought of it in the heat of the moment. Lucas probably didn't have decent medical insurance or he wouldn't be in the situation he was in with his mom's medical bills.

"Thank you," I murmured to Zed. "I probably would have just pulled a gun and made the whole thing a million times worse."

He arched a lopsided smile at me and bumped my shoulder with his. "Nah, you'd have done the same." He shifted his attention to Cass, who sat silently by my side. He hadn't said a single word since we'd arrived at the hospital but still made it abundantly clear he wasn't going anywhere. "Are you sticking around for a bit? I need to change my shirt and check in on Seph."

I flinched. Seph. Jesus Christ, what was she going to say when she found out? When I'd realized Lucas had been taken, I'd had Cass drop her off at Madison Kate's mountain home some three hours away. Surrounded by Archer and his boys, she was as safe as she could be without me and Zed physically watching her. But sooner or later, she was going to find out—not just about Lucas being hurt but about *why* he was taken in the first place.

Fuck. She was going to murder me, and I'd deserve it for not fessing up the *second* I found out Lucas was her high school crush. In my own defense, I had been in shock. But this was firmly on the shittiest-sister-alive list of things to do.

"Not goin' anywhere soon," Cass replied, shifting into a slouch that looked impossibly effortless in the uncomfortable plastic chair.

"I'm just fine here on my own," I told them both with an edge of irritation. "Or did I suddenly transform into a helpless princess without noticing? Last I checked, I was a hell of a lot bigger and badder than you two."

Zed arched a brow at me but didn't reply. Instead, he gave Cass a nod and strode out of the waiting room. He had a fair point, given that his white button-down was coated in Lucas's blood from carrying him out of the tunnels, but part of me didn't want him to go. Codependency built from years of trusting no one but each other, I supposed.

"You can go," I told Cass after a few moments of silence. He just gave me a long side-eye, and I let out a frustrated sigh. "This is pointless. I have shit I should be doing. I've got traitors in the Wolves that need to be eradicated and tunnels to seal up underneath Anarchy. Not to mention—"

"Stop it," he growled. "None of that is so urgent it can't wait a couple of hours."

I ground my teeth together, wanting to disagree but coming up blank. My brain was too fried.

"Besides," Cass continued in a low, quiet voice, "that kid took a knife in the chest tonight. He deserves to see your face when he wakes up."

That statement, from Cass of all people, gave me pause. I bit my lip to hold back my stubborn denials and swallowed heavily. Fucking hell, Lucas didn't need me messing up his life. I should have listened to Demi when she told me not to corrupt him.

Cass cleared his throat, pulling my attention once more. "So... how old is he?"

I stiffened, turning my head slightly to peer at him. "Excuse me?"

He met my gaze and dragged his thumb over his lower lip thoughtfully. "Lucas. How old is he?" When I didn't respond, he continued. "Because when Seph was on the phone with you at the yogurt shop..."

I cringed. Hard. Oh *fucking hell*. Seph had said to me on the phone that Lucas had come over to study with her. Even if Cass hadn't seen him arrive in his Shadow Prep uniform—which he likely had as well—there was no avoiding the fact that Seph had *told him* Lucas went to school with her.

"He used a fake ID when I hired him," I muttered, fighting to keep the embarrassment from showing on my face. "I didn't know until *after*."

Cass showed no signs of judgment but also no signs of *anything* really. Fucker had a better poker face than me some days. I'd kill to play a game against him one day.

"What I would have done to see your face when you found that out," he muttered with an edge of amusement. "So, eighteen?"

I groaned and ran my hand through my hair. Obviously, this was a secret that was bound to come out sooner or later, but if I was honest, I hadn't really been thinking long-term when I agreed to keep seeing Lucas. I hadn't even been thinking more than one day at a time. Fucking hell, Zed was going to have a field day.

"Nineteen in a few weeks," I replied, as though that somehow made it all better. I mean, he was legally an adult; we weren't doing anything *wrong*. If our roles were reversed, no one would even bat an eyelid at the age gap. Hell, Archer's wife was four years younger than him and that was just accepted as *normal*.

Cass grunted a sound, his eyes still glued to my face. "Shit, Red. I'm old enough to be his father."

I snorted a laugh, not having thought of that. "Well, good thing you're not fucking him then, huh?"

His lips tugged into a micro-smile, and I bit the inside of my cheek to keep from blushing like a girl. For a man who barely ever smiled, goddamn, he made it a sexy expression, all sly and sexual whether that was his intention or not.

"You look like shit," he told me in a rapid change of subject that had my brows hitching in surprise. "Let's grab coffee while we wait."

My eyes narrowed. "For one thing, it's rude to tell a lady she looks like shit, Cassiel Saint."

Another smirk. Damn him. "Oh, you're a lady now, *sir*?"

My glare darkened. "And for another, if that's your idea of a peace treaty—"

"It's not." He cut me off with a short headshake. "It's just coffee because we both need it. We've got time."

I mulled it over for a quick moment, then sighed. "Yeah, I suppose we do. Or something stronger. There's an all-night diner across the street that doesn't make terrible coffee." I stood up from my chair and made my way over to the nurses' station to let them know where we would be and make sure they had my phone number in case Lucas woke up sooner than the doctor's estimate.

Cass followed my lead out of the waiting room and across the road to the diner in question, but paused me with a hand on my arm before we entered.

"Here," he murmured, shrugging off his leather jacket and draping it over my shoulders. I made to object, but he gave me a hard look. "I figure you might not want to attract any police attention tonight."

"Oh," I replied with a nod, realizing what he meant. With my Desert Eagle strapped under one arm, a Glock under the other, and three throwing daggers strapped to my thigh, I was far from inconspicuous. So I threaded my arms into the sleeves of Cass's jacket and pushed through the door to the diner.

He was only carrying one gun, tucked into the back of his

jeans, and he'd pulled his T-shirt over it, so the jacket was much better served hiding my weaponry.

"This isn't going to do wonders for my reputation," I muttered under my breath as I slid into a booth. Cass took the seat opposite me and quirked a brow in question.

"Having coffee with me in the middle of the night?" he asked.

I shot him a deadpan glare. "Wearing a Reaper's jacket."

He scoffed. "Big bad Hades cares what people think?"

"When it could potentially destabilize my hard-won seat of power and lead foolish upstarts into thinking I've lost my edge? Yeah, I care." I glowered, then sighed. "But you're right. Too many of the SGPD are no longer under my control, and I really don't need some Good Samaritan reporting me as a threat tonight."

Our waitress came over then and took our orders for coffee. We both remained silent until she came back with our steaming mugs and placed them down with the bill.

"So, what else do I need to know about this Chase Lockhart situation?" Cass asked in a quiet rumble when we were alone again.

I frowned, then sipped my coffee. "Nothing," I replied firmly. "I appreciate your help getting Lucas back, but this has nothing to do with the Reapers. I'll deal with it, just like I deal with anyone who threatens my business."

That clearly wasn't the answer he wanted, because his jaw tightened and I could almost hear his teeth grinding.

"Red—" he started, but my phone vibrated in my pocket.

"Not up for discussion, Cass." I cut him off, pulling my phone out to check who it was. Then I released a long breath and declined the call. "Seph," I admitted when he gave me an inquiring look. "She wants to know what's going on, and I have no idea what I'm going to tell her."

Cass huffed a sound. "I can relate," he grumbled, clearly sour that I still wasn't spilling all my deep dark secrets with him. After he'd dropped Seph at Madison Kate's last night, he'd returned to help Zed and me without being asked. So we'd given him *some* information…like the fact that we'd dug up Chase's grave and found it empty. And the fact that we suspected he was still alive and waging war on me. On us. I still couldn't work out if it was just me he was targeting or Zed too. After all, they'd been as close as brothers once.

But the rest of it? My history with Chase and what all had led us to the Timberwolf massacre five years ago? None of his fucking business.

My phone vibrated again, this time with a call from Zed, which I accepted.

"All okay?" I asked, holding the phone to my ear as I toyed with my coffee mug.

"Yeah, fine," he replied, then gave a short yawn. "I just spoke to Seph, and she said you're ignoring her calls. What do you wanna do about that?"

I wrinkled my nose. "Dunno. She's still safe with MK, right?"

"Yes, sir. I spoke with Archer, and he's aware of the risks. She's safe there as long as we need."

A small sigh of relief rushed out of me. As much as I was avoiding my sister's calls, her safety was—and always would be—my number one priority. Always.

"Good. Get some rest and meet me at Copper Wolf in the morning. I've told Alexi to come in for a meeting." Just the thought of that meeting was making me tired. In reality, though, I was going to need a meeting with my entire freaking gang. First an undercover FBI agent, and then a traitor guarding Lucas? I didn't believe for a second there weren't any other moles.

Zed scoffed a laugh. "Rest. Sure. Call your sister and stop her blowing up my phone. It's past her bedtime."

I rolled my eyes and ended the call. He was right, though; I couldn't avoid Seph forever.

"Everything all right?" Cass asked when I drummed my fingertips on the table a couple of times, thinking.

I arched a brow. "Of course."

"I wish you'd let me help." He scowled.

With a bitter laugh, I ruffled my fingers through my hair, then took a long sip of my coffee to collect my scattered thoughts. "Somehow, Saint, I doubt you can help me explain to Persephone that I've been fucking her *high school* crush for the last two weeks without telling her. And that because of me he was abducted, tortured, and almost killed. Oh, also that my ex-fiancé—who she doesn't know played a heavy hand in her near-sale to a Saudi pedophile—is back from the dead and gunning for me." I bit my tongue to stem the flow of words that suddenly wanted to pour out of me, then took a deep breath. "If you can help with that, by all means, I'll happily listen to suggestions."

His only response was to stare at me intently. Sometimes I seriously wished I could crack his skull open and see what in the hell was going on inside there during moments like this.

Then other times, like when he'd declared that I *needed* to come to the hospital, his words hit far too close to the truth and I'd rather he kept them inside.

My phone buzzed again, this time with an unknown number, and I answered cautiously. To my relief, it was the hospital calling to let us know that Lucas had been transferred to a private room and we could visit if we wanted.

I quickly downed the rest of my coffee, and Cass tossed some money on the table before following me out of the diner.

"This is stupid," I muttered to myself as we crossed the street back to the hospital. "He's not going to want to see me right now."

Cass gave me a slightly pitying look, shaking his head. "You always lie to yourself like that, Red? Or is this a new thing?"

I flipped him off and stalked ahead of him, making my way straight over to the nurses' station to get directions to Lucas's room. Clearly Cass wasn't going to let up until I actually *saw* Lucas, and... yeah, if I was honest I also wanted to see he was okay with my own eyes. It didn't change the fact that I was probably the last person on earth he would want to see right now.

"The doctor asked me to give you this," the nurse told me, holding out a plastic bag containing a folded-up green butterfly knife.

My stomach flipped, and I needed to swallow heavily before I could take it from her.

Cass grimaced when he saw it in my hand, too. "That's one of Phillip D'Ath's blades," he correctly observed.

I gave a jerking nod. "Yep."

"Let me guess," he rumbled, walking with me over to the elevators. "This one belonged to Chase Lockhart?"

"Close, but no," I replied reluctantly as we stepped into the elevator and Cass stabbed the button for the seventh floor. "This one was Zed's."

CHAPTER 4

Lucas wasn't awake when we reached his room. Cass still nudged me inside, though, then waited in the hallway to give me... I don't know what. Privacy? To talk to an unconscious guy I barely knew but had almost gotten killed?

Awkward didn't even begin to touch on how I felt standing there looking down at Lucas's bruised face, still and calm in sleep.

"Nope," I muttered to myself. "This is weird." It wasn't like he was my boyfriend; he was just a guy I was fucking. Right? Right. He was just an addictively good lay who had gotten caught in the crosshairs of a burgeoning gang war.

"Hayden." His hoarse voice stopped me dead in my tracks as I tried to sneak back out of the private hospital room again. Despite how I'd just mentally labeled him as nothing more than a *good lay*, the sound of his voice hit me like a thousand volts of electricity. "You're here."

With a cringe, I turned back around to face him, guilt flooding through me harder than any drug I'd tried. Nothing could have prepared me for the look on his face, though.

"Yeah," I replied, backing up a step, getting closer to the door and my escape. "I just wanted to make sure you were...you know... alive."

The pure, unfiltered look of relief and joy on his face only got more intense as he smiled. Wow. Just *wow*. It should have been illegal for a guy to have that good a smile while beaten and bruised in a hospital bed after a near-death encounter. Straight-up illegal.

Not a flicker of hurt or accusation showed on his gorgeous face, and that only made me feel all the more guilty for my part in his torture. He didn't blame me, and he should. He should be goddamn terrified. He should be running as far and as fast as he possibly could. But no... No, all I saw when I met Lucas's sea-green eyes was something scarily close to love. Which, obviously, was insane.

No one fell in love at first sight. That shit was reserved for fiction—and fiction *only*.

He stretched out a weak hand to me, his fingers limp but the gesture clear that he wanted me to come closer. The *last* thing I wanted to do was get any closer to Lucas than I already was. Physically and emotionally. Yet my traitorous feet moved me across the room without my permission, and I stifled a small gasp when our fingers met.

Fuck. Fuckity-fuck shit, I was doomed.

With a groan of despair, I sank into the chair at his bedside and dropped my forehead to the mattress. "Lucas, I'm *so* sorry," I mumbled into the sheets.

"For what?" he asked, his voice rough like he'd been screaming all night. Hell, he probably had. That brand on his chest would have been straight-up blinding agony. His fingers trailed through my hair, gently offering *me* comfort, like I deserved it in the least. "You're not the one who did this. It was that deranged fucking eye-patch dude."

My shoulders stiffened, and I lifted my head to look at him. "What?"

He blinked sleepily at me, that soft smile still on his lips. "Fuck, you're beautiful," he mumbled. "I thought for a second I had died when you appeared in that room. You looked just like an avenging angel."

His words were slightly slurred, and there was a glassiness to his gaze that betrayed how heavily drugged he was for the pain. *Shit.* He probably had no idea what he was even saying. Still, I was desperate to know what he might have seen or heard.

"Lucas," I whispered, linking my fingers through his and squeezing gently. "What eye-patch dude? Did he tell you his name?"

His smile slipped a little, a small frown touching his brows. "No. No, he was..." He gave a small headshake, then blinked a couple of times like he was trying to fight the urge to sleep. Shit, I should just leave him alone. I was already pretty confident I knew what he would tell me, anyway.

Just as I was about to make my exit, his fingers tightened on mine. "He kept calling you *his*. He kept talking about his *darling*."

Bile rose in my throat, and I shoved it back down with Herculean effort. "Chase," I whispered, my voice full of dread and five-year-old fear. "He's alive. How..."

"He was pretty messed up," Lucas told me, his voice still a sleepy mumble. "Did you do that to him, angel? Did you take his eye and scar him up like that? I hope so."

That made me bark a short laugh. His lids dropped closed, but another smile touched his lush lips.

"I'm so happy you're here," he whispered. His fingers tightened on mine again, and even when his breathing had evened out into sleep, it took me a long time to force myself to pull away.

When I finally did, I sat back in the chair and just stared at him for the longest time. He was so...*innocent*. It should have been a major turnoff for me. It should have creeped me out and made me run a mile in the opposite direction. Everything about him screamed *nice guy*, and that was firmly *not* my type.

And yet...here I was, watching over him as he slept in a hospital

25

bed, wrapped in bandages and covered with the marks of my ex's wrath. Here I was, dreading the thought of ever pushing him away, even if it was to keep him safe.

I couldn't even put a finger on when it'd happened, whether it'd been the night we met, or just now, but he'd firmly surpassed the just-a-good-lay category. He'd become a weakness...because goddamn it all to hell, I cared about him.

The soft click of the door opening behind me interrupted my train of thought, and I tilted my head up to see Zed there. Then glared at him.

"I thought I told you to rest," I whispered.

He just gave a casual shrug and nodded to Lucas's sleeping form. "Had to check on my little brother. How's he doing?"

I grimaced, then pushed up out of the chair. We could speak outside the room so we didn't wake Lucas up, seeing as he'd just come out of surgery. The best thing for him now—aside from painkillers—was sleep.

Zed closed the door behind us again when we stepped out, and Cass looked up from where he waited, leaning on the wall opposite. The tilt to his head was questioning, and I indicated he should follow us down to the end of the hall.

"He's pretty foggy and shit," I told them, crossing my arms under my breasts. I still wore Cass's jacket, which was so big on me it probably looked ridiculous, but it was also comfy as all hell so I hadn't offered to give it back.

Zed noticed it, too, giving the Reaper patch on the left shoulder a hard look before frowning at me with irritation painted across his face.

"To be expected," Cass said, responding to my statement and ignoring the way Zed was glaring at me. Or I thought he was ignoring it until he shifted his position to lean on the wall a whole hell of a lot closer to me than he'd been a moment ago. "General anesthesia takes a bit to recover from."

I gave a sigh, rubbing at my temples where I could feel a blinding tension headache building. "Yeah, well, he was lucid enough to mention he'd been hurt by a *scarred man with an eye patch.*" I winced just at the thought of Chase surviving the bullet I'd put in his face. "Oh, and the nurse gave me this." I pulled the bagged knife from my pocket and handed it to my second.

Zed just grimaced and pocketed the bagged blade without even looking at it. He already knew what it was; he'd had to stare at it sticking out of Lucas's chest the whole way to the hospital.

"So Chase is alive," he murmured, resigned.

"It would seem so," I agreed.

Zed just nodded, silent. Cass said nothing, but watched me with an intensity that made a shiver run down my spine.

"We need to send someone to check on Lucas's mother," I finally said, breaking the tense moment between us all. "She uses a wheelchair, and he's her primary caregiver."

Zed jerked a nod. "On it. You want someone posted to keep watch or…?"

I thought on it for a moment, then shook my head. "No, see about getting her moved to a care facility, even just temporarily while Lucas heals. Then have Dallas run a health check on the security at the facility in case Chase decides to target her there."

"Yes, sir." Zed was all business as he pulled out his phone and got to work.

"What can I do?" Cass asked, seeming to move closer still. Or maybe that was just my imagination now that I'd met his dark gaze.

A handful of completely inappropriate ideas flitted across my mind, but I kept them to myself. Not the time or the place. So I just smoothed out my face and pushed aside my baser instincts to focus on business.

"Nothing," I told him firmly. "We've got this from here. You have a gang to run. How's that search for a second-in-command going, anyway? It's been over a year."

27

Cass's glower was pure death, because he knew damn well what I was doing. I was reestablishing the political lines that had become so very muddied in the last day and a half. He had his place, just like I had mine. It was about damn time we stepped back into them.

"I'm taking my time," he answered after a few beats. "No one has impressed me enough so far, and I'd hate to accidentally appoint a turncoat now—especially given how many people seem to be secretly working for the resurrected Chase Lockhart."

I shrugged like it didn't make an ounce of difference to me if he had a second or not. "Your funeral, Cassiel. Not having a second makes you an easy target. Make smart choices."

His lips curved in that sly, sexy smirk, and he huffed a short laugh at his own advice on my lips. "Cute. This isn't over, Red."

I tilted my head to the side, playing dumb. "What isn't?"

His eyes narrowed. "This. Us. I know you've got bigger things on your mind right now, but I'm not taking no for an answer."

The audacity of some men was astounding. After all the chances I'd given him... I shrugged. "Well, you know what to do, then."

He gave a brief frown of confusion, then quickly realized what I meant. "I thought you were joking about writing you that letter."

I had been. But he didn't need to know that. "And I thought you weren't interested." I started along the corridor toward Zed, who was on the phone sorting out my requests. He gave me another hard look, and I understood his silent reminder.

Pausing, I slid Cass's jacket off and tossed it back to him.

"See you around, Saint."

CHAPTER 5

It was harder than I'd expected to force myself away from Lucas's hospital room. But sitting in his room watching him sleep simply wasn't an efficient use of my time. There were plenty of other things I could be doing, plenty of things I *should* be doing. So I left.

"I've got Boris and Rixby here watching the hospital," Zed informed me as we exited the building. "One of them will head up to Lucas's room now and keep physical eyes on him until further notice. The hospital staff will send through any and all updates from his doctors when they check on him in the morning too."

I drew a deep breath, feeling the ache of stress in every damn muscle of my body. "Good. Good thinking. Thanks, Zed." I yawned heavily, then scraped my hair up into a high ponytail to try to stop messing it up. Running my fingers through it was a stress fidget and tended to result in me looking like a lion.

He unlocked his Ferrari with the key fob, then held the passenger door open for me to get in. I didn't argue at the chivalrous gesture; I was pretty used to it from him by now. Instead, I just sank into my seat and cranked the heater up while he circled around to the driver's side.

"Did you call Seph back?" he asked as he drove us away from the hospital and in the direction of our neighborhood.

I wrinkled my nose. "No. She should be asleep, anyway."

He just gave me a sidelong glare, calling me on my bullshit without even needing to say a word. Yeah, whatever.

"Why aren't you telling her about Lucas anyway?" he asked, his eyes back on the road but his attention fully on me. "She knows something has happened."

Ah crap. Zed was going to be totally insufferable when I told him Lucas was in high school with Seph...and that she had a huge crush on him.

I wasn't in the mood to deal with that, so I just shrugged and avoided looking at him while I lied. "No reason. I'll talk to her in the morning."

Zed slammed his foot down on the brakes hard enough to make me jerk against my seat belt, then moan in pain at all my bruises.

"Shit," he muttered, cringing. "Sorry. But did you just fucking lie to me?"

Wincing, I rubbed my chest where the belt had just assaulted me. "What? No."

Zed gave a dramatic gasp. "You did it again!"

Rolling my eyes, I huffed. "Like you're one to talk right now, Zayden. Can we please just go? I want to get home and sleep for about six years."

His frown dipped low, but he did as I asked and accelerated once more. Except he wasn't heading in the direction of my apartment anymore.

"Zed..." I said his name in a low, suspicious growl.

"I'm not taking you back to an apartment that Chase has already proven isn't secure. You can stay at my place until this shit gets sorted." His tone was firm and unyielding, and I was too tired to argue. So I just shrugged and settled in for the ride. Seph was safe with Madison Kate, Lucas was safe in the hospital, and *hopefully*

Demi was on a plane to Italy with her wife by now. Everyone I cared about was safe.

Or as safe as they possibly could be in our world.

Besides, Zed had a point. My apartment was no longer secure, while he lived in a veritable fortress. His house was on acreage outside Shadow Grove and had been built to mimic a Scottish castle, but in a modern, architect's wet-dream kind of way.

About half an hour of silence passed until we reached his front gate, within which time I had fallen asleep and jerked awake about a dozen times. I hated sleeping in cars.

Zed had a similar biometric access panel at his gate to allow access, and I yawned heavily as we waited for the decorative wrought-iron gates to open.

"Take my room," he told me as we headed into the house. He didn't have any staff because of trust issues, but his lights were motion-activated so the house lit itself up before we got inside. "I haven't made up any of the guest rooms, and you look way too tired to wait for me to find sheets."

I should have declined, but fuck it. What were best friends for if you couldn't occasionally claim their nice, cozy bed? So I just nodded, yawned, and started up the grand staircase without waiting for him.

In his room, I helped myself to one of his old T-shirts that'd been stuffed into the back of his closet behind a million and one designer button-down shirts and suits. I changed and left my dirty clothes in a crumpled pile that I knew would annoy the shit out of him and climbed into his bed.

Before letting myself crash, I set my alarm for the morning... then groaned when I saw it would only allow me three hours sleep. Still, it was better than nothing, so I tossed my phone onto the other side of the bed and closed my eyes.

I could have sworn that barely a minute passed before Zed shook me awake, and I snarled insults at him before my eyes adjusted to the *daylight* and my brain processed the fact that I had, in fact, slept.

"Whoa, Dare." Zed interrupted my mumbled abuse with a smirk. "That was all a little harsh after I let you hog my bed all freaking morning."

Huh? I blinked about a thousand times to try to find my bearings and slowly remembered I was at Zed's house. In Zed's bed. With him...shirtless...and...

Fuck's sake. This was *far* from the right time to start developing feelings for him. Far *fucking* from it. I needed a slap. Or a cold shower.

"What time is it?" I asked in a sleep-thick voice as I sat up.

Zed was already propped up on one arm, his bicep curled under him like—

"Shit, you asshole," I snapped, noticing the sheepish look on his face. "You turned my alarm off, didn't you?"

He just gave a shrug like he didn't feel all *that* bad about it. "You needed the rest and Alexi could fucking wait."

Fair point. "So why the fuck am I awake now?" I muttered, climbing out of the bed and groaning at how stiff and sore my whole body was. In fairness, it hadn't been *that* long since I was thrown across the 7th Circle parking lot by a gas explosion.

"Because Seph is blowing up my phone trying to get ahold of you," he replied with a cringe. "And she sounds *pissed*. I figured you might want to call her back before she shows up here and sets fire to my house."

Crap's sake. I exhaled heavily and raked my fingers through my hair. Where did I leave my clothes? I was only wearing underwear under one of Zed's shirts...

A moment later, I spotted my clothes from the night before neatly folded on the chair in the corner and smirked.

"Yeah, all right," I said as I tugged my ripped, black skinny jeans on. "I'll call her back."

Zed wrinkled his nose at me in disgust, still propped up on his elbows in bed. "She can wait five minutes while you shower. I'll reply and let her know you're here."

I glared back at him, not missing the implication that I was dirty. But he was probably right, given how our night had ended up going after we'd worked out where Lucas was being held. There was every chance I had blood crusted in my hair somewhere.

So I just flipped him off, grabbed the rest of my clothes, and headed into his bathroom to shower. Seph could definitely wait. So could that explanation about why Lucas was in the hospital right now.

I kept my shower quick, then roughly towel dried my hair when I was done. With clean skin, I was less than excited about putting dirty clothes on. But I had shit that needed to be done today, and it wasn't going to wait. Nor was it going to get done while wearing borrowed clothes from Zed. Dirty clothes would do.

My phone was sitting on the bedside table when I emerged, so I grabbed it and scrolled for Seph's number while I made my way downstairs. It only rang twice before she picked up, and I steeled myself against whatever she wanted to say.

"Seph, what's going on?" I asked her, slightly annoyed at her persistence in getting ahold of me. For all she knew, we'd had a break-in at the apartment and she was staying at Archer's house until the security could be reset. That was the best story I'd come up with in the heat of the moment on Friday night.

"I'm five minutes away," she snapped down the phone at me. "Tell Zed to make me breakfast."

I coughed a laugh. "Tell him yourself, Your Highness. Jesus, Seph, what's with the attitude?"

There was a pause, then I heard her sigh. "Please? He'll tell me to make it myself, but he won't say no to you."

A grin tugged my lips as I walked into the kitchen and found Zed—as Seph correctly guessed—standing at the counter and mixing up his family waffle recipe. "I'll think about it," I replied to my sister, teasing. "Looks like he's only making enough for me right now."

Seph gave a whine of protest. "Don't be mean! Oh, also, I've got Kody with me because apparently I need a twenty-four-seven bodyguard right now?" She phrased it like a question, and I grimaced. No wonder she was blowing up our phones to talk. I was usually a little more subtle with her protection detail, but I should have known Archer had told MK and in turn... Yeah, not surprising she was worried. Or suspicious.

"See you soon, brat." I chuckled, then hung up on her and gave Zed a raised brow. "You'd better double that batch. Seph's on her way with Kody."

Zed didn't complain, just jerked a nod and set about mixing up a second batch of waffle batter.

"You wanna tell me what's going on before she gets here?" he asked quietly as he poured the first batch into his waffle iron.

I wrinkled my nose and slid onto a stool at the kitchen island. "Not really," I muttered. He'd already poured me a huge mug of coffee and added a heavy splash of real cream.

He just gave a slow nod, his eyes on the cooking waffle. "Fair enough," he replied after a moment. "So you don't want to tell me about how Lucas is actually an eighteen-year-old high school senior at Shadow Prep?"

I'd been taking a sip of my coffee when he said that and promptly choked on it. Zed barely reacted to my coughing fit, just cocked a brow at me while I spluttered and turned red in my attempt to expel the fluid from my windpipe.

"What?" I squeaked when I could draw enough air into my lungs.

"What?" he replied, blinking at me innocently. "You think I don't run my own background checks on our new employees?"

"Since fucking *when*?" I exclaimed, slamming my mug down

on the stone countertop. "Did Demi give you that information? I'll fucking kill her!" And for once, I only meant that as a figure of speech. I loved my aunt like a second mother.

Zed just shot me a glare. "No, I had someone *else* run a check on my *little brother*, and I'm sure you can imagine my surprise when I found out the truth."

My cheeks were flaming, and nothing I could do would make them cool. Fucking *hell*. I really badly had *not* thought things through before becoming involved with Lucas.

"Since *when*?" I demanded again. He'd never run a double background check on our dancers before, at least not to my knowledge. Hell, we hardly ever ran background checks at all if they were only being employed by Copper Wolf as a legal worker. It was none of our business if Aphrodite the exotic dancer was actually Diane Green, a bored housewife from the Rainybanks suburbs.

Zed's cool snapped, and he smacked his hand down on the counter with a flare of anger in his stare. "Since you decided to give him additional job perks, Boss. That's when. When did *you* plan on telling Seph that you're fucking her classmate?"

Uh…never. Probably. If I could get away with it…

"Why didn't you say anything sooner?" I asked in a cool voice, deciding that I wasn't gaining any ground by letting him drive the conversation.

He just glared at me for a long, tense moment, his gaze full of judgment and accusation. Frustration. "I only got the report while you were in the shower," he admitted after a heavy pause. "I requested the search last night to check for his health records."

Well shit, now I felt like an asshole. He hadn't been prying into my love life; he'd been taking care of business. Just like he always did.

I swallowed my pride and ducked my gaze back to my coffee. "Well…trust me, it's worse than you think."

He gave a grunt of disbelief, flipping the first cooked waffle out of the iron and pouring in fresh batter. "It can get worse?"

As if the universe was laughing at me, his gate buzzer sounded right then, announcing that my little sister had arrived. Was it too early to start drinking? I definitely needed something stronger than straight coffee.

CHAPTER 6

Zed buzzed Seph and Kody in, and a minute later my far-too-energetic sister burst into the kitchen where I was gulping coffee and quietly thinking about the easiest escape routes out of Zed's fortress.

"Wow, you look like total crap," she announced when she laid eyes on me, wrinkling her nose in disgust. Then she shifted her gaze to the cooking waffles. "Oh, Zed...you're making breakfast? I had no idea."

My second just snorted a laugh and shook his head. "Sure. Sit down, Seph. Where's Kody?"

Seph slid into the seat beside me and waved her hand in the direction of the front door. "He's waiting in the car. Apparently, you guys are that unpleasant in the morning, and he didn't want to risk getting shot."

Zed and I both glared death at my little sister, and she snorted a laugh.

"Kidding. He had some work calls to make for KJ-Fit so he said he'd wait outside, then drive me back to MK's place later. Unless you want me to come stay here? The security doors won't take that long to fix at home, right?"

The hopeful look she gave me was actually gut-wrenching. I couldn't lie to her forever… It was only going to get worse the longer I kept my mouth shut.

Zed came to my rescue, though, breaking the silence when no words left my frozen lips.

"Actually, it's a bit more complicated," he said as he plated up a waffle for each of us. With deft movements, he chopped a banana and several strawberries to scatter over the hot waffles, then drizzled them with maple syrup. To top it all off, he added a scoop of ice cream, and Seph bounced in her seat like an excited three-year-old.

"Complicated how?" she asked as she took a big forkful of food.

Zed shot me a look like he wanted me to take the opportunity and explain…but I really preferred to eat my breakfast before Seph tried to claw my eyes out. So I just filled my mouth with food like a big old coward.

He glowered at me, then shifted his attention back to Seph. "The security breach is likely part of a bigger situation we're currently dealing with. Until it's contained, it's not safe for you to go home. For *either* of you." This was added with a sharp look directly at me, and I narrowed my eyes in response. I'd agreed to stay one night because I was exhausted and hurting. I sure as fuck hadn't agreed to move in with him indefinitely.

"Wait, what?" Seph squeaked. "How long are we talking? I can't stay with MK forever, you know."

"Yes, you can," I mumbled around my food. "Already cleared it with D'Ath."

She scowled. "No, I mean, I *really* can't. I love MK, don't get me wrong, but holy shit, she's *loud* in bed. I actually got Kody to buy me earplugs this morning on our way over. If I have to hear my friend begging for one of the guys to fuck her ass one more time, I'm gonna puke."

Zed gave an exaggerated cough as he turned his back on us,

and I suspected he was trying to hide a laugh. I didn't blame him, and only Seph's outraged stare kept me from snickering myself.

"Well...too bad." I shrugged. "It's not safe to be at the apartment."

Seph pouted. "What aren't you telling me?"

"Lots of things," I replied with a grimace. "But all you need to know is that Archer and the boys will keep you safe while we deal with this...threat."

She huffed but ate her breakfast in silence for a short while. When she finished, she slid off her stool and took our dirty dishes to the sink to rinse. Then she turned back to face me with a troubled frown creasing her brow and something quite clearly on her mind.

"I'm...going to go shower," Zed announced after an extended pause. When neither my sister nor I responded, he gave a nod and made a speedy exit from the kitchen.

"What's up, brat?" I asked Seph when we were alone. "You're not seriously that grossed out by MK's sex life, are you?"

Seph shook her head, giving a dismissive wave of her hand. "No, that's...whatever. Good for her, right? Hashtag girl power and shit." She folded her arms tightly, like she was comforting herself, and her gaze skittered all around the kitchen but never met mine.

"Okay..." I paused. "So what's going on?" She couldn't know about Lucas already. She was too...calm.

She drew a deep breath, then let it out in a heavy sigh as she returned to her seat beside me at the counter. "It's Lucas."

Oh shit.

"Uh..." I had nothing constructive to say here.

"It's not what you think," she rushed to say, and I mentally replied, *Fuck, I hope not.*

"Okay... Why don't you explain?" I suggested, licking my lips when my whole damn mouth went dry.

She gave another dramatic sigh. "I know he has a girlfriend and stuff, I totally get it. And I know I was being super inappropriately pushy, too, which was totally not cool of me because, like, what if that was me and some girl was constantly hitting on *my* boyfriend, right? So, *so* not cool." She was talking at a million miles an hour, but I was happy to let her word vomit and save me the need to respond.

"Mm-hmm," I offered by way of agreement. She was right. Even without my involvement, it'd been a dick move on her part when he'd already told her he wasn't interested.

"Right. So that's half the reason I asked him over to study on Friday night. I wanted to apologize and, like, be friends. You know? Because he's a really cool guy and we could totally just be platonic friends. Couldn't we?" She gave me a pointed look, and I gave a slight shrug.

"I suppose..." *Where the fuck is she going with this?*

She gave me a pained frown. "Did he say anything when you dropped him home the other night?"

I'd told her it was a minor break-in attempt on our apartment, someone trying to pick the lock while Lucas was still there, and that I had dropped him home so I could deal with it. Yep. Big old liar.

"Like what?" Fuck it, I was playing dumb. It seemed like the easiest course of action.

Seph shrugged, oblivious to my anxiousness. "I dunno. But he hasn't replied to any of my messages, and I'm sort of worried he finally got scared off. Did *you* say something?"

Oh geez. Of course he hadn't. His phone was still in our apartment amidst the destruction caused by his fight with my double-crossing Timberwolf. Also, he was in the hospital recovering from a full twenty-four hours of beatings, a brand, and a stab wound.

Blowing out a long breath, I peered down at my empty coffee cup. I needed to rip the Band-Aid off before Seph did something dumb out of ignorance and got herself in danger.

40

"Seph, there's something I've been meaning to tell you about Lucas," I reluctantly gritted out. "I probably should have told you when I first realized he went to school with you."

Probably? Definitely.

"I already know," she said quickly, cutting me off before I could speak again. I jerked my gaze up from my coffee mug to look at her in alarm, and she gave me a sheepish smile. "Cass told me."

My brain short-circuited. "Cass did *what?*"

Seph wrinkled her nose. "Don't be mad, he didn't know it was a secret. He assumed I already knew that Lucas was a stripper, and I mean it totally explains his body, right? And I know Zed does all the hiring and shit so you probably didn't even have anything to do with hiring him, but anyway, I totally would never judge him for stripping. It's just a job, right? And he needs the money for his mom, so it's kinda admirable."

"Right." I blinked at her slowly. "Cass told you…"

She gave a small frown of confusion. "That Lucas was a stripper at 7th Circle. Why? Was there something else?"

Crap.

That was my opening. I really, *really* wouldn't have any excuses left if I didn't tell her now. She was going to completely blow her lid. I already knew it. But the nice thing about Seph was that her temper worked like magnesium. It burned white hot in a flash, but quickly extinguished. Once she'd screamed and thrown shit, she'd get over it.

I hoped.

"Yeah," I finally forced myself to say, "so…okay, I'm going to preface this by saying he gave a fake ID to get the job at 7th." Seph's eyes narrowed, and I looked away. I could stand up to the biggest bad guys around and not even bat a lash, but my little sister? Nope. "So, in saying that…" I drew a deep breath, then ripped the Band-Aid off. "I've been sleeping with Lucas."

For a second, I thought she hadn't heard me. Then she blinked, frowned, and shook her head. "What? No, you haven't. He has a girlfriend."

I winced. "Uh, yeah. Me."

She shook her head again, a confused smile on her lips like she thought I was messing with her. "No, because…" Her voice trailed off when I just met her gaze and didn't laugh. Her expression slipped quickly, and her frown deepened. "You've… You're the girl on his phone. H. She was saved as *H*…" She blinked in disbelief, and I braced myself for the screaming.

But it didn't come.

Instead, she just pursed her lips and swallowed heavily.

"I didn't realize you were in the habit of fucking your dancers," she finally said with an edge of bitterness in her voice.

I groaned. "I'm not. It was a one-off thing that just…kept happening."

"And you never thought to tell me? After I poured my heart out to you about how much I liked him? You never thought, 'Hey, maybe I should tell Seph that it's *me* who is screwing him'?" Then her brows shot up, and she looked at me in horror. "Oh my god. *That's* why he kept coming over to study? Because he wanted to see you?" She let out a bitter laugh and slid off her stool. "I'm such an idiot," she muttered under her breath, starting toward the door.

"Seph, where are you going?" I asked, sliding off my own seat.

"Anywhere but here," she snapped back, but it wasn't the diva tantrum I'd been expecting. No, this was just cold fury. Fuck me, she was handling this completely unlike *her*. She was handling it like *me*…and that was way worse.

"Fuck's sake," I growled, following after her. "Seph, that's not everything. You need to know—"

"Was there really a break-in?" she demanded, whirling around to face me with a stonelike expression hardening her features. "Or was that some bullshit excuse to get me out of the way so you could fuck Lucas all over the apartment?"

My brows shot up and my pulse raced. "Okay, you're upset, so I'm not going to point out how insulting *that* was. But now that you know about Lucas, I'll give you the whole truth, shall I?"

She folded her arms and gave me a sarcastic look like she wasn't going to believe me no matter what I said.

I forced myself to set aside my anger and frustration, though. She was upset, hurt, and the last thing I needed was her ending up in danger for doing something dumb like running away.

"The apartment *was* broken into, not just an attempt. They'd gotten in and left before I called you that night." I paused, gritting my teeth against the fresh anger and guilt over Lucas's torture.

Seph just curled her lip in disbelief. "Oh yeah? And where was Lucas during all this? I wasn't gone *that* long."

"They took him," I bit back, clenching my fists at my sides. "And then they tortured him for over twenty-four hours while Zed, Cass, and I tried to find him. Lucas isn't returning your texts because he's in the *hospital*, Seph. He almost died because he was sleeping with me, and my first reaction was relief that it hadn't been *you*."

She said nothing for a second, then tightened her jaw and gave me a hard look. "Who? Who took him?" She tilted her chin up in determination like she was daring me to try to lie to her. "Who are you trying to protect me from this time?"

I swallowed heavily again. "Chase," I croaked, hardly believing myself.

Seph looked stunned for a second, then she shook her head with a harsh laugh. "You're a piece of fucking work, Dare. You wanna tell me your *dead* ex tortured some high school kid that you've been fucking? For what? You sure as hell aren't in love. You've been using him, just like you use everyone you meet. And when they're no longer *useful*, you kill them. Just like you killed Dad when he wouldn't give you the power you wanted. You're fucking sick, Dare. You need professional help."

Her bitter accusation left me speechless, and I made no move to stop her as she rushed out of Zed's house like hellhounds were snapping at her heels.

I just stood there shocked and hurt, turning over what she'd said in my mind even as the sound of Kody's car faded into the distance.

"She didn't mean any of that," Zed murmured from somewhere close behind me. The sound of his voice made me flinch, and I shuddered to know he'd heard the whole thing.

I cleared my throat, then turned to face him. "Yes, she did. But that's okay. She can think whatever the fuck she wants about me so long as she's alive and thriving." I wet my lips and ran a shaking hand through my hair. "Give Archer a call and let him know that he's to keep her safe indefinitely. I don't want her around here until Chase is dealt with."

Zed jerked a nod, but concern was painted all over his face. "She's *wrong*, Dare. You know that, don't you?"

I let out a bitter laugh and shrugged it off. "Doesn't matter if she is or not. I can't change the past, and I wouldn't even if I could. All we can do is keep moving forward. Right?" I made to move past him, intending to grab my phone from the kitchen, then head into Copper Wolf for our meetings. But he grabbed my arm before I could pass, stopping me. His hold on my arm was tight, and he used his other hand to grip my chin, forcing me to look up at him.

"Hayden. She. Is. Wrong. You're the bravest, most selfless, determined, and caring woman I've ever known. There is *nothing* you wouldn't do for that girl, and she needs to figure it the fuck out soon." His gaze locked on mine with soul-deep intensity that did horrible things to my flickering interest in him beyond our solid friendship. "The next time she tries to cut you like that, I'm setting her straight. I've had enough."

A small, humorless smile tugged my lips as I gazed up at him. "You'll do nothing of the sort, Zayden De Rosa," I whispered, totally lacking the emotional strength to push my voice any louder. "I don't care if she thinks I'm Hannibal fucking Lector, I won't rob her of the father she thought she had." Because Seph had forever been daddy's little princess. She'd never seen through his mask to the monster lurking beneath. Never. "My word is law, Zed, and you'd do well to remember that."

His gaze flicked away from mine for the briefest second, flashing down to my lips a scarce few inches from his own. Then his thumb stroked my cheek ever so softly before he released me.

"Of course, Boss," he murmured, already turning away from me. "We should get going. Alexi is at Copper Wolf HQ already."

There was a strange tightness to his voice as he said that, and I frowned at his back as he walked ahead of me. Something weird was going on with him.

CHAPTER 7

Zed and I stopped by my apartment on the way to Copper Wolf, and I carefully ignored the trashed furniture, broken glass, and dried blood as I passed through to my room. All I needed was a change of clothes, a lick of makeup, and a hairbrush.

"I'll have someone come by and pack up your things later today," Zed told me as I dressed in a skintight leather pencil skirt, deep-purple silk camisole, and deadly spiked heels. And my gun holster, of course, but that pretty much went without saying as I never went anywhere public without it.

"Absolutely not," I replied as I peered into my mirror and painted black winged eyeliner on. "I'm not having a random creep handling all my shit. And I don't remember agreeing to move in with you, Zayden De Rosa."

He met my gaze in the mirror as I arched a brow at him. "You're not moving in, Dare, just staying while Chase is out there waging psychological warfare on us. Safety in numbers and all that. Besides, the security is already compromised here. You're not moving back in, and we both know it."

I huffed, but he was right. After one break in—regardless of whether Lucas had opened the door himself—the whole vibe of my apartment was fucked. I was never going to get that same sense of comfort and safety within these walls again.

"Whatever," I conceded, pissed as hell that Chase had screwed up the home I'd built for Seph and me. With my makeup finished, I gave my reflection a once-over. The bruises and patched burns on my shoulders and left forearm were obvious as hell, but easily hidden by the addition of a cropped leather jacket.

On our way out, I deactivated the biometric scanners on the front door and just left it key-code locked. I wasn't storing anything particularly valuable in my apartment; only idiots kept a safe full of diamonds behind a Renaissance painting. My wealth was all secure in investments, offshore bank accounts, and safety deposit boxes. So I wasn't concerned about the decreased security on the door. Biometrics were there to keep Seph and me safe when we were home, nothing more.

"Let's take my McLaren," I said as we rode the elevator down to the parking garage.

Zed twitched a smile at me. "You gonna let me drive it?"

"Wash your mouth out, Zed," I hissed back with disgust. "You can't be trusted not to scratch her again."

His small smile spread wider into a chuckle. "Well then, we'll take my car. You shouldn't be driving for at least a couple more days. Or did you forget that you were recently almost blown up along with 7th Circle?"

I glared but couldn't argue. My body was *aching*, and I was too damn stubborn to take the prescribed painkillers. Now, more than ever, I wanted to keep my wits about me—at least until *after* I'd confronted my head of security about the traitors in our ranks.

So I just grumbled my irritation and let Zed open the passenger door to his Ferrari for me to get in. At least he was a decent driver and I didn't feel like I was taking my life into my hands when he was behind the wheel…like when I let Seph drive.

"What are you going to do about Lucas?" Zed asked as we drove over to Rainybanks and the Copper Wolf main office.

I gave him a sidelong glance. "What about him?"

He shot me an accusing look. "Chase took him to hurt you, which means he *knows* you care about the adorable little gumdrop."

I couldn't help the snort of laughter at that description of Lucas, no matter how insulting it might be. He *was* a bit of a gumdrop, all sweet and innocent. Flammable too.

"What can I do?" I replied with a small groan. "This is the point in the movie where the heroine is supposed to push the innocent victim of collateral damage away to protect them and keep them away from the dangerous criminal life."

Zed gave me a skeptical look. "Babe, I don't wanna be the guy to break bad news...but you're no heroine."

I gave him an eye roll. "No shit, Sherlock. Nor am I selfless or noble or morally irreproachable. Chase probably wants to tear down my support, take away all the people I care about. And he started with the easiest target."

Zed nodded. "Gumdrop."

"Stop it," I murmured with amusement. "But nonetheless, he wants me to be so consumed by guilt that I push Lucas away and retreat into myself. Put my walls back up. Second-guess my choices. Well, fuck that. All he's done is reminded me to keep the few I care about closer than ever."

Zed grunted a sound that could have easily been agreement or otherwise but didn't say anything to clarify his response. Instead, we drove in silence for some time until his phone rang.

He answered it on the car's internal speakerphone after giving the caller ID a cursory glance.

"Nico, what's the progress?" he asked, not waiting for pleasantries from the caller. Nico was one of Zed's higher-ranking team members, a man with a lot of loyalty to the Timberwolves and one of the least likely to be a double agent. Then again, no one was above suspicion these days.

"All sorted, sir," Nico replied. "The nurse that went by last night is getting Ms. Wildeboer ready for transportation this morning. Sunshine Estate is preparing her room as we speak."

I let out a small breath of relief to hear Lucas's mother was getting the appropriate help. "Did you have any trouble explaining things to her?" I asked, not caring that Nico knew he was on speakerphone.

"No, sir," he replied, not skipping a beat. "The nurse told Ms. Wildeboer that her son had sent her, as instructed. She apparently wasn't happy to be leaving the house today, but when it was explained that renovation crews will be working on wheelchair accessibility, she accepted it."

"Good work," Zed replied. "Make sure she gets settled into Sunshine and leave a protection detail on watch."

"Yes, sir," Nico responded. "On it."

The call ended, and I ran a hand over my hair. I'd woven it into a tight Dutch braid to keep it off my face, but the habit was still there.

"I need to call the hospital and check on Lucas too," I murmured, then stiffened when I realized I'd said that aloud. The mere fact that I was thinking about him, was worried for his well-being, made me vulnerable. Then again, if I couldn't let my walls down around Zed of all people, maybe I really was the broken, heartless bitch Seph thought I was.

Zed didn't question me, though. "We can stop by on the way back from Copper Wolf," he suggested. "I'm sure Gumdrop will be ecstatic to see you."

He said it with a heavy dose of teasing that made me smack him on the arm, but he just laughed and shrugged. "What? I would be, in his shoes. I don't blame the poor kid for falling head over heels in love at first sight."

I rolled my eyes. "He's not in love. It's just…lust. Or something. Anyway, let's discuss a game plan for dealing with our Timberwolves because I sure as fuck don't have time to personally interrogate all three hundred and eighty-seven members to find more traitors working for Chase."

Zed grimaced. "Agreed. But I had a thought about that earlier."

We spent the rest of the drive to Rainybanks discussing how we could both deal with Alexi—he needed a test of loyalty—and weed through our ranks at the same time. When we arrived, I wouldn't say we'd come up with the most airtight of ideas, but it was something and that was better than nothing. So, it'd do.

Alexi was waiting for us outside my office, his foot tapping a nervous rhythm on the tiled floor and his temples glistening with sweat. When he saw us approaching, he shot up out of his seat like it was made of cacti.

"Boss," he greeted me, his eyes darting between Zed and me.

I just gave him a small head tilt, a silent command to follow us into my office, which he did. He shut the door behind himself, then cautiously approached the desk as I shrugged off my jacket and sat down.

"Alexi, I trust you're already up to speed on everything that happened last night." I cocked a brow at him as he hovered over the guest chair like he didn't know if he should sit or not.

"Yes, sir. Absolutely. Fully informed." His expression implied he really would rather *not* have that information, but that was his job.

Zed let out a sigh as he leaned against the bookshelf at my back. "Sit down, Alexi. You're making me irritated hovering like that."

Alexi jerked a nod and dropped into the vacant seat in front of my desk. Out of habit, I pulled my Desert Eagle from my underarm holster and placed it down on the desktop. Yes, it was an intimidation move, but it was also a comfort thing, considering how badly bruised and scraped up I still was.

"What the fuck happened, Alexi?" I asked in a cool voice,

50

cutting straight to the chase. "My dancer was held and tortured underneath Anarchy for twenty-four hours, and none of us knew. You know who I found guarding the cell door when we got in there?"

My head of security grimaced. "Reggie. Yes, I heard. Wish I could've got my hands on him personally and draw that death out for days."

I was inclined to agree. "This is the second traitor in the ranks, Alexi. Last week it was an undercover FBI agent, who I'm not altogether convinced wasn't also there under someone else's orders. Now this?" I paused, letting the tension build in the room. "I'm going to need a fucking golden explanation, Alexi. This is happening on *your* watch. Under *your* authority. Give me one reason why I shouldn't shoot you right now."

Alexi tilted his chin up slightly, meeting my eyes despite the nervous sweat on his brow. "Honestly, sir, I don't have a good enough reason. This happened on my watch, and I need to bear responsibility. All I can do is apologize sincerely and swear to you that I'll do whatever it takes to prove my loyalty. I can't explain how this has happened so far, but I can ensure it won't happen again, sir, if you allow me the opportunity."

I held his gaze for a long moment, unblinking, then tilted my head to Zed. Fortunately for Alexi, he'd given us the one and *only* reason not to kill him. He hadn't lied or backtracked or shifted blame into anyone else's lap. He easily could have, too, given it was Zed's forged signature that had allowed the undercover FBI agent to infiltrate our ranks in the first place. But nope, Alexi had pulled his big-boy pants up and taken responsibility.

It was admirable and ballsy. I appreciated it.

"We're willing to allow you a chance to prove yourself, Alexi," Zed told him. "Take a deep dive into the Timberwolves, personally speak with *everyone* under our umbrella, and weed out anyone else that has been corrupted. No one believes for even a second that

51

these two were isolated incidents. Where there's smoke, there's fire. Smother that fire, Alexi."

Our head of security nodded firmly, relief clear across his face. "Yes, absolutely. Yes. I can do that. Thank you, sir." He directed his thanks to me, and I just nodded to the door.

"You can go," I ordered. "Don't fail me, Alexi. I'd hate to put a bullet in your brain."

He knew me well enough that he didn't fuck around babbling more thanks. He just stood up, gave us both a respectful nod, and beat a speedy exit out of my office. The door closed softly behind him, and I spun in my seat to look at Zed.

"What do you think?"

He shrugged, his hand resting on the gun at his belt. It was just a casual pose, one he affected pretty damn often. Yet...why was it suddenly striking me as sexy? Was that intentional on his part?

"I think he's solid," he replied, his eyes steady on mine. "Alexi has too much to lose to try and fuck us. But you're right that he's the best resource we have to weed out any other traitors. Hopefully, he finds them before any more damage is done."

I nodded, then winced as I pushed myself up out of my chair.

"You didn't take any painkillers today, did you?" Zed asked, the accusation clear in his voice and his expression as I tried to put my jacket back on with stiff arms.

"You know I didn't." I tucked my gun away and gave him a pointed look. In other words, *Don't fucking start with me here, Zed.* Not in my office with a phalanx of staff lurking just outside the door.

He took my silent reminder and held the door open for me to exit. I knew him too well to believe he was dropping the subject, though. He had that stubborn look on his face that promised me it was just on pause until we were alone.

Fucker. Lucky I loved his argumentative ass so much or he'd have been shark food ten times over by now.

CHAPTER 8

Zed and I detoured via Anarchy on our way back to his place to make sure everything had been efficiently cleaned up from the mess of the night before. I was pleasantly surprised to find a couple of the mid-rank Timberwolves had taken my orders quite literally and had spent all morning mapping out the hidden tunnels and checking their structural integrity to ensure my repurposed amusement park wouldn't collapse into a hole one day.

"They know," I commented to Zed as we left Anarchy some hours later.

He arched a brow at me. "That someone is gunning for our seat?"

I jerked a nod. "Not surprising, but irritating nonetheless. We need to hurry up and deal with Chase before anyone decides to plan a mutiny."

"Agreed, but that lot won't be the ones leading it." He gave a nod in the direction we'd just come from, indicating the Wolves who'd been working on Anarchy. "They sense the danger in the air, and they're using it as an opportunity to step up and prove themselves to you, Boss. The Timberwolves—for the most part—are all like that. A few bad eggs don't mean we throw the whole basket out."

I frowned. "I never planned to throw the whole basket out."

Zed gave me a look but said nothing. His meaning was clear enough without needing to voice it because it wouldn't be the first time I'd thrown the basket out. There was no doubt in my mind that a lot of the deaths the night my father died weren't necessary. I slaughtered a lot of people that night who'd been innocent of the crimes that'd forced my hand, but I'd been too paranoid, too *angry* to offer any benefit of the doubt. Anyone who'd remotely seemed suspicious had been killed.

"We're not there yet," I said quietly, staring out my window. "Not even close. Besides, we built this version of the Timberwolves ourselves, Zed. We personally selected every single one of them for the first three years. I'm fully aware that loyalty is strong within the Wolves. But...I wouldn't have expected Reggie to be a traitor."

He'd been one of the security guards at 7th Circle, not in my upper ranks but not all that much lower. He'd been with us since the beginning...but maybe that was the problem. Maybe he'd had ties to Chase that I hadn't picked up on in those early, blood-soaked days of my rule.

"Do you want to stop by the hospital and check on your boy toy?" Zed offered, changing the subject.

I scowled. "Don't call him that. You're *hardly* in a position to judge, given the dubious ages of your prior conquests. Pretty sure Seph told me one of those girls only recently graduated Shadow Prep."

Zed smirked. "At least she'd graduated."

I bit my lip to hold back my smile. He did *not* need encouragement. "Yes, let's stop by quickly. We need to let him know what's happening with his mom."

"You got it, Boss," he replied with a nod, taking a turn that would take us toward the private hospital where Lucas was being treated.

The closer we got, the more I worried at my lip with my teeth.

For all my tough talk with Zed this morning about refusing to back down and let Chase win…I was second-guessing myself. It was selfish of me, no two ways about it. I wasn't holding Lucas close out of some altruistic sense of protection for him. It was because I liked him and didn't want to let him go.

Like Zed had pointed out, I was no heroine.

"We'll keep this quick," I told him as we parked.

"If you say so," he murmured, walking beside me into the hospital. We bypassed the nurses' station and headed straight up to the floor Lucas was staying on. "I've got some calls to make. You go ahead."

I jerked to a stop a few feet away from Lucas's room. "What calls?"

Zed gave me a deadpan glare. "Are you being a chicken right now? Quit being such a girl and get your ass in there. Gumdrop took a knife to the chest for our shady history. You at least owe him a personal visit."

My lips parted in surprise. "Zed—"

"Dare." He all but growled my name at me, and I couldn't keep pretending things hadn't *drastically* changed in recent weeks. Not only was he talking to me with casual disrespect, but he was frequently using my nickname. Somehow, Chase rising from the dead was bringing Zed and me back to each other…and I wasn't even slightly mad about it.

So when he pointed at Lucas's room, I just flipped him off and made my way inside. He was right. Lucas deserved to see me, even if it was just to tell me he never wanted to see me again.

Deep down, though, I knew he wasn't going to say that. So when I entered his room and a smile like fucking sunshine lit his face, I wasn't shocked.

"Hayden, you came back," he croaked, then cleared his throat and winced. "I wasn't sure you would."

"Neither was I," I admitted, crossing over to the chair beside his bed.

He struggled a bit to sit up straighter, then used the mechanical bed remote to do the rest of the work. "Well, I'm glad you did," he told me with a wide smile.

It was making me all kinds of squirrelly, having him so damn *open* with his emotions. Who the fuck was so confident in their own skin in this day and age?

Lucas was. That's who.

"I had your mom moved to a care facility," I blurted out, sidestepping the awkward, unfamiliar feelings that he was stirring up in me. "Just temporarily, if she doesn't like it. But I figured it was better for you to know she was being taken care of while you heal."

His brows had shot up with my first statement, and for a moment he seemed speechless. Then he let out a long sigh of relief. "Thank you," he whispered, running a hand over his face. "Thank you, that was… You didn't need to do that. She is still semimobile and would have been okay on her own for a couple of days." He cringed as he said that, and I knew he didn't believe what he was saying. Not to mention how worried she would have been when he just didn't come home.

"Well, it's done. Zed's got some of our guys finishing the renovations to your place, but it might take a couple of weeks while they wait on parts." I'd had several conversations with the freshly appointed contractor while we'd been at Anarchy and approved all the costs.

Lucas gave a small frown. "The ramps were completed last week, though."

I gave him a long look. He'd had ramps installed over any steps or ridges between doorways, but that was it—which was understandable when money was tight. But the work my guys were doing would mean his mom wouldn't just be *making do*, she'd be comfortable.

"Has your doctor given you any updates on when you'll be

discharged?" I asked instead of explaining myself. I could already tell he'd only protest what he'd undoubtedly see as charity.

He gave a small nod. "Maybe tomorrow. He just wants to make sure the, uh, the burn on my chest isn't getting infected." He wrinkled his nose, and my shoulders tightened with tension.

"Lucas..." I let my voice trail off with a sigh. Out of habit, I bit the edge of my thumbnail as I searched for the right words, but Lucas reached out and gently tugged my hand away from my mouth.

"Don't bite your nails," he told me with mock scolding.

I stared at him a moment, stunned, then gave a sharp laugh and shook my head. "Fucking hell, you just perfectly imitated Zed for a second there. Anyway, I was going to ask what you remembered about the man who took you. The one who did all this." I waved to indicate his hospitalized condition. "You weren't super lucid when I saw you last night."

He grimaced but didn't let go of my hand. He just linked our fingers together over the stiffly starched bedclothes. "It was Reggie that attacked me at your place," he said, confirming what I'd already guessed. "I checked the video monitor like you told me, but I recognized him from 7th Circle and assumed—wrongly, of course—that it was okay to open the door."

Fury burned through my veins, and I once again wished I hadn't killed Reggie so damn quickly when we'd found Lucas last night.

"Was he there for you?" I asked, swallowing past my anger. "Or for Seph?"

Lucas gave me a firm nod. "Definitely for me. The eye-patch dude who came in after Reggie had beaten the shit out of me spouted some crap about how I deserved it for daring to put my hands on *his* woman." He quirked a bruised eyebrow at me, and I blew out a long breath.

"I'll tell you," I whispered, answering his silent query.

He gave a small nod. "But not here. I can accept that. Is Seph okay?"

I groaned. "She's fine. Safe. But…kinda pissed at me. Or *us*."

Lucas's brows shot up. "She knows?"

"It was unavoidable, so yeah. And she's far from happy with me right now, but she'll get over it. Eventually." Or maybe she wouldn't, and she'd hate me forever. But I could live with that, knowing she was still safe from the sins of our family.

"Fuck, I'm so sorry, Hayden," Lucas murmured, his eyes full of sincerity and guilt. "I should have said something from that first moment…"

I just shrugged. "Can't change the past, Lucas."

"I have to confess something," he said, then bit his lower lip in a way that was far too distracting. There was a scabbed split on one side, but it did nothing to detract from how lush his mouth was.

A flutter of dread spawned inside me. "Is this the part where you tell me you're some kind of double agent working for my enemies?" I said it like a joke, but part of me still wondered if it might actually be the truth. It was such coincidental timing to have met Lucas the same night Chase triggered his first attack on my business… Before he'd been attacked and nearly killed, all signs had pointed to Lucas being more than he seemed.

His brow dipped at my suggestion. "Uh, no. Is that what you think? No, I was gonna admit that I'd guessed you and Seph might be related before I got into your car that day. That first night at 7th Circle? I thought I recognized you from school, but before you even spoke, I'd known I was off the mark. Then…I dunno. You looked at me and I was just…gone. That sounds stupid, huh?"

My mouth had gone dry, and I needed to swallow before I could respond. Our fingers were still linked together, and suddenly I was hyperaware of every place our skin touched.

"Not stupid," I finally managed to say. "Just…unfamiliar. I'm not used to people in my world being as good as they seem, and you…" I let my voice trail off with a small laugh, shaking my head as his thumb traced a pattern over my inner wrist. "You seem better. It scares me that you're gearing up to rip my heart out." I whispered that confession so quietly it was barely audible, then instantly panicked that I'd given away too much of *me*.

I tried to pull free of his hand and stand up, but Lucas wasn't letting me get away so easily. His fingers tightened on mine, and he tugged me forward. It was a move I hadn't been expecting, especially considering his injured state, so I lost my balance. Only quick reflexes had me hit the bed and *not* land my entire weight on top of him.

"Lucas!" I protested, trying to push myself up again. He just grinned, though, threading his hand into the back of my hair and kissing me. I mean *kissing* me like I was his entire freaking world. Like my lips were the only thing sustaining him.

Fuck it. I kissed him back. After all, he *had* taken a hell of a beating thanks to me and my mistakes. I owed it to him. Not just to kiss him, but to stop *lying* to him about how I felt. Long story short, I liked him. I liked how I felt when I was with him. I barely even recognized the girl he brought out of me, and that was a good thing. So I kissed him back until we were both hot and bothered, our breathing rough when we broke apart.

"Dammit, Lucas," I muttered, our faces still just a scant inch away from each other. "That's not what I came here for."

His grin spread wide. "Are you sure, though?"

Unable to help myself, I smiled back at him as I reluctantly straightened up and untangled myself from his hold. "Pretty sure. I just wanted to see that you were okay, that's all."

"Because you care about me," he whispered, teasing.

I rolled my eyes. "You're not bad, I guess. Anyway, I've got guys keeping an eye on the hospital, so you're safe while you're here and your mom is safe at Sunshine Estate."

His eyes widened. "Sunshine Estate? That place costs—"

"Lucas," I growled, giving him a firm headshake. A soft knock on the door announced Zed a second before he entered the room. "Just rest up and get better. I'll sort out a safe place for you to stay after you get discharged."

"He's already got one," my second offered, folding his arms over his chest. He'd rolled his shirtsleeves up at some point during the afternoon, and his strong, tattooed forearms looked all kinds of incredible. "He can stay in one of my guest rooms until Chase is dealt with."

My jaw hit the damn floor.

"Uh..." Lucas was just as speechless as I was.

Zed gave a small shrug. "You're a weakness for Hades, Gumdrop. We can't risk Chase snatching you again to play bait in a trap. So you'll stay at my place, and for the love of liquor, you'll learn how to protect yourself better. Clear?"

What in the *fuck* was happening?

"Um, yes. Clear. Thank you, sir," Lucas stammered, giving Zed a wide-eyed nod of thanks.

Zed gave him a small nod in response. "Good. We'd better go, Boss. Our errand boy is almost back to my place with your things."

Still stunned, but not totally hating this idea, I gave Lucas a quick kiss and told him to rest, then followed Zed out into the hall. He walked beside me out of the hospital like nothing weird had just happened, and I pinched myself before we got into his car, just in case I was trapped in some weird fever dream.

I wasn't. It was just my life, for better or worse.

CHAPTER 9

Zed's so-called errand boy was already waiting at his front gate when we pulled up, and I couldn't stop the snort of laughter that escaped me when I saw who it was.

"Errand boy, huh?" I commented.

Zed shot me a smirk. "What? He wanted to be useful." He unlocked the gates, and Cass followed us up to the main house on his bike.

"Did you get what I asked for?" Zed barked at Cass as we got out of the car.

The big biker swung his leg over his bike and shot Zed a scathing glare. "I'm not an idiot," he growled back, unclipping some tightly packed bags from the sides of his bike. "Not exactly a hard request."

Zed didn't elaborate on that, just led the way into his castle-like home. Giving Cass a curious look, I started to follow. He cocked a brow at me in response, then ran his dark gaze over my outfit, lingering appreciatively on my tight leather skirt, before he gave me one of those microsmiles that made me all hot and bothered.

"After you, sir." He gestured for me to cross the threshold ahead of him, and I rolled my eyes. I'd definitely lost my scary edge around these men. And I didn't totally hate it either.

I brushed past him and threw a little extra swing in my step as I led the way into Zed's foyer. In fairness, I was wearing stiletto heels, so it would have been hard *not* to walk with at least a little sexiness.

We headed through to the open-plan kitchen-living area where Zed was already grabbing drinks from the fridge for us all. Cass dropped the bags he was carrying, then took two steps closer to me. He dipped low, brushing his lips across my ear.

"Tease," he accused in that gravelly rumble that set my nipples tingling.

"Food should be here any minute," Zed announced, tossing a bottle of beer across to Cass. The grumpy fuck caught it easily, then popped the cap off with his teeth. Ugh. That was *so* bad for his enamel but also so damn sexy.

"Dare," Zed said, jerking my attention away from the way Cass's lips were wrapped around the mouth of his beer. Cass shot me a wink, knowing damn well I was staring.

"Hmm?" I focused on Zed and tried really hard to pretend Cass wasn't smirking at me.

Zed rolled his eyes, seeming exasperated. "I've got pinot noir or Malbec. What's your poison tonight?"

I wrinkled my nose, considering the options, then shook my head. "Neither, unless you want me to fall asleep on the couch. Just give me some whiskey."

"Yes, sir," he replied, putting away the wineglass and exchanging it for a rocks glass.

I gave the bags Cass had brought in a curious glance, then tilted my head toward him. "What's with the luggage, Grumpy Cat? You moving in, too?"

He raised a brow at his nickname, then gave a slight headshake. "Nope, those're yours. Zed told me to pick up your clothes and shit so you wouldn't need to go back to your apartment. I could only fit so much on my bike, though, so I'll grab the rest tomorrow when I've got my car."

Surprise rippled through me, and I gave Zed a confused look. He shrugged. "You didn't want some rando going through your shit, and I didn't trust Alexi not to steal your panties or something. Cass seemed like the logical choice."

"How's the kid?" Cass asked, changing the subject as he sat down on one of Zed's barstools with his beer in hand.

Zed slid my drink over to me, and I took the stool beside Cass. Somehow the whole area seemed to shrink, though, because there wasn't enough space to sit without our knees touching.

"Stop calling him a kid," I chastised after a sip of my liquor. "Next time I have to remind you, I'll deliver the message with a right hook. Clear?"

Cass looked awfully like he was about to smile but swiped a hand over his mouth instead and gave a small nod. "Fair enough. How's *Lucas* then?"

"Gumdrop," Zed muttered under his breath, and I threw a piece of ice from my drink at him. Damn. That only left me two cubes, and I really liked three. Odd numbers sat more comfortably with me than evens.

"He seems to be doing well," I said, replying to Cass's question. "Getting discharged tomorrow and in pretty good spirits."

Zed scoffed. "That's one way to put it. He looked like he wanted to fuck you right there in the hospital bed after nearly dying yesterday. Gumdrop has stamina, I'll give him that."

I shot him a sly smirk. "You don't know the half of it."

Zed choked on the sip of beer he'd just taken and coughed violently for a moment. Served him fucking right.

The gate buzzer sounded, and Zed took the opportunity to escape and answer it. If he'd ordered us food, I was willing to bet it was wood-fired pizzas from Massimo's. Zed's heritage was Tuscan, and although he'd never actually *been* to Italy, he always seemed to find the authentic eateries wherever we were.

"Let's head out to the patio," Zed called out to us as he headed for the door to collect our food.

I didn't question his suggestion, just slid off my stool and carried my drink outside. Zed had an impressive outdoor lounge area set up with a gas firepit. It was cold enough out in the night air that I paused to flick a switch on, and a moment later the fire was crackling away with a warm glow. For all Zed's love of medieval architecture, he was a sucker for conveniences.

Cass sat down closer to me than he might have a month ago, and I didn't shift away. Fuck it. I *liked* him showing his hand…even if I was still stubbornly refusing to make another move on him. Let him do the chasing. It was about damn time.

But then there was still Lucas. He *said* he didn't care that I had something going on with Cass…but did he mean it? Or was he just saying what I wanted to hear?

Ugh. This wasn't me. I wasn't the girl who second-guessed her actions. I was the woman who took what she wanted and consequences be damned.

"Here," Cass murmured, pulling a leather pouch from his pocket. He unzipped it and took out a rolled joint, then handed it to me and tossed the pouch on the table between us and the open flame of the firepit.

I eyed the joint, then quirked a brow at him. "I don't know if this is the best idea under the current circumstances."

He leveled me with a hard stare. "I know that you refusing to take painkillers is a pretty fucking bad idea, Red. Your body needs a break. This or meds, your choice."

My pulse sped up at the thinly veiled threat behind his words. "Oh yeah? What are you going to do, Grumpy Cat? Hold me down until I comply?"

His dark eyes flashed with something all too suspiciously like amusement. "If I have to. You either look after yourself or we will do it for you. No one needs you turning into a martyr,

Hades. That's not going to get this fucking cockroach caught and killed."

Shock rippled through me. "*We?*"

"Yes, Boss," Zed answered, striding over the pavers carrying a stack of pizza boxes. He always ordered too many. "We. Cass and I apparently have something in common after all."

I scoffed a bitter laugh. "I'd say you have plenty in common."

Neither of them responded to that, just exchanged a *look* as Zed placed the pizzas down in front of the fire.

I silently cursed the two of them for ganging up on me but gratefully accepted my pizza from Zed when he located it. Authentic margherita with buffalo mozzarella and added prosciutto and garlic. So tasty.

Curious, I peered over at the pizza Zed handed to Cass, then gave him a quizzical look. "Really?"

He gave me a level stare. "What? I like what I like." Holding my gaze, he took a huge bite from his vegetarian pizza topped with grilled eggplant, sun-dried tomato, mushrooms, and artichokes.

Zed took the joint from the table, brought it to his lips, and lit it. He took a long drag but made no move to hand it over when I glared. Instead, he just held eye contact with me, unblinking and intense as he released the smoke from between parted lips.

How the fuck was he making my pulse race so hard? He was my friend. My *best friend*. I needed to stuff my libido back in its cage before I ruined that.

Instead of handing the joint to me, he passed it to Cass. When the hell had those two become so friendly? It was weirding me out. But...I also kind of enjoyed it. I liked that the three of us could hang out like this...like friends. Even if Cass did have his own gang to run.

Cass shifted in his seat, reclining his long body back against the cushions and letting his thigh rest against mine. The couch was *not* that small.

Okay. So, friends with a whole truckload of sexual tension filling the air. And a small part of me wished Lucas was there with us…even if I was having a hard time seeing how in the hell he could ever fit into our dynamic, sweet innocent gumdrop that he was.

Cass propped a boot up on the edge of the table, and I could *feel* his eyes on the side of my face as he took a drag on the joint. I stubbornly refused to look, though. I was too worried my own control would snap and I'd launch myself at the sexy fuck.

Exaggeration, for sure. I wasn't generally prone to thoughtless acts of pure hormones and desire. Then again, I also wasn't prone to developing feelings for a guy five years younger than me, yet here we were.

"Everything okay with Mini-Red?" Cass asked after some moments of silence. I'd somehow managed to inhale almost half my pizza in that time and wasn't even sad about it. What I *was* sad about was that I'd run out of liquor. Despite Cass's insistence that I dull my pain with weed, he wasn't actually going to force me into doing anything I didn't want to do. He was smarter than that, and respected me enough to make my own smart choices.

I wrinkled my nose at the empty glass in my hand, then gave Zed my best pleading look. He didn't even make me ask, just took the empty glass and headed inside to refill it.

"She's…safe," I answered Cass's question, placing my pizza box on the table and shifting slightly so I could look at him. "She's also not my biggest fan right now, and I don't expect that's going to change anytime soon." His brow quirked in silent question and I stifled a small groan. "I told her about Lucas."

He just held my gaze for a long moment, then understanding seemed to dawn on him and the corners of his mouth twitched. "Oh dear," he murmured with more than a heavy dose of amusement. "Something tells me Seph might have had a bit of a crush on your boy toy."

"Stop it," I muttered. "He's not a boy toy. He's almost nineteen."

66

Cass scoffed. "Uh-huh, that makes so much difference. She's staying with Arch and the boys?"

I nodded. "Yep, and they're aware of the situation. She's well protected there."

Cass took another drag off the joint and blew out the smoke in a long exhale. "Well, that's one less thing on your mind. She'll come around."

I wasn't so sure. But then again, it wasn't like she'd been *dating* him. It didn't matter anyway, so long as she was safe. We could iron out our differences after Chase was back where he belonged: six feet under.

"Are you going to share that or what?" I demanded, nodding to the joint between his thumb and forefinger.

A sly smile touched his lips as he handed it over. "And here I was thinking you'd make me follow through on that promise."

That utter fucknut had to wait until I'd taken a deep draw on the joint before saying that. So when it clicked about what he meant, I choked on the smoke like some kind of total first-timer.

"You okay, Boss?" Zed asked, coming back over with my refilled glass. This time it was just a fingerbreadth from the top and had five ice cubes.

"Fine," I replied in a strangled voice, handing the joint back to Cass, who looked far too fucking smug for his own good. Whiskey probably wasn't the recommended way to recover from a coughing fit, but it suited me just fine.

With the liquor burning a happy path all the way to my stomach, I closed my eyes and leaned back in my seat. As much as I hated being told what to do, Cass was right. I needed *something* to take the edge off my bruises and muscle aches. It'd barely been five days since the explosion at 7th Circle, and pushing myself so hard to find Lucas had taken its toll.

Zed sat back down on my other side, this time a whole lot closer than before he'd left, and I tilted my head to give him a small smile. Shit was completely blowing up in my life—literally—but I was having a hard time regretting it. Obviously, I wished Lucas hadn't been hurt. I'd never have wished that on him. But I liked suddenly feeling like *me* again. Like a real fucking person and not the hard-edged, cold-blooded murderess that *Hades* was.

Cass and Zed fell into quiet conversation about gang shit, and I let the low sounds of their voices just float over me while we passed the joint back and forth for a while, replacing it with another when the first burned out.

"I appointed a second," Cass informed us at some point when my glass was nearly empty again.

I cracked one eye open—when had I even closed them? "Oh?"

It'd been over a year since he'd taken over the Reapers, and I was beginning to think he didn't trust anyone in his own gang enough to appoint them as his second-in-command. Not that I blamed him. After the snake that was his predecessor, I wouldn't trust so easily either.

He inclined his head. "Roach."

It took me a moment to muster up a face for that awful name. "The scrawny kid?" I asked, frowning with confusion.

Cass smirked. "Older than Lucas, but yeah, that's him. I've had my eye on him since before Zane's fuckup. He just needed a bit more time under his belt. Now, I reckon he's ready to step up."

I peered at him from sleepy eyes. "Interesting choice," I murmured. "But a good one."

He met my gaze with heavy intensity. "I'm glad Hades approves of my decision."

I was too high and drunk—what a combination—to form a snappy reply, so I just drained the rest of my glass and closed my eyes once more. The two of them continued their conversation, discussing Roach's promotion in the Reapers and how things were going with the former Wraiths that Cass had added to his ranks.

Slowly, little by little, I slouched lower on the couch until my head was resting on Zed's shoulder. Then I started getting a pain in my neck, so I shuffled my sleepy butt around until my head was in his lap with my legs extended across Cass. I was still wearing my skintight leather skirt, which stifled my movements enough that this was the most comfortable I was going to get, short of taking my ass to bed.

One of them snorted a soft laugh, but I wasn't sure which of them it was. It didn't matter, because within a second they were back to their chatter—this time about the stats of upcoming fights scheduled at Anarchy. As they talked, Zed played with my hair, loosening it from the tight braid and twisting it around his fingers absent-mindedly. Cass's hands rested on my calves, and after a few minutes, he started tracing a soft pattern over my bare skin.

Yeah, I was in heaven.

CHAPTER 10

When I woke up in Zed's bed once again, it took me a hot second to remember how the hell I'd ended up there. Then it slowly came back to me, and I remembered leaving Cass and Zed drinking and smoking in front of the firepit to hunt for a guest room. None of them had been made up with bedding—of course, Zed and I had been gone all day—and I was tired enough that I'd just headed back to Zed's room and claimed a T-shirt and stolen his bed.

Perks of being his bestie, I figured.

I was alone in bed, and I took a few minutes to wake up, stretching my arms over my head and testing my muscles. Thankfully, I wasn't hurting anywhere near as much as the day before. My bruises and scrapes were *finally* healing up enough that I could feel normal. Or semi-normal. Normal enough.

Eventually, I sat up and looked around for my phone. I spotted it where I'd left it, plugged into Zed's charger beside the bed. But I also found a folded sheet of paper with *Red* scrawled across it in messy handwriting.

I blinked at it a couple of times, wondering if I was still half-asleep, then reached over and picked it up. For some unexplained reason, my heart was racing at a million miles an hour as I unfolded the paper and stared down at the thick block of messy handwriting in front of me. Then I started reading, and I couldn't wipe the smile from my face.

He'd taken me *so* literally. It was a love letter in every sense of the word…with a distinctive Cassiel Saint twist. Several parts made me snort with laughter, and more parts than that made my nipples hard and my pussy clench. By the time I got to his signature at the bottom, I was more worked up than I'd been since…uh, since I'd been grinding all over Lucas on the dance floor at Scruffy Murphy's three weeks ago.

"Shit," I breathed, flopping back down into Zed's pillows with the letter still clutched in my hand. My whole body was aching, turned on like I never knew ink on paper could get me. But… goddamn. For a man of so few spoken words, Cass had a *way* with the written word.

For a hot second, I contemplated handling business myself right then and there, but before I could get my hand into my own panties I remembered where I was. Zed's bed.

As much as my friend liked a bit of exhibitionism, I doubted he'd appreciate finding me masturbating in his bed—especially while I was thinking about another guy. Or, hell, maybe he'd be into that?

With a groan, I sat up and raked my fingers through my hair. I needed to pull my shit together. I *needed* to go find Cass and tell him—*show* him—exactly what I thought of his love letter. Maybe then I could stop acting like a horny teenager. Or maybe it'd make me worse, but I was willing to give it a try.

Climbing out of Zed's comfy bed, I spotted Cass's bags near the door. He must have delivered them along with his letter after I'd already fallen asleep. No shock that I hadn't woken up, considering how stoned I'd been.

I rifled through, searching for some clean clothes, and pulled out a pair of black skinny jeans, a charcoal-gray bodysuit that showed off a decent amount of side-boob, and…no underwear. Not a single pair of panties were to be found in either bag. Nor had he packed me any shoes. Fucking men were so dense sometimes.

With a sigh, I figured I could make do, so I took my clothes with me into the bathroom. I showered quickly, not washing my hair, then dressed as my stomach loudly rumbled and twisted with hunger. I'd grabbed my makeup when Zed and I had stopped at my apartment yesterday, so I made quick work of my face, then finger-combed my loose curls to tame my mane.

When I looked pretty damn presentable—even with my yellow-green bruises showing in the sleeveless bodysuit—I made my way downstairs with bare feet in search of food.

Zed never fucking let me down. Never. He was already hard at work in the kitchen cooking up what smelled like omelets and freshly baked bread. Was he for freaking real?

I padded over to where he stood at the stove, an apron tied around his neck and earbuds blasting music in his ears, and wrapped my arms around his waist in a tight hug.

He leaned back into me, reaching up to tug his earbuds out. "Good morning, Sleeping Beauty."

"Zayden…did you *bake bread* this morning? What the fuck, dude?" I smiled up at him when he grinned wide.

"Technically, no. The bread maker did. I just threw the ingredients in last night and set the delayed start so it'd finish in time for breakfast." He arched a cocky brow at me, flipped the cooked omelet out onto a waiting plate, then spun around to loop his own arms around my waist.

His thumbs hooked in the loops of my jeans, and a slight tug pulled me in closer so we were chest to chest.

"Still counts," I told him, tilting my neck to hold his soft gaze. "Thanks for letting me steal your bed again. I was wrecked last night."

His lips curled in a teasing smile. "No shit. You snored too." I pulled away slightly, a little horrified, but he tugged me back into his hold with a laugh. "I'm kidding, you sensitive petal. Hungry?"

My stomach howled. "Starving," I groaned.

Zed's gaze darkened. "I know that feeling." His words were barely more than a murmur, but the sound of a door slamming startled me out of his embrace.

"Who—"

"Good morning, Red," Cass rumbled, loping into the kitchen in nothing but a pair of low-slung jeans with the top button undone. Water dripped from his floppy Mohawk haircut and ran in a tantalizing line down his ripped, ink-covered chest.

Zed brushed some hair away from my face, then brought his lips to my ear. "Careful, Boss, you're drooling all over my kitchen floor." My jaw snapped shut, and Zed snickered a soft laugh. "Subtle. Real subtle."

"Fuck you," I hissed, turning my back on Cass and reaching for the omelet Zed had just finished.

My friend shot me a wink. "One of these days, I might call your bluff on that." Then he just continued making omelets like *nothing* had happened.

And there went my appetite. How the shit was I supposed to enjoy my breakfast while psychoanalyzing what the ever-loving shit he meant by that? Oh yeah, that's right. Zed was an incredible cook. I'd suffer through my delicious breakfast and shove that weird comment aside to unpack later.

"How come you're still here?" I asked Cass instead as I carried my plate over to the island and perched on a stool.

He quirked his scarred brow at me. "It's not safe to drink, smoke, and drive a motorbike, Red. You know that."

I hummed a sound of agreement. It was a fair point.

"How'd you sleep?" he asked, sliding onto the stool beside me and making no attempt to put a shirt on. Where even *was* his shirt? More to the point, was that a nipple piercing?

73

Focus. On. Food. Must keep my focus on the food and not the half-naked man beside me.

"Great, thanks," I replied, taking a bite of my breakfast to save myself from giving any more information than that.

He ran a hand over that short beard. Or long stubble. It was somewhere in between, and despite my usual distaste for beards on men, Cass was seriously rocking that look. "Hmm," he murmured. "Read anything good lately?"

I'd been expecting *something*, so I managed not to choke on my food. I chewed, swallowed, then met his heated gaze with a perfectly collected expression. "I did. Some very...*enlightening* material, thank you. The author seemed to have a lot to say for himself, which was rather surprising."

Cass gave an amused sort of grunt. "Sounds like he was inspired."

"Sounds like he has a filthy fucking mind hiding under all that ink, and I need brain bleach to erase the pure smut I was subjected to in delivering that letter." Zed gave an exaggerated shudder and slid a freshly made omelet over the island to Cass.

My face flamed hot and a strangled sound escaped my throat as I stared at Zed. He'd *read* it? Oh...fucking hell.

"Shouldn't read shit not addressed to you, De Rosa," Cass rumbled, totally unapologetic.

Clearing my throat, I decided I really wasn't in the mood for... whatever the fuck seemed to be going down between the two of them. It felt awfully like some kind of pissing contest, and I wasn't here for that.

"Have we heard anything from the hospital about Lucas's release?" I asked Zed, firmly changing the subject as he tipped a fresh, steaming loaf of bread from his bread maker.

"Nothing yet," he replied as he cut some thick slices. "I'll call and ask for an update after breakfast."

I jerked a nod, shifting my brain into business mode. "I need an update from Alexi, and I'm hoping like hell he isn't a traitor, too."

Cass scoffed. "Alexi? No way. Loyal to a fault and totally in love with you, Red."

Zed shot me an I-told-you-so look, which I brushed off.

"Don't you have a gang of your own to be running today, Saint?" I quirked a brow at Cass, who seemed to have no fucking issues with holding my gaze in return. So much for being turned off by my cold *Hades* face. Or maybe my bare feet that didn't quite reach the floor were killing my badass vibe.

He shrugged. "Nah, my new second needs to get his feet wet."

I rolled my eyes. "How convenient."

"Besides," he continued, shifting subtly closer to me so I could legitimately feel his body heat radiating from his bare flesh. That was definitely a nipple piercing. "I promised I'd pack up the rest of Seph's and your things today."

I met his eyes with a whole lot more cool and calm than I was actually feeling. "I think I can handle it, big guy. But we appreciate the assistance last night."

"And the weed," Zed added, oh so helpful this morning. "That was good shit. But we've probably got it from here."

Cass arched his scarred brow at Zed, a flicker of disbelief on his face. Then he turned to me with a hard, accusing glare. "Oh, hell no."

I tilted my head to the side, a spark of amusement warming me as I saw the defiance in his eyes. "Excuse me?"

He glared harder. "I said *hell no*. You two are not shutting me out again now." He slid off his stool and carried his empty plate to the sink like the politest houseguest. "Come on, Red. We'll go swap my ride on the way."

Without waiting for me to agree—or decline—he sauntered his fine ass out of the kitchen. I assumed he'd gone to find the rest of his clothes, but with Cass nothing was certain.

"Stubborn fucker," I muttered, not shifting from my seat but letting my eyes drift in the direction he'd just disappeared like I could see through the walls and eye fuck him as he dressed.

Zed huffed a sound of agreement, or irritation, then dropped a hot slice of bread onto my plate. It was covered in melting butter, and my mouth watered at the sight of it. Not to mention the *smell*. Nothing smelled as good as freshly baked bread.

"You're the best, Zed," I groaned before taking a bite of the buttery bread.

He shot me a smirk and a wink. "I know how you like your bread buttered, Boss."

What the fuck?

He was lucky I'd already swallowed that mouthful or I would have choked on it. Prick. Was he just messing with me for fun? When had we slipped back into this teasing shit? Not that I was complaining... I was enjoying it.

"Perv," I muttered, then took another bite, trying not to think too hard about the vaguely flirty comment. "I bet you don't." I sent him a wink of my own, and he didn't laugh like I expected.

Instead, he just held my gaze as he rubbed his palm over his shadowed jaw. "Sounds like a challenge."

My brows shot up. But before I could dig myself into a deeper hole with pseudo-flirty Zed, Cass yelled from somewhere vaguely in the direction of the foyer, "Red, move your fine ass. Let's roll!"

"Screw you, Saint!" I shouted back. "No one orders me around." Still, I was entertained enough that I hopped off my seat and went in search of my gun and shoes. Fuck riding bitch on the back of his bike again, though.

"I'm borrowing a car," I told Zed when I returned to the kitchen to snag the rest of my bread.

He didn't argue, just pulled open a drawer and tossed me a set of keys. "Take the Audi, but don't scratch it."

I snorted a laugh. "Coming from you, who scratched my

76

McLaren? Cute. Real cute. I'll be quick on this. Can you arrange a meeting with Dallas? I'm ready to go hunting."

Zed jerked a nod, folding his arms over his apron. "You got it, Boss."

"Come on, Saint!" I yelled out to Cass. "I'm driving."

CHAPTER 11

Close proximity to Cassiel Saint after reading his version of a love letter? Terrible, *awful* idea. We'd barely made it out of Zed's garage before my skin was prickling with the sexual tension in the car.

To my relief, though, he got a call from his newly minted second, Roach, just a few moments after we turned out of Zed's gates, and I was spared the awkward silence. Not that I had any intention of pulling over to jump his bones on the side of the road; I had shit to do and a not-so-dead ex to hunt down. No matter how badly my cunt was begging for a bit of Cass's dick, it could wait.

When we reached my apartment building, there was a space directly across the road from the front door, so I didn't bother parking in the underground garage.

"What day is it?" I muttered mostly to myself as I climbed out of the car. Everything since the explosion at 7th Circle had turned into a whole big blur in my mind, and I'd totally lost track of time.

Cass tilted his head to the side, giving me a curious look. "Monday. You okay?"

"I'm fine," I replied with a small sigh. I was physically fine, but my mental health was in shreds—no doubt exactly what Chase wanted, that sick fuck. It wouldn't be the first time he'd gotten off on my fear and mental deterioration.

I suppressed a shudder as dark memories tried to worm their way out of the iron box I kept them locked in. Hell no. Nope. Not on my watch, not ever.

And yet, instead of entering my building, I took a detour to the newspaper stand a little farther down the street. It hadn't even been a conscious thought; I just *needed* to check the obituaries. Either there would be another creepy fucking message or reading strangers' death notices would calm me down, help me feel grounded once more after such a chaotic few days.

"Sudden desire for the daily news?" Cass asked as I flipped through the stacks, hunting for the weekend paper. It always had the best obits.

"Something like that," I muttered, still searching.

"Good morning, Daria!" someone called out, and I looked up from the stack of papers I'd been sorting through.

I carefully shifted my expression from cold-hearted bitch to pleasant Daria Wolff and tugged my jacket closed to cover my rather obvious handgun.

"Good morning, Jeanette," I responded to one of my downstairs neighbors. She was out walking her dog, a little yappy thing that liked to pee when it was excited, and she paused when she got closer.

Her smile was genuine, but the way her eyes trailed over Cass made me want to punch her in her cute nose. In her midforties, Jeanette was still a total babe with a body to die for. She'd regret it if she tried flaunting that body in front of Saint, though.

"I heard about the break-in on Friday night," she told me, wisely shifting her gaze back to my face. "Oh gosh, were you home?" She reached out to touch the side of my face where I still had a fading bruise, and I flinched away before her finger reached me.

"No," I responded quickly, giving a tight smile to cover my flinch. "No, this was just a clumsy boxing accident at the gym last week."

She looked instantly relieved at my excuse. "Oh, phew. I'm glad. Anyway, I hope you get everything sorted on insurance." With another smile, she carried on her way with her yappy dog trotting happily along beside her, totally carefree. Lucky bastard.

When I turned my attention to Cass, he was watching me with a mixture of curiosity and amusement that instantly made me suspicious.

"What?" I snapped.

He shrugged. "You have neighbors."

I frowned. "So do you." He lived in a Reaper-owned block on the west side of town, but it was still an apartment building.

"My whole building is Reaper occupied," he informed me with a small headshake. "Your neighbors are normal people who think your name is actually *Daria Wolff*. It's..." His voice trailed off, and my mood soured. If he was about to have another mood swing like when he'd seen me transform from Hayden to Hades, we were about to have *issues*.

"It's *what*?" I growled with a clear edge of warning.

"Fascinating," he replied in an equally dark growl. Then he leaned forward, brushing past me to snag the paper I'd been looking for. "Here. Saturday's, right?"

"Right," I murmured, taking it from his hand, then paying the vendor before tucking it under my arm. Ignoring Cass's questioning look, I started back toward my apartment building, then paused when a car I didn't recognize exited the parking garage. Given how many of the building's parking spots I owned, there weren't many other cars that parked down there. And that...that wasn't one belonging to any of the residents.

That wasn't totally unheard of, I supposed. Maybe someone had gotten a new car or it was a visitor they'd given access to. But in light of everything *else* going on, it made me hesitate.

"What's wrong?" Cass asked, pausing with me.

I scowled at the car as it waited for traffic to break so it could turn into the street. The windows were tinted dark enough that I couldn't make out the driver—beyond what I'd think was a legal tint—which made my paranoia prickle.

"Something…" I murmured, still frowning at the car when it turned, entering traffic. "I don't know. Maybe nothing. Just—"

I cut my sentence short at the muffled sound of an explosion, accompanied by the ground trembling. Then another. And another.

I counted them even as Cass threw his considerable weight at me, wrapping me in a human shield and dragging me behind a car. Seven. Seven explosions, then silence.

"What the—" Cass started to say through the ringing in my ears. I shrugged free of his hold and pushed to my feet, needing to see my building. That's where the bombs had gone off, I was *certain* of it. That mysterious car…seven explosions… I had left seven vehicles on my parking level, six cars and my motorcycle. That mother*fucker* had blown up my cars.

"Get in!" I shouted at Cass, already sprinting toward Zed's car. Fuck the damages, I was catching that bombing fucknut before he escaped this time.

Cass didn't question me, just dove into the passenger seat as I pulled out of the parking space. Another explosion had me slamming my foot on the brake, though. This one was louder than the others. Bigger.

My heart shuddered and my breath caught as I swung my gaze back to the building. Almost as if in slow motion, the walls began to crack and fall, the entire structure collapsing in on itself.

I didn't stick around to watch the rest. There was nothing I could do to fix it now, but I *could* chase down the most likely suspect. So, steeling my aching chest against the loss of life that'd just happened, I pressed my foot down on the accelerator and sped after the disappearing black sedan in the distance.

For a second I lost sight of the car, and my stomach sank. But then I spotted it between a break in the traffic ahead and increased my speed to narrow the gap.

Cass didn't speak, just reached over and buckled my seat belt for me, then did his own before he pulled out his phone to text someone.

Moments later, I needed to swerve sharply to avoid colliding with fire engines and ambulances screaming down the street, no doubt headed for the remains of my apartment building. They were too late to do anything, though. Whoever had been home when the bombs had gone off was dead.

"He's going to take the freeway," Cass told me as I wove between cars. The darkly tinted car knew I was on his ass now and had sped up accordingly. If that didn't confirm my suspicion…

"I know," I replied, my eyes glued to my target. He was sticking to the outside lane, furthest from the on-ramp, but I'd put money on it that he'd make a last-minute switch. Sure enough, a second later he darted across three lanes, clipping the back of a minivan and mounting the curb to make it onto the on-ramp.

"Idiot," Cass grunted as I followed with ease, having already positioned myself in the correct lane in anticipation.

"How good of a shot are you, Saint?" I asked with grim determination as I matched pace with the black car. Luckily, traffic was light on this road and no chance of crashing into innocent bystanders.

Cass huffed a sound. "Don't insult me, Red."

I mentally rolled my eyes, a touch of amusement breaking through my cold determination. "Well then, what the fuck are you waiting for? Shoot out his tires."

"Yes, ma'am," he murmured, and I flicked him a quick look. Was he…? No. Surely not. This was *not* the time for flirting. Must have been my imagination.

Shaking it off, I switched lanes and accelerated harder to bring us as close to our target vehicle as I could get without endangering *us* when he spun out. Cass rolled his window down and pulled his gun.

Before he could shoot, though, I spat out a curse and pressed my foot on the brakes, letting the black car pull away.

"Red, what—" Cass started to protest, then saw what I saw. "Oh, for *fuck's* sake."

I seethed but maintained a safer speed as we passed three school buses full of elementary-aged children. Must have been a field trip, and I sure as fuck wasn't tempting karma any more by deliberately shooting at a speeding vehicle right behind them.

"Fuck, fuck, fuck, fuck it all to fucking hell," I whispered as I glanced in my mirror to make sure all three buses were safely behind me before hitting the gas again. "Where is he?"

Cass took a second to reply, his dark eyes searching the road ahead of us before shaking his head. "Take this exit," he told me.

"You sure?" I glanced at him, needing to make the decision in less than a second.

"No." He looked back at me, his brow furrowed.

Fuck it. I jerked the steering wheel sharply, flying down the off-ramp at about four times the legal speed. The sharp turn at the base of the ramp made our car skid out slightly, but I was able to regain control easily while frantically searching the road ahead for any sign of that blacked-out car.

"There!" Cass barked, pointing to the grass shoulder. I slowed down to see what he'd found, and sure enough, right where the grass met the road, there were tire tracks.

A surge of satisfaction ran through me, and I gave a grim smile. "Found you, sneaky fuck."

We followed the tracks into the forest by the side of the road but didn't need to go far to find what we were looking for. Only about fifty yards in, there was the black car with its front end crumpled against a tree and the engine smoking.

I barely even remembered to put the car in Park before leaping out. Cass beat me over to the smoking vehicle, though, his gun out and ready as he approached the driver's side. My own gun was already in my hand, and I had no recollection of even pulling it. Muscle memory.

"Shit," Cass spat out as he peered inside. A second later he lowered his weapon and reached for the door handle. I didn't question him as he yanked it open, because he immediately stepped aside to let me see.

Our driver was still inside, but he was very much dead. Blood and chunks of brain decorated the interior of the car, and when I nudged his lolling head back, a bullet wound decorated his forehead. The front windscreen of his car was totally smashed in and the hood totally crumpled.

"You've got to be fucking kidding me," I hissed. A cursory glance around didn't reveal a gun that he might have used, which either meant it'd fallen between the seats…or that someone else had shot him and gotten away.

I let out a string of creative curses, then spotted a folded piece of paper in the dead man's hand. "For the love of *fuck*," I breathed, eyeing the paper with distaste. I had to see what was on it, though. *Had* to.

Cringing, I put my gun away, then tugged the paper free of the dead driver's fingers and unfolded it.

I scanned the message scrawled there, already half anticipating what it might say and not surprised when I was right.

"What is it?" Cass rumbled, his gun still drawn and his shoulders bunched with tension.

I gave a small sigh, then read it aloud. "*Sorry I scratched your car, Darling. Still love me?*" I folded the paper again and tucked it into my back pocket. "Let's go. This was a setup. He's just playing with me."

Cass blinked at me like he was trying to understand that note. "Chase Lockhart?"

I jerked a nod, already stalking back over to Zed's car. He followed, sliding back into the passenger seat and buckling his seat belt as I backed out of the trees once more and headed back toward town.

"Are you going to tell me the whole story, or are we still playing this secret-keeping game?" Cass demanded after a few minutes of tense silence.

My first instinct was to tell him to shut the fuck up and kick his ass out of the car. But then a heartbeat later, I desperately *wanted* to tell him everything. Would it really be so bad to let him in? So far, only Zed knew what had really happened the night I took over the Timberwolves. Only Zed...and Chase.

Fucking hell. Chase had just destroyed my entire apartment building with dozens of innocent lives inside. He'd just killed... *all* those people and laid the weight of guilt squarely across my shoulders.

I tried to speak to answer Cass, but all that came out was a panicked sort of gasp. Shit. *Shit.* My grip on the steering wheel tightened to try to hide the tremors in my hands, but I wasn't fooling Cass for even a second.

"Pull over," he ordered, and I did. That, in itself, spoke to my level of shock.

Cass climbed out of the car, circled around the hood, then popped my door open. He even reached over and unbuckled my seat belt, then jerked his head to the seat he'd just vacated. "Shift over. I'm driving."

The desire to kick back rose up on instinct, but I had to admit how stupid I would be to continue driving in my state. My heart was racing so hard it physically hurt, and my entire body felt like a live wire. So I bit back my stubborn refusal and climbed over into the passenger seat.

Cass didn't comment on my easy acceptance, either, which helped. He just got in and buckled my seat belt—which apparently I'd forgotten to do again—and his own.

85

"Where are we going?" I asked in a hollow voice as he turned us back onto the road.

He glanced over at me, those dark eyes of his all kinds of intense and thoughtful. "My place," he rumbled and didn't elaborate any more than that.

CHAPTER 12

"What are we doing here?" I finally asked after Cass closed and locked the door to his apartment behind us. His place was exactly what I'd pictured it might be: a small, one-bedroom, minimalist-style unit with exactly zero personality anywhere in sight. Like he'd never really moved in.

Cass didn't answer, just tossed his jacket over a chair, then went to his fridge. He pulled out two bottles of beer and tossed one to me.

"Sit down, Red," he told me, nodding to the couch, which looked brand new. Did he never spend any time here? Or just never have company?

With a sigh, I crossed over to the couch and twisted the top off my beer to take a sip. It wasn't even noon, but who gave a fuck? I needed *something* to settle my nerves and regain my calm.

Cass dropped down on the sofa beside me and lounged in that typical tall-guy sort of way, all sprawling legs and arms. Hot as hell when Cass did it, not so much when it was some random dude in a public space.

Ignoring him, I set my beer down on the table, then shrugged out of my leather jacket. It was cute with my outfit and functional, as it stored spare clips for my gun and a couple of knives, but not amazingly comfortable.

The garment thudded heavily when I tossed it onto the coffee table, and Cass quirked a brow at me in question.

"Like you don't carry spare weapons in yours," I muttered, picking my beer up once more. I still had my Desert Eagle strapped under my arm, but I wasn't exactly here for a pool party. It could stay put.

Cass just scoffed and tipped his beer back. Damn, he even made that look sexy.

"Why are we here, Saint?" I asked again. "Because this is probably not the best time to hang out and get stoned."

A microsmile touched his lips. "That's cute."

Sometimes his lack of verbal skills really irritated me. "What's cute?"

"That you want to hang out and get stoned with me." His gaze dipped to my lips on the mouth of my beer bottle. "But that's not what I had in mind."

Sick of trying to pry answers out of him, I just sat back and drained half my bottle with one gulp, then wiped my mouth on the back of my wrist like a really classy bitch.

"What did the note mean?" Cass asked after a long pause.

I huffed a humorless laugh. "It meant Chase is crazier now than he ever was. That's my guess, anyway." The beer soured in my stomach, and I regretted drinking it so fast. Tension vibrated through me, and my fingertips danced an anxious pattern on the side of my beer. This wasn't me. I wasn't this jittery, scared woman. Every message from Chase was making me forget more and more of who I was *now*. I kept backsliding into the weak, easily manipulated *victim* I'd been back then. Back when I'd been stupid enough to think he loved me.

"He blew up all my cars," I said eventually. "Those seven smaller explosions? My cars. And Fat Bob. The note was his way of taking credit for it." I pulled it out of my back pocket and smoothed it out again.

"I'd say that was a little more than scratching them," Cass muttered, then gulped his own beer.

I gave him a weak smile. "Zed taught me how to drive when I was sixteen," I told him. "But he didn't trust me not to crash *his* car, so we would take Chase's instead and just…not tell him. Until one night I thought a cat was on the road, and I swerved to miss it. Crashed right into a tree." I swallowed heavily as the old, venomous emotions clinging to my memories of Chase tried to surface. "I knew he was going to be *so* mad, so I wrote him a note and left it taped to the windshield after the car got towed back to his place."

Cass nodded his understanding. "Gotcha. Word for word, I assume?"

I wrinkled my nose. "Pretty much."

He was quiet for a long time. I had nothing else I wanted to add to the story, so I just tossed the note on the table beside my jacket and finished my beer.

Cass's phone beeped and he checked it, then nodded to me. "Zed's trying to get ahold of you."

Oops. My phone was on silent. I found it in the pocket of my jacket and saw the screen flashing with Zed's name already, so I slid my thumb across the answer button.

"I'm fine," I said before he could even get a word out. "He waited until we were right outside to blow it."

There was a pause on the other end of the phone. "To blow what, Boss?"

I don't know why, but I looked over at Cass in confusion. Not that he could hear Zed on my phone, but I was *confused*. "The… Wait, what were you calling about?"

"The hospital called me to come pick Lucas up. I thought you'd want to know. Dare, *what blew up?*" Zed sounded like he was just one step away from shouting at me, which was new for him.

I rubbed a hand over my face, cursing myself for not letting him speak first. "My building. Landon House. Chase fucking blew up my cars, then took the entire building down for good measure."

Another pause. Then a muffled string of obscene curses. "Where are you now?" His voice was shaking with fury, and I guessed part of that was over the loss of my McLaren. Or maybe the fact that Mrs. Greenbriar had almost certainly been inside at the time of the explosion. In fairness, I was simply avoiding thinking about all those deaths. It was the only reason I hadn't given in to my panic attack in the car earlier.

I let out a sigh. "I'm with Cass. We followed the guy from the scene and caught up with him just outside Shadow Grove. Chase got there first, though."

"Shit," Zed said with a groan. "Where are you? I'm getting in my car now."

I shot a glance at Cass again, but he was just watching me with an unreadable expression. His long fingers toyed with the label on his bottle, and I found the small movement strangely mesmerizing.

"I'm fine here," I told Zed, evading his question for some reason. "Go pick Lucas up, and I'll meet you at home." I stiffened, my pulse racing. "I mean, at your house."

Another pause. "Sure thing, Boss." He ended the call, and I tossed my phone back onto the table.

"You okay?" Cass asked after a moment.

I blew out a breath, running my hand over my hair. "Yeah. I should go. Thanks for…" I gave a shrug. Thanking people was still an uncomfortable concept for me. I wasn't used to giving a shit about social niceties.

Cass leaned forward and slammed his beer bottle on the table. "Stop," he snapped. "Stop *doing* that."

His sudden anger gave me a small jolt of shock, but not in a bad way. Just…it was surprising to see a raw emotion out of his

90

perpetually stonelike state…and fascinating in a way that made me want to poke the bear with a stick.

But not now. Now, I had to deal with the destruction of my building, set up death benefits for my neighbors who were killed, and, somehow, hunt down Chase.

"Spare me the tantrum, Saint," I told him in a cool voice. "I don't have the time or the patience for this." Grabbing my jacket and phone from the table, I stood up and started toward the door.

"So, we're not going to talk about it?" he demanded before I could even get my arms into the sleeves of my jacket.

Spinning around to face him, I flipped my hair out of the collar. "Talk about what?"

His eyes blazed. "The letter. You demanded I write you a letter, so I *did*. But you still don't trust me enough to let me help."

I gave a bitter laugh before I could catch myself. "I don't trust anyone, Cass. Don't take it personally."

Silly me for thinking that would be the end of it. I turned my back on him and reached for the door handle. But I'd barely gotten the door open a couple of inches before his huge palm slammed it shut again.

"You trust Zed," Cass rumbled, his lips so close to my ear that his breath warmed my skin. How the shit had he moved so freaking fast? Then again, he'd trained with Phillip D'Ath, just the same as Zed and me. It really wasn't *that* surprising.

I drew a slow breath, trying to calm my racing heart. "Zed's my second. My best friend." I grimaced and amended that statement. "My only true friend."

Cass left his hand planted against the door, fencing me in on one side. His other hand brushed the hair away from my neck, and I shivered involuntarily as his fingertips brushed my skin.

"You trust Lucas." His voice had dipped to a husky whisper, and my whole body was responding.

I gave a small headshake, my eyes still glued to his tattooed hand pressed against the door. "Do I, though? Lucas knows nothing about me. He has no idea why he was taken and tortured. All I trusted him with were my orgasms. And look where that landed him."

Cass shifted closer, his chest brushing my back and his facial hair tickling my neck as he bent low over me. "That's still trust, Red. What do I have to do to earn the same?"

I gave a sharp laugh, spinning around abruptly to face him. "You wanna give me orgasms, Saint?" I tilted my head back, mocking him as our eyes locked.

He didn't flinch. "I thought I was pretty clear about that in my letter, Red."

My lower belly fluttered. He really fucking had been. But that *wasn't* all he was asking for here. I knew it. He knew it. But apparently we were both just pretending this was only about sex.

I dragged my lower lip through my teeth, sorely tempted. "I've got too much shit to deal with right now, Cass. I don't have time for this."

He wasn't backing down. In fact, he just leaned in closer, his mouth hovering over mine like he was waiting for me to kiss him again. "I'm not asking for forever, Red."

Like a magnet, my body arched closer to him, and I mentally chastised myself. I wasn't that girl. I wasn't ruled by my dripping cunt like some airheaded twit.

Cass was done messing around, though. That subtle signal from my body must've been all the answer he needed because his mouth crashed onto mine with an intensity that knocked the breath clear out of me. My back hit the door, and I turned to putty in his hands. Whether he intended to or not, he'd just stumbled over my Achilles' heel. I *wanted* him to take charge.

With a small moan, I kissed him back, letting my tongue meet his as my fingers dug into the hard flesh of his back. His huge hand gripped my face, holding me firmly when he pulled back from our kiss, his eyes burning with heat as he stared straight into my soul.

"I'm not *asking* you for forever, Red," he murmured in that deep, husky voice that all but dripped sex. "But you'll give it to me anyway."

I scoffed, genuinely amused by the size of his ego. "We'll see."

A wicked smirk touched his lips. "Damn right, we will." He used his grip on my face to bring my lips back to his, this time kissing me slowly and with undeniable purpose.

It scared me. It legitimately *terrified* me. Cassiel Saint didn't just want a quick fuck; he wanted commitment. There was no way I was ready to give him that. Not now, probably not ever. But I also wasn't pushing him away and walking out the door.

When his hand shifted from my face to my neck and gave a light squeeze, I moaned in a way that would put a porn star to shame. His response was just to crush me tighter against the door until the hard length of his dick trapped in denim was unmistakable against my hip.

His fingers slid under the collar of my jacket, and his other hand at my waist tugged me slightly away from the door so he could push my jacket off. I let it fall from my arms, hitting the floor with a heavy thud. I quickly unclipped my gun holster and tossed it onto the decorative table near his door.

"You've got fifteen minutes," I told Cass in a breathless whisper as he hitched his hands under my ass and lifted me clean off the floor. "Make them count."

He just grunted an amused sound and responded by striding through to his bedroom with my legs still wrapped around his waist. "That's cute," he told me, kicking the door shut and then dropping me onto his bed. He planted his hands on either side of me on the bedding and brushed a light kiss over the side of my neck, making my head tilt back in invitation. "I'll take as long as I want."

His teeth scraped my pulse point, and my breath caught in a sharp gasp. Damn it. Damn it all to hell. I wasn't even wearing any

93

panties to destroy, but that alpha-male asshole comment would have done it. As it was, my jeans and the snaps of my bodysuit were taking a solid soaking, and I gave zero shits. Cass seemed to know exactly what made me tick.

My back arched as his hands skated down the thin fabric of my body suit. I kicked my heels off as he flicked my jeans open like they were made of Velcro. Then he peeled them down my legs and tossed them across the room in one smooth, very practiced motion.

Cass paused then, his heated stare on my body and his chest rising and falling with heavy breaths.

"Problem?" I taunted, running my own hands over my breasts to tease my hard nipples and let them show through the thin fabric. "Clock's ticking, Saint."

He huffed a short laugh. "Fuck your clock, Timber. You're a damn goddess, you know that?" His face dipped low again, and he dropped a teasing kiss at my collarbone. "The number of times I've pictured you like this..." His knee wedged between my legs, pushing them wider.

"Cass," I groaned, rolling my hips forward so that he'd be perfectly situated, if not for his jeans and my bodysuit. "Quit talking about it and *show* me."

A low, sexy laugh rumbled from his chest as he pulled away and sat back on his heels. "Such a smart mouth, Red. Makes me want to fuck it." He tugged his shirt off in a one-handed motion, and his ink-covered muscles rippled as his hands dropped to his belt.

I watched him eagerly as he unbuckled it, sliding it from the loops of his jeans slowly enough that it had to be for dramatic effect. As badly as I wanted to give him another quip about taking his damn time, I was mesmerized. I bet he knew how to use that belt for more than just holding his pants up.

He clucked his tongue at me when I licked my lips, a sly smile on his own. "All the times I pictured fucking you, Red, I never guessed what really turned you on."

I gave a small shrug, pushing myself up on my elbows to get a better view of his tattoos disappearing under his waistband. There was no need to offer up explanations; it was pretty damn obvious I was panting all over him right now. He'd thought I needed control in *every* area of my life—bedroom included. He'd been wrong.

Here... This was one place I was happy to step back. Or at least I was willing to give it a try. So far no one I'd slept with had been ballsy enough to even *try* to take charge, but I didn't think Cassiel Saint would have that issue.

"Take it off," he told me, nodding to my bodysuit. "As hot as that is, I wanna see you naked, Red."

No argument here. The snaps holding it together opened with one swift tug, and a second later the garment hit the carpet beside the bed. Cass inhaled sharply.

"Well?" I coaxed when he did nothing but stare at my body sprawled across the bed in front of him. "You taking those jeans off or what?" Because I *really* wanted to see how far those tattoos extended.

Cass's eyes jerked back up to meet my hungry stare, and the corners of his mouth curved up. "Turn over."

I did as he asked, feeling a small part of my constant tension ease at the simple act of following a direction from him.

"Shit," he breathed, smoothing a rough hand along my bare back. I had a tattoo running down my spine, and he loosely traced the lines of it before grabbing a handful of my ass. "This ass..."

I arched my hips, wiggling my behind at him in invitation. Smack it, fuck it, I didn't care. I just wanted him to take whatever the fuck he wanted from my body. Use me, abuse me, make me forget my own goddamn name.

His weight shifted on the mattress, and I turned my face to watch him unzip his fly. Then my mouth went dry and I needed to swallow several times as he palmed his dick and met my eyes with a dark, hungry gaze.

"I bet that hurt," I murmured, breaking away from his stare to eye his inked cock.

Cass responded by stroking himself, his thumb highlighting the designs decorating the base of his shaft.

Then we both jerked when someone knocked loudly at the front door.

Cass's expression hardened with anger, and I couldn't help the laugh that bubbled out of me.

"What the fuck is so funny, Red?" He leaned over me and bit my shoulder teasingly.

I smirked at him, then smacked a light kiss on his lips. "Sounds like reality is knocking. Time's up, Saint."

With a smooth motion, I rolled off his bed and swiped my clothes up in my hand. Whoever was at his door was knocking again, and I wasn't in the mood to lie there with my legs spread, desperate and waiting while he dealt with whoever it was.

Nope, that was the universe's way of reminding me that my life was already far too complicated without adding any extra dick to it.

"Get your fine ass back here right now, Timber," Cass ordered with a rumble of frustration underscoring his words. "We are *not* leaving it at that."

I snorted a laugh, totally at odds with the internal turmoil I was struggling to contain. "Yeah, we are." I turned to face him, then gave his hard dick a pointed look and licked my lips. "Guess you'll have to keep using your imagination." Goddamn, I did *not* want to go.

Some dark emotion flashed across his face, and he unfolded off the bed with the smooth grace of a shadow—or a *reaper*. "Don't you dare walk away. We're not even close to done." He seemed to pay no mind to whoever was at his door; his focus was on one thing and one thing only. Me...leaving.

Just because he'd told me not to, I opened his bedroom door and took a very deliberate step through it while flashing him a wide grin. "Moment's passed, Cass. You've got a visitor." I was still naked—there was no way I was actually running out of his apartment until I got dressed—but I couldn't pass up the opportunity to push him.

"Fuck that," he rumbled, prowling after me with long strides. He caught me in just a couple of steps, grabbing my clothes from my hand and throwing them out of reach.

I arched a brow. "Really? That's your plan to stop me from leaving?"

He huffed another husky, pure-sex laugh. Then he shoved me against the wall and kissed me until I was breathless and shaking. But whoever was at the door was determined and knocked again. When Cass wrenched his lips from mine to glare at the door, I took the opportunity to push him away.

I made it all of three steps before he caught me again, this time with his fingers tangled in my hair. A surprised yelp escaped my throat as he pulled me backwards against his hard chest with a twist of his wrist, tightening my hair around his fist and holding me prisoner.

"No, Red," he growled in my ear as he walked me forward. "I don't have to stop you because you don't *want* to leave. You just want me to take the decision out of your hands." His free hand caressed my bare belly, then dipped lower to stroke my throbbing pussy. His fingers spread me open as he pushed me against the wall right beside the front door. Right where this had all started. Except this time, someone was on the other side, knocking persistently like they urgently needed his attention.

I started to deny his accusation, but my words failed when he pushed two thick fingers into me, rough and demanding.

"Isn't that right, angel?" he murmured in my ear, then bit my lobe in a way that made me shudder with pure desire.

The knocking sounded again, louder this time. "Boss!" a man shouted through the door. "It's Roach."

Cass paused a moment, and I tried to wriggle free of his grip. That movement, though, only made him tighten his hold on my hair, jerking my head back to an almost painful angle. It gave him access to my lips, though, and he kissed me so hard I knew my lips would be swollen and puffy for hours.

I moaned as he roughly finger-fucked me, making me writhe and buck against his tight hold.

"Quiet," he growled in my ear with an edge of anger when he released my mouth. "I don't want my asshole second knowing what you sound like when you come."

"Boss!" Roach shouted again, accompanied with more knocking. "I know you're home and I'm guessing this is shit timing, but something's happened. It's urgent."

This time, Cass withdrew slightly, clearly considering what to do.

"Deal with it," I told him, my voice quiet but firm. "Our world doesn't just stop because we want to fuck."

His muscles bunched against my back, his frustration a palpable thing, but a second later he released me with a growl of anger. Shaking out my hair, I turned around and leaned my shoulders against the wall as I watched him.

With a deep scowl, he yanked his jeans up over his hard dick, then gave me a narrow-eyed glare. "Don't even fucking *think* about getting dressed, Red."

I didn't fight the smirk that crept across my lips. "We'll see."

More knocking. Cass gave a growl of fury and jerked the door open. He stepped out into the corridor and slammed the door shut behind him, ensuring there was no way Roach could have seen me.

As tempting as it was to follow directions and just sprawl naked across his bed, waiting for him to come and finish me off, my messed-up brain wouldn't let me make it so easy on him. I *liked* pushing him away and making him pull me back in so fucking hard. I *liked* challenging his dominance. It turned me on. So I grabbed

98

my jacket from where I'd dropped it earlier and went in search of the rest of my things. It took me all of two minutes to get dressed, all the while listening to the low rumble of voices outside the front door.

I was clipping my gun holster back on when Cass yanked the door back open and stormed inside like a thundercloud. When he saw me standing there, fully dressed, he froze.

"What the *fuck* are you doing?" he demanded.

"Leaving," I replied with an eyeroll, biting back my smile. "Hot as all that alpha-dom crap is, we both have empires to run and people to protect. Sounds like yours just came knocking, literally, and mine got bombed this morning."

Something shifted in his expression, and a delicious thread of anticipation rippled through me.

"You think I'm playing?" he asked in a dark voice, stalking closer to me. For some goddamn reason—call it a moment of temporary insanity—I backed up a couple of steps into the kitchen before I caught myself and stood firm with my chin up.

My expression hardened into *Hades* again, and I met his blazing stare with ice. "You think you're not?"

He huffed a laugh, and it struck me somewhere deep. God, that was a sexy sound, and the fact that he didn't back down at that hardness spoke volumes. Instead of answering, he reached out and stroked the backs of his fingers over my exposed décolletage. I shivered and leaned into his touch, feeling the power behind such a gentle gesture.

In a flash his hand was around my throat.

A shock of excitement, of exhilaration, ran through me like a lightning strike, and my heart galloped against my ribs as his fingers tightened and his lips brushed over mine.

"I told you not to get dressed, angel," he murmured, his grip just a fraction away from cutting off my air, but loose enough that I could still reply.

"What are you gonna do about it, then?"

Silly question. Cass kept his grip on my throat but circled around behind me until my back was pressed to his chest once more. Slowly, letting me anticipate his actions, he reached out and plucked a filleting knife from the block on the counter. Then, in a series of quick, precise cuts, he shredded my bodysuit but left my gun holster intact.

"I swear," he murmured in my ear, "I've never seen a woman make weapons look so fucking hot." Satisfied with the way he'd destroyed my bodysuit, he stabbed his knife point-first into the wooden cutting board in front of me.

Releasing my throat, he flicked the button of my jeans open, then gripped the sides of my open fly in each hand and *ripped*. The already distressed denim tore like wet paper down the entire length of my crotch, and Cass shoved them down my legs with rough movements before I could get anything more than a startled sound of protest out.

"Cass—" I started to say, somewhat irritated but still exceedingly turned on at how he'd just destroyed my clothes. But he cut me off with a hand over my mouth. With strong movements, he kicked my legs wider and bent me over the counter until my aching nipples touched the wooden cutting board right beside his knife.

One hand still over my mouth, his other grabbed my hip. He pulled me back against him as his cock found my cunt, shoving inside and making me scream against his palm.

For a moment, it felt like my brain had short-circuited. Stars exploded in my vision, and my whole body quaked, shaking with raw arousal and pent-up tension. Then I bit down on his fingers, and he grunted a curse.

"Bitch," he growled as he removed his hand from my mouth. Somehow, he made it sound like the highest compliment, though, and I bucked my hips. "Fuck, you feel incredible, Red."

My sassy retort dissolved on a wave of euphoria as he started fucking me properly. His fingers bit into the fading bruises on my hip as he nailed me against the counter, and I moaned under his touch.

"Holy shit," I groaned as he slammed into me, harder and harder. "Cass…"

"Roach will be back any minute," he grunted, wrapping his free hand back around my neck once more. I shuddered with waves of pleasure as the edge of the counter bit into my waist and Cass pumped faster. "So be fucking *quiet* when you come."

I snorted a laugh, then moaned when his grip tightened. He wasn't fucking around, and I was in freaking heaven. Planting my hands on the counter, I pushed back into him, frantically chasing the climax that was teasing me.

"Harder," I moaned, louder than I really needed to.

He cursed and gave me exactly what I wanted. He went harder on my cunt and on my throat, squeezing in just the right place to make my vision dance and my lungs scream as I came with soul-shattering convulsions.

He barely even waited for me to finish before jerking out of my pussy and shoving me to my knees. His fingers tangled in my hair, he shoved his cock so far down my throat that I couldn't breathe.

"I told you to be quiet," he grunted as he fucked my mouth.

If I'd been able to, I'd have smirked. As it was, I just grabbed onto his tattoo-covered hips and sucked his dick like I was trying to win a prize. A few moments later, he jerked and used his grip on my hair to force himself deeper as he came.

When he released me, I sat back on my heels with my chest heaving and my lips throbbing.

Cass stared down at me a moment, his eyes slightly stunned, then that sly, sexy grin crossed his lips.

"Get up," he ordered. "Go to my bedroom while I get rid of Roach. I want to taste your sweet cunt and feel you come on my face before I let you leave."

My breathing hitched, and my pussy tightened with excitement. Slowly, I climbed to my feet and kicked my shoes aside. Holding Cass's dark gaze steadily, I licked my lips, then uttered the words that irrevocably shifted our power dynamic.

"Yes, sir."

CHAPTER 13

Striding back into Zed's house, I kept my head high and my spine strong despite the puffiness in my lips betraying exactly what I'd been doing. Not to mention the way my hair barely covered the marks on my neck.

"Nice outfit," Zed commented, spotting me before I could sneak upstairs to change.

My shoulders tightened, and I hardened myself against his teasing before changing direction. "Thanks," I snapped back. "Designed it myself."

My outfit, as my second so amusingly called it, was one of Cass's black hoodies. That was it. Just a hoodie. But I was short enough compared to Cass's six-foot-five that it fit me like a dress. And really, I'd had no other options considering the shredded mess he'd left my clothes in.

"You smell like sex," Zed informed me as I brushed past him. There was no teasing in his tone, though. In fact, he sounded pissed off.

I stopped and shot him a scowl. "What's your problem, Zayden?"

His answering smile was pure sarcasm. "Nothing, Boss. Just

commenting on the fact that you've clearly been riding that Reaper's dick while I was out collecting your boy toy from the hospital. Oh yeah, and thirty-six people died in the collapse of your apartment building."

A wave of guilt ripped through me so hard I wobbled on my heels. "Zed—"

"Whoa, no!" Lucas cut me off, pushing up from the couch with a grimace. I hadn't even seen him sitting there, but he'd clearly heard what Zed just said to me. "Not cool, Zed. Hayden didn't set that bomb off. Don't go dumping those deaths on her shoulders."

Zed looked stricken, frowning between Lucas and me, then gave an angry shake of his head. "Fuck this," he muttered, then started to storm away.

"Excuse me?" I barked after him, the sharp edge in my voice making him freeze in his tracks. "You want to try that again?"

Ever so slowly, Zed rolled his shoulders, then turned back around to face me with a carefully shuttered expression. "My apologies, sir," he said, the words still underscored with anger. "I have some calls to make." He held my gaze steadily, and I swallowed a frustrated sigh.

"That's better," I snapped, dismissing him.

Zed's answering glare was darker than I'd seen from him in a *long* time, but he said nothing else before leaving the room and heading upstairs.

As soon as he was gone, I let out a long sigh and let my shoulders sag. Something really strange was going on with Zed, and I needed to get to the bottom of it sooner rather than later.

"What was that about?" Lucas asked quietly, touching a gentle hand to the small of my back.

I shook my head, not even knowing where to start explaining the complicated relationship between Zed and me. "Doesn't matter," I lied. "How are you?"

Shoving Zed's temper tantrum into the back of my mind, I

focused on Lucas and inspected the colorful bruises decorating his face.

"I'm fine," he told me with a smile. "Better now that you're here." He looped his arms around my waist and pulled me close in a hug. After a moment's hesitation, I reached my arms up around his neck and relaxed into his hold.

Lucas buried his face in my hair and tightened his arms around me, then gave a soft laugh. "You really do smell like sex." I tried to pull away, instantly worried that he was hurt or upset, but he didn't let me go. "I didn't say I hated it."

A fact he reinforced by nuzzling my hair out of the way and kissing my neck right over the teeth marks and light bruises Cass had left.

"Lucas," I groaned, sliding my hand around to cup his face. I pulled back far enough that I could meet his eyes and see the open honesty in his gaze. "You're unbelievable."

He grinned that cheeky, mischievous smile of his. "In a good way, right?"

I rolled my eyes but couldn't fight my answering smile. "For one thing, I'm almost positive you're not allowed to have sex so soon after surgery to reinflate your lung—"

"I don't remember the doctor saying that." He gave me a thoughtful frown, like he was searching his memory. "Hmm, nope, no recollection."

Still grinning and unable to wipe it off my face, I just gave him a headshake. "And for another, I smell like sex because I've been fucking someone else. That doesn't bother you? Because it should. You deserve better than me, Lucas. I'm only going to—"

"Break my heart?" He finished the sentence for me, and I gave a weak shrug. He drew a deep breath, then released it as his arms loosened around my waist. Instead of pushing me away, he took my hand and led me over to the couch to sit. "Yeah, you probably will."

My brows shot up, and my stomach knotted. "And you're okay with that?" I had a hard time believing him, and it showed in my voice.

Lucas just met my eyes with a calm that seemed far too mature for his years. "I'm okay with that. It doesn't bother me that you smell of sex with Cass because *you* smell like *sex* and that's just a straight-up turn-on."

All my skepticism must have shown on my face because he just laughed and grabbed my hand. With a quick movement, he shoved my hand inside his gray sweatpants and wrapped my fingers around his hot, hard length.

"Tell me I'm lying, Hayden," he challenged me in a husky voice. "Tell me I'm not thinking about how badly I want to fuck you right here on Zed's ugly-ass couch. I *dare* you."

I huffed a short laugh at his play on my name. "Cute."

"Not the vibe I was aiming for," he muttered, releasing my hand. I didn't immediately withdraw it, though, and his breathing spiked. "So no, it doesn't bother me. But if you want to know whether it makes me jealous?"

I tilted my head to the side, curious.

Lucas swiped his tongue over his lush lips, his cheeks flushed as he tried to continue his conversation while I stroked his dick. "Insanely jealous," he admitted in a hoarse whisper. "I want to know everything he did to you, then I want to do it all myself and make you scream harder. Louder. I want to make you forget his fucking name while my dick is inside you."

Somewhat shocked by his answer, I removed my hand from his sweatpants and searched for an appropriate response. No words came to mind, though, so when he leaned over and kissed me, I simply melted into his touch.

A crash of something breaking upstairs jolted me out of the fuzzy haze of *Lucas* that I'd just so comfortably slipped into, and I looked to the ceiling with a grimace.

"I need to go and deal with him," I said with a sigh. "I don't know what his fucking problem is, but I'm not putting up with it."

Lucas gave a soft laugh. "You really don't know what his problem is?"

I frowned at him in confusion as I peeled myself out of his warm embrace to stand up. "Uh, no. He's been acting strange for fucking weeks and keeps fobbing me off with stupid excuses whenever I push the issue."

Lucas sprawled out a bit on the sofa, cupping his dick to rearrange it. "Since when? The night you and I hooked up?"

I took a moment to consider his question, then shook my head. "No, his attitude has nothing to do with you. Him trying to sabotage our night wasn't some kind of misplaced jealousy. He's always meddled when he's seen me with guys, but I do it to him with chicks. It's just a thing we do." I grinned, remembering an incident a few months ago. I'd caught Zed fucking a girl against a wall at Club 22, so I'd convinced a waitress to "trip" and "spill" a whole pitcher of sangria all over his white shirt.

Zed had been livid but had never even known it was me. By some stroke of luck, the waitress I'd picked was one of Zed's former conquests, and he'd assumed it was an act of jealousy. Hah.

Lucas was just watching me with a bemused smile as I took that quick trip down memory lane; then he gave an unconvinced shake of his head. "If you say so." Another crash of something breaking upstairs made us both look to the ceiling. "Maybe you should just let him work through it alone."

His concern made me grin, and I leaned back down to kiss his lips. "That's cute that you think Zed would ever hurt me. Don't worry, I'll be quick. He probably just found out he caught an STD from his latest bed buddy or something." I kissed him again, letting my lips linger as my pussy throbbed with need. "Just make yourself at home, okay? And ignore any gunshots from upstairs."

Lucas made a panicked sound of protest as I left the room,

and I just laughed in response. I wasn't *actually* going to shoot Zed for throwing a temper tantrum, but I wasn't averse to scaring him a bit.

It was pretty obvious all the crashing was coming from Zed's room, so I marched down the corridor and threw the door open without bothering to knock. Inside, I found Zed standing on the small balcony with his back to me and his shoulders heaving. I approached without any hesitation but took note of how white his knuckles were on the balcony railing and how the thick muscles in his forearms were flexed hard.

"You wanna tell me what the fuck is going on with you, Zayden?" I asked in a dry voice, propping my shoulder against the doorframe and folding my arms.

He spun around, his lips parted as though he had a million and one sharp retorts just waiting on the tip of his tongue. But then his blazing, furious glare met my calm gaze, and his mouth snapped shut.

"None of your business, Hades," he growled instead, his brows dipping in anger.

He was trying to push my buttons, but lucky for him I was still riding the euphoric wave of Cass's parting kiss so my usual quick temper had been cooled.

Spoiler alert, his kiss hadn't been on my mouth.

Instead of snapping back and exerting my authority like Zed clearly expected me to do, I just raised my brows and tipped my head to the side. "Why don't you talk to me anymore, Zed? I thought we told each other everything."

His eye twitched with rage. "Like you're one to talk."

"What's *that* supposed to mean?" Okay, now he was starting to piss me off.

He advanced a couple of steps, getting all up in my personal space and forcing me to tip my head back so I could maintain eye contact. I *despised* when men did that to me. Usually. Somehow,

I was okay with it when it came to...certain men. Zed was one of them.

"This shit with Cass and Lucas," he growled in a low voice still underscored with raw emotion.

"What *shit* with Cass and Lucas?" I replied when he didn't elaborate. "I'm fucking both of them. So what?"

His eyes narrowed. "So what? *Seriously?* You've got genuine feelings for both of them? How do you not see how dangerous that's becoming for you? For us?"

My jaw dropped slightly. "What? Zed, chill. It's just sex. Don't read so much into it, drama queen. Is that what all this is about? Fucking hell, I thought there was a real problem."

A little of Zed's anger seemed to slip, and he studied my face with an expression of disbelief. Then he barked a sharp laugh and shook his head. "Just sex, huh?" He continued searching my eyes for long enough that I shifted uncomfortably. "You're so full of shit, Hayden. I know what you look like when you've let someone into that glacier-cold heart of yours."

Fear spiked through me, and I lifted my chin in stubborn denial. "Oh yeah?" I scoffed a sharp laugh. "How?"

Zed's eyes flashed with pain, and his mocking smile faded completely. "Because you used to look at me like that." His voice was quiet and full of bitterness and regret. But regret about *what?*

As quick as his mood had shifted, he snapped his gaze away from mine and brushed past me. "I'm heading out," he announced, already grabbing a clean shirt from his closet and swapping it for the wrinkled one he'd been wearing.

"Zed, what the fuck? Don't you dare walk away from me. We're in the middle of a conversation." I started after him, reaching for his arm, but he shrugged out of my grip.

"I've got shit to take care of," he snapped, not meeting my gaze anymore. "Do me a favor, though?"

My heart thumped hard against my chest, and a dark emotion

I couldn't name welled up within me. "Anything," I murmured, meaning it with total sincerity.

Zed grabbed his gun from the dresser and strapped the holster at his waist, then shoved a spare clip in his pocket. "Don't fucking *trust* them. The timing is too damn coincidental…especially for Gumdrop."

My brows rose. "You think he's a plant? Demi ran his check, and—"

"Demi's good, but she's not the best." He cut me off, his tone harsh as he finally spun around to face me. "There's something more going on with that kid. Maybe with Cass too. They're using you, Hayden, and you're falling for it because you're so desperate for some good dick."

And that was as far as my patience extended. My fist snapped out, catching Zed in the face with a sharp jab. He barely even flinched, though. He just clenched his jaw and drew a deep breath before opening his eyes once more.

"Speak to me like that again, Zayden," I hissed at him. "I fucking *dare* you. Maybe all the excellent orgasms I've been getting have taken the edge off my violence, but I am *more* than fucking happy to remind you why I am who I am. Do *not* test me."

His blue eyes blazed in anger, but he didn't reply, just gave a sharp nod and stormed out of the room. A few moments later, the front door slammed and his tires squealed as he peeled out of the drive.

When I was confident he was gone, I let the strength seep out of my bones and crumpled to the floor in a shaking heap. What the *hell* had all that been about? Zed and I didn't argue like that. We just didn't. So what the fuck had just tipped his anger? I didn't believe for a second it was just knowing Cass and I had fucked. That would mean his feelings for me had shifted dramatically in recent weeks, and that…that just wasn't fathomable. Not him. Not my best friend.

I refused to even consider the possibility, because I refused to lose the most important person in my life. So there must be something else going on.

Maybe he was on to something…

CHAPTER 14

Lucas was still in the living room when I eventually made my way back downstairs, and he looked up in question when I joined him.

"I didn't hear any gunshots," he offered with a lopsided smile. He looked tired and in pain.

I gave a weak smile in reply. "Not yet, anyway. Has Zed sorted you out with a bedroom yet?" Better to change the subject than try to explain Zed's confusing anger toward me today.

Lucas shook his head. "We got here not long before you. The hospital paperwork took forever to fill out."

"All right, let's go sort one out. You need to rest, and I need to deal with..." I let my voice trail off with a heavy sigh. I needed to deal with the unexpected demolition of my apartment building. It was just one more lead weight of guilt added to the already staggering weight I carried on a daily basis.

Lucas stood up and brushed a stray lock of hair behind my ear. "You kinda look like you need to rest, too."

Zed must be on crack. Lucas wasn't some kind of undercover spy sent to seduce and kill me. He was just a genuinely nice guy who was incredible in bed. Nothing more, nothing less.

"I'll rest when I'm dead," I whispered back, only half joking.

"Come on, we need to find linens for the spare room." Linking my fingers with his, I led the way upstairs and showed him to the guest room down the hall from Zed's room.

He tried to help with the sheets, and I had to scold him into submission. Weirdly, I got a spike of arousal when he obeyed my command and sat his ass down in the armchair. Maybe I was just still hypersexed from my tryst with Cass earlier.

After making the bed up and fetching him a stack of fresh towels for the shower, I ordered him into bed and ran downstairs to fetch his medication, which I'd seen sitting on the counter. Then I made a stop in Zed's room to quickly shower, change clothes, and remove my gun holster.

When I returned to Lucas's room in a pair of comfy sleep shorts and my favorite Blink-182 T-shirt, he was fast asleep. His long lashes fanned over his high cheekbones, and his face seemed so damn serene as he slept. Zed had hit the mark too damn well in his rant. Lucas was more than *just sex* to me already. If he turned out to be a traitor, it'd hurt more than I even wanted to consider.

Biting my lip and swallowing the emotions that threatened to overwhelm me, I tiptoed across the carpet and drew the curtains against the setting sun. I made it halfway back to the door, intending to leave him in peace, but the sound of him shifting in bed made me pause.

"Hayden..." he mumbled, and I cringed. I hadn't wanted to wake him up.

"Sorry, Lucas," I whispered, changing direction to cross back over to him. Then I realized his eyes were still closed and he was just mumbling in his sleep. He was dreaming about me. And if the smile on his lips was any indication, it was a good dream.

I couldn't help myself. I leaned over and pressed a light kiss to his lips. But that must have just played into his dream because a moment later his hands threaded into my hair, and he dragged me into the bed with him.

Then he froze, his eyelids lifting and a grimace of pain on his face.

"Idiot," I whispered with a soft laugh, trying to extract myself from his grip. "You must have forgotten your injuries in that dream, huh?"

His response was just a low groan, but his fingers tightened on mine before I could fully climb off the bed. "Lie with me for a bit?"

Ugh, how could I refuse that angelic face? I lifted the blankets and climbed into the warm bed beside him, slotting perfectly into the side of his body like we'd been created as a matching pair. Neither of us spoke; Lucas just curled his arm around me and drifted back to sleep within seconds.

I envied the way his whole body relaxed in sleep.

My entire being was exhausted, yet after lying there listening to the peaceful, calm sound of Lucas's heartbeat for hours, I had to admit that sleep wasn't coming for me. Not yet. Not when I had so many dark and depressing thoughts swirling around in my brain.

Ever so carefully, I slid out from under his arm and padded from the room.

My phone was downstairs on the kitchen counter where I'd tossed it earlier, and I groaned when I saw how many notifications and missed calls were waiting for me. But one of the numbers made my brows shoot up in surprise, and I hit redial.

"Ms. Timber," the woman greeted after the second ring. "I'm glad you called back."

I clucked my tongue, the gears in my mind whirling. "Special Agent Hanson. I'll admit I'm surprised to hear from you."

"And why is that?" the FBI agent asked, sounding irritated. "You didn't think I'd want to speak with you after your entire apartment building was blown up this morning? Hell, half the law enforcement in the state is currently hoping to have a word with you, Ms. Timber."

Anger simmered in my belly, and I sat up straighter. "It's Ms.

Wolff to you, Special Agent," I corrected her, "and I assumed you were dead. After all, you set me up last week. I can't imagine why he left you alive." I was genuinely confused. I'd told the special agent where I would be and when, and then my club had been blown up with me very nearly still inside. There was no way that was a coincidence.

"Ms. *Wolff*," Agent Dorothy Hanson responded in a tart voice, "if you're implying I had something to do with that accident at your club last week—"

"I'm not implying shit, Agent Hanson. I just can't work out why you're still alive." Staring at the marble countertop, I tapped my fingernail against my lip while I thought it through. "Or maybe he wanted to see if I would kill you myself and do his dirty work for him."

"Excuse me?" Agent Hanson squawked in my ear. "Did you just threaten my life?"

I snorted a laugh. "Hardly." I pushed the conundrum aside to dissect another day. "So, what can I do for you today, Hanson?"

The FBI agent made a sound like she could hardly believe what she was hearing. "I need to speak with you in person, Ms. Wolff. You were at the scene right before the bombs went off in your building. If you're not responsible, then you know who is." Her voice was thick with frustration and irritation. It made me laugh.

"Careful, Hanson. You're showing all your cards at once." I was mocking her, and she knew it. "But no, I won't be arranging any more in-person chats with you. Call me crazy, but I'd prefer not to get blown up this week."

She sucked in a sharp breath. "I had nothing to do with your club exploding, Ms. Wolff. The mere fact that you're suggesting I did is—"

"I don't have time for this, Hanson," I said, cutting her off. "But it was nice chatting. Watch your back, you're on my shit list now."

I ended the call before she could splutter any more bluster, then drummed my fingernails on the countertop in thought. She genuinely seemed offended by my accusation, but her actions and lack of follow-up after last week's bomb didn't ring true for a legitimate FBI agent.

Not coming up with any immediate answers, I checked all my other messages. They were mostly just work-related updates: check-ins from all my venue managers with their balance sheets and nightly reports attached, updates from the various Timberwolf leaders in different parts of my territory, and even a message from the Death Squad's leader.

Vega: Feels like something is brewing. It's too damn quiet.

I rolled my eyes and tapped out a quick reply.

Hades: No shit. Keep your damn eyes open and your ear to the ground. I won't tolerate another fuckup from you, Vega.

His reply came quickly.

Vega: Understood.

There was also a message from the Timberwolf I'd appointed to oversee Vega's business as punishment for breaking my rules. Nothing exciting from him, so I didn't reply.

After I cleared all my work messages, I scowled down at the empty inbox. Nothing from Cass, despite his promise to *talk later* when I left his apartment earlier.

Also, nothing from Zed. It wasn't like him, and it set my nerves on edge all over again.

I sat there for several minutes, debating whether I should message either of them, then ultimately decided not to. Regardless of how I'd let Cass take control in the bedroom, I was still the boss outside of that unique situation. He could come to me, not the other way around.

Instead, I tapped out a message to Archer D'Ath, checking on my sister. He replied promptly, confirming she was still safe, and I left it at that. She could contact me when she was ready, and I wouldn't push her. Besides, her words from yesterday still stung and sat like a lead weight in my heart.

Frustrated and edgy, I went to Zed's freezer and pulled out a bottle of vodka. I wasn't that fussy about my spirits, but vodka needed to be cold for shots. I didn't bother to measure it out, just free-poured a double shot into a crystal tumbler, then knocked it back in a huge gulp.

The liquor burned a fiery path down to my empty stomach, and my gut cramped in protest. I needed to put some food in me before alcohol, but I sure as hell wasn't in the mood to cook. Vodka would do, at least until the morning.

I poured another and drank it quickly, then headed upstairs once more. Just because I hadn't been able to sleep next to Lucas didn't mean I couldn't just lie there and soak up his calm.

"You're back," he murmured when I slipped beneath the covers. His eyes were still closed, but he shifted over to give me more space and, when I'd settled, wrapped his arms around me in a warm hug.

"I didn't mean to wake you," I whispered back, shivering as his warmth enveloped me. On habit or instinct, I pressed a kiss to his neck.

He gave a contented sigh and dipped his head to find my lips with his own. "You can wake me up anytime you want, Hayden." He mumbled the words between kisses that were quickly getting me heated up all over again.

"Lucas," I groaned, pulling away with mammoth effort. "I didn't come up here to take advantage of you. Just go back to sleep." In an attempt to demonstrate my point, I rolled over to face away from him, while still snuggled under his arm.

Lucas shifted onto his side, too, spooning me with his strong forearm banded over my chest. He held me tight against him, and his lips caressed my neck like he was worshipping me.

"You're not taking advantage, Hayden," he murmured in my ear, then dragged my lobe between his teeth teasingly. "I just can't get enough of you." A statement supported by the hard length of his erection crushed against my backside.

I gave a small laugh, playfully biting the forearm across my chest. "Lucas, you *just* got out of hospital. You're injured."

He hummed a sound, his lips trailing down my neck and his free hand sliding my shorts down over my hip. I still had no panties—thanks to Cass's shitty packing skills—and he inhaled sharply when his fingers brushed over my bare pussy.

"I *am* injured," he agreed with a heavy breath as he slid a finger down my seam, searching for my clit. He found it too. No treasure map needed. I gave a small groan, my hips rocking into his touch without my permission. "But you know what would make me feel a million times better?"

His finger slid lower, pushing into me. "I bet I could guess," I replied with a lusty laugh. "Lucas…" This time his name was said with a plea, and I didn't know if I was asking him to stop or keep going. Probably the latter.

"I'll be so careful," he promised in a dark whisper, pumping two fingers into me and making me quake. "You're already so hot, so fucking wet…"

Shit. He had me and he knew it. I reached behind me and tugged his sweats down, giving in to what he and I both so clearly needed.

His breathing rough, he lifted my top leg slightly and pushed into my cunt from behind with small, rocking thrusts that made my whole body flood with heat. Only when his hips were flush with my ass did he release my leg.

"See?" he whispered, his voice rough with arousal. "So careful.

I won't pull any stitches if we take it slow." Demonstrating his point, he started fucking me with the slowest, most deliberate strokes that were already driving me nuts.

"This is definitely against doctor's orders," I protested, then groaned when his fingers found my clit once more.

Lucas just gave a low, sexy chuckle as he fucked me carefully and drove me straight up Mount Orgasm. "Rules are made to be broken, Hayden."

Fuck, that was hot as hell coming from his lips.

Moaning, I relaxed into his hold and let him have his fun. Over and over, he brought me to the edge of orgasm, then backed off as his thick cock pumped in and out of me with that maddening pace. Only when I was ready to spontaneously combust did he finally start fucking me harder. With his huge shaft slamming into my cunt, all it took was the lightest of touches to my swollen clit and I detonated.

Lucas whispered curses as I came hard, my pussy clenched around him like a vise, then he was coming too. His hips bucked and rolled as he forced himself deeper inside me, spilling hot cum as I continued to climax.

The whole encounter was intense and sweaty and insanely relaxed, and even after our breathing slowed and our fevered skin cooled, neither of us moved. I fell asleep with Lucas's dick still buried inside me, so it was no great shock when I woke up sometime later to him hardening once more. Who needed sleep when you could lazy-fuck all night long?

Zed had no idea how right he'd been when he said Lucas had stamina. Fuck his paranoia, Lucas was exactly what I needed in my life. And if he turned out to be a double agent, then at least I'd gotten some epic sex out of it. Right?

Yeah. I didn't believe me either. I'd be fucking crushed.

CHAPTER 15

Despite my conversation with Special Agent Hansen, I wasn't a total asshole. I wasn't just ignoring the destruction of my building and pretending it hadn't happened. When I woke at dawn and carefully extracted myself from Lucas's sleeping embrace, I headed back through to Zed's room to grab clean clothes.

His bed was still perfectly made, the broken pieces of the lamp he'd smashed still littering the floor. Either he hadn't come home last night or he'd simply not slept. With an irritated frown, I rifled through my bag. There weren't many options left, so I made myself a mental note to pick up new shit when I was in town.

I helped myself to Zed's shower, washing my hair and scrubbing myself down thoroughly before getting dressed. Zed didn't have a hairdryer, which wasn't ideal, but I dragged his comb through my wet locks and gave them a rough towel dry instead.

On quiet feet, I made my way downstairs and inhaled deeply at the smell of bacon cooking. Apparently Zed was home after all.

"That smells incredible," I groaned, joining him in the kitchen as he pulled the crispy bacon from a pan and laid it out on a slice of waiting toast.

He was shirtless and sweaty, his knuckles red and puffy like he'd been boxing without gloves on. Without answering me, he just assembled the bacon and egg sandwich, added a slice of cheese and a drizzle of barbecue sauce, then added another slice of toast as a lid. He looked up at me then, meeting my eyes with a cool gaze as he lifted the sandwich to his mouth and took a huge bite.

The message was crystal clear, and I glowered.

"Real mature, Zed," I sulked, looking longingly at the empty frying pan on the stovetop. He'd very deliberately only cooked for one. Prick.

I didn't need breakfast anyway, just coffee. So I shoulder-checked him out of the way to access the coffeepot, which was already full of dark gold. He didn't step away, though, just made me lean past him to grab a mug and fill it up.

"You used my shampoo," he muttered, sounding annoyed.

I finished making my coffee, then turned back to face him with a no-shit look on my face. "Mine is somewhere underneath a thousand tons of rubble right now. Is that a problem for you?"

His answer was just to hold my gaze and take another huge bite of his breakfast sandwich. He even gave an exaggerated moan, like it was the best thing he'd eaten in a long time.

Because I was feeling childish, I grabbed his wrist in an iron grip, holding the sandwich still as I took a shark-like bite from the other side of it.

"Mmm," I mumbled around my mouthful of food. "Tasty."

Zed just stared at me like he could hardly believe I'd just done that, and I snickered a laugh while I chewed. "I'm heading to Copper Wolf," I told him when I'd swallowed. "You coming?"

His gaze dipped, taking in my black laced-up pencil skirt and loose satin blouse with my gun holster strapped over the top. My shoes were somewhere in the living room, as I'd kicked them off talking to Lucas last night, and right now they were my only pair. I really needed to restock my wardrobe today. Big bad Hades couldn't be getting around in men's T-shirts and sweats. Neither could Daria Wolff. More's the pity; they were goddamn comfy to wear.

After taking *way* too long perusing my attire, Zed gave a small headshake. "I've got some shit to follow up on today. Don't worry, though, your Gumdrop is perfectly safe here on his own."

I arched a brow. "I wasn't worried. Good to know what's on your mind this morning, though." With a pointed look, I went in search of my shoes while sipping my coffee. Was it too early for scotch? I squinted out the window at the sun, which hadn't fully risen. Probably yes.

Zed just remained in the kitchen, watching me with an unreadable expression as I stepped into my shoes and finished my coffee.

"I expect a progress update from Alexi today," I told him as I returned my mug to the sink and rinsed it out. "And we need to arrange a meeting with the mayor of Cloudcroft. Our gambling license for Timber still hasn't been approved, and I think it's time we applied a little extra pressure."

Zed jerked a nod of understanding but remained silent. Fucking melodramatic shit.

I was tempted to just leave and let him sort out his emo feelings on the punching bag, like he'd clearly been doing already this morning. But he was still my best friend, and it didn't sit right to have this animosity between us.

With a sigh, I propped my butt against the counter and folded my arms over my chest. "Zed…what the fuck is going on with you? I haven't seen you all moody like this since you watched the last episode of *Supernatural.*"

I was joking, trying to ease the tension in the room, but he just shot me a furious scowl. "That ending was *fucked*, Dare, and you know it. Total fucking bullshit."

A smile touched my lips, and I rolled my eyes. At least I was back to Dare and not *Hades* this morning. That had to be a step in the right direction.

"Look, I get that you don't trust Lucas—" I started gently, trying to broach the subject that was clearly pissing him off so much.

Zed scoffed a bitter laugh. "You wouldn't either if you weren't—"

"Do *not* insult me again, Zed," I barked, straightening up and glaring ice-cold death. "You didn't have any issues offering Lucas a place to stay here. In *your home*. You vouched for him as his fake brother. You seemed to actually like him a few days ago, so what the fuck changed?"

Zed's smile was brittle. "Keep your friends close and your enemies closer, Boss. Better to have him right here under my nose so I can figure out what angle he's working."

I stared back at him for a long moment, confused as all fuck. He was lying...at least partially. "And Cass? Why do you suddenly have such a vendetta against him? Two days ago you two were all fucking buddy-buddy."

Zed's jaw tightened, and his gaze flicked away from mine. "Just because I trust him to pick up some clothes for you or bring us quality weed doesn't mean he's *trustworthy*. He's the leader of a rival gang, and he's clearly got an agenda."

I huffed a laugh. "The Reapers are not our rivals, Zed. I could take them out just as easily as I wiped out the Wraiths. Or did you forget who I fucking *am*? Cass is not a threat to us, Zed."

He gave an angry shake of his head. "Respectfully, *sir*, I disagree."

I rolled my eyes, tempted to be a petty bitch and ask if it was really him who felt threatened by Cass getting closer to me. But I bit my tongue and kept that accusation to myself because it would only be a bullshit swipe to piss him off. Like when someone says "calm down" in the middle of an argument and it only fans the flames.

So instead I drew a deep breath and gave him a short nod.

Professional lines needed to be reestablished. "Well then, I expect you'll present me with your evidence when you have something conclusive. Until then, I suggest you keep your opinions to yourself."

Zed's brow furrowed at the shift in my tone. He'd have to be deaf and blind to have missed it. "Dare—"

"Save it, Zed. Until you're ready to either show some hard evidence or fess up to whatever other secrets you're holding, I don't want to hear it. Just because you have an *opinion* doesn't mean I need to hear it." Brushing past him, I grabbed the keys to his Audi from where I'd left them last night. "I'll meet you at Anarchy this afternoon, usual time."

I made my way out of the kitchen. He shouted a curse behind me, but I didn't stop. Fuck it. He could head down to Anarchy early and deal with his male PMS on the trainee fighters there.

The drive over to Copper Wolf was quick and easy from Zed's property, and when I arrived, I asked Hannah, my accountant Macy's assistant, to join me in my office.

"Did you want a coffee, sir?" Macy asked as her assistant blinked up at me with huge eyes. Poor thing thought she was in trouble. "Hannah was about to run down to the kiosk for me."

"Yes, please, that would be great." I softened my severe expression and gave Hannah a small smile. "There's no rush, Hannah. Just come in when you get back. I won't deprive Macy of her caffeine." I shot my accountant a knowing look, and she returned it with a nod.

In my office, I lost myself in piles of emails and spreadsheets until Hannah tapped on my door about fifteen minutes later.

"Come in," I urged her, and she approached my desk with a tall coffee cup in her hand. "Thanks, Hannah. Take a seat."

She gave me a nervous smile and perched on the edge of a chair, tucking her curly black hair behind her ears. Damn, and here I was thinking my Daria Wolff face wasn't as intimidating as my Hades one.

"Don't look so worried, Hannah," I chastised in a gentle tone. "You're not in trouble. I just wanted your help on something, and I don't have my own assistant. I hope Macy won't mind me borrowing you for the day." Actually, come to think of it, I should have checked with my accountant first.

Hannah nodded quickly. "I'm sure it'll be fine, sir. What can I do for you?"

"You seem like you've got a good eye for fashion, Hannah. You're always so well dressed when I come into the office." It was half the reason I'd thought of her for this task. Her style seemed to echo mine quite well, if on a slightly lower budget.

She beamed. "Thank you, sir. I interned at a fashion magazine for a year, and it taught me a lot about personal presentation."

I cocked my head, interested. I'd never really spoken to Hannah before, but she'd been Macy's assistant for over a year. "What made you leave there? I thought that was the sort of job fashionable women dream of."

She quirked a smile. "Uh, yeah, I prefer to work for blood-thirsty criminals who don't try to hide behind fake smiles and clouds of Chanel perfume."

I arched a brow, and she gave a horrified gasp, clapping a hand over her mouth.

"Oh my god," she squeaked in panic. "I didn't mean—"

Unable to fight the smile creasing my lips, I waved off her frantic backpedal. "You did, and it's absolutely fine. I think I like you, Hannah."

Her eyes widened, and her fingers trembled as she returned her hands to her lap. "Th-thanks," she replied in a strangled whisper.

"Anyway, I need you to help me out. My home was destroyed yesterday." Hannah gave a shocked gasp, and I shrugged. "So I'm in need of a new…uh…everything. Clothes, shoes, underwear, makeup, toiletries. Everything." I pulled my desk drawer open and fished out the corporate credit card I kept in there. "I don't have the time or patience to deal with it myself. Do you mind doing it for me?"

I was being more polite than I usually was because the poor thing already looked like she was on the verge of a panic attack. Her eyes flipped from my face to the black metal credit card I held out for her to take, then back to my face.

"I—" she started, then swallowed and wet her lips. "You want me to go shopping?"

I gave her what I hoped was a reassuring smile. "Yes, please. Is that something you can do for me?"

She gaped for another moment, then nodded quickly and took the credit card from my hand. "Yes, absolutely. Yes, leave it to me, sir. I can definitely sort you out. Do you, um... Can I get your sizes?"

I scribbled all my sizes and makeup and toiletry preferences down on a piece of notebook paper and handed it over to her along with a business card for a corporate car service I'd used on occasion.

"Call this guy. He can drive you around and carry bags and whatnot. Then have him deliver it all to this address." I scribbled down Zed's address. "There's a gatehouse where he can leave everything."

Hannah took the extra note from my fingers and tucked it into her skirt pocket. "Absolutely, leave it with me, sir. Do you also need furniture and...all that?"

I shook my head. "Not yet. I'm staying with Zed until I can sort out new living arrangements." I watched her carefully as I said that, but her expression didn't change. Maybe she hadn't yet fallen prey to Zayden De Rosa, which seemed odd when she was easily pretty enough to meet his standards. Somehow that made me like her a little bit more.

"Got it," she acknowledged with a firm nod. "Thank you for the opportunity, sir." With a wide smile, she stood to leave.

"Wait." I scribbled another note. "This is my mobile number. Text me if you have any questions along the way."

Her eyes almost bugged out of her head, and her fingers shook when she took the paper from me. She gave another nod of understanding, whispering that she was sure it'd be fine, then made a speedy exit out of my office.

That taken care of, I picked up my phone and dialed my aunt. She'd damn well better be drinking wine under the Tuscan sun or there would be hell to pay.

"Finally," she snapped on answering my call. "Took you long enough to call me, hon. You're lucky Zed already told me you were alive or I'd have been on a plane straight back to Shadow Grove by now."

I gave a soft laugh. "Sorry, Demi. Things have been crazy. Are you and Stacey staying safe over there?"

"Of course," she huffed. "Now I'm guessing you need legal help?"

"I do," I agreed with a sigh. "I was identified at the scene right before my building collapsed. I've already had a call from one sketchy FBI bitch, but I'm thinking it's best to get ahead of the ball on this."

Demi made an annoyed sound. "I'll handle it," she told me. "I've had my eye on a promising young lawyer in the DA's office. I think it's about time she got a new job offer."

"You're my favorite aunt in the whole world, Demi," I replied with a grin.

She huffed again. "I'm your only fucking aunt, you brat. You killed the other ones."

"They deserved it," I murmured, my smile slipping.

"Damn right they did," she agreed with a sigh. "Now, can you tell me why your sister has messaged and asked if she can come stay with us in Italy?"

I winced, rubbing my brow. "Actually, that might not be such a bad idea," I thought out loud. "Have you got space there for Madison Kate's crew? I'd feel better keeping a close guard over Seph until this mess is sorted."

"I'll make space, but you didn't answer the question, hon. Why did Seph make it sound like you'd just—"

"Stolen her boyfriend?" I cut Demi off with a sharp laugh. "I didn't. She's just being…a teenager." There was a long pause on the phone, and I sighed. "She had a crush on a guy that was already taken."

"Mm-hmm," Demi replied, perceptive as always. "I'm going to guess he was taken by you."

"Seph is upset that I didn't tell her." That was basically it in a nutshell. No one had cheated on anyone. She was just hurt that I'd kept secrets from her.

Demi didn't say anything for a moment, then clucked her tongue. "I'll sort out some guest rooms and tell Seph to sort out her flights. As for you? Stay alive. Understood?"

"Thanks, Demi," I said with a sigh. "You really are my favorite aunt. Give my love to Stacey."

She mumbled something about how I was going to give her a stress heart attack, then ended the call to sort out my new legal counsel.

CHAPTER 16

The rest of my morning was completely eaten up with Copper Wolf business, and I didn't even notice the time until my phone lit up with Alexi's name.

Lucas didn't have a phone, so I had no way to call and check in on him. So when I saw it was already after noon, a spike of worry rippled through me.

"Alexi," I snapped, answering the call. "I hope you have good news for me."

"I have news," he corrected. "Zed said you were at Copper Wolf. Do you want me to come there?" The sound of padded gloves hitting sandbags echoed in the background of his phone.

"Are you at Anarchy?" I asked, closing down the windows on my computer.

"KJ-Fit," he replied, "but I can head over to Anarchy now."

"Good, I'll meet you there. I'm leaving Copper Wolf now, so I'll be an hour or so." I ended the call and left my office. I paused a moment to chat with Macy, then bade her farewell and headed for the elevator.

I checked my phone while waiting and replied to a message from Hannah, who was awkwardly asking if she was working with a budget. Cute.

The elevator dinged, announcing its arrival, and the doors slid open. Not looking up from my phone, I stepped in. A strong hand closed over my wrist and jerked me forward, pulling me against a hard, leather-jacketed body.

"I almost fucking stabbed you," I muttered, meeting Cass's dark eyes as the elevator doors closed behind me. "Don't surprise me like that."

His lips curled up in a microsmile. "You don't even have a knife on you, Red." He used his grip on my wrist to spin us around, pushing my back to the wall of the elevator.

I tilted my chin up, holding his gaze. "I'm resourceful, Cassiel. I'd have managed."

He made an amused sound, then lowered his lips to meet mine in a harsh, bruising kiss. I kissed him back just as hard, my free hand reaching up to cling onto the back of his neck as I molded my body against his.

Then the elevator dinged to announce we'd reached the parking level, and I pushed him away forcefully.

"What are you doing here?" I asked as I stepped out and fished car keys from my bag. "I generally like to keep Copper Wolf fairly free of known gang leaders." He arched a brow at me, and I explained. "Daria Wolff is just a businesswoman, Cass."

His gaze ran over me, hungry and lustful. "Well, I was coming to see if *Daria Wolff* wanted to come to lunch with me."

I jerked to a stop in the middle of the parking lot. "You came to…take me to lunch?"

He met my eyes, cool as a damn cucumber. "You need to eat, so do I. I was in the area already…" He tipped his head to the side. "You like steak?"

I didn't fight the smile creasing my lips, but at the same time I shook my head. "You're full of fucking surprises, Saint. But I have an appointment at Anarchy in an hour. Rain check?"

His brow creased, but he gave a short nod. "Fine. Dinner instead, then."

A surprised laugh escaped my chest. "Cass—"

"I wasn't asking, Red," he growled in a quiet, commanding voice. "I'll pick you up at eight."

Damn it all to hell, my pussy instantly heated and my breath caught. I was still aching and bruised from our rough escapade the day before, but that didn't deter me in the least. Goddamn, I was turning into an addict.

Biting back a smile, I gave a shrug. "I don't know if I'll be back by eight. I've got a lot of shit to deal with today."

Cass knew I was being deliberately difficult—I could tell by the way his eyes glittered—and he crowded me against the door of Zed's car. His inked fingers wrapped around my throat, but he didn't choke me. Instead, he just leaned down and kissed me until I forgot whose air I was breathing.

"I'll pick you up at eight," he growled with sex-drenched promise, and his lips brushed over my cheekbone before he released me and stepped away. "Wherever you are."

I didn't reply because I was too busy getting my breath back and clenching my thighs tight. Damn Cass... I badly needed replacement underwear. Skirts weren't ideal when my cunt was getting so wet around him.

His lips curved in an arrogant smirk as he backed up a couple of steps toward his bike, and I rolled my eyes. I'd never realized just how big Grumpy Cat's ego was, but he was giving Zed a run for his money now.

Flipping him off, I popped my car door open and slid inside before I could do something stupid—like throw myself at him for a quick fuck right there in the parking lot. As hot as that was in my imagination, it was just a straight-up terrible idea in reality.

While driving back to Shadow Grove, it took me longer than I'd have expected to get my shit under control once more. Then I started questioning everything. Was Zed right about Cass having an ulterior motive? If so...what? He surely wasn't working with

Chase. The timing was simply coincidental in that it was *me* who'd made the first move on *him*. That couldn't have been manipulated. Hell, I hadn't even known I was going to do it until it happened.

By the time I pulled into the parking lot of Anarchy, I was an irritable mess and itching for a fight.

To my disappointment, though, neither Zed nor Alexi was in the training center. A couple of younger Timberwolves were there lifting weights, and they scrambled to greet me politely. But it didn't seem fair to take out my bad mood on them.

With a sigh, I left them and headed over to the security office beside the big top. Zed was sitting at one of the desks looking freshly showered, and Alexi sat opposite him with a grim expression on his face.

My head of security was in workout clothes, like he'd come straight from the MMA gym without wasting time on a shower or change of clothes, which probably meant his news wasn't good.

"Boss," Zed said with a tight smile as I approached. "Good of you to join us."

"Bite me, Zed," I hissed under my breath as I reached him. "Get out of my chair."

It wasn't *my* chair, it was just *a* chair. But there was power in positioning, and while I was all for a power exchange in the bedroom—apparently—I wasn't interested in it in business settings.

Zed raised a brow at me, the desire to push my buttons all over his damn face. But after a moment, he stood up and brushed a hand over my lower back as I swapped positions with him.

"Alexi," I said, addressing my grim-faced employee. "What do you have for me? Or have you already filled Zed in?"

Alexi shook his head, his eyes locked on my face. "No, sir. I waited for you to get here."

Zed huffed with irritation, and he rested a hand on my shoulder. "Alexi apparently doesn't think I could relay the information correctly, Boss."

Alexi's brows shot up. "What? No, that's not—"

"Oh, shut up, both of you," I snapped before the conversation could turn any more childish.

Alexi's lips tightened, and he frowned at Zed's hand on my shoulder. Actually, why the fuck was Zed's hand on my shoulder?

His fingers tightened, and Alexi's face darkened.

Seriously?

I tilted my face, giving Zed a scathing glare. He knew damn well what he was doing and that I wasn't in the fucking mood. But it didn't stop him from shooting me a sly smirk as he withdrew his *possessive* hand from my shoulder.

Alexi was an idiot for being riled up by that. Everyone knew Zed and I were purely platonic *and* that I wasn't remotely interested in Alexi.

With an irritated sigh, I turned my attention back to my trusted Timberwolf. "Get on with it, Alexi. I've got a lot to do today."

"Yes, Boss," he replied, chastised. "I've been conducting interviews like you requested."

I jerked a nod. "And?"

"And so far only found one questionable suspect that I'd like to review in more detail. But I have plans to head further abroad this afternoon and personally meet with the regional Timberwolf leaders." He paused, his jaw tight and his eyes nervous. "But something strange came up, and I think you need to know."

I raised one brow, and Zed shifted beside me, folding his arms over his chest.

"Boss…someone recently dug up Chase Lockhart's grave." Alexi looked genuinely disturbed by this news, and the tension inside me eased.

Leaning back in my chair, I kept my gaze glued to his face. "Why do you think someone would do that?"

His brows hitched. "Honestly? I have no idea. It's bizarre. The body was missing too. So…" His voice trailed off as he shook his head in disbelief. "I can't work it out, Boss. But considering every-thing else going on, it seemed relevant."

"Thank you for letting us know, Alexi." I kept my expression neutral and gave him a small nod. "Is there anything else?"

He flicked a confused gaze between Zed and me, clearly taken aback by our lack of reaction to this news, then shook his head. "Uh, no, sir. No, that's everything so far."

"Good. We appreciate you informing us of this. Please con-tinue to keep us updated no matter how irrelevant the information might seem. You can go now."

Alexi hesitated a moment longer, then gave us each a polite nod and started out of the office.

"Hold up," I called after him. "The suspicious interview you conducted... Send Zed the info, and we will handle the follow-up."

"Absolutely, Boss. I'll send it right over."

When he was gone, I spun around in my chair to pin Zed with a hard glare.

"What?" he asked, feigning innocence.

"What the fuck was that?" I jerked my head toward the door, indicating where Alexi had disappeared.

Zed knew full fucking well what I meant and just gave a shrug. "He was eye-fucking the shit out of you, Boss. I figured it didn't hurt to remind him that you're not interested."

I scoffed a laugh. "You're so full of shit. Alexi has been eye-fucking me for *years*, that's nothing new. And last I checked, I wasn't interested in you like that either."

In a move that surprised me more than I cared to admit, Zed leaned down and placed his hands on the arms of my chair, getting all up in my personal space.

"Maybe you need to check again, Dare. You're usually more self-aware than this," he whispered so softly that if it weren't for the crazy-intense look in his eyes, I'd have thought I'd heard him wrong.

Then just as abruptly, he pushed away and stalked out of the office like the hounds of hell were snapping at his heels.

"Zed!" I shouted after him, surging out of the chair. "What the *fuck*?"

"Marketing team is waiting for us inside the fun zone," he replied, tossing the words over his shoulder without slowing down. "We're late."

Vaguely I recalled seeing a meeting with our Fight Night promoters scheduled in my weekly planner but had dismissed it as unimportant right now. Apparently, Zed hadn't canceled it, though. But since when did either of us give two fucks about keeping people waiting?

Weird. So damn weird.

CHAPTER 17

After meeting with our marketing team, I got the call I'd been waiting for from my new legal counsel. Her name was Genevieve Le Clair, and I was willing to bet Demi had made her a jaw-dropping offer to make the move. After speaking with her for half an hour, I was thoroughly impressed and confident Demi had chosen well in her replacement.

Gen assured me that she would handle everything with law enforcement on my behalf, and in return I assured her that she'd be well compensated for her effort. Those were the easy transactions with smart people that made me love my job.

When I finished my call, I decided to leave dealing with the rest of our meetings to Zed. Lucas had been asleep when I'd left for the day, and the more time that'd passed, the more anxious I was getting about checking on him.

I shot Zed a text to tell him I was going back to his place, then called Dallas to arrange another phone for Lucas. I hated not being able to text him and also didn't want to investigate that feeling too closely.

Dallas, however, was fast becoming one of my most useful recruits. He assured me that he'd bring over a clean phone for Lucas after he picked up baby Maddox from day care.

I passed a familiar black SUV on my way up Zed's street, and when I paused at the gate to key in the access code, I found an enormous pile of shopping bags stacked neatly beside the gate. I popped the trunk to load them all in.

"Lucas?" I called out upon letting myself into Zed's house. "Are you here?"

He didn't answer immediately, and I checked my phone out of habit. There was nothing to explain his absence—of course—but there was a message from Hannah letting me know she'd sent over a carload of purchases.

I smiled as I replied that I had them, and she quickly added that she would send more at the end of the day.

Hannah was fast making me wish I had my own assistant instead of relying on Zed for everything. Not only was she efficient and took initiative, she was also polite and upbeat.

Tucking my phone away, I wandered upstairs. Maybe Lucas had gone back to sleep. I wouldn't have blamed him if he had. Sleep was the best thing for healing.

The guest bed where I'd left him was vacant, though, and I'd almost walked out before I caught the floral scent of bath products.

"Lucas?" I called out again, and this time the bathroom door opened.

"You're back." He smiled wide, standing in the doorway in nothing but a towel. Steam wafted out from behind him, and I needed to bite the inside of my lip to keep the drool in my mouth.

A thick gauze patch covered half of his chest, and I focused on that rather than his wet, rippling abs as I crossed the room toward him.

"Sorry I left so early," I said with a weak smile. "How are you feeling?"

Dark bruises covered almost the whole side of his body where he must have taken some kicks, and his black eye was fading to a greenish purple.

"I feel great," he replied, not even seeming to be joking. "I mean, it wasn't the easiest to bathe without wetting this dressing, but I figured it out." He looked down at the gauze and frowned. "Or I thought I had."

I reached out and ran my fingertip over the sticky edges of the bandage where it was lifting from his skin. He'd definitely gotten it wet.

"I can replace this for you," I told him with a smile. "Wait here. I'm almost certain Zed has these same dressings in the medical kit downstairs."

Leaving Lucas to get dressed, I ran back down to the kitchen and retrieved the supplies I needed. When I returned to the bedroom, he was pulling on a pair of sweatpants, and I *really* needed to keep my tongue inside my head. What was it about sweatpants on a gorgeous man?

"Sit," I told him, pointing to the end of the bed.

He did as he was told and sat perfectly still as I used the edge of my fingernail to peel his soggy dressings off the wounds on his chest. There were two that needed covering. One was from the stab wound and subsequent surgery to save his life, and that was still covered with surgical tape. It seemed to be an impeccably precise incision line—from what I could see through the translucent tape—and I had no doubt it'd heal easily and leave minimal scarring.

The other…was a different story. I drew a deep breath as I stared down at the burn on Lucas's otherwise smooth chest, and fury built up deep within me.

"They should have removed this and skin grafted it while you were under general," I muttered in outrage. The design was almost perfectly untouched. One side had a small shadow where it looked like the brand had moved against his flesh, but otherwise it was perfectly recognizable as my Darling logo.

Lucas breathed a soft laugh, placing his hand on my waist and giving me a small squeeze. "I think they were more concerned with making sure my lungs were working properly, babe."

My gaze shifted up to his face, and I quirked a brow. "Babe? Seriously?"

His grin spread wide over his face. "What? Just 'cause I'm younger doesn't mean I can't call you 'babe.' You *are* a babe. Have you seen you? You're—"

I shut him up with a hard kiss, then pushed him back onto the bed with a firm hand to his good shoulder. "Stay still. I need to stick this dressing in place."

He smirked, his hands still clasping my hips as I leaned over him. "Yes, ma'am."

Rolling my eyes, I didn't try to fight my smile. I loved his playfulness. I loved that Chase hadn't managed to extinguish even the tiniest piece of the light inside Lucas. And I hated that Zed was now making me question whether it was all an act.

My smile slipped at that thought, and I kept my eyes on Lucas's chest as I finished replacing his dressings, then took a step away.

"What just happened?" Lucas asked in a quiet voice, sitting up once more.

I gave a small sigh and shook my head. "Doesn't matter."

He reached out and grabbed my waist again when I tried to retreat further. "It *does* matter. Hayden, whatever is on your mind, you can talk to me about it. I know I'm not as useful as Zed, but I'm a pretty good problem solver. And I can listen like a pro if you just need to talk something out."

Sometimes I could swear Lucas wasn't even real. He knew exactly what to say to slide past my defenses to the point where I was wondering why I even bothered trying to keep those walls up around him.

Wavering, I let him tug me gently closer until he could wrap both arms around my waist and look up at me with total adoration.

Goddamn. That look should have scared me straight, but it just made me more invested.

"Would it make you feel better if I told you a secret in return?" he offered, and something suspiciously close to panic flashed over his face.

It didn't make me instantly guarded and cautious like my better sense told me I should be. Instead, I just felt like an asshole for making him think he needed to trade in order to pry inside my head.

"Zed thinks you're playing me," I told him honestly. "So now I'm wondering if everything you do, everything you say...is an act."

Lucas's brows rose, but he didn't look offended. Instead, he just gave a slow nod of understanding. "I can see how he might think that," he murmured, holding my gaze with open sincerity. "I get the feeling you don't really do relationships?" He tipped his head to the side, and I wrinkled my nose in confirmation. "And Zed's been your right-hand man for...forever, right? You guys are close."

"Yeah," I said on a sigh. "We've been friends for thirteen years. He's been my second since the day we took over the Timberwolves. He knows me better than I know myself."

Lucas hummed a small sound. "I doubt that. But I get why he's suspicious. For one thing, the timing is awful. Me meeting you the same weekend as someone starts attacking your power structure? Uh, yeah. I'd be confused if you guys *didn't* think I was involved." He said it with a laugh, showing he was perfectly comfortable with the accusation. There was no defensiveness to his body language, just an eagerness to disprove Zed's suspicions.

"For another thing," he continued, his fingers tightening on my waist to pull me closer. His head was tipped back, and I couldn't stop myself from running my fingers through his damp hair. "Zed's probably feeling threatened."

A small sound of surprise escaped my throat. "Threatened?" I gave a laugh. "Nah, I don't think that's it. He's just..."

Lucas arched a brow. "Protective?"

I gave a small shrug, uncomfortable discussing my friendship with Zed. "Yeah. We've been through a lot together. I'd probably be the same way if he was seeing a girl seriously." Not that he ever had. The girls he picked up were for one thing and commitment wasn't it.

"Serious, huh? Is that what we are?" Lucas didn't look at all panicked, only amused. Meanwhile, I'd just heard what I said and was quietly dying inside of embarrassment.

"That's not what I meant," I muttered, feeling my cheeks heat. But...it kind of was. Not that I was sneaking off to plan our fucking wedding, but things between Lucas and me were a whole hell of a lot more *serious* than I'd ever been with anyone since Chase. "Besides, he's also getting paranoid about Cass. So I'm pretty sure he's just on his period or something."

Lucas scoffed a laugh. "Yeah, and you want to tell me he's not threatened?"

I glared at him, deep in denial. "Don't you owe me a secret in return?" Not that I really *needed* an information exchange, but shit if I wasn't curious to know what secrets this unicorn guy was carrying.

The teasing smile slipped from his lips. "Yeah, I guess I do. But I have one more question first. Or, actually, two."

Curious, I tipped my head. "Go on then."

He wet his lips, and it drew my attention like a magnet.

"Okay, first question, will you take me to see my mom in the care facility? I didn't want to leave here earlier without telling you where I was, but she must be so worried and—"

"Yes, of course," I cut him off, cupping my hand around the back of his neck. "You don't need to explain. I should have offered to take you last night."

Relief washed over his face, and it made me feel like a big asshole for not realizing he'd want to see her for himself. It was a testament to how far I'd distanced myself from my own loved ones that it hadn't even occurred to me.

"Okay," he replied with a small exhale. "Maybe that will help you see that I'm not some undercover spy with a fabricated past." He smirked like that was a crazy suggestion in the first place. Little did he know...

"What's your second question?" I redirected.

In answer, Lucas reached up and guided my face down to his. He kissed me until I was dizzy and breathless, my knees weak and my heart pounding, then pulled back just far enough to ask his question in a low, husky voice.

"Does that feel like an act to you, Hayden? Because to me, it feels like the most real thing I've ever experienced."

Holy fuck.

Clearing my throat, I released his neck, then swept a shaking hand through my hair. "So, what's your secret?"

He cringed slightly, dragging his lush lower lip through his teeth as his thumb stroked circles over my hip. "Uh, okay. I mean I *have* told you before, but I think you maybe misunderstood... You were my first."

I blinked a couple of times, waiting for him to finish his sentence. Then it hit me like a wrecking ball. That sentence *was* complete.

"Get fucked," I murmured in utter disbelief.

An embarrassed smile crossed his face. "Uh, yeah, I sure did. With you. In...a supply room at Scruffy Murphy's."

CHAPTER 18

My knuckles were white on the steering wheel as I turned us sharply into the visitor parking at Sunshine Estate. We hadn't spoken for the entire drive over, and I was still at a loss for words.

Okay, that wasn't strictly true. Lucas had tried to talk to me several times, and I'd shut him up with a pointed glare.

"You're freaking out," he said with a sigh as I shifted the car into Park and killed the engine.

Gritting my teeth, I shook my head. "I'm not."

Lucas gave a sharp laugh. "Yes, you are."

Blowing out a breath, I turned to face him properly for the first time since he'd admitted that I took his fucking virginity. After realizing what he'd meant, I'd sort of just…panicked. I'd panicked. And mumbled something about needing to leave before Sunshine Estate visiting hours were over. Then hadn't said a word since.

Yeah, and people thought Hades was always so cool, calm, and collected. If they could see me now…

"Okay, I am." I gave him a hard look. "Why didn't you tell me sooner? Why did you let me—"

"I did," he cut me off with a gentle laugh. "I told you it was my *first time*."

My jaw opened, but no coherent words came out for a second. Then I just made a strangled sound of exasperation. "I thought you meant it was your first one-night stand! Or…your first time for public sex! Lucas, *how?*"

His brows hitched. "How…what? How was I an almost nineteen-year-old virgin applying for a job in a brothel?"

Jesus *fuck*, I'd totally forgotten that he'd initially wanted a back-of-house position at 7th Circle. I cringed. Hard.

"You wanted to lose it before becoming a prostitute, then?" That made a little more sense as to why he'd been so willing to fuck a strange woman in a supply closet.

But Lucas just shook his head with a short laugh. "Uh, no. Actually, I hadn't thought it through all that well. I knew I'd be a good dancer. I knew I could make good money as a stripper. But I *also* knew Swinging Dick's was only hiring for both positions, and I was…am…desperate." A pained look crossed his face, and I drew a sharp breath as understanding dawned. He'd taken the job at 7th Circle because he needed the money. Now the club had gone up in flames and Lucas's injuries would prevent him from dancing again until he'd healed.

Not that I was letting his bills pile up thanks to *my* fuckups. His mom's debts had already been cleared, and her stay at Sunshine was fully paid for. But Lucas didn't know that, and I got the feeling he wouldn't be happy about it either.

"I don't get it, Lucas," I groaned, resting my head on the steering wheel. "You're…*you*. There must have been girls panting all over you for *years* in school—"

"Homeschooled, remember?" he interrupted with a flash of a grin.

I rolled my eyes. "Okay, then just in general. You must have had girlfriends before. Hell, Seph was ready to make a damn fool of herself over you even when she knew you were taken."

He shrugged. "None of them have ever interested me like that," he admitted. "I've been on a few dates, but it never went that far. There was always just something missing. For a while I thought maybe I was gay." He gave me another smile. "Now I know better. I was just waiting for the right person."

That statement did crazy things to my insides, and it was all getting a bit too heavy for my liking. So I unbuckled my seat belt and popped the door open.

"We should get in there before the visiting hours end," I told him, changing the subject so hard I almost gave myself whiplash. "Your mom will be dying to see you."

"Actually," he said, getting out of his side but leaning against the car when I started toward the entrance. "At the risk of reminding you *more* of my age...I'm supposed to be at school this week."

I jerked to a halt and blinked at him in shock. "Oh fuck. I totally forgot about that."

He winced. "Damn. I was sort of hoping you'd pulled rank on the principal or something so I wouldn't get expelled."

I flashed him a grin. "I'm kidding. I had to excuse Seph, so I took care of yours too. In case anyone asks, you have glandular fever. You've still got to do the coursework, but it's being emailed to you to do at home."

A visible rush of relief washed over his face, and he strode forward to grab my face and kiss me. "You're fucking amazing, Hayden."

I rolled my eyes. "Uh-huh. Maybe some time you can tell me why you even went to Shadow Prep instead of just getting a GED." I arched a brow at him, and he nodded.

"Absolutely, yes." He threaded his hand together with mine and we made our way through the grand entrance to the care facility. We paused to sign in at the guest registry, and then a male nurse showed us the way through to Sandra Wildeboer's room.

Before we entered, Lucas hesitated. A quick look at his face told me he was tense—maybe even scared—and I took a guess that he was worried his mom might have deteriorated in the past few days. Or maybe he was scared what her response would be to his visible bruising. Either way, I acted on instinct. My fingers linked through his, and I gave him a small squeeze of reassurance.

The way his shoulders relaxed told me it was the right move, and he reached for the door handle with renewed confidence.

His mom was sitting near the wide picture window, her back to us as we entered, but her head tipped in a way that said she'd heard us.

"Mom?" Lucas spoke up, heading toward her with my hand still tightly clasped in his own. "It's me."

"Of course it is," the woman replied, her speech slow and slightly slurred. "No one else would be visiting." Her words were harsh, but her tone wasn't unkind. Just...sad.

The room she'd been given was lovely and not at all like a hospital, if you ignored the nurse call buttons and safety rails. Otherwise, it just felt like a room inside a country bed-and-breakfast. A vase full of sunflowers sat on the small table, and the bed was made up with a floral comforter.

"Mom, this is Hayden," Lucas offered, tugging me closer to introduce me to his mother. "She's my...uh..."

"Girlfriend," I finished for him, swallowing hard against the spike of panic that word caused. It seemed like a more palatable explanation for Lucas's unwell mother to grasp, though, so I went with it.

She turned her wheelchair slightly so she could look up at us, a small smile on her lips. A ripple of surprise ran through me at seeing how young she was. She couldn't have been more than forty-five at most, her dark hair showing only the thinnest streaks of gray and her face only holding lines around her eyes.

Sandra Wildeboer was gorgeous. I could see where her son got his looks, no question.

"Hayden," she greeted me with a resigned sigh. "I should have guessed."

Confused, I flicked a glance at Lucas. He looked just as puzzled as me, though, so I turned my attention back to his mother. "Uh, guessed what, ma'am?"

It never hurt to be polite when meeting your boy-toy's parent, right? Sure. That sounded legit.

"I should have guessed," she repeated, her slow words deliberate, "when that *nice nurse* showed up at my house with a Timberwolf tattoo."

My brows shot up and my lips parted. Her speech might be impaired and her body confined to a wheelchair, but the look in Sandra Wildeboer's eyes was sharp as a blade. She knew exactly who I was...but *how*?

"You look like her," she told me, her gaze running over my face with familiarity. "And him. That hardness in your eyes... It's all your daddy." Her tone went cold and hard with that comment, and anger swelled in my chest with my inhale.

"Lucas," I murmured. "May I have a moment alone with your mother?"

"No," he replied without hesitation. "Sorry, but no way."

Incredulous, I gave him a hard stare, but he just shook his head and met my gaze with stubborn defiance.

"Luka, baby," his mother said with a small laugh, "go and get me a coffee."

Lucas glared down at his mother. "What? No, you can talk with me here."

I swallowed back the laugh that wanted to bubble out of me, but I gave his fingers a reassuring squeeze. "I promise I'm not going to hurt your mom, Lucas. I just want to talk with her a moment." And find out how in the hell she knew my parents. What connection did the Wildeboer family have to the Timbers?

"That's not what I was worried about," Lucas muttered, but he seemed to know he was outnumbered. He gave his mom a hard look. "Be nice, Mom. I like her."

Sandra just smiled and waited for her son to leave the room before indicating that I should sit down. I pulled over a chair from the small table and sat facing her as she eyed me from her wheelchair.

"Hayden Timber," she murmured. "I'd have thought Luka too young for the likes of you."

I sat back, tucking my ankles over one another. "Why, because I'm a woman? No one has a problem when a man dates younger." I arched a brow at her, silently questioning her feminist standpoint.

Her lips curled in a sly smile. "Good answer. I bet you want to know how I knew your parents, huh?"

I inclined my head. "That would be nice. I wasn't aware Lucas had any connections to my world."

She grunted an annoyed sound. "He doesn't. But I did. Once." She drew a shaky breath and let it out slowly. "I should warn you, my mind isn't what it used to be. Sometimes things get a bit…lost."

"You seem pretty sharp to me, Ms. Wildeboer." It was a somewhat dry accusation, and she huffed a laugh.

"Right now, yes. You got me on a good day, Hayden." She tilted her head to the side, her eyes inspecting my face. "Do you remember much of your mother? She died when you were very young."

I swallowed past old, bitter emotions that tried to surface, holding onto my calm mask like a life raft. "I remember more than my sister does," I answered, not really answering the question at all. I remembered a *lot* of my mother; I just chose not to think about her. I chose to keep those memories locked up tight, and no matter how curious I was about Lucas's mom, I wasn't pulling them out for a trip down memory lane.

"We were friends," Sandra told me in a nostalgic whisper, her eyes misty as she gazed at me. I got the feeling she wasn't seeing me at all, but my mom. "Natasha was too good for your father. He knew it too."

My jaw tightened. "She didn't die in a car accident, did she?"

Sandra gave a sad sigh. "No. He shot her. She tried to leave him, tried to take you and your sister, and he shot her."

Those words were like a knife in my already bleeding heart. "How do you know?" I asked, my voice hoarse.

"Because I saw it happen," she murmured. "And I was so scared. I had Luka to think of, so I ran. I made some bad choices, trusted the wrong people to keep me safe…" Her words trailed off, tears gathering in her eyes.

I waited, tense with anticipation, but she didn't continue. Instead, she just gave me a pleading look and held out a weak, trembling hand. "Keep my boy safe, Hades," she whispered, the slur to her words making it hard to understand. "Please. You owe me nothing, but—"

"Of course I will," I said, promising her despite the danger Lucas had already landed in, thanks to me. "But you need to tell me more. What happened after you ran? How were you and my mom friends in the first place?"

Sandra shook her head, her eyelids fluttering. "I'm sorry, it's just…" She grimaced, clearly annoyed. "Will you call the nurse for me, Tasha? I'm not feeling so good."

Shock held me immobile for a second, then I slowly replied, "It's Hayden. I'm…I'm not Natasha."

Sandra blinked at me, then nodded with a laugh. "Yes, sorry. Of course. I knew that, Hayden. Things just get a bit foggy sometimes."

Frustrated but biting back my feelings, I reached for the nurse call button and pressed it for her. "That's okay, Sandra," I assured her. "It's all in the past anyway." The door opened then, but instead of the nurse, it was Lucas returning with a coffee in each hand. "Look, Luka is back with your coffee."

He gave me a questioning look, but I just retreated to give him some time with his mom. A nurse passed me as I was leaving the room, and I briefly described how Sandra had just had a moment of confusion.

The nurse nodded knowingly. "Pretty normal," she told me with a smile. "Thanks." She continued into the room, and I made my way outside.

As badly as I wanted to know more about Sandra's connection to my mom, I wasn't cold enough to push an unwell woman for answers that would ultimately give me nothing. She'd known my mom before she died, and—if I was to understand correctly—had left Shadow Grove a *long* time before I came into power. Nothing she could tell me of my deceased parents would be relevant to my current struggles.

More importantly, none of it implicated Lucas as being anything more than he seemed. He would've only been four when Sandra ran from Shadow Grove, and I didn't care how deeply involved she'd been in the Timberwolves, he was innocent.

Lucas didn't stay long before rejoining me in the car, and I gave him a concerned frown as he closed his door.

"You can stay longer," I told him. "I just didn't want to intrude."

He shook his head. "Nah, she needs rest." His jaw tightened, and he seemed to be searching for the right words to say something more. Eventually he ran his fingers through his hair and let his shoulders droop on a long exhale. "Thank you," he said. "For this." He waved a hand at the entrance to Sunshine Estate. "She needed more care than I could provide, but this...this was way out of reach."

I quirked a lopsided smile, not used to being thanked so genuinely. It was awkward, but in a good way. "Considering you almost died because of me? It really was the least I could do." Acting on instinct, I reached out and threaded my hand around the back of his neck, pulling him in for a kiss.

He kissed me back without even a shadow of hesitation, letting his full lips explore mine in a way that made my whole body hot with need.

"What was that for?" he murmured with an edge of surprise.

I licked my lips, starting the car up. "I like you too, Luka."

CHAPTER 19

Zed called me before we got back to his house, asking me to head back to Anarchy. The tone of his voice told me it wasn't a casual request, and I didn't push him for further information on the phone. I just changed direction and drove back to the creepy old repurposed amusement park.

Lucas grimaced as I drove in under the enormous laughing clown face, and I shot him an amused glance. "Not a fan of clowns?"

He wrinkled his nose, rubbing a fingertip over the yellowing bruise around his eye. "Is anyone? That shit is creepy as fuck. What made you buy this place anyway?"

I barked a laugh. "Why not? It was going cheap and already had a reputation for hosting cage fights. Easy choice."

Getting out of the car, I headed for the fun zone, where I usually found Zed at this time. It was past dusk, the drive to and from Sunshine Estate having taken longer than I anticipated. The main bar would have opened a couple of hours ago, so I expected to find him sitting at the bar with a drink in hand.

The bouncer on the door greeted me respectfully, then directed me down to the lower level, where our private dance rooms were.

It was also where our dancers registered as back-of-house workers could take clients for more than just a lap dance.

Anarchy was predominantly to host fight nights, so the basement of the club only had a couple of private rooms, but that was where I found Zed waiting for me.

Two of my high-ranking Timberwolves, Fang and Jim-Bob, flanked one of the doorways and gave me respectful nods as I pushed the door open.

"Boss," Zed greeted me, then shifted his gaze to Lucas with a subtle narrowing of his eyes.

I folded my arms over my chest, taking in the scene in front of me.

"What's going on here?" The question was quite clearly for Zed, and the other occupants of the room knew it. The near-naked woman sitting on the bed with her arms around her knees just blinked up at me, her cheek puffy and red with a handprint. The man who was no doubt responsible for that handprint? Well, he couldn't have answered me even if he'd wanted to. Zed had him on the floor, hog-tied and gagged, but not in a fun sort of way.

"Gigi's client thought he could take liberties that he hadn't paid for," Zed told me in a cold voice of disgust. He gave the hog-tied man a swift kick that rolled him over and revealed a bleeding wound in his side. "Apparently he didn't realize all our staff are trained in self-defense. Gigi disarmed him before he could cut her and raised an alarm."

I looked over to the woman on the bed. She was clearly shaken, but nowhere near a blubbering mess. "Good work, Gigi," I praised her, taking a couple of steps closer to inspect her face a little better. She understood what I was doing, raising her face up to show me the handprint and some red marks around her throat. "Jim-Bob!" I called out to one of the door guards. "Go and fetch Gigi an ice pack from upstairs. Go get dressed, you can take the night off." I gave this last order directly to Gigi. She was a beautiful girl, maybe a year or so younger than me with long blond hair and huge tits. I was pleased to see she'd been able to defend herself.

She gave me a defiant shake of her head, a flash of worry showing across her face as she drew a breath.

"You'll be paid out for the whole night," I told her before she could protest, and relief washed over her. "Jim-Bob will escort you home too."

"Thank you, Hades," she said in a small voice, scooting her sequined-thong-wearing ass off the bed and giving Lucas a wide-eyed look of appreciation. She made no attempt to cover her bare breasts as she brushed past him, and an acidic bubble of jealousy formed inside me.

Lucas didn't look, though, and placed his hand on the small of my back like a silent declaration that he was *with* me. Smart boy.

"So, you want to tell me why you called me down here?" I asked Zed after Gigi was gone. "Clients getting rough with the staff is something the security can handle themselves." Usually with a baseball bat or steel-toed boot. Assholes learned *real* fast not to hurt my workers. I didn't care how much they were paying, consent was key, and last I checked Gigi wasn't into those kinks.

Zed gave an irritated glance at Lucas, then nudged the bound guy with his boot again. "See that?"

The man wasn't in the best shape, with a heavy layer of fat around his belly and a thick coating of hair across his shoulders. He'd also inked himself up in pseudo-gang tattoos, shit that *looked* like he was in a gang but were just vanity pieces. Except for one.

With a groan, I crouched down to get a better look at the one-inch-square design on his shoulder. "Mother*fucker*."

"My thoughts exactly," Zed agreed.

I sat back on my heels, a million thoughts racing through my brain. Then I pulled my phone out and scrolled for a familiar contact.

"Getting impatient, Red?" Cass answered on the first ring,

and I bit back a smile at his greeting. "I'm on my way to pick you up now."

Ah shit, our dinner date. It must be almost eight. "Rain check, Grumpy Cat. I need you to come to Anarchy."

"Be there in ten," he replied, not questioning me. I appreciated that.

Ending the call, I stood up again and raked my fingers through my hair. "Fang, come help Zed move this prick down to the cold room," I ordered. "Then don't take you damn eyes off him until I get back."

"Yes, sir," Fang replied, stepping aside to let me out of the small room before he entered. Lucas followed me, questions rolling off him in waves, but he bit his tongue nonetheless.

"I'll meet you down there," I told Zed.

He jerked a nod of understanding, and I led Lucas back up to the main club. We paused briefly at the bar so I could advise the manager not to venture into the cold room for a while, then made our way back out to the parking lot.

"What's going on?" Lucas asked when we were safely away from anyone who might be listening. "Was that tattoo on his back what I think it was?"

I wrapped my arms around myself, wishing I could lie to him. But…something about Lucas made me *want* to be honest with him. "The same design that got branded into your chest by a madman last week? Yeah. Who gave it to him remains to be seen, but…I have a fair idea."

He nodded silently, his jaw tight, and a wave of guilt washed over me. I still hadn't explained to him exactly what had happened when he was taken. I hadn't told him *why* he was taken or who I was pretty sure had been responsible. Nothing.

Fucking hell, Lucas deserved better than my messed-up ass.

"I'll explain everything when I get home," I told him in a soft voice, reaching out to place my hand on his cheek. Tilting his face back toward me, I rose up on my toes to press a light kiss on his lips.

He gave a frustrated sound as he weaved his fingers into the back of my hair. "You're sending me back to the house, aren't you?"

I nodded, hearing Cass's motorcycle rumble closer by the second.

"I can stay," Lucas tried to tell me, a frown creasing his brow. "Maybe I could be useful somehow."

Instead of answering him—because the answer was a firm *hell no*—I kissed him again. He knew what I was doing, but kissed me back hard, his fingers in my hair holding me tight as he devoured my mouth. I lost myself in his kiss for a moment, my body arching into his. Then I reluctantly peeled myself free and shot a guilty look at Cass—who'd just pulled up beside us on his bike.

"You got a death wish or something, Wilder?" Cass growled, glaring pure death at Lucas.

"Quit it," I snapped before that confrontation could escalate. "Cass, I need you to take Lucas home to Zed's place."

The big biker shifted his gaze to me, his scarred brow rising slightly. "What's going on, Red?"

"That's what I'm about to find out," I told him with a grim expression. "Here, take Zed's car." I held the keys out to him, figuring he probably didn't want to cozy up to Lucas on the back of his bike. "Just…make sure Lucas gets back to Zed's safely. He's still an easy target for Chase."

Cass wrapped his hand around my wrist rather than taking the keys from my fingers. With a sharp tug he pulled me close and planted his lips against mine in a clearly possessive move.

I kissed him back for a moment because I *craved* his kisses like a drug. Then I pushed free of his grip and clucked my tongue in warning.

"If you two are both quite finished pissing on me like a tree, I have someone waiting to be tortured in the basement." I leveled a warning glare at the both of them. "Stay alive. Both of you. Or you'll have me to answer to."

Leaving them to *hopefully* not kill each other, I strutted my ass back inside the fun zone and headed for the cold room.

Several more of my more trusted Timberwolves were posted along the corridor, no doubt tasked with stopping my Copper Wolf bartenders and waitresses from accidentally stumbling into what was quite definitely Timberwolf business. Some days the two facets of my business blended so smoothly, while on others the lines were clearly drawn.

Fang hauled the heavy refrigerator door open for me as I approached, and I gave him a tight smile of appreciation. I was glad to know all the faces I'd just passed had been cleared in Alexi's investigation. It would have pissed me right off had my judgment been faulty on any of those men.

"Gumdrop safely on his way home?" Zed taunted as I stepped up beside him. The man who'd thought he could lay hands on Gigi was now bound to a metal chair in the middle of the walk-in fridge, the ropes holding his arms and legs tied in a decidedly decorative pattern. Either Zed was showing off or I'd taken longer handing Lucas to Cass than I realized.

"You're acting like a jealous girlfriend, Zayden," I muttered with an eye roll. "Maybe you just need to get laid. I'm sure Zoe would make time for you when we're done here."

Zed scowled. "It's Chloe. And I stopped seeing her weeks ago when she asked if I would meet her parents."

I snickered. "Well, whatever. You've got enough random pussy in your contact list, I'm sure you can sort it out."

That comment seemed to piss him off more, and he folded his arms with a huff that created steam in the cold air. A deep shiver ran through me, as if my body had just remembered we were standing in a cool room, and I rubbed my upper arms.

"Fucking hell. Let's get on with this." I eyed our victim and grimaced at my lack of equipment. My metal woven gloves had been in my apartment when it went up, which was just fucking great.

"Here," Zed muttered, handing me a set of brass knuckles from his pocket. I arched a wide smile at him, and he rolled his eyes. "You've looked like you were itching for a fight all damn day. Have at him." He nodded to the hairy man tied to the chair. He was still gagged, but neither of us was bothered by that fact. They never talked on the first hit anyway.

Threading my fingers through the metal loops, I gave a soft laugh. "You know me so well, Zed." I took a step closer to the bound and gagged man and swung a vicious punch that made a sickening crunch and sent blood arcing across the cold room.

"Better than anyone, Dare," Zed muttered behind me. Then he stood back and watched intently as I indulged in my own form of therapy and shook some information free at the same time.

Disappointingly, it was only a few minutes before the hairy-shouldered wannabe gangster was screaming muffled pleas behind his gag. Zed tugged the gag away, letting the creep talk, and boy, did he feel chatty.

To our disappointment, though, he knew very little of importance. He'd been recruited after he was picked up for assault and battery against his ex-wife, then released by a dirty cop. A man whose description I didn't recognize was the one who'd given him the tattoo and assigned him this task.

When Zed and I were satisfied we'd extracted everything of use from the piece-of-shit woman basher, Zed put a bullet through his skull.

"Thanks," I muttered, wiping thick blood-goo from my chest. "Couldn't have waited until I'd moved a little farther away?"

Zed's lips twitched like he was trying not to laugh at me. "You've got a little something here, Boss." He indicated his forehead, and I swiped a hand over my own. It came away wet with blood, but given how thoroughly I'd beaten the shit out of that guy before he'd died, it was no great shock.

Shooting Zed a glare, I stepped over the mess we'd made and pushed the cold-room door open.

Fang was still waiting outside, and his brows shot right up when he saw me. Zed must not have been bullshitting, because Fang's eyes went to my forehead straightaway. I bet I had a chunk of skull or something stuck in my hair.

"Uh, Boss, we didn't want to interrupt earlier," Fang said, stepping aside to let Zed and me pass. "But Cass from the Reapers sent one of his men over. Dropped this off for you." He indicated to a nondescript duffel bag against the wall. It looked largely empty, so I gave Fang a confused look. "Dunno, Boss. We told him he couldn't be here and shit, but he said Cass ordered him to deliver that."

Zed swiped the bag up and tugged the zipper open before giving a short laugh. "What a smooth motherfucker," he muttered, handing the bag to me.

Inside was a clean set of clothes and a thick packet of wet wipes. Smooth motherfucker indeed. That was one way to show he was thinking of me.

Cassiel Saint was really living up to the promises in his love letter.

CHAPTER 20

As thoughtful as Cass's care package had been, the wet wipes weren't totally necessary. Zed and I headed through to the dancers' changing rooms and borrowed the showers there to rinse off the worst of the blood. The change of clothes *was* appreciated, though, and I threw my silk blouse straight in the trash.

"Oh my god," Zed groaned when I emerged from the changing room squeaky clean. My hair was wet—there had been no avoiding washing it—and my makeup gone, and I was wearing activewear—skintight yoga pants and a cropped sweatshirt that showed off my toned stomach.

"What?" I demanded, slinging the bag, now containing my bloody skirt and heels, over my shoulder.

He just arched a brow and shook his head. "Nothing. Let's get out of here before our staff see you looking like a real human being."

We took the service corridors to get out to the staff parking lot, where Zed opened the passenger door to his Ferrari for me.

"I should probably drive Cass's bike back for him," I commented, but Zed prodded me to get into his car instead.

"He probably got his guys to pick it up earlier," Zed said

with a shrug, climbing into his own seat. "Besides, I like driving you."

I snorted a laugh. "Driving me crazy, more like. You ready to talk to me about that temper tantrum yesterday?"

His hands tightened on the steering wheel until the leather creaked. "Nope."

"Cool. Good chat, Zed."

I'd been joking, but apparently he wasn't. He didn't say another word for the whole drive home, and I was too busy muttering insults at him in my head to attempt any change of topic. Anyone who wanted to come at me for being childish could kiss my ass. Everyone did it, no matter how old they were.

By the time we'd parked in Zed's garage, I was in a shitty mood myself. I slammed his car door way harder than necessary and bit back a smirk at the angry mutter it extracted from him in response.

Snatches of conversation echoed through the halls toward us, making me pause midstep. When it sounded like someone *laughed*, I gave Zed a puzzled frown. He just shrugged in return and nodded for me to precede him toward the kitchen as he pulled his gun out.

Suspicious fuck. Not that I was arguing; something felt seriously off.

As we approached the voices got louder until I recognized them. Then I needed to second-guess my own hearing because I could have sworn I just heard Cass *laugh* at something Lucas had said.

What in the—

"Babe!" Lucas was the first to see me as I entered the kitchen with Zed on my heels.

Cass looked over at me with a lazy smile on his lips and a half-smoked joint between his fingers. Ah. That explained that.

Zed put his gun away, brushed past me, and turned around to mouth *babe* in the most infuriatingly condescending way known to man. Prick. I flipped him off, then headed over to the dining table where Cass and Lucas had apparently been playing with knives.

"What...is going on?" I asked them both, eyeing the seven-inch hunting blade currently sticking out of Zed's wooden table-top. A deck of cards sat off to the side in a messy pile, and a couple of half-empty beers completed the scene.

"You're buying me a new table, asshole," Zed snapped, glaring at Cass as he pulled out a chair and sat down.

"Just killing time until you got back," Lucas told me with a grin, accepting the joint from Cass and taking a drag. Based on his droopy eyelids, I'd guess it wasn't their first.

Cass sat back in his chair, slouching in that sexy, tall-man kind of way as he blatantly eye fucked me. "Everything okay at Anarchy?"

"None of your fucking business," Zed grunted, answering for me. Cass leveled a threatening glare at my best friend, and Zed met it stubbornly.

Mother-shitting tit balls. That drama needed to be nipped, and I was having a hard time seeing any better moment than the present.

Pulling out a chair, I sat down and plucked the remains of the joint from Lucas's fingers. I took one long drag, finishing it, then dropped the butt into one of the mostly empty beer bottles.

"All right," I announced. "Let's clear the air before our secrets and miscommunications lead to one of us being kidnapped, tor-tured, or possibly killed. Shall we?"

Lucas coughed a small laugh. "Yep, that seems like a sound plan, babe."

I wrinkled my nose. "Sorry. I meant *again*. I can't even remem-ber who knows what at this stage, so I'm just going to...lay it all out there and make sure we're all on the same page."

Zed gave a sound of protest, shaking his head. "Dare, they're not—"

"I know," I snapped, shooting him a vicious glance. "I *know*. They're not even Timberwolves. Hell, Cass is *the* Reaper, for fuck's sake. But sue me, I like them both. So whether you agree or not, they're involved in this."

Zed wasn't backing down so easily, though, his eyes flashing with stubborn defiance and his chin lifting in a way that said he was ready to fight me over this decision. He'd have lost. So it was a damn good thing the gate buzzer sounded and broke our staring contest.

"Who the fuck is that?" Zed demanded, swinging an accusing glare at Lucas.

He raised his hands defensively. "Don't look at me."

Cass just shrugged and sipped his beer. "I was hungry. Figured you might be too." He eyed me carefully as he said that, like he was trying to see inside my mind.

Zed grumbled shit about his privacy and security but went to answer the gate buzzer anyway. As usual, he waited with his gun ready for the delivery driver to drop the food at the front step. Only once the driver was gone did he step out and collect the bags.

Paranoid? Sure. But better safe than sorry.

"Where the fuck did you even order from?" Zed demanded, carrying the food back through to us in the kitchen. "This isn't one of our restaurants."

By *our*, he meant a Timberwolf establishment. We had slowly bought up all our favorite eateries in the area so that we knew—or had more confidence—that we wouldn't get poisoned ordering takeout. And I didn't mean that as a euphemism; there had been an incident in the past where a gang leader was assassinated through arsenic in his Chinese food.

So Zed and I tended to stick with places we knew and controlled.

"It's safe." Cass...man of many words.

Zed arched a challenging brow. "Says who? You? For all we know, you deliberately ordered a *special* meal to take out the competition."

Cass scoffed a husky laugh—damn, that was a sexy sound—and shook his head in disbelief. "If I wanted you dead, De Rosa, you'd—"

"Stop it!" I snapped, slamming my hand down on the table. "I've had *enough*. Sit down, shut up, and don't fucking speak unless you're spoken to."

With fire in my eyes, I glared all three of them into submission—not that Lucas needed it—then stood up and dragged the bags of food closer to inspect.

I recognized the logo on the napkins as I pulled out cardboard boxes of food and gave a small smile. "I didn't know Nadia's delivered."

Nadia's Cakes was an awesome coffee and cake shop in Reaper territory, but she also did delicious meals and burgers.

"They don't," Cass replied. "I just thought you might want some real food when you got back, rather than frozen dinners or whatever the fuck Zed has in his kitchen."

I bit back the urge to laugh, and Zed was clearly having a hard time not reacting to that dig.

"Quit it," I scolded Cass. "Zed's a fucking fantastic cook, and you damn well know it. This smells amazing, though. Thank you."

I pretended to ignore the antagonistic looks passing between Cass and Zed because, for *fuck's* sake, they weren't teenagers. Hell, the only teenager in the room was acting the most emotionally adjusted out of the lot of us.

After opening all the boxes of food to display a range of mouth-watering steaks, chicken wings, fries, and various other sides, I went to the kitchen to retrieve plates and cutlery. Lucas—shocker—got up to help me, and when I murmured my thanks, he informed me that his mother had raised him with manners.

At that comment both Cass and Zed turned their glares on Lucas, and I couldn't fight my snort of amusement.

"Okay, calm down," I told them, rolling my eyes. "Eat your food before it gets cold. I'll talk and you three can just listen."

No one argued with that, but Zed did keep glaring in my direction like he wanted me to kick Lucas and Cass out and keep our problems private. Too bad. Things had already escalated past that point. Way, *way* past that point.

"All right." I drew a deep breath, then released it in a long sigh. "Where do I even begin on this?" It was rhetorical, a filler phrase while I tried to gather my thoughts.

But Cass answered me anyway. "Start with Chase Lockhart. Start at the beginning. How'd you two meet?"

My gaze flicked up instantly, locking with Zed's pained eyes across the table. Cass didn't realize it, but he'd struck right on *the* turning point in my life. So yeah, what better place to start explaining than my fucked-up history with Chase Lockhart?

A grim smile curved my lips as I held Zed's sad gaze. "In hindsight, I should have seen this whole violent mess coming," I said with a small laugh. "I met Chase—and Zed—when they tried to kill me."

Zed's face softened with nostalgia, and I grinned at the stunned expressions on Cass's and Lucas's faces.

"In fairness," Zed added, rubbing his palm across the stubble on his cheek, "I was just along for the ride."

I rolled my eyes but couldn't fight the smile on my face. "Yeah, whatever. Anyway, knowing what I know now, that was a really big red flag for how things would turn out with Chase." I grimaced and combed my fingers through my damp hair. "I was ten. After that, my father decided to send me to Phillip D'Ath's training camp so I wouldn't ever be an easy target for his enemies again."

Zed gave a grim smile, taking over my story. "Little did Garrett Timber realize Chase and I were enrolled in the same session. Because we'd failed to execute the Timber princess, our families had lost faith in our potential to lead the next generation of criminal syndicates." He pushed his half-eaten plate away and went to the kitchen to grab a beer.

I rubbed a hand over the back of my neck, remembering. "Chase and I bonded over our mutual interest in learning how to kill a man seventeen ways without a weapon."

"Seventeen ways with just your hands?" Lucas asked, an amused smile playing across his full lips.

Shit. He was so stoned. Maybe this wasn't the best time to have this discussion after all.

"I'm gonna fast-forward this," I decided out loud, "and just hit the key points for now. We can go into details another day."

Cass jerked a nod of understanding, but I could see a million questions buzzing behind his eyes.

"Chase Lockhart," I explained for Lucas's benefit, "was the oldest son, the heir to the Lockhart fortune. They were known on paper as an old-money family who'd made their fortune in the stock market. In reality they ran drugs and dabbled in human trafficking."

Lucas's brows rose in surprise, but he didn't interrupt. I appreciated that.

"He and I started dating when we were really young—too young to have any fucking clue what we were doing." I heaved another sigh, bitter at my own past self.

Zed placed a beer down in front of me, then touched his leg to mine under the table. "You were," he corrected. "Chase wasn't. He knew, he just didn't care."

I hummed a sound that was neither agreement nor disagreement. Sad fact of the matter was that by the time I'd worked it all out, it was far too late. Kill or be killed, and we all knew which option I'd taken to escape.

My lips parted to explain more of my relationship with Chase, how he'd made me fall in love with him, how I'd let our fathers push us into an engagement right before my fifteenth birthday, how Chase had slowly morphed into a goddamn fucking monster thanks to his free and easy access to drugs. But no words would leave my tongue. They just froze there, trained to stay silent from years of denial and suppression.

Eventually I closed my eyes and took a moment to regroup. A warm hand crept into my lap, linking fingers with my fingers and giving a reassuring squeeze. Lucas.

Letting my lids open once more, I gave him a small smile, then skipped straight ahead in my story to the part I knew I could tell. The part that I'd well and truly hardened my heart over.

"I did something stupid when I was eighteen," I told them, swallowing heavily against the rising tide of emotion. "I fucked up, and as a result Seph almost paid the price. Our father listed her for sale on a darknet site that dealt in what they considered top-tier human auctions. Through some investigation, I discovered that this wasn't the first time my father had dealt in stolen girls. He and the Lockhart family had been smuggling countless children into the country for *years*. But the part that flipped my switch was when I discovered it'd been Chase, my fucking *fiancé*, who had given Garrett—or *Claw* as he liked to be called—the idea to sell Seph to *remind Darling who really holds the power.*"

A deep shudder ran through me as I heard Chase's voice so damn clear in my mind. Apparently, I wasn't as closed off to those memories as I'd thought.

After a long pause, Cass cleared his throat and leaned forward on his forearms. "So you killed them all." It wasn't a question, because he'd been deep enough into the Reapers by then that he would've seen the aftermath with his own eyes.

Refusing to feel guilt over what I'd done, I raised my chin and met his eyes. "I did. With some help. I personally shoved a knife in my father's back during a Timberwolf monthly meeting, then slit his throat. Chase wasn't there, though. Somehow, he'd found out what I had planned, and none of the Lockharts were at the meeting like they were supposed to be."

Lucas's hand still gripped mine, but I couldn't bring myself to look at him as I spoke. I couldn't handle seeing fear in his eyes as he heard about my pivotal moment in becoming Hades. It was much easier to speak directly to Cass, who stared back at me with a totally unreadable expression. What he really thought of my actions was a mystery. I was fine with that, for now.

"So, I left my backup to execute the Timberwolf massacre, then Zed and I went hunting. We caught up to Chase in the Lockhart manor. He was packing his shit, cleaning out the family safe, and there was a helicopter waiting for him on the lawn, ready to whisk him away to safety. He wasn't even taking the rest of his family with him, just looking after himself. As usual." Bitterness burned through my veins like acid, and I shook my head to clear the vivid, blood-soaked memories from my mind.

It was no use, though. Over and over I saw myself shooting Chase's father in the face after I kicked the door in. I saw the arc of blood splattering the white marble tiles as I yanked my dagger from Eleanor Lockhart's throat after she tried to attack me from behind. Their screams of terror and the pleas for mercy fell on deaf ears. I smelled raw, hot flesh and the acidic tang of disembowelment.

"Long story short…" Zed took over for me, his leg pressed firmly against mine and his gaze intense on my face. "Chase put up a hell of a fight, but ultimately we won. Dare put a bullet straight in his face, then dragged me out of the house while calling for help."

"What had happened to you?" Lucas asked in a quiet, husky voice. This story was definitely taking the edge off his buzz.

Zed leaned back in his chair and lifted his shirt up to display his toned chest. Carefully, one by one, he ran his fingertip over the thirteen individual scars, each an inch long and all hidden by his tattoos.

"That bastard stabbed me half to death," he told Lucas before tugging his shirt back down. His eyes returned to mine, and I no longer had a voice to say all the things I'd always wanted to say about that night.

Silence fell around the table for a tense moment, then Cass scraped his chair back from the table and ambled into the kitchen. He returned a moment later with a bottle of scotch and four glasses. Wordlessly he poured a heavy splash into each, then handed them out to us.

"I understand the Lockhart manor exploded that night," the big guy rumbled, still totally expressionless. "Gas leak."

I jerked a nod, swallowing half my drink in one mouthful.

"The gas line was damaged in our fight," Zed elaborated. "We had no idea."

Another gulp of scotch and I started getting more of a grip on my spiraling emotions. "And now Chase is apparently back," I told them in a hollow voice. "Zed and I didn't believe it, so we dug up his grave last week."

Lucas choked on his drink.

Cass's brows rose in surprise. "And?"

I shrugged. "And it was empty."

He ruffled a hand over his semi-Mohawked hair. "Doesn't mean he's alive."

"Also doesn't mean he's *not* alive," I countered, reaching for the bottle of scotch. "The evidence keeps stacking up. The personal notes, blowing up 7th Circle with a gas leak, kidnapping Lucas... There's no way it can be anyone else."

Cass grimaced. "It seems that way, but maybe that's deliberate."

"Does it matter?" Lucas asked, jerking my attention over to him. His fingers were still twined together with mine under the table, and it didn't seem like he wanted to let go anytime soon. So...that was something.

"How fucking stoned are you?" Zed asked, an edge of anger

to his voice. "Of course it matters. Or did you forget how you got taken, tortured, and almost killed less than a week ago?"

Lucas flinched at Zed's harsh tone, and anger flared up hot inside me. "Zed, cut it out."

"Believe me, Zed," Lucas snapped back, clearly having had enough of his bullshit, "that's not something I'm going to forget in a hurry. But does it actually matter whether this is Chase himself or someone else acting out a vengeance plot in his name? The end result is the same, right? We're going to hunt this sick fuck down and make him pay. Aren't we?"

The raw determination in his tone made my jaw drop, and I stared at Lucas in shock. That...hadn't been how I'd thought he'd react.

Zed snorted a laugh, shaking his head and rubbing a hand over his chest like his old scars were aching. "Yeah, Gumdrop. That's exactly what we're gonna do. Make that fucker pay."

CHAPTER 21

Unsurprisingly, my sleep was fraught with nightmares of the past. I'd wanted to be alone after spilling all those memories for Cass and Lucas, but after the fourth time I woke with my heart racing and my skin coated in cold sweat, I admitted defeat.

Silently, without turning any lights on, I made my way along the hall from the guest room I'd claimed and visited the bathroom. Not even ice-cold water on my face helped me stop trembling, though.

With a quiet groan of frustration, I headed downstairs. It was only a few hours before dawn; I may as well just wake up properly and hit the gym. All the sex in the world wasn't going to keep me in shape if I kept skipping training like I had been in the last few weeks.

To my surprise, the living room was lit by the flickering blue light of the TV, and I found Zed sprawled out on the couch in front of it. He looked up from where his head was propped on the arm of the sofa when I approached, his eyes just as haunted as I felt.

"Hey," he murmured, reaching out a hand in invitation.

I took it and climbed onto the sofa with him, snuggling into his warmth and letting him draw a blanket over both of us.

"What are we watching?" I asked, using his bicep as a pillow. The brunette actress on the screen looked familiar, but my sleep-deprived brain couldn't quite place her. With my luck, I'd probably just walked in on Zed watching porn or something.

He wrapped his other arm around my waist, pulling me closer into his body. "*High School Musical*," he mumbled, then yawned.

For a second I thought he was joking. Then the characters on screen started singing and dancing in the middle of a basketball court, and I snickered a laugh.

"Shh," Zed told me, "I love this part."

I didn't need to make fun of him out loud; he knew I was doing it inside my head. So I just relaxed into his hold and watched the ridiculous G-rated movie about singing and dancing high-school basketballers.

Zed was onto something, though. I drifted into sleep easily there on the couch with him, and only woke slightly when the movie ended and he switched the TV off.

"Go back to sleep," he whispered when I yawned. His arm returned to my waist, hugging me tight as his face rested against my neck. Maybe it was my groggy, sleep-hazed imagination, but his lips brushed my skin in a kiss that seemed unusually intimate.

I didn't question it, though. I just leaned into his embrace and let the fog of exhaustion pull me under once more as Zed whispered more words that I couldn't make out.

In the light of morning, things almost seemed better. I'd woken up still wrapped in Zed's arms on the couch, and he'd dropped all the bitchy attitude of the past few days. He got up with a yawn and stretched, then dropped a quick kiss on my hair before announcing he'd cook breakfast.

Maybe he just needed a chill session with good weed and shitty kids' movies to level out his bad temper every now and then. I'd remember that.

Somehow, I was totally unsurprised when Cass rolled up on his motorcycle as Zed was sliding a plate of bacon and eggs under my still half-asleep nose.

Zed didn't comment, just buzzed Cass in and served up another plate of breakfast for the big grump. Now it made sense why he'd cooked up an entire tray of eggs.

"Morning, Grumpy Cat," I teased when Cass entered the kitchen.

He shot me an amused look, sliding his jacket off his arms and dropping it over the back of a chair like he fucking lived here. "Morning, Red," he replied, then swooped down to kiss me. His fingers slid into the back of my messy hair, gripping my head tight in a silent reminder of how rough he was in the bedroom. And how much I loved it.

Zed cleared his throat deliberately, reminding us we weren't alone, but Cass was in no hurry to let me go. Hell, I could almost feel the amusement rolling off him as he continued to kiss me senseless for another few seconds before letting go. It gave me a small stab of guilt to kiss Cass like that when Zed had displayed concerns about this new relationship, but part of me wanted to push him. Force him to either speak up or shut up.

"De Rosa," Cass said with a husky voice, swiping his thumb over his glistening lower lip. "Sorry, man, didn't see you there."

Zed's glare said exactly how much he believed that bullshit. "And here I was about to give you breakfast. Probably just changed my mind."

Cass slid into a seat and reached for the plate of bacon and eggs. "Don't be a sore loser, Zed."

Whatever the fuck *that* was supposed to mean. I gave Cass a hard glare, but he didn't react, just took a forkful of his eggs.

Zed didn't lose his shit like he would have yesterday, though.

He just snickered a conspiratorial laugh and shook his head. "Can't lose when you're still in the race, Saint."

An uncomfortable feeling crept through me, and I narrowed my eyes in suspicion. "I don't know what the fuck you two are talking about"—or I damn well hoped I didn't—"but it's too early for bullshit. So cut it the fuck out."

Zed poured a mug of coffee and held it out to me with a smirk. "Yes, sir." The mocking tone was there, as it always was, and his fingers seemed to linger longer than necessary against mine when I took the mug. Weirdo. No doubt he was playing territorial games with Cass because it amused him to rile up the older gang leader.

"Where's Gumdrop this morning?" Cass asked between bites of breakfast.

I settled in with my own food, tasting the Parmesan and chives Zed had mixed into his scrambled eggs. So damn good. "Still sleeping," I told him. "And don't you fucking start with the Gumdrop shit too. His name is Lucas. Get used to it, he's not going anywhere in a hurry."

Cass quirked a microsmile in my direction. "He's a gumdrop, Red. Get used to it."

I sent my death glare in Zed's direction, seeing as he was responsible for that name, and he just grinned back at me while sipping coffee.

"What are you doing here anyway, Saint?" Zed asked, changing the subject. "Don't you have your own gang to run? Or is your new second suddenly so competent you can retire already?"

Cass pushed his empty plate away and slouched in his chair, so fucking comfortable. "I'm here because I woke up alone in my bed with a raging hard-on and an undeniable *need* to see my woman."

I choked on my food. Just a little. A couple of coughs and a sip of coffee sorted me right out, but *that* hadn't been what I'd expected Cass to answer. Neither had Zed, apparently, because the look he leveled at Cass was pure violence.

"As for Roach," he continued, "not yet. And if retirement was a thing Reapers could do, believe me, I'd have done it already."

His irritated tone sparked curiosity in me, and I tilted my head to the side as I peered at him. "Why *are* you in the Reapers, Cass? Some things never quite added up to me, like why the fuck you were content to serve as second to that shitbag Zane D'Ath for so long when he was so clearly incompetent."

Cass held my gaze as he took a sip of the coffee Zed had just poured for him. "That seems a lot like insider trading, Hades, blurring the lines between entities and all that."

I rolled my eyes. "Screw off. I *own* the Reapers, and you damn well know it."

Lucas shuffled into the kitchen then, looking all sexy and sleep-rumpled in a pair of sweatpants and nothing else. Goddamn, he was a vision, even with the bandages still stuck to his chest and bruises coloring his entire rib cage.

"Jesus, Gumdrop." Zed cringed. "That hurts to even look at. Did you put up a fight at all?"

Lucas scowled, helping himself to a coffee mug and filling it from the fresh pot. "Unlike *some* people, I never went to a top-secret training camp for killers and other criminals."

My brows shot up at the angry tone of his voice, and I exchanged a quick warning glance with Zed before sliding out of my chair. "Hey, Zed was just teasing." I crossed to where he stood against the cabinets and looped my arms around his waist. The ease of that simple gesture made my pulse race, and confusion washed though me at how comfortable I'd grown around Lucas.

Lucas didn't notice my weirdness, though. He just heaved a sigh and rubbed the back of his neck in a gesture that was way too sexy to be real.

"I know," he muttered, his lips slanting in a slight pout. "I'm just in a bad mood. Hearing those bits of your history last night, all the shit you and Zed went through… It's made me fully appreciate why Zed called me a liability."

I shot Zed an accusing glare, and he just shrugged, unapologetic. That only pissed me off, and I glowered. "Yeah well, tough shit," I snapped. "We can't change the past, but we're also not throwing you away. We're *more* than capable of keeping you safe."

Lucas grimaced. "You shouldn't have to."

"I shouldn't *have* to do a whole list of shit right now, Lucas, but none of that is your fault." I rose up on my toes and combed my fingers through his soft hair. "I'm sorry you got dragged into it, though."

He let out a long breath, shaking his head. "I'm not." He leaned down to kiss me but paused when Zed interrupted.

"I cooked breakfast, Gumdrop. Eat some food, then let's start dealing with your abysmal lack of fight training." Zed arched a brow at me as I let Lucas go so he could sit and eat. "We may not be able to change the past, Dare, but we can better equip him for the future."

I folded my arms and frowned. "Look at him." I indicated with my chin to the mess of bruises and dressings decorating Lucas's body. "We're not teaching him how to fight in that state."

Zed, the shithead, just gave me a challenging look. "Why not? You've trained in worse shape, and it didn't kill you."

Both Lucas and Cass gave me long looks at that comment, and I seethed. He'd put me in an impossible situation there, and he damn well knew it.

"Fine," I hissed. "But when his doctor wants to blame someone for split stitches, I'll be sure to let him know that Lucas's *brother* is responsible."

Zed just grinned his victory, and Lucas, damn him, beamed twice as wide.

What was it with men enjoying hurting themselves?

CHAPTER 22

Despite the happy little dynamic on that first day of Lucas's training in Zed's home gym, we all eventually needed to get back to real life. Cass still had the Reapers to run and a newly minted second to train. Zed and I had the Timberwolves *and* Copper Wolf to deal with, not to mention the insurance paperwork for both 7th Circle and my apartment building.

Still, Zed made time in his day, every day, to train Lucas. Considering how suspicious Zed'd been of him, it confused the hell out of me…until I saw the shrewd way Zed watched him when his back was turned. Then I remembered what he'd told me about keeping his enemies close.

Giving up on the latest stack of insurance reports I was trying to fill out, I set them aside and pushed to my feet. I'd been sitting in the corner of the gym in an armchair I'd dragged in there a week ago to try to get work done while overseeing Lucas's training, but now I was getting tired of watching Zed pound on Lucas.

"All right. Give me a go," I told Zed, kicking my shoes off. I'd gone into the Copper Wolf office this morning, so I was in full corporate clothing, including pantyhose with a sexy seam up the back.

Zed arched his brow at my outfit and gave an amused shake of his head. "Dressed like that?"

I sent him a mocking smile. "What's wrong, Zayden? Scared I'll flatten you without wrinkling my blouse?"

Lucas let out a low whistle, then unstrapped his gloves as he backed away from the mats he and Zed had been gently sparring on. "Kick his ass, babe," he whispered, smacking a kiss on my cheek.

Zed rolled his eyes but sauntered over to the shelves at the side of the room to grab a set of wraps. "I don't need Cass coming at me ·for you splitting your knuckles," he said, tossing them over to me.

I grinned but made quick work of wrapping my hands up in the fluorescent yellow fabric. Cass had often come by to visit over the past week since our chat but seemed distracted and quick-tempered every time. He also hadn't tried to get in my pants again, and that was starting to really piss me off.

"You guys aren't going to wear gloves?" Lucas asked with a thread of concern.

Zed and I both grinned at that one, and I bounced on my slippery silk-covered toes. Hand-to-hand combat while wearing pantyhose on a vinyl mat was probably not at the top of the list of smart things to do. But it made it more fun. And if I'd given Zed time to strategize while I was getting changed, he might not be so easy to beat.

"You ready, Boss?" Zed teased, his wrapped hands raised and his feet shifting into a boxer's stance. He was shirtless—something he seemed to be doing a lot lately—and wearing just a pair of loose basketball shorts. He and Lucas had been working out for almost two hours, so a light sheen of sweat coated his hard muscles in a way that almost seemed fake.

I gave a short laugh as I shifted my weight, scanning him for weaknesses. Not that I needed to look to know; I had all of Zed's old injuries and weak points mapped out in my brain like they were my own. Trouble was, he knew all of mine too.

"Bring it on," I replied, excitement and adrenaline zapping through me. "I'll let you take the first swing." I shot him a teasing wink, and he gave a short laugh as he shook his head, relaxed.

That was my chance, and I snapped out a sharp left hook, catching him clean across the cheek.

Lucas gave a shout of surprise from the sidelines, possibly protesting the dirty trick. But Zed knew the score. He just laughed and rubbed his face as he circled away from me.

"Come on, that was an *old* trick," I mocked him with a snicker. "Can't believe you just fell for that."

Zed shook his head as if he could hardly believe he'd fallen for it either. His eyes were sharper now, though, like he'd just remembered exactly how dirty I liked to fight. Yep, I was in for a real fight now.

I didn't even try to hide the grin of enjoyment on my lips as we started trading blows for real. Neither of us pulled our punches—much—but we were both experienced enough that we could dodge or deflect the majority of strikes.

More of mine landed on Zed than the other way around, but I could see he was eyeing me for a takedown move.

Not today, Satan. No way was I losing this after bragging that I could wipe the floor with him in my pencil skirt and silk blouse.

I struck before he got the chance to, sweeping his legs from under him, and heard my skirt rip all the way up the side seam. Whoops. Still, there was no sense in wasting my advantage over damage already done, so I followed through by tangling Zed up in an arm bar that tested the limits of how far his elbow would bend.

The stubborn fuck didn't tap out, though.

"Uh, Hayden, you're gonna break his arm," Lucas informed me, watching with wide eyes and his hands on his slim, toned hips.

I flashed a smile. "Nah, I won't break it. Zed just needs to man up and accept he's been beaten."

Zed chuckled a breathless sound, turning in a way that only intensified the angle of my arm bar. "Do I, though?" he taunted. His free hand reached around and slid up the side of my bare thigh. That in and of itself was almost enough to make me loosen my grip, but I quickly realized he was just playing dirty to unnerve me.

Prick.

Then his fingers hooked under one of the tight straps of my garter belt and snapped that fucker against my thigh.

The shock of it made me yelp and jerk. My grip only loosened for a split second, but it was enough for Zed to wriggle free like some kind of overgrown python.

"God*dammit*," I groaned, rolling to my feet and stepping back into fight stance.

Zed smirked, smug as fuck. "Told you not to fight in that outfit."

We traded a few more blows, and then the gate buzzer rang and distracted Zed enough that my foot caught him straight in the face.

"Dare!" he roared from the floor, his hand to his nose.

"I'm sorry!" I shouted back, swallowing my laughter. "I thought you were going to dodge!"

"You two are insane," Lucas muttered, coming over to offer Zed a hand up. "You'd better get some ice on that." He winced as Zed took his hand away and revealed a bloody nose.

The glare Zed sent in my direction was pure malice, and I couldn't help laughing back at him.

"You're so fucking lucky you're you," he grumbled, making his way out of the gym to answer the buzzer and, probably, to ice his face.

Meanwhile, Lucas turned to face me with a certain level of respect in his eyes. "I've never seen you fight before," he commented, stepping closer and taking my hands in his to unwrap the yellow fabric.

"These days I generally use bullets to deal with my problems," I admitted with a small shrug, "but I'd be an idiot to let my skills get rusty simply because I have other people to do the dirty work for me. Complacency is what gets people in my profession assassinated."

Lucas gave me a look that bordered on adoration and dipped his head to kiss me lightly. "That's why you're Hades," he murmured. "Because you actually think these things through. I'm all kinds of impressed."

"Oh yeah?" I replied, rising up to kiss him back. "How impressed?"

His arms banded around my waist, pulling me against his hard body as his lips answered my question. I groaned into his kiss and hooked a leg up around his waist in a clear invitation to pin me against the nearest flat surface and fuck me stupid. But Zed's and Cass's voices echoed down the hallway, and I reluctantly peeled myself off Lucas. Not that I was trying to hide anything, but Cass was still being odd, and I needed to get to the bottom of that without pissing him off first.

"You responsible for this?" Cass asked Lucas, jerking a nod at Zed's face—or, rather, at the ice pack he held to the bridge of his nose.

Lucas grinned. "Nah, that was Hayden."

One of those sly, sexy smiles curved Cass's lips. "That makes more sense."

"Screw you, Saint," Zed snarled. "I'd like to see you spar with her. She'd have you begging for mercy in no time."

Cass's eyes met mine, flaring with a heat that went straight to my pussy. Fuck *me*, I didn't need to be a mind reader to see exactly what was going through his mind as his gaze traveled down my body, taking in my ripped skirt and ruffled hair. I doubted it would be Cass begging for mercy if we were alone right now.

"On the topic of fighting," he said slowly, his eyes still hot on my body while he ran a hand over his short beard, "I heard Crusher got checked into rehab today."

My brows shot up, and Zed spat a curse. Crusher was one of our headliners for a fight night at the end of the month. It was one of the biggest events on Anarchy's books to date, and the big top was completely sold out. If he was in rehab…

"What for?" Zed asked, his brow creased with frustration. "Is it something that just needs a quick detox or—"

"Nothing so innocent," Cass cut him off with an irritated grunt. "He's in for PCP addiction."

"What the *fuck*?" I shouted, losing my cool before I could grab ahold of it.

It was a total frame job, though. One of the fighters in the event my club had been promoting for *months* suddenly has an addiction to angel dust? Of all the fucking drugs on the market… Nope, I didn't believe it was a coincidence for even a second.

"Why is this the first we're hearing of it?" I demanded, spearing Cass with a hard look. "How did you find out before we did?"

He quirked his scarred brow. "I've got people in the right places, Red. And I came here with a proposition."

I folded my arms, still radiating suspicion regarding how he was more in the know than my own team. Crusher not being able to fight was a huge problem. "Go on then."

He folded his arms over his chest, mirroring my stance. "Let me take Crusher's place in the fight."

Of all the propositions I could have imagined Cass bringing forth, that definitely wasn't one of them—so much so that I just stared at him in shock for a moment.

Then Zed coughed a laugh and clapped Cass on the shoulder. "Good one, Saint. You had me going for a second there."

I didn't see any trace of joking in Cass's expression, though. My brows hitched, and I tilted my head to the side. "You're serious?"

A small, arrogant sort of smile touched his lips, and he gave a soft laugh. "I forget sometimes that you two are relatively new to Shadow Grove, not to mention how young you are." Zed made a sound of annoyance, but Cass ignored him. "Trust me, Red, my name on the billing will more than match the interest you had for Crusher. I'm doing you a favor."

Lucas cleared his throat, pulling our attention. "Uh, he's not joking, babe." His gaze shifted to Cass with admiration. "Didn't you retire on an injury about eight years ago, though?"

Cass gave a small shrug. "Officially. Then I went on to train punk-ass Reaper kids like Kody and Archer." He gave me a meaningful look, and the pieces started clicking together in my brain. Eight years ago would have been around the time he started getting groomed for his position as Zane's second within the Reapers.

Now, Archer was one of the hottest UFC fighters in the world and his best friend Kody was the founder of KJ-Fit, an MMA training gym—but I'd sidelined them both on babysitting duty with Seph.

Cass wouldn't be suggesting this if he wasn't more than up to the fight, though. So I gave him a small nod. "You sure you can beat Johnny Rock? It would be terrible PR if the leader of the Reapers got his ass kicked by a twenty-one-year-old shithead with anger management problems."

Cass scoffed. "That punk? Yeah, Red, I can handle him." His confidence legitimately made my cunt wet. It was surreal.

Neither Johnny Rock nor Crusher were pro; they fought way too dirty to ever be considered for official sponsorships. But goddamn, they had huge followings. And that meant money. Fight nights could clean so much dirty money through betting and alcohol sales that it was almost laughable.

"All right, then." I turned my attention to Zed. "Set it up."

Zed gave me a skeptical look but shrugged. "Yes, sir."

My phone started ringing in the corner, so I left the guys talking so I could answer it. When I saw the caller ID for my new legal counsel on the display, my stomach sank. Something told me she wasn't calling for a casual check-in.

"Shit," I breathed, biting my lip as I slid my thumb over the phone to answer. "Gen. What's happened?"

"Hades, sir," she responded in a clipped voice. "I just heard back from the insurance company regarding 7th Circle. They've denied your claim."

Mother*fuckers*. Seven million dollars invested in that venue... up in smoke.

CHAPTER 23

To my absolute frustration, Gen didn't have many more details than that. She ended the call with a promise to look further into it, and I very nearly threw my phone across the fucking room.

Furious at the insurance company, and at *Chase*, I ordered Zed and Cass to go to Anarchy and deal with the fight-night changes. Otherwise, I was likely to end up in a blazing fight with one or both of them and end up stabbing someone.

"What can I do to help?" Lucas asked when the guys were gone.

I gave him a long look, my fist clenching and unclenching at my side. It hit me suddenly how rare it was for me to express my emotions around other people, whether good or bad. Yet when I'd just been given that bad news, it hadn't even crossed my mind to internalize my fury and frustration. It'd just felt so natural to let it out, to let these men see me and everything I was feeling.

Fuck. It shook me.

"Nothing," I said after a moment to take a calming breath. "Nothing. Just…there's nothing I can do until I hear back from Gen with the official report. I'm going to get changed, then come work out down here for a while."

He nodded, rubbing the back of his neck. "Want company or..."

I started to shake my head, then paused and reconsidered. It was about damn time I let Lucas in. He so badly wanted to be the shoulder I leaned on when I was stumbling, and maybe I needed to let him.

"Sure," I replied with a brittle smile. "If you're not too wrecked already, maybe I can teach you a few things that Zed glossed over."

Lucas's face brightened. "I'd love that."

I ran upstairs to my borrowed bedroom, the guest room I'd claimed as my own by unpacking all my new clothes and personal items into it, and changed out of my ripped skirt. It only took me a couple of minutes, and I ran back downstairs with a renewed sense of determination. All week, watching Zed teach Lucas how to throw a punch or a kick or how to dodge and block, I'd been itching to give my opinions.

Besides, any excuse to have Lucas all hot and sweaty with his hands on my body sounded like a good idea in my mind.

Back in the gym, Lucas sat on the end of a weight bench, wrapping his hands up carefully like he'd been taught. He looked up when I walked in, his full lips curling in the sexiest of smiles.

"Goddamn, Hayden, how do you make work-out clothes look so fucking sexy?" He stood up, and the outline of his dick against his shorts echoed the primal look on his face.

My breath caught, and I licked my lips. "I changed my mind. I know exactly how you can clear my head."

Lucas gave a low, irresistibly sexy chuckle. "Uh-huh, I bet you do." He stooped down and swept me up with a strong hand under each side of my ass, crushing me against him as his mouth found mine.

"Lucas," I groaned against his lips as he walked us over to the wall. My back against the cool surface, his hot erection ground against me teasingly as he kissed me stupid. Literally. Sometimes I felt like I was losing IQ points when I let my pussy take control… but then again, who gave a fuck? Who the hell would say no in my shoes?

"Lucas, you shouldn't be lifting me like this," I chastised, peeling my lips away from his only to move them to his neck. I couldn't resist dragging my teeth over his tight trapezius, and he shivered against me with a curse.

"I'm fine, Hayden," he assured me in a husky voice, "I promise. Almost completely healed up already."

I ran my hand over his chest where the Darling brand sat red and raised but was healing incredibly quickly. His stab wound now only had a thin strip of surgical tape covering it too. The human body was fucking astounding.

"Still," I protested on a sigh, "I don't want to risk hurting you." Pushing him away, I dropped my feet to the floor, then nodded to the armchair that I'd abandoned earlier. "Go sit down, and I'll ride your dick."

His eyes widened, and a grin spread over his face. "Yes, ma'am."

He hurried to do as he was told, kicking his shorts aside and sitting back in the chair as if it was a damn throne, his huge dick sticking straight up in the air like an invitation. His hands were still wrapped, and his sneakers still on, but I sure as hell wasn't nit-picking. I stripped off my leggings and panties in one motion and placed a knee to either side of his hips on the chair.

"Shit yeah," Lucas groaned as I lined him up with my core and worked my way down onto him. "This is the kind of workout I can get on board with."

I would have come back with something dazzlingly witty, but my brain was in the process of short-circuiting and my breath was already coming in short, sharp gasps.

Lucas gripped my hips, pulling me down deeper onto him and making me cry out at the way he filled me up. When my butt rested on his thighs, I shifted my grip on his shoulders to clasp onto the back of his neck. I needed to kiss him like I needed air, and he obliged without hesitation.

When I started moving, I only rose and fell ever so slightly, keeping most of Lucas's cock buried deep within my tight cunt and relishing the ache there. I circled my hips with each rock of my body, grinding on him and moaning when my clit rubbed against him.

"Hayden," Lucas said with a pained chuckle, "are you trying to torture me? Because this is seriously testing me right now."

I grinned into the side of his neck, sucking and biting the skin there, leaving my mark like a jealous teenager. "A little anticipation is good for the soul, Lucas."

He laughed, then groaned again as his fingers flexed on my hips. He wanted me to speed up; I could feel the way he was just barely holding back from taking charge. It made me all kinds of hot, though, knowing he was waiting for me to set the pace.

Probably in an attempt to distract himself from my maddening grind, he tugged my tank top over my head and tossed it aside, then unzipped the front closure of my sports bra and sucked in a sharp breath.

"Fuck, your tits are incredible," he whispered, palming them with reverence.

I grinned wide, arching my back to give him better access. In fairness, I was driving myself just as crazy by not fucking him as hard as I wanted. Just as I shifted my position, readying myself to ride him for real, a familiar ringtone pealed through the room.

Lucas and I both froze.

"Shit, that's my phone," I said, unnecessarily. "It might be Gen. I've got to take it." I started to scramble off Lucas's dick, but he caught me with a hand around my waist, holding me in place. I started to protest, but he just leaned over the side of the chair and used one of his long arms to reach my phone on the floor.

He handed it over to me where I sat, and I glanced at the caller ID.

"Oh, it's just Zed." That was significantly less urgent. I debated declining the call until we were done but then hesitated, wondering if something else had blown up. Literally.

"Trust me?" Lucas asked, meeting my eyes with a heavy dose of sincerity and a small part mischief.

I gave the most honest answer I was capable of while his dick was still fully encased in my pussy. "Within reason, yes."

He flashed a smile. "Fair." He swiped my phone out of my hand and slid his thumb over the answer button.

My eyes bugged out, but he clapped his hand over my mouth, telling me with his eyes to be quiet as he took the call and switched it to speaker. "Hey, Zed."

There was a pause on the other end, and I writhed against Lucas's hold on my face—not to get free, but because I was suddenly a thousand times more turned on and I hadn't even known that was possible.

"Gumdrop," Zed replied, and I rocked my hips. "Where's Dare? Why are you answering her fucking phone?"

"Uh, she's just a bit busy," Lucas replied with a smirk. He carefully balanced the phone on the arm of the chair, then pressed a finger gently to his lips. The message was loud and clear. Stay. Silent.

I nodded, willing to play the game, and he removed his hand from my mouth. It was only so he could grip my hips, though, and encourage me to ride him like I'd been about to do when the phone rang.

Oh fuck. He wanted me to fuck him while he was on the phone with my best friend? That was…so hot. I mean, totally messed up. But also…fuck me, I was *soaking*.

"What do you mean, *busy*?" Zed snapped. "What the fuck is she busy doing?"

Lucas tipped his head back, his hips bucking up to meet me as I bounced lightly on his cock. Holy hell, there was no way I could come silently. And there was also no way I was lasting longer than a few minutes.

"She's working out," Lucas told Zed, somehow keeping his voice totally neutral as I flexed my legs harder, fucking him faster. "What's up? Did something happen?"

He dropped one of my hips and slipped that hand down my front to find my clit as I rode him. Because apparently Lucas woke up this morning and chose to be wicked.

Zed grunted a sound on the phone. "Figures. That sounds like she's hitting the punching bag. Just stay out of her warpath until she calms down."

Oh god. I almost laughed. Almost. But Lucas pinched my clit, and I needed to clap a hand over my own mouth to stop myself from screaming.

"Ah, I reckon she'll be okay," Lucas told Zed. "Just needed to work off a bit of steam." He shot me a wink, and I couldn't decide if I wanted to punch him or kiss him.

It sounded like Zed had sighed on the phone, and I was about to detonate. My orgasm was so fucking close. *So* close.

"Well, if she's not likely to gut you for getting close, can you hand the phone over? I need to discuss some legal shit."

I froze. Lucas grinned.

Frantically, I shook my head at him, and he just shrugged and picked up the phone once more.

"Sure thing," he said, and I just about died. There went my orgasm. Poof. "Just give me a sec." He hit the mute button on the call, made a point of showing me, then tossed the phone onto the training mat.

"Lucas," I murmured, suspicious as fuck. "What are you—"

In a move that surely only a gymnast could pull off, he scooped me up off his lap and stood up, then sank gracefully to his knees and lay me flat on my back on top of the padded training mat.

"I didn't believe you could be quiet for this part," he whispered back at me, his face pure mischief. Then he hitched one of my legs up so my knee touched my shoulder and slammed his monster cock back into me hard enough to make me see stars.

He was goddamn right. He fucked me hard and fast, nailing me into the mat and making me scream like a fucking banshee when I came.

His own release was only a split second behind, his hot cum filling me as I thrashed and moaned all over his dick like a strung-out junkie.

I barely got a second to catch my breath, though, before he picked the phone up and unmuted it with a challenge written all over his sexy fucking face.

"Zed," I snapped, my voice rough from screaming and my breathing still elevated. "What's up?"

"I've got some guys looking into our insurance provider for 7th Circle," he informed me. "Just had a weird feeling about them denying the claim."

Lucas eased out of me and collapsed onto the mat at my side where he pressed gentle kisses to my sweaty skin.

"Okay," I replied, still breathless. "And?"

"And the underwriter for Allied Host Insurance was bought out by a shell company six months ago." Zed's tone was grim, and I sat up sharply.

"Bought out by *who*?" I demanded.

He gave an irritated cluck of his tongue. "Not sure yet. I've asked Dallas to do some digging, though. Wanted to check if that was okay with you, first."

I frowned, ruffling my fingers through my hair. "Yes, of course. Let me know the second he finds something."

"You know I will. I'll let you get back to your workout, but maybe don't go so hard. You're panting like an old lady." He said it with a teasing laugh, and I groaned inwardly.

"Bye, Zed," I growled, then ended the call. Then I shot Lucas a sharp look. "You're in *so* much trouble, Wilder."

He grinned. "You gonna punish me, Hades?"

Fuck if that didn't make my pussy flood with warmth all over again. I really was messed up.

CHAPTER 24

Lucas had visited his mom almost every day since he'd gotten out of the hospital, and at first I'd gone with him in the hope that she'd tell me more about her history with my parents. But it'd quickly become clear that my being there stressed her out, so I started waiting for Lucas in the Sunshine Estate rose garden.

Today, though, I was more on edge that usual. My foot tapped an anxious rhythm on the gravel path as I spoke with Gen on my phone. She'd handled everything with law enforcement with regards to my apartment building, but she wasn't optimistic about the outcome of my claims on the cars. I'd used the same insurer for all my properties, and the recent sale of the underwriter was starting to stink like a dead rat.

The crunch of shoes on gravel made my eyes jerk up, and I spotted Lucas making his way over to me.

"Gen, I need to go," I told her with an irritated sigh. "If you need copies of invoices, get in touch with Hannah at Copper Wolf. I'll authorize her access to the files now so she can get you whatever you need."

"Understood, sir," Gen replied. "I'll be in touch."

I ended the call and tilted my head back to look up at Lucas. "All okay? That was quicker than usual."

A frown creased his brow, but he gave a small nod. "Yeah, fine. Let's go."

Things were quite clearly *not* fine, but I didn't argue with him. I just stood up and wrapped my arm around his waist as we walked back to the parking lot and the Audi I was still borrowing from Zed.

Once we were inside, I gave him a raised brow. "Want to talk about it?"

For a moment, I thought he was going to decline. But then he blew out a heavy breath and scrubbed his hands over his face. "I'm just really confused," he admitted with a groan of frustration. "I asked her today about why she left Shadow Grove."

I glanced at him in surprise as I drove us back toward Zed's house. I'd filled him—and Zed and Cass—in on what Sandra Wildeboer had told me. But when I'd tried to talk to Sandra again after that day, she'd played dumb with me.

"She got really angry at me for asking," Lucas confessed. "Told me that she'd left to keep *me* safe, and the more I dug around in the past, the more attention I'd bring."

That phrasing seemed curious, and I bit the edge of my lip as I ran it through my mind. "That sounds like something to do with *you*, specifically, and not the Timberwolves," I commented, still thinking. "So maybe we were being too closed-minded. Maybe her leaving here when my mom died was just coincidental timing..."

Lucas drummed his fingertips on the door handle, clearly irritated. "That's what I thought too. It would explain why she moved us around so much. I always thought it was because she couldn't keep a job and needed the health insurance, but now I'm wondering if she was running from someone."

"Or hiding *you* from someone," I offered in a soft voice. "What do you know about your dad, Lucas?"

He gave a bitter laugh. "I asked her exactly the same thing. Then she threw a coffee mug at the wall and started yelling at me to get out."

My brows rose. "What do you think that meant?"

He shrugged. "Either something secret…or she was just really offended that I basically suggested she'd lied about my father all these years and he *wasn't* the upstanding gentleman she'd told me he was." He gave me a wry smile. "My mom does have a flair for the dramatic. I don't put a whole lot of suspicion behind that reaction."

I didn't respond to that. My natural instinct was to be suspicious of fucking *everything*, and the evidence was stacking pretty heavily in favor of Lucas's daddy being involved in something shady.

"I take it that wasn't good news from Gen when I interrupted you?" Lucas asked, changing the subject. He'd met my new lawyer earlier in the week when I stopped for a meeting with her at Copper Wolf on our way home from Sunshine Estate, and he seemed to genuinely like her.

I shook my head. "Nope." Then another thought popped into my brain. "Hey, yesterday when Cass suggested fighting in the event with Johnny Rock, you seemed to know more about that than Zed or me."

Lucas grinned. "Um, yeah, because I clearly do know more." He gave a teasing laugh when I shot him a glare. "What? Let me have my moment of glory. It's not often I'm the one with the information."

I rolled my eyes, but he had a point. "Fair call," I muttered with a sigh. "So, tell me what you know. Please?" I threw that polite addition on with an exaggerated flutter of my lashes, and Lucas snickered.

"Cute. But I'm pretty sure Cass should be telling you about himself, you know, *himself*? I will say that I'm not against a bit of casual Google stalking when I want to know more about someone, and Cass seemed like he was important to you when we first met. So I did some searching." He gave a small shrug. "It wasn't a thorough background check or anything, just normal Googling."

I was a little impressed. "And you discovered he used to be a fighter?"

Lucas nodded. "A really good fighter. Like, I've seen some of Archer D'Ath's fights on TV, and Cass would probably flatten him."

"Huh." I was almost speechless. I knew Cass *could* fight, of course. But I didn't realize he was actually *good*.

Lucas grinned. "You should ask him about it sometime. I bet he'd like to tell you all about his glory days. Isn't that what old dudes like to do?"

I groaned but couldn't fight my answering smile at his teasing. "Say that to his face, Gumdrop. I fucking dare you."

"Aw, come on, not you too! Fucking worst nickname on the planet." He pouted and slouched back in his seat as I laughed silently.

"Actually, I think he's over at Anarchy training with Alexi today," I commented, tapping the steering wheel with my index finger. "Want to head over there?"

Lucas shifted in his seat, turning slightly so he was looking at me while I drove. It was both unnerving and flattering all at the same time. "Sure thing. Maybe you can work out why Cass has been all cagey and secretive this week."

I flicked him a quick look. "You noticed that too, huh?"

He inclined his head. "Hard not to. I mean, I'm more than fine with having you all to myself, but I'm a bit more realistic than that. I know you're not going to be happy with just me...not when you're already so invested in them, too."

I frowned, guilt rippling through me at his words. Although he'd said he was fine with me and Cass, I hadn't exactly *asked* before jumping into bed with another guy. Did that make me a cheater? Fuck. I despised cheaters.

"Lucas..." I started to say, then let my voice trail off because I simply had no idea what the fuck to say. It wasn't that he was not enough. It was just...Cass had a very particular hold on my heart that I was tired of ignoring.

"Hey." He reached over and linked our fingers together like he always seemed to do when I needed the emotional support. "I didn't mean anything by that comment. Please stop frowning like that. It was just a statement of fact, not a guilt trip, okay? I'm good with this, with the way we are. But I hate that Cass is being a secretive shit, and I can see it's getting under your skin."

I gave a soft laugh at that because he was dead right.

"So," Lucas continued, lifting my hand to his mouth and kissing my knuckles. "Let's go to Anarchy, and best case, you get some answers out of the big grump. Worst case..." He let his voice trail off with a sly smile.

I flicked him another suspicious glance. "Worst case *what?*"

His eyes glittered with mischief. "Worst case, you get all hot and bothered watching Cass beat the crap out of Alexi in the training room, and I get to reap the rewards afterward. It's a win-win if you ask me."

Well...when he put it like *that*, how could I argue?

I'd barely wiped the silly smile from my face by the time we pulled into Anarchy, and Lucas managed to sneak in a quick make-out session before we exited the car.

Walking into the training room, I was surprised to find Cass fighting Zed, not Alexi. I was also uncomfortably surprised at how fast my heart started pounding at the sight of those two, shirtless, inked-up, and sweaty, trading punches like...well...like professionals.

Lucas gave a low chuckle, swiping a hand over his mouth as if to hide his smug grin. "This ought to be interesting," he murmured, shooting me a knowing look.

I glared back at him, refusing to pick up what he was putting down. "Don't stir shit, Lucas. We're not fucking up a good thing."

He didn't reply, just smirked and turned his attention to the fighters locked in a sparring match that seemed a whole lot more serious than it needed to be.

Folding my arms, I settled in to watch with him, analyzing

Cass's form more than anything because it was the first time I'd really seen him fight. Zed I could probably fight in my sleep, but Cass was an unknown entity. And holy shit, Lucas hadn't been exaggerating; he was a *weapon*, even if he was a little rusty.

At some point Cass caught sight of me watching, but instead of being distracted, he just seemed to come at Zed harder and faster. Trying to prove something?

Eventually the fight ended when Cass slammed a hard uppercut into Zed's diaphragm, knocking the air from him in a grunt, then nailed a right hook into the side of his face.

They wore gloves, yes. But even gloves couldn't rein in the power behind those strikes, and Zed hit the mat like a puppet with his strings cut.

Lucas sucked in a sharp breath, cringing. "I'll go find some ice," he suggested, shooting me a worried glance.

I just smiled back at him and nodded in the direction of the locker room. "There's a freezer just inside the men's changing room. Should be ice packs in there."

Lucas hurried off to do that, and I strolled over to where Cass was helping Zed up off the mat. My second still had a distinctly dazed look about him, the one that confirmed Cass had definitely turned his lights out for just a few seconds.

"Nice moves, Grumpy Cat," I commented, giving him a slow clap. "Who'd have thought a retiree such as yourself had skills?" Yeah, I was just taking my stick and smacking it straight into the hornet's nest. Danger and I liked to flirt on a regular basis.

Cass tossed his gloves aside and scooped me up with one strong arm around my waist, lifting me clean off my feet. "I'll fucking show you skills, brat."

"Ugh, spare me the show," Zed groaned, rubbing the already bruised bridge of his nose and glaring at the two of us. "You're adequate, Saint. But you'd better put in the fucking hours if you want to beat Johnny Rock in three weeks."

Cass flipped Zed off, then kissed me with a level of primal possession that made my insides turn to jelly and my nipples hard against his hot chest. Fucking hell, there went another few brain cells.

Reluctantly, I pushed away from Cass and located the floor with my toes as Lucas came jogging over with an ice pack in hand.

"Thanks, Gumdrop," Zed grunted, taking the ice from Lucas. He headed over to the well-worn couches at the side of the room, sat down with a groan, and clapped the ice to his face as he leaned back in the seat.

Cass sat on the edge of another chair and meticulously unraveled his hand wraps, rolling them back up on themselves rather than letting them spool all over the floor like wet spaghetti—like I did. "How was your mom?" Cass asked Lucas, shooting him a curious glance. He, like the rest of us, was suspicious about Sandra's past.

Lucas gave an uncomfortable shrug and sat on the couch beside Zed. "Same as usual," he replied, keeping it vague. As well as the three of them seemed to get along, not one of them trusted the others as far as he could throw them. To be expected, I guessed. It could have been worse.

"Jesus, Zed," I muttered, crossing over to him and snatching the ice pack from his hand. "You didn't even have it on the bruise." I reapplied it directly to the rapidly swelling mark on his cheekbone where Cass's knockout blow had landed, and Zed hissed in pain.

"What the fuck, Dare?" he growled, grabbing my wrist like he wanted to push me away.

I just snickered. "You're such a crybaby." I pressed the ice harder against his face, and he glared death at me. Instead of taking the ice from my hand, though, he yanked me into his lap and let me hold it there while he ground his teeth together loudly enough to hear.

"Lazy shit," I muttered, but kept the ice on his face anyway as I rebalanced myself on his lap with my foot up on the sofa near Lucas.

My sexy stripper just grinned at me like an asshole and fanned himself with his hand. "Is it just me, or is it hot in here?"

Death glare didn't even begin to describe the look I sent in his direction. Lucky for him, he was saved by the interruption of my phone ringing.

Keeping the ice on Zed's face with one hand—none too gently, mind—I fished my phone from my jacket pocket and answered the call.

"Rio," I said, greeting the contractor assigned to Lucas's house renovations.

"Boss," he replied, sounding nervous, "I think you better come over here to the Wildeboer house."

I frowned, confused, and switched the call to speaker so I wouldn't need to relay the information like a parrot. "Is everything okay there?"

"Yes, Boss," Rio replied, his accent stronger than usual. "But, uh, we found something you're gonna wanna see, you know, in person and shit."

I locked eyes with Lucas, questioning, but he seemed just as lost as I was about what Rio might have found.

"Fill me in a bit, Rio," I demanded, my voice sharp. "What did you find?"

He cursed softly in Spanish, then returned to the call. "Guns, Boss. Fucking shitloads of guns. More than I've ever seen in one place."

My eyes widened, and Lucas jerked like he'd been electrocuted.

With my spine stiff and my shoulders tense, I stood up from Zed's lap and drew a deep breath. "I'll be right there, Rio," I snapped. "Don't touch a single fucking thing, you hear me? Seal the house up until we arrive."

"Yes, Boss," Rio replied. "Absolutely."

He hung up, and Zed exploded from his chair. "I *knew* it!" he shouted, pointing an accusing finger at Lucas. "I *fucking knew it.*"

CHAPTER 25

Calming breaths were a distant memory as I clenched the steering wheel with white-knuckled hands. "Lucas, if you know *anything*—"

"I don't!" he cut me off, shaking his head.

Zed and Cass were tight on my ass in Zed's Ferrari, and the fact that the Audi was only a two-seater was the only thing that'd saved Lucas from the Spanish Inquisition on the way over to his house.

"Hayden, I swear to you I have *no* idea what guns are at my place, and I sure as fuck didn't put them there. I wouldn't lie to you about this. You *know* that." His tone was firm and even with just an edge of a plea.

I raised one hand from the steering wheel, rubbing my temple where a huge-ass stress headache was building. "I want to believe you..." That statement sounded weak even to my own ears.

Lucas jerked a sharp nod, shifting to turn his attention out the window. "But Zed doesn't."

Fucking hell. Zed was *painful* on the best of days when he was right about shit. This, though? This was going to be a whole new level of infuriating. Not to mention he was probably going to kill Lucas if this revealed him as some sort of double agent for Chase.

I needed to admit to myself how much my feelings for Lucas

had developed when I'd already decided I couldn't kill him. Even if there *was* something—even if he'd deliberately targeted me in the first instance—I didn't believe it was all fake. His feelings for me were genuine now. So did it matter how that had come about?

Yes. Short answer, yes. It *absolutely* mattered. And yet I still didn't want to kill him.

Shit. I'd totally lost my edge. I'd never known I had the emotional capacity left to care about anyone other than Seph and Demi. I'd thought I'd salted and burned that part of my soul five years ago.

Apparently, I was wrong.

"Just…" We pulled up in front of Lucas's house where several trade vans were parked in the driveway and a bunch of my Timberwolves in orange vests and hard hats stood around on the front lawn. "Just don't fucking speak, okay? Don't do anything to get in Zed's way until we sort this out."

Lucas flicked a sharp look at me, confused, but nodded his understanding anyway as we got out of the car.

There was no real opportunity for him to steer clear of Zed, though. The Ferrari parked directly behind us, and Zed clamped a strong hand on the back of Lucas's neck before we even approached the building team.

"This bastard should be chained up in the basement of Anarchy right now, Boss," he spat out, shoving Lucas ahead of him with furious motions.

Cass rumbled a grunt that sounded awfully like agreement. "He should, if he's guilty, be choking on his own blood right now." Then he paused and narrowed his eyes at Lucas. "*If* he's guilty."

"Which we don't know he is," I snapped, "and the fact that he is cooperating should go a long way here." I gave Lucas another warning glare, begging him not to antagonize Zed *or* Cass right now. I'd underestimated how seriously Cass was taking my safety since we'd fucked, but he was almost as bad as Zed.

"Hades, sir," Rio, the foreman, greeted me as I strode up the path to his group of workers. I cast my gaze over all of them, checking that I recognized each and every face, no matter how vaguely. I might not know names for all of them, but I was confident there were no new sneaky plants within the crew.

"Show me," I ordered Rio, indicating he lead the way into the house. The guys could follow or wait outside, I didn't much care so long as they were keeping Lucas alive for the time being.

Rio strode through the front door and headed for the back of the house. "We found it while we were installing the elevator, sir," he told me, glancing over his shoulder. "We needed to knock out this side of the house to allow for the box shaft and, well, shit, hang on." He held aside a heavy piece of plastic sheeting and indicated for me to enter their current work zone. "One of my boys somehow managed to let go of his sledgehammer, fucking moron, and it smashed through the floorboards over here."

I frowned at the section of flooring he pointed to where there was now a hole considerably larger than a sledgehammer would have made.

"Anyway, the hammer dropped straight through. Made us fucking suspicious, you know? The plans don't show a basement level." He raised his brows at me, totally ignoring the three muscular shadows at my back. Smart man. I knew there was a reason I'd taken him into the Wolves.

"So you investigated." It was rhetorical because of course that's what he'd done. I would have, too.

He grimaced and ran a hand over his thick moustache. "Yes, sir. We cut the hole bigger and then… Well, then that's when I called you, Boss."

"Thank you, Rio." I held out my hand, and he passed me the flashlight from his tool belt. "I'll take it from here."

"I've got a bigger floodlight in my truck, sir. I'll get the boys to bring it through if you want." He jerked his head at the hole in the floor. "Pretty dark down there otherwise."

I nodded my acceptance, and he hurried away to do what he'd offered. Alone with the guys, I arched a brow directly at Lucas and tilted my head to the hole in the floor.

"I *don't know*," he answered my silent question. "I'm just as shocked as the rest of you."

Zed scoffed a laugh, his fingers digging into the back of Lucas's neck. "Or you're a fucking excellent actor, Gumdrop."

With a sigh, I kicked my high-heeled shoes off as I approached the hole and shone the flashlight inside. It was a deep enough drop that I would need my hands, so I held the flashlight out for Cass to hold. With him training the light on the darkness below, I gripped the rough edges of the broken floor and lowered myself down. The drop when I let go wasn't significant, and I landed in a crouch.

"Throw the light down," I called out to Cass. I held my hands out and caught the heavy flashlight when he dropped it, then spun it around to inspect my surroundings. "Holy shit."

Rio hadn't been exaggerating.

"What is it?" Zed yelled down at me as I made my way deeper into the room and ran my pissy little flashlight over walls stacked with an entire arsenal of weapons.

"Come down and see for yourself," I yelled back. "I'm not your fucking secretary." That didn't even make a whole lot of sense, but my attention was entirely focused on working out why in the hell there were so many fucking *guns* under Lucas's house.

There was some muttering of men's voices above me, and a moment later Zed dropped through the hole to join me.

I flashed my light over him, giving a small chuckle. "Knew you couldn't resist. You let go of Lucas, finally?"

Zed scowled at me in the eerie shadows. "Cass is holding him." He took the flashlight from my hand and ran the beam across the walls just like I'd done, then let out a low whistle.

"Dare...if this doesn't convince you that kid is a plant, I don't know what will." His voice was pitched low, his tone disappointed like he actually hadn't wanted Lucas to be anything more than he seemed. I knew the feeling.

But this wasn't evidence of guilt. "Zed, don't be so narrow-minded," I chastised, stepping closer to him in the darkness so we could speak without being overheard. Why it mattered I had no idea. But old habits died hard. "Lucas and his mother have been in Shadow Grove for less than two months now, and the past eight days he's been staying with us and workmen have been here. You want to tell me he built this…massive weapons cache under his uncle's house within that time and imported all these guns undetected?" I clucked my tongue. "There's no way."

Zed huffed an annoyed sound. "Sure, *if* that's how long he's been here."

"Or doesn't it make more sense that this was his uncle's doing? Demi said he was squeaky clean, but this suggests otherwise." I nudged him in the ribs, making him look at me rather than scowl at the guns. "Zed. Come on. You've spent a whole lot of time with Lucas this week. Do you *honestly* think he knew about this?"

Zed's eyes blazed with stubborn defiance, the flashlight casting all kinds of harsh shadows and emphasizing his tight jaw. "I just…" He broke off with a sharp exhale. "I'm worried you're going to regret this later, Boss. I'm scared you'll trust the wrong man with your heart and be burned for it." He all but whispered the confession, and it struck me right in the chest.

Something had shifted between us, something important, and I was starting to think maybe I was okay with it.

I reached up, placing my palm against the rough of his cheek as anxious energy buzzed through me like electricity.

"So who *is* the right person to trust with my heart, Zayden?" I tipped my chin, trying to meet his eyes in the darkness. "You?" I said that word so softly, but it shocked through me with the force of a freight train. Had I seriously just said that out loud?

Luckily—or unluckily, depending on your perspective—a loud

scraping and thumping upstairs sounded a split second after I'd asked that heavy fucking question, and I stiffened. It was entirely possible Zed hadn't even heard me, so I was freaking out over nothing.

"Floodlight incoming!" Cass shouted down to us, and I stepped smoothly away from Zed, heading back to the hole where a large floodlight on a tripod stand was being lowered on ropes.

"Got it!" I yelled back when the light touched down. Zed and I quickly untied the ropes from it and repositioned it away from the entry hole. Cass tossed an extension cord down, and Zed plugged the light in.

The brightness that flooded the room made me flinch and cover my eyes, but Zed's surprised curse made me blink rapidly to adjust.

The room was enormous, probably covering the entire footprint of the house with structural pillars at regular intervals to support the building above. After several moments of staring around, silent, I turned to Zed with an eyebrow arched.

"Yeah," he admitted softly. "You might have a point."

I rolled my eyes. Might. *Might* have a point. This basement had quite clearly been built before the house itself, meaning it predated Lucas by at least a decade, if not more.

"Oh shit," Cass's voice echoed down to us. He was crouched down, peering through the hole. Lucas was beside him, looking damn shell-shocked.

"Come down," I called up to them. "Zed's going to play nice for the time being."

My second huffed in annoyance, shooting me a glare. "That's not to say he didn't *know* about this. He inherited the house, who's to say he didn't inherit some Timberwolf vendetta from his uncle?"

I didn't have a response to that because he posed a relevant question. Telling him I wanted to trust my gut probably wasn't going to fly either. So I just ignored him and watched Cass and Lucas drop down through the hole.

Lucas's face was the definition of shocked as he stared around at the massive armory in awe. "Fucking hell," he murmured. "I had no idea."

"Didn't you, though?" Zed muttered with a dark glare.

"Fuck off," I hissed at my second. "Go look around a bit. Find me some answers about why Lucas's uncle needed all this firepower."

Zed shot a pointed look at Lucas, still radiating suspicion, then stalked off to do as I asked. The air smelled clean, and not a speck of dust covered the weapons. A slight breeze clued me in to the fact that there was an air-purifying system keeping the weapons in pristine, dust-free condition.

"Gumdrop, I'm gonna say this now," Cass rumbled, giving Lucas a skeptical look. "If you knew anything about this, you'd better start fucking talking."

Lucas threw his hands up in frustration. "Jesus Christ, Cass. I didn't. I don't. This is... I'm just as confused as you guys. More. My uncle wasn't in any gangs or...anything. He was a fucking accountant."

Cass twitched a microsmile. "I thought accountant was code for sex worker, not hit man."

As amusing as that observation was, his comment struck something in me, and my brows hitched.

"Shit," I breathed. "I reckon you nailed it, Cass."

He wasn't following my train of thought, just squinting at me across the bright stream of light. "Nailed what, Red?"

I waved my hand around, indicating where we were. "This. Lucas's uncle with the squeaky-clean background check and the secret arsenal underneath his house. He wasn't an accountant... He was a fucking mercenary."

Cass stiffened, his eyes wide. Lucas looked more confused than ever, and Zed? Zed yelled from farther into the room, pulling my attention toward him.

"I think you might be right, Boss!" he called out. "Look what I found." He tossed a sheathed dagger to me, and I caught it easily.

Turning it over in my hands, I let out a groan when I recognized the ancient crest inscribed into the handle.

"Lucas," I said, licking my lips and holding the knife up for him and Cass to see. "Did you know your uncle was in the *Guild*?"

CHAPTER 26

It didn't take us long to work out exactly how the secret basement was accessed without the need for a huge-ass hole in the floor. There was a staircase further down the room that ended in a false back to the closet in the downstairs guest room. Based on the level of dust in that room, it was an easy guess as to why Lucas had never found the hidden door. I'd have been surprised if he had ever even stepped foot in the guest room.

Even then, it would have only taken five minutes to find the access had we not been locked in an argument about whether Lucas's uncle being in the Guild also meant Lucas was and whether it was possible he somehow didn't even know he was doing their work.

Eventually, I'd reached the point where I either had to shoot Zed in the knee for being such a contrary dick or walk away from the conversation. Based on the fact that Zed was following me out of the house with two perfectly hole-free legs under him, it wouldn't be hard to guess which option I'd taken.

"Seal up the floor," I told Rio as I approached his team all sitting around smoking on the lawn. "No one goes in there without my permission, understood?"

The foreman jerked a sharp nod, and I ran my eyes over his men to reinforce my order.

"Seal the floor and forget what you fucking saw, Rio. Trust me on this one. I'm not the scariest bastard out there."

His eyes widened, but he was firm in his assurances that they'd do exactly as instructed. Satisfied with his response, I made my way back to the cars.

I didn't wait to see if the guys had all followed or not, and Lucas slid into the passenger seat a split second after I turned the ignition.

Neither of us spoke, and Zed's Ferrari roared past me when we hit the highway on the outskirts of Shadow Grove, heading toward his estate.

My lips twitched in a smirk as he accelerated faster ahead of us, and I gave a short laugh. "Fucking show-off," I muttered.

"Okay, so, I really don't want to tempt fate here or anything," Lucas said, breaking the tense silence as I drove. "But...am I... Are we...?"

I flicked a glance at him and saw his brow was furrowed with genuine anxiety. His hands were balled into fists in his lap, and his whole posture was tighter than a piano string.

As instinctual as it was to immediately reassure him, to put his fears to rest, I couldn't do that. Not truthfully. But I owed him more than my silence and suspicions.

"I really want to tell you that we're fine, Lucas," I finally said, my grip on the steering wheel easing. "There's no question in my mind that your uncle was in the Guild, that much we're unanimous on." The copious number of fake IDs and passports we'd found with his uncle's picture added weight to that theory. "But Zed's not wrong in being paranoid about whether you knew."

Lucas just blew out a long breath and rubbed his hand over the back of his head. "Yeah, I can understand that," he said in a resigned voice. "The evidence does look pretty damning, and you guys are used to people being more than they seem."

I quirked a brow. "That's a very mature response to a shitty situation, Lucas."

His lips curved up as he tipped his head to the side. "I figure I have a moral responsibility to act more like an adult than Zed, if only to show him up when he's being a jealous fucknut."

I couldn't fight my laugh at that statement.

When we pulled up outside Zed's house, I leaned over and pressed a quick kiss against Lucas's lips. "You're a little bit amazing," I murmured, my hand cupping his face. "I think that's why I'm still so suspicious. I haven't done anything in my life to deserve someone like you."

His brow creased, and he slid a hand around the back of my neck to hold me close a moment longer. "That breaks my heart that you believe that, Hayden. I think out of anyone in this fucked-up town, you're the most deserving of everything and more."

At a loss for words, I kissed him again, then climbed out of the Audi to head inside.

Zed was in the kitchen, angrily slamming cabinet doors and throwing food onto the counter like it had personally offended him, and Cass was nowhere to be seen.

I raised a brow, looking around and not finding anywhere that sexy, tattooed biker-man might be lurking.

I propped my hip against the counter and folded my arms. "Where's Grumpy Cat?"

Zed paused to glare at me with a deadly sharp chef's knife in his hand and a handful of vegetables on the board in front of him. "Why? You worried I shot him and stashed the body while you were busy making out with Gumdrop in the car?"

I rolled my eyes. "Yeah, 'cause you totally know how to clean up a scene that quick."

Zed huffed a short laugh, slicing into the vegetables. "He got a call from someone and took off to deal with it. Reaper shit, I guess."

"Is it just me," Lucas asked thoughtfully, "or does Cass seem like he'd rather *not* be the Reapers' leader?"

The glare Zed sent toward Lucas was pure acid, and I swallowed a frustrated sigh.

"Lucas, do you mind giving Zed and me a moment to talk? We have some things to discuss." I kept my tone friendly, but the look I gave Zed told him just how pissed off I was getting with his attitude.

Lucas wasn't stupid, either. He saw it and wisely must have realized Zed had it coming, so he left the kitchen without another word.

Zed set his knife down on the chopping board and scowled at me in disbelief. "Dare—"

"No, Zed," I snapped, cutting him off with a glacial stare. "Just *shut up*. I've had it up to fucking here with your bad temper lately." I indicated a point somewhere around my eye level, showing him just how close I was to truly losing my shit at him entirely. "I get it, okay? I fucking *get it*. You want to protect me. It's your job to second-guess anyone getting close to me because it's quite literally in the job description, both as my second and as my best friend. And trust me, Zed, I appreciate the hell out of you for it. You've always had my back. Always. But this is getting out of hand, and it needs to stop."

At the hard edge in my voice, his eyes hardened with anger and his jaw tensed, but I wasn't done.

"Everything we just discovered at Lucas's house implicates his *dead uncle* of being in the Guild. That's it. Anything more is just… speculation." I gave a frustrated headshake, my pulse racing with the need to fix this uncomfortable tension between my best friend and me. "Nothing says Lucas is or was ever involved. Short of making him take a polygraph, what more can be done, Zed? At some point, you're gonna have to judge him based on his *actions*, not your *suspicions*. And nothing Lucas himself has done leads me to think he's anything but honest." I paused, giving a small frown. "Except, you know, about his age. But that was a white lie at best and not intended to harm anyone."

Zed drew a long breath through his nose, glaring daggers at me as he leaned on the countertop. "You done?"

"Not even close," I bit back, narrowing my eyes. "But for now, sure."

That touch of sass only seemed to infuriate him more, but I gave zero shits about his temper. He was way out of line with his attitude toward both Lucas and me, and enough was enough.

"I don't like this, Hades," Zed growled, his forearms flexed hard against the counter on either side of the cutting board with his half-chopped veggies. "I hate it. For five years you've been so closed off and cold. Totally unshakable. Untouchable. Nothing seemed to crack your walls even the slightest bit. Fuck, you were even closed off and distant with *Seph*. Trust me, she noticed. Then..." He shook his head, the frustration and anger clear across every plane of his face. He wasn't making any attempt to hide what he was feeling from me, and that in itself should have scared me more than his words.

But it didn't. It just made me more determined to crack him open and work out what the hell was going on.

"Then, what?" I pushed. "Then I started fucking Lucas and you got territorial?"

Zed didn't flare up at that swipe, he just gave a bitter laugh and pushed away from the counter. "Territorial? That's what you're gonna call it?"

I shrugged, at a loss for any other way to explain his mood shift.

"Let me put you in my shoes for a hot second, Dare. In the space of *one night* you decided to break your track record of anonymous, emotionless one-night stands and make a pass at Cassiel fucking Saint, a man you've been quietly crushing on for years and never acted on. If that wasn't out of character enough, you then picked up some random hot guy at the bar, made out with him in full view of the staff, then proceeded to *fuck him on camera* at Scruffy Murphy's to make Cass jealous." He paused to draw a breath and scrub a hand over his stubbled face, as if he could still hardly believe what had happened.

I ground my teeth together in outrage. "So it's okay for you to fuck countless random girls *inside our clubs* but not okay for me to do it in a Reaper bar? Ever looked up the definition of hypocrisy, Zed? It'd have a big old picture of your face right now."

He gave a bitter laugh. "Except they weren't random hookups for you, Dare. In one night, you went from being an iron fucking fortress of solitude to suddenly throwing your heart on the line with two different dudes."

I squinted at him, disbelief practically oozing from my pores as I interpreted slut shaming in his words. "So what? What business is it of yours what I do with my heart *or* my pussy? If I wanted to fuck both of them at the same time tonight, then confess my undying love, I damn well could. It'd be nobody's business but *mine*. Sit the fuck down, Zayden. You're overstepping."

My idea of hashing things out was backfiring pretty hard. We weren't sorting through jack shit. If anything, I was making it worse because Zed looked like he wanted to punch a hole straight through his pantry door.

"You know what?" I said, my voice dripping bitterness. "This is fucked. I'm going to find somewhere else to stay for a while."

"No." Zed barked that one word with a hard-edged authority that rivaled me in Hades mode.

I paused on my way out of the kitchen, spinning around to give him an incredulous stare. "Excuse me?"

Fists clenched at his sides, he took two steps closer. "I said *no*. No, I will *not* sit down. Not about this. I'm not goddamn overstepping, Dare, because I fucking *love* you. Okay? I love you."

His words drained the fight out of me like he'd pulled a

plug, and my shoulders sagged in exhausted defeat. He wasn't being combative for fun; he was just trying to protect me. Like he *always* had.

"I know," I replied softly. "I love you too. You're my best—"

He cut me off with a sharp laugh of disbelief. "No, you dense bitch. I *love* you." And then, because clearly I'd missed the emphasis he was placing on that statement, he grabbed me by the front of my shirt and crashed his lips down on mine.

The shock of it froze my brain, and for a moment I acted on pure instinct and kissed him back. His mouth devoured mine with an intensity that made my entire being ache and beg for more. Then better judgment took hold, and I shoved him away hard enough that he staggered a bit.

"No," I gasped out, wiping a shaking hand over my mouth. "No, you do *not* get to play that game, Zayden De Rosa. You made your choice years ago. You don't get to suddenly change your mind the second I start falling for someone else."

I started to leave the kitchen, and he spat out a curse, then followed and grabbed my arm to stop me. "Dare, that's not—"

"Not *what*?" I screamed, jerking my arm free and whirling around to give him the full force of my years-old hurt. "You broke my heart, Zed. Is that what you want to hear from me? You're the *only* person to ever break my heart. But I sucked it up and dealt with it. You offered me friendship and I took it. You're my best friend and *nothing* more."

"Jesus, Dare, that was six years ago, and you were engaged to my best friend! What the fuck was I supposed to do? I didn't know. I had no idea what he was—" He broke off, scrubbing a hand over his face. "I thought I was doing the right thing."

The backs of my eyes burned, but no tears welled up. I seriously wondered if I'd lost the ability to cry like a normal human. "Well, look how that turned out," I whispered, my voice choked with bitterness and accusation that was totally misplaced. It wasn't

Zed's fault, and I knew it. But seventeen-year-old me had *so* badly wanted him to see through the lies and come to my rescue.

"Dare…" Zed stepped forward, reaching out for me again. His eyes were pleading and his brow creased with pain, but I was too far gone with my anger and hurt to acknowledge it.

"Forget it," I spat out, my mouth twisting with regret. "It's in the past, and it needs to fucking stay there. Don't try this shit again, Zed. Don't push this. You're too important to me to lose over misplaced jealousy."

I started to walk away, but he called after me. "I can't do that, Dare. You feel the same way for me, and you damn well know it."

I had nothing to say back to that because he was right, so I just continued out of the kitchen and raced upstairs to my temporary bedroom. By the time I locked the door, my knees were weak, and I dissolved into a crouch on the floor, my arms around my knees.

Zed had the best of intentions. He wanted to push that delicate relationship balance between us in a way I'd been quietly hoping he would do for ages. Yet all it'd done was resurface my badly patched trauma and thrown me straight back into the past to when I was seventeen, naive as fuck, gaslighted at every waking moment, and abused behind closed doors by my sociopathic fiancé.

The night I'd gone to Zed had been one of my worst mistakes. Not only had he rejected my feelings, making me think I'd imagined our connection, but Chase had found out. And he'd made me *pay.*

Deep shudders ran through me as I struggled to box all the memories and emotions back up inside my mind once more. Time lost all meaning as I huddled there in a ball on the carpet, fighting with my inner demons and exerting the mental strength I'd worked so damn hard to build.

Eventually, though, the quaking in my limbs subsided and my harsh breathing slowed. I carefully relaxed my grip on my knees, pulling deep breaths and releasing them slowly as I let the calm fill my body. It left me exhausted, though, and I tipped my head back to rest against the door.

"I'm here." Zed's quiet voice traveled through the wood to me like he was sitting in a mirror position on the other side. "I'm here if you need me. I always will be."

My throat tightened with emotion, and I swallowed heavily. Then I pushed up from the floor and unlocked the door. Opening it, I looked down at my friend sitting on the floor, his button-down shirt rumpled and his brow creased in concern.

No words passed my lips, but I pushed the door open wider, then retreated over to the big bed and burrowed under the covers. The door closed softly a moment later, and Zed crawled in beside me, wrapping me up in his familiar embrace.

"I'm sorry," he whispered, and I knew he wasn't talking about kissing me, because he'd seen the tapes from Chase's room and he *knew*.

CHAPTER 27

Zed's gentle hand on my shoulder and his whispered voice in my ear shook me awake, and I groaned when I saw it was still dark out. Then I sat up with a jerk and stared at him with wide eyes.

"What is it?" I asked. "What's happened?"

The relaxed smile on his face reassured me before he responded. "Nothing. I didn't mean to startle you like that. Just…get up. We've got somewhere to be."

I frowned my confusion, and he tugged me out of bed by the arm. "Come on, get in the shower. I'll grab you some fresh clothes. Just be super quiet so we don't wake the Gumdrop. This is a job only for us."

"Well, color me curious," I muttered, then covered my mouth as I yawned heavily. "Fine, I'm going."

We'd both fallen asleep fully clothed after our fight the night before, and I had sore points where my seams and zippers had pressed into my flesh all night. So I wasn't arguing all *that* hard about showering and changing.

After I'd washed, I found a stack of my new clothes waiting on the edge of the vanity and gave Zed's choices a curious look. Wherever we were going, I doubted it was on Timberwolf business, not if I was wearing dark denim jeans and a plain, long-sleeved black top.

"Here," Zed whispered, handing me a pair of flat-soled boots when I emerged. He placed a finger over his lips, reminding me to be quiet, and we silently made our way downstairs. The clock on the foyer wall showed it was about an hour before dawn, and I gave Zed a suspicious look as he led the way through to the garage.

"Shouldn't we tell Lucas we're going out?" I asked, hesitating beside the Ferrari.

Zed gave me an exasperated look. "I left him a note, he'll be fine. Kid always sleeps in unless you wake him up, anyway. He probably won't even notice we're gone."

He had a point there. With a shrug, I slid into the passenger seat and buckled my seat belt. "All right, fess up, what are we doing?" I ruffled my fingers through my hair, yawning again. I hated mornings.

Zed just grinned and revved the engine. "Patience is a virtue, *sir*. You'll see."

I rolled my eyes at his teasing tone, turned my attention out the window, and propped my head on my hand. So far it seemed like we were just pretending that whole argument from last night had never happened. That Zed hadn't kissed me…or that I hadn't kissed him back before spiraling into a meltdown.

Cool. I could handle denial.

Zed cranked the stereo up loud, eliminating the need for conversation, and I settled in for a drive. I wasn't worried about where he was taking me or why he was being secretive because I trusted him implicitly. He might have been feeling threatened, but surely he knew how much of my heart he already owned.

We pulled to a stop at a lookout high up in the hills behind Shadow Grove right as the first glow of sunrise started cresting the horizon, and I turned to Zed with a knowing smile.

"Really?"

His smile was sly as he reached behind the seats to retrieve a picnic basket. "It's not *quite* the same," he said with a shrug, popping his door open. "But it's close."

We got out, and I grinned when Zed sat on the hood of his Ferrari and patted the spot beside him. When we'd done this as teenagers, our cars had been considerably less expensive and we didn't much care if we dented them.

Still, I wasn't going to argue, so I hopped up beside him and accepted the thermos of coffee he took from the picnic basket.

We were silent for a long time, sharing the coffee and watching the sun rise over Shadow Grove. I couldn't speak for Zed, but for the first time in a long time, I just let my mind empty out and allowed a heady sense of calmness and serenity fill me up.

When the coffee ran out, I sighed and rested my head on Zed's shoulder. He wrapped his arm around me, and the strength of his grip reinforced exactly what he'd told me last night. He would always be there for me, no matter what.

"Thank you, Zed," I murmured after a while. "I needed this more than I even knew."

It was something we used to do a lot, back when we were still new to all the violence and tension of gang life. When it all started to get overwhelming, we would sneak out in the early hours of the morning and drive to a lookout to watch the sun rise. It was our thing, Zed's and mine, and Chase had hated that he was never invited. Ultimately, though, he'd never needed it like we did. Chase Lockhart was born for that life; he thrived in it. The killing, the violence, the threats and tactics—none of it weighed on his mind like it did on ours. It never stained his soul, because you couldn't stain something already so black.

"We're not done yet," he told me with a lopsided smile, checking his watch for the time. "Get in."

Smiling and feeling like a lead weight had been lifted from my shoulders, I climbed off the hood of the Ferrari and returned to my seat. The look Zed gave me as he accelerated back out onto the road was pure excitement, and I couldn't stop the rush of emotion it stirred up in me.

He'd been accurate last night when he accused me of feeling exactly the same way as he claimed to. But because of that, I was more determined than ever to keep the status quo between us. Messing with a good thing was only going to end in heartbreak.

It didn't make it any easier, though. Now that I knew how he felt, it was worse than ever. I was reading more into every glance, every touch, every smile…

Shit. What had he done?

I bit the inside of my cheek, trying to give myself a mental pep talk as we drove to our next location, but then I started laughing as we pulled into a driveway marked by a sign that read *Stealth Hunter Paintballing*.

"Zed…" I turned to him with a wide grin. "You're taking me paintballing?"

He gave me a wry smile. "You're not fucking shooting me, if that's what you're thinking. I've taken enough bruises for one week, thank you." He grimaced and rubbed his face where both Cass and I had left our marks.

We parked in the mostly empty lot, but straight away I spotted the busload of SGU frat boys unloading near the entrance, laughing and whooping, talking trash about kicking each other's asses.

"Wanna shoot some loudmouthed idiots without all the messy body disposal?" Zed offered, tilting his head to the side. "This is an open course, us versus whoever else is playing."

I let out a low whistle, quickly counting frat boys. "Two against twenty-six? Seems like unfair odds." I quirked a brow. "Maybe we should do it blindfolded."

Zed scoffed a laugh and led the way into the paintball park.

A few of the frat boys spotted us patiently waiting our turn to register and started making stupid jokes about how there wouldn't

221

be much competition on the field today. By the sound of things, they were regulars at the paintball park. Poor darlings.

A familiar face in the group caught my eye, and I tilted my head slightly in question. He casually made his way over, separating himself from his friends, and stood slightly to the side of Zed and me as he pretended to look at the noticeboard.

"Morning, Boss," he greeted me quietly, then inclined his head to Zed, "and Boss."

"I never picked you for a frat boy, Rixby," I replied just as quietly, biting back my amused grin. "It's an interesting look for you."

His usually spiky, gelled hair was combed flat, and a buttoned-up polo shirt covered a lot of his tattoos. The edges of the Timberwolf mark on his bicep were visible, but unless someone *knew* what the mark was, they'd never guess it was a gang symbol.

Rixby shot Zed a look, which told me that my second was fully aware and had possibly even inserted him into the frat in the first place.

"He's looking into some new campus drug dealers," Zed murmured softly. "But today, he's setting his frat brothers up for a bloodbath, aren't ya, Rixby?"

The preppy undercover Timberwolf scoffed a laugh. "They need the ego check. Go easy on me, Boss? I have a reputation to keep intact."

Zed shook his head. "Good fucking luck on that one."

Rixby gave a groan but was grinning when he made his way back into the group of his "friends" to get kitted out.

Folding my arms, I gave Zed a long look, and he just smiled back at me, smug as fuck in the knowledge that we would wipe the floor with these poor fools.

Yeah. This was *exactly* what I needed.

Zed had been right when he said we would probably get home before Lucas even knew we were gone. When we returned to the house covered in paint splatter—but no direct hits—Lucas was on his way downstairs, still looking half-asleep.

"Hey, what's with the note?" he asked Zed, frowning at a scrap of paper in his hand, then reading aloud, "*Gone out with H. Do your homework like a good Gumdrop. Boss Man.*"

I snorted a laugh. "That's cute," I told Zed with a wide grin. "You think *you're* the boss around here." Reaching up, I gave him a condescending pat on the head, then headed through to the kitchen.

"What?" Zed asked, following. "I *am* his boss. Or...was. You're probably not a hot commodity on the stage right now, kid."

Lucas scowled back at Zed as I slid onto one of the barstools at the island. "Yeah, keep lying to yourself like that, Zed. Chicks dig scars. I'll be ten times as popular whenever the *actual* boss lets me get back to work." He gave me a pointed look, and I shook my head firmly.

"Not a chance, Lucas. Your bruises haven't even healed, let alone that burn." I frowned at his chest like I could see the brand through his T-shirt. It was healing well, and his doctor speculated that the branding iron may not have been as hot as it could have been. Chase had rushed it, and for that I was glad.

"Actually, I had an idea about this," Lucas told me, tapping the spot with his index finger. "So don't stress. I got it handled. Just say the word and I'll happily get back to work in any of your other clubs."

Zed arched a brow at me behind Lucas's back, and I flicked a look at him before shaking my head. "We can discuss it when you've had another checkup."

Lucas gave a long sigh and braced his hands on the counter beside me. He leaned in close, his lips brushing over my ear. "I guess I'll have to keep my skills sharp with private dances in the meantime." His whispered words were full of sex and promise, and his teeth nipped playfully at my neck.

I sucked in a sharp breath as my body responded, but my eyes

223

locked with Zed's. He wasn't angry, though. Just…sad. Resigned.

Fucking hell. That was the *last* thing I wanted. Had we already broken our once ironclad friendship with that one kiss? Or had this already been a long time coming?

The gate buzzer sounded, saving me from doing something really dumb—like asking Zed if he was cool entering into a polyamorous relationship with me, Lucas, and Cass.

Zed went to answer it, and Lucas seized the opportunity to kiss me properly while we were alone. His hands clasped my waist, and his full lips were soft and unhurried against mine as I kissed him back.

I could seriously kiss Lucas forever; he had some crazy natural talent with that mouth of his.

"Are you okay this morning?" he murmured softly when he released me a moment later. "I couldn't help overhearing a bit of that argument last night…"

I cringed, hating that he'd possibly witnessed such a raw wound on my soul. "Yeah. Zed and I have…history."

Lucas snorted a laugh. "No shit. But that wasn't quite how I thought it was going to play out."

My brows rose. I wanted to ask what he meant by that comment, whether he had known Zed was going to spontaneously declare his love and kiss me. But footsteps on the tile floor cut our quiet conversation short, and Zed walked back into the kitchen with Dallas following behind him.

"Dallas," I said with surprise. "I didn't know we were expecting you this morning."

He gave me a tight smile and a nod of respect. "Sir. No, you weren't. I thought this was important enough to warrant discussing in person, though."

His laptop was tucked under his arm, and he placed it down on the countertop to open the screen up.

I shot Zed a curious look, but he gave me a small headshake

in response, telling me he also had no clue what Dallas had come to tell us.

"Okay, I'm just going to cut to the chase and pray you two aren't in the mood to shoot the messenger," Dallas muttered, flicking Zed and me nervous glances as his fingers flew over the keyboard.

"We took the edge off at the paintball park this morning," Zed replied with a wry smile. "What have you found?"

"The purchaser of your insurance underwriter," Dallas replied with a grimace. "That shell corporation took a bit of hammering to crack, but sure enough…" He heaved a sigh, then spun his laptop around to show us the document on the screen. "Locked Heart Enterprises."

My whole body stilled, and my heart rate seemed to pause for a second.

"You're kidding me," I responded in a hoarse whisper, my gaze locking with Zed's. "That's not even remotely subtle."

Zed nodded his agreement. "He wanted that shell cracked."

"Uh, okay, maybe," Dallas murmured. "Anyway, this is your CEO of Locked Heart. I did some digging into his background, of course, and—"

"And you found affiliations to the old Timberwolves," Zed finished for him, scrubbing a hand over his face with a groan. "As well as a familial tie to the Lockhart family. Wenton Dibbs was, what? Chase's cousin?" He looked to me for confirmation, but I was shaking my head in disbelief.

"Yeah, he was," I replied, licking my suddenly dry lips as I stared at the data sheet on the laptop screen. "But he's also dead."

Dallas frowned. "Um, not to contradict you or anything, sir, because that seems like a supremely stupid idea…but Wenton Dibbs is very much alive. He's been filing tax returns every year, paying rent, getting parking tickets…" He let his voice trail off with a shrug.

I arched a brow at him. "Do you have a picture of him?"

Dallas's expression tightened. "No. Or nothing clear enough

for facial recognition software. Just these, lifted from a security camera outside the Locked Heart office in Cloudcroft." He clicked a couple of times, bringing up some grainy images that simply showed a tall man with light hair and broad shoulders. His face was averted in all the shots, like he knew where the cameras were and deliberately avoided them.

They had been cousins, so without seeing his face, there was no way to conclusively tell whether it was Chase or Wenton. Except for one thing.

"Wenton Dibbs is dead," I said again, rubbing my forehead. "Chase shot him on the back of his dad's yacht and tossed the body overboard."

Zed gave me a startled look. "How come I never knew about this? Didn't the family blame their feud with the Montaguires on them killing him?"

I shrugged. "I forgot all about it until just now. I wasn't..." My voice broke, and I needed to swallow. "I wasn't fully lucid when it happened."

I met Zed's eyes, and he gave a knowing nod.

"If that's everything, Dallas, I think we need to discuss this in private." He arched a brow at our resident hacker, who smoothly collected his laptop and jerked a nod.

"Understood, Boss. I'll send a copy of all of this over to you and keep hunting for better images of Dibbs. Or whoever." He gave me another nod, then hurried out of the house once more.

After the front door closed, echoing through to us in the kitchen, Zed folded his arms and gave me a worried look.

"Want to tell us the story?" His voice was calm and unemotional, but his eyes were swimming with concern. He'd seen my meltdown last night, and this would be wandering awfully close to those same memories. But one word in his question grounded me back in the present. One word choice threw me a lifeline to cling to and remind myself that things were different now.

226

Us.

He'd asked if I wanted to tell "us" the story...him *and* Lucas.

Lucas heard it too and slid his arm around my waist in a silent reminder that he was there for me. I wasn't that scared, drugged-up teen anymore. I had a support network, and dammit, I needed to start using it.

I only wished Cass were here too. Where *was* he?

CHAPTER 28

Clenching my teeth, I tried to force my hand to stop shaking as I raised my coffee to my lips. Zed had just poured it for me, then pulled out the bag of assorted pastries we'd picked up on our way home from paintballing.

"Zed already knows my horrible history," I told Lucas in a dry voice, wrinkling my nose, "so just…interrupt if I confuse you. Otherwise, I'm just going to gloss over the details, if that's cool?"

He nodded, his brow creased in concern, but his hand on my knee was nothing but reassuring.

I drew a breath. "Okay, so in a nutshell, Chase Lockhart was an unrestrained, sociopathic psychopath. I mean…if a clinical psychologist got their hands on him, they'd either write a thesis or wet themselves." Zed snorted a laugh but didn't interrupt. "He used to…" I let my voice trail off, then gave myself a mental slap to pull it together. "He thought it was entertaining to drug me. PCP was his family's cash cow, and he found the hallucinations that a strong dose could induce to be… I don't know. Amusing. He got off on fear, so trust me when I say that my experiences with angel dust were quite firmly the stuff of nightmares."

"That's fucked up," Lucas muttered, and I gave him a lopsided smile.

"You have no idea. Anyway. Wenton Dibbs." I cleared my throat and tugged nervously on a lock of my hair. "It was during some event or other that the elder Lockharts were hosting. We'd gone out on his father's yacht, and Chase was in the mood to celebrate some promotion his father had given him. He was drinking and doing lines of coke and pressuring me to do it with him."

Zed grunted an annoyed sound. "He was good at that. Manipulative fuck."

"Yep. Eventually he decided I wasn't being *fun* enough and dosed me up on angel dust." I detached myself from the story, focusing on the warmth of Lucas's hand on my knee, of the rich scent of coffee under my nose, and the intense, blazing blue of Zed's eyes locked on mine. "The altercation with Wenton happened when Chase decided to share me around. Wenton refused, then stood up to Chase and told him…" My voice trailed off, the details fuzzy. "I don't know what. But it ended up with Wenton punching Chase and Chase shooting him in the head."

I paused, taking a sip of my coffee and letting the distorted memories play out in my mind like a TV channel with bad reception. It was all fuzzy, and broken flashes of my drug-induced delirium intermingled with reality. My stomach churned and twisted like I was stuck on a roller coaster after drinking milk.

Nope. No way. That was a ride I was more than capable of getting off. So I did. I shut it down and shook my head to clear the scene before refocusing on Zed's eyes once more.

"Chase panicked that he'd be in trouble for killing a member of the family, so he shoved Wenton's body into the ocean, then paid off the other witnesses, Ivan and Dennis, before we got back to shore." I gave a small sigh. "I was so messed up that it all just… disappeared in my mind."

Zed's shoulders were tight with fury, his hands clenched into fists at his sides as he stared back at me. The guilt and pain in his gaze was almost too much to bear, so I looked away, turning to Lucas, as I cleared my throat.

"Do you have any questions?" I asked it gently, meaning did he want more details or would that suffice to explain what an unbalanced mess I'd been.

Lucas's forehead was deeply lined with disgust, but his grip on my knee was strong and comforting. "Yeah, actually, I do," he replied, his voice rough with emotion. "I in no way want to doubt your version of events, but my first thought here is… Are you *sure* that's what happened? On all those drugs, already hallucinating… You said Chase got off on your fear, so I'm going to assume he did shit to deliberately scare you, probably orchestrated situations to mess with your head and terrify you."

I jerked a nod. He'd nailed it.

Lucas winced, probably hoping I'd say it wasn't like that. "Well, yeah." He ran his free hand over his floppy, model-esque hair. "How do you know that wasn't a setup to scare you or keep you in line? Like a warning to you not to fuck with him?"

The cold chill traveling down my spine turned to ice.

"It's possible," Zed said softly, leaning across the counter and tugging my thumbnail from between my teeth. I hadn't even noticed I was chewing it. "I remember that event. I wasn't there that night because I was out with some random college chick, desperately trying to convince myself I wasn't in love with my friend's girl." He gave me a long look. "If I'd been there, he wouldn't have tried that shit."

I gave a small shrug, refusing to let myself wallow in that victimized feeling any longer. "He'd have just done it later, when we got home."

"But it's possible Wenton wasn't shot," Lucas reiterated. "A whole lot more possible than Chase surviving a bullet to the face. Right?"

My skin prickled, and I glanced over at Zed. *Was it?*

My friend gave a one-shouldered shrug. "Only you have any hope of answering that, Dare. How positive are you that your memory was reality and not a dust-induced fakery?" He ran a hand over the back of his neck, wincing. "Because I witnessed you shoot Chase. But both Ivan and Dennis are dead now, so we can't check with them about your memory of Wenton."

I ran that information over and over in my mind, inspecting it from an outsider's perspective. From Lucas's point of view. Eventually, I swiped a hand over my face and exhaled long and hard.

"Fuck," I whispered. "I don't know."

Lucas gave my knee a squeeze. "That's okay, babe. You don't have to know. Whether it's Chase himself or Wenton Dibbs, we're still gonna kill him for real this time. He's declared war on Hades herself, so there's only one way to end this."

Zed gave a grim laugh. "With total *anarchy*."

I groaned and rolled my eyes at his dumb play on words. But it shifted my mind onto a more worrying subject.

"Have either of you heard from Cass today?" His absence was increasingly irritating me. Not that I expected him to be hanging around like a lovesick fool simply because we'd fucked once, but something seemed off about him not being here. Maybe that said more about how deeply I'd already let him under my skin than it said about anything else. Prior to hooking up, I'd been lucky to see Cass once a week. He had his own life, his own gang to run. But I was uncomfortably aware how much of his life had previously involved random, beautiful women, and we hadn't exactly drawn up an agreement about what we were.

Lucas shook his head, taking a bite of a chocolate croissant. "Nope."

Zed refilled my coffee mug and pressed an oh-so-casual kiss on my cheek as he leaned in. "It sounded like some teething pains with the Wraith takeover." He spun away before I could give him a hard look for that slightly more-than-platonic gesture. "But I'm supposed to see him at Anarchy for training in a few hours, if you want to come spectate."

I grinned, nodding to the bruise on the side of his face. "You that eager for me to see you get KO'd again, Zayden?" I clucked my tongue, teasing. "I think you might have let your skills slip a bit in recent years. I might need to throw you into a fight night too."

He narrowed his eyes, setting the coffeepot back down and folding his arms over his chest. "Pick a date. I'll do it. I was just going easy on the old man yesterday so he wouldn't break a hip."

Lucas started laughing and choked on his mouthful of pastry. He coughed hard, his face red as he tried to get himself under control, but Zed just glared ice-cold death at him throughout.

"If you say so," I told him with a wide grin, thumping Lucas on the back to help him out, even though it was a proven fact that did *nothing* to help.

Zed glowered, picking up his own coffee mug to drink from it. "Fucking shit stirrer," he muttered at Lucas. The dark look he cast at my Gumdrop said he would be getting revenge during training later, poor darling.

"All right, I need to go wash some of this paint off," I announced, sliding off my stool and taking my empty mug to the sink. "You two play nice and don't kill each other in some kind of misguided dick-measuring competition."

Lucas smirked. "I'm secure enough not to need measuring."

I rolled my eyes, but he was probably right. That snake he was smuggling in his trousers was a one in a million.

Leaving them in the kitchen, I made my way back upstairs while texting Dallas. I wanted the details of the Locked Heart offices so I could pay the CEO a visit in person. After all, it seemed like the easiest way to answer the Wenton-or-Chase question once and for all. Positive, firsthand identification.

But I had to admit to myself as I washed fluorescent paint from my hair under the shower stream that it was seeming a hell of a lot more likely this was Wenton, and that gave me some measure of relief. I could handle Wenton Dibbs back from the dead. He wouldn't break me like Chase could.

CHAPTER 29

Zed seriously taught Lucas a lesson about laughing at him. When they finished their training session in the downstairs gym, Lucas was groaning curses at my second.

I gave Zed a half-hearted reprimand on account of Lucas's still-healing wounds, but ultimately, Lucas was just as much to blame.

Dallas had gotten back to me earlier to let me know that Wenton Dibbs, CEO of Locked Heart Enterprises, was currently out of the country, so I'd had to put my confrontation plans on ice for the time being.

After Zed left to check on the clubs and meet Cass at Anarchy, I settled down beside Lucas on the sofa in the living room. He was freshly showered and changed and flicking through the streaming channels in search of a movie.

I snuggled under his arm. "What are you looking for?"

He gave me a sly smile. "Research," he replied, then clicked on the movie he'd been hunting for. "Gotta work on some new routines so I'm ready when my boss puts me back on the schedule."

I snickered as *Magic Mike* started playing on the big screen. Call me curious, though. I wanted to see what inspiration he was going to draw from Channing and his guys.

We'd just settled in to watch when my phone vibrated in my pocket and I gave a frustrated sigh. I was starting to think I'd be better off without a phone…but that probably wouldn't work amazingly well for running my empire.

I pulled it out and sat up with a jerk when I saw the caller ID.

"Everything okay?" Lucas asked, arching a brow at me.

My eyes flew from the phone to him, then back to the phone screen in an instant. "Yeah. Yes. I have to take this." I rushed out of the room, sliding my thumb over the "accept call" button, and brought the phone to my ear. "Seph? What's wrong?"

There was a heavy pause, and I desperately wished I could climb through the phone. Then my sister sighed. "Hey, Dare," she finally said.

She didn't sound like she was panicked or in pain or being held against her will. What the fuck?

"I'm still *so* mad at you," she informed me, her tone hard and edged with hurt. "But you're still my big sister."

The air rushed out of my lungs, and I sagged against the wall of the foyer. I'd texted Seph several times since our fight, but she hadn't responded and I hadn't pushed her. Demi had kept me updated that they were all fine in Italy, and I'd left it at that, hoping distance and time would scab over the wound of my shitty actions.

"Of course I am, Seph," I whispered. "I'll always be your sister, even if you don't want me."

She huffed a sound. "Yeah, well… Demi might have had some words with me about…things." She paused, sounding awkward. "Lucas and you. And how I reacted."

"You don't need to apologize, Seph. I never should have lied to you," I told her in a rush, and she barked a laugh.

"I wasn't fucking apologizing, you narcissist." She snapped the words at me, and I grinned. "You're damn right you shouldn't have lied to me. You made me feel like a total idiot! But…a little perspective has made me accept the fact that it wasn't *that* bad. It's not like Lucas cheated on me. It was just a stupid crush."

I was genuinely surprised at her maturity. "That's what you were calling me to say?"

"No, not entirely," she admitted. "I might have, um, accidentally overheard Demi talking with Archer about you."

Ah, shit. My spine stiffened, and I raked my fingers through my hair.

"What did you hear, Seph?"

"Not much," she admitted, sounding annoyed about that fact, "but I heard them say that the bomb at our building had something to do with Chase."

I had nothing to say to that. I could kill Demi and Archer for being so careless around Seph. I never, ever wanted her to know what I'd gone through while our father was alive—or what she'd very nearly ended up suffering.

She let out another small sigh. "Look, I'm starting to understand that I don't really know what you dealt with back then. But…I know *you*, Dare. I know how strong you are and how fiercely you protect the new Timberwolves. And I remember how you were back then when you were dating Chase." Her voice was small and quiet, making my eyes heat and my throat thicken. "You weren't you back then. The look in your eyes got hollower, *deader* every fucking day I saw you, and I knew it was because of him. I used to sneak into your room while you were sleeping just to check your pulse and make sure you hadn't killed yourself when it all got too much." Her voice broke over that confession, and I could hear the tears in her breathing.

Try as I might, I couldn't find the words to reassure her. I couldn't tell her she was wrong, that I hadn't thought about ending it all hundreds of times. But I never did it because of her. If I was gone, who would save my little sister from the same fate?

Seph sniffed loudly and drew a breath. "But then shit changed.

236

You…did what you did. And even though you withdrew and became all cold and mean, I was relieved because since that day, you've never once looked like you were giving up again." Her voice stopped wobbling, and I could practically see her pulling herself together. She was a fucking strong woman in her own right; I just never told her that.

"It's not Chase," I whispered to her, not trusting my voice fully. "I don't think so, anyway. It's…complicated. I guess. But even if it were him, he'd be in for a nasty surprise if he expected to push me around again."

Seph gave a sharp laugh. "No shit. You'd flatten his ass. Anyway, what I wanted to say is that I think this weird cougar thing you've got going with Lucas is good for you. You've changed since you met him, and even though I thought it was Zed you'd been fucking, I knew *someone* was being good to you. Someone had finally been let in and showed you that you were worth loving. 'Cause you are, Dare. I hope you know that."

A hot tear escaped my eye and rolled down my cheek, rendering me speechless.

"I'm just…" Seph continued, oblivious to the way her words had just struck me dead in the heart. "I was angry at you for Zed and Cass. You were screwing a high school senior while those two gods among men have been pining after you for-freaking-ever, and I thought you were making a big mistake. But I dunno. Now I'm choosing to accept anyone who can make you smile like Lucas clearly does."

I gave a harsh chuckle, sniffing back the tears that welled behind my eyeballs. One more heartfelt statement from my bratty little sister and I was likely to dissolve into a puddle of emotions.

"Well, don't write them off yet," I told her with a dry groan. "Things are…complicated."

There was a pause on the phone, then Seph let out a high-pitched squeal of excitement. "Oh my *god!*" she shrieked. "You're totally fucking all three of them! Ugh, Dare, did I ever tell you you're my idol? Maybe now you'll stop cunt-blocking me so I can get a reverse harem relationship of my own. I'm so left out right now."

I could hear the exaggerated pout in her voice, and I grinned. "Don't count on it, little sister."

She whined a protest, then yawned. "Okay. I need to go to bed. It's, like, one in the morning here. Demi is taking us into Florence tomorrow to visit the Galleria dell'Accademia and look at some giant stone dude's tiny dick. Reckon that's okay, or did you want to go threaten the statue of David not to show me his junk?" The sass was back, and my chest flooded with warmth.

"Don't tempt me, brat," I warned her. "Is Archer around somewhere to talk to me?"

She made a grossed-out sound. "Trust me, you do *not* want me interrupting him and MK right now. I'll tell him to call in the morning."

I snickered again. "Fair enough. I love you, Seph." My voice was hoarse, and as I said it, I realized how painfully infrequently I told her.

Enough that there was a stunned silence before she reciprocated. "I love you too, Dare. Don't die on me, okay? I still need you to teach me how to shoot, and Demi refuses to let me touch her guns."

I rolled my eyes and shook my head, even though she couldn't see my reaction. "Sweet dreams, kid. Send me some pictures from Italy, okay?"

"You got it," she promised, then ended the call.

I sat there in the foyer with my back pressed to the wall for a long time, replaying my conversation with Seph in my head over and over until I decided maybe I didn't need to murder Demi and Archer after all. Despite how bad Seph's eavesdropping could have ended, I couldn't stay mad considering how it'd turned out.

Eventually I pushed back to my feet and made my way through to the living room, where I found Lucas shirtless and grinding on the coffee table as music poured from the speakers.

He froze when he spotted me watching, then grinned. "Hey, babe," he said, sending me a suggestive look. "Wanna help me work on this combination? I need a focus point."

Seph's words about how Lucas had changed me for the better echoed through my mind again, and as I ran my eyes over him, my whole body seemed suddenly warm and floaty with an emotion I was totally unused to.

"I've got a better idea." I raised the hem of my T-shirt and stripped it off. "Show me that move you were just doing…upstairs."

His eyes widened with eagerness. "Upstairs, huh?"

I nodded, unhooking my bra to toss aside with my shirt. "Yup. So you have a soft landing if you fall."

"Oh," he replied, prowling across to me with a wicked smirk on his full lips. "Well, if it's in the name of safety." He stooped, swooped, and scooped me up in his arms, drawing a surprised yelp from my throat.

"Lucas!" I objected. "Put me down. You're still healing!"

He just laughed and kissed me as he carried me upstairs. Damn it if his disregard for doctor's orders wasn't still turning me on. I loved a bad boy, and Lucas was quickly losing his angelic shine.

Every day he spent with me, with Zed and Cass and the Timberwolves, his halo was becoming more perfectly tarnished. Perfect for *Hades*.

CHAPTER 30

Lucas was more than happy to show me just how much his range of motion and stamina had returned, fucking me stupid well into the night until we both passed out from sheer exhaustion.

He really was setting the bar high, I had to admit. Cass was going to have his work cut out if he wanted to get back into my panties after this week's strange behavior. And as for Zed... Well, I was still too much of a stubborn bitch to fully consider what it'd be like to fuck Zed for real. I didn't want to get my hopes up, even inside my own mind, only to have him buck the idea of sharing me in real life.

Zed simply didn't play that nicely with others. He was too territorial, despite how cordial he'd been with Lucas and Cass so far.

Unfortunately, no one sent that memo to my subconscious. So later that night I found myself deep in the throes of a sex dream starring me and three to-die-for sexy men, all naked and sweaty and—

A gentle clink of metal jerked me from my delicious fantasy, and my eyes popped open to find a large, shadowed figure looming over the side of the bed. Lucas's arm was still heavy over my waist, his soft breath tickling my back, so I acted on instinct and struck out silently.

My foot shot out of the blankets, catching my surprise visitor square in the crotch. He uttered a quiet *oof* as he crumpled but still reached out to drag me down with him as he hit the floor. The movement was so quick, so smooth, I slid straight out from under Lucas's arm and tumbled on top of my attacker without a sound. He rolled, locking me under his huge form and clapping a hand over my mouth with an almost silent chuckle.

"Hi, Red," Cass rumbled in my ear. His teeth nipped my lobe, then he suck it into his mouth. "I missed you."

So I could tell. Despite the direct hit his junk had just caught from my foot, he was having no trouble getting it up now that he had me naked and pinned beneath him.

I bucked under him as quietly as I could, trying to dislodge his weight but also not wanting to wake Lucas up. So okay, sure, I wasn't trying *that* hard. Sue me, I liked having Cass's body pinning me to the carpet and his lips on my neck.

His kisses trailed down the line of my throat, sucking and biting my skin like he wanted to devour me, but his hand stayed tight over my mouth to prevent me from cursing him. Smart man, he really did know me well. So surely he'd have seen it coming when I bit his fingers to make him release me.

He snatched his hand away with a hiss, then bit my shoulder in retaliation. Prick.

"Screw you, Saint," I said in a harsh whisper, shoving at his strongly muscled torso. "You're on my shit list. You don't get to maul me in the middle of the night."

He raised his head slightly, peering at me in the moonlight leaking through the half-closed windows. "Hmm, I see."

In a smooth motion he rolled off me and surged to his feet, pulled me up along with him.

"Cass—" I started to protest, but he was already pulling me out of the room.

I shot a quick look back at Lucas, but he was still sound asleep and hugging a pillow where I'd just been—proof he'd had a hell of a lot less darkness in his life that he could sleep through the quiet noises Cass and I had just made.

Once we were out of the room, Cass closed the door with a barely audible click, then turned to me with a flash of determination across his face.

"Don't give me that look, Grumpy Cat," I snapped—quietly—and folded my arms under my breasts. The fact that I was totally naked sort of changed the whole tone of that gesture, though, something Cass must have agreed with because a second later I found myself slung over his shoulder as he strode down the hall to the bathroom I'd adopted as my own.

"Cass, put me down," I ordered as he stepped inside and shut the door. He didn't bother turning on any lights, and he didn't really need to. The full moon outside was bright enough that we could still see.

He didn't answer me and didn't put me down. Instead he reached into the shower, cranked the water on, and stuck his hand under the stream to check the temperature. When I struggled against his strong grip around the backs of my thighs, he slapped my ass with a wet hand, and I gave an embarrassingly sexual moan.

Whoops.

He heard it too, if his dark chuckle was any indication. His fingers kneaded my stinging butt cheek, caring but rough as fuck.

Dammit if I wasn't soaking for him, despite my irritation at his absence all week.

"What are we doing, Cass?" I demanded, letting my voice rise slightly louder now that we were away from Lucas's bedroom. "How'd you even get in here? Did Zed bring you home?"

He tested the water again, then turned his face to give my hip a teasing bite. "Nope. Last I saw him, he was still at Anarchy, beating the shit out of some punk-ass kid for being caught with angel dust."

Alarm shuddered through me, and I tried to push out of Cass's grip. "What? Why didn't he call me?"

Cass stepped straight into the shower—still fully dressed—and deposited me under the warm stream of water. "He did. You didn't answer." The water quickly soaked through his T-shirt and jeans, plastering the fabric to his body like papier-mâché, and I was glad for the darkness to hide the way I eye-fucked him.

I frowned, wanting to argue his point, but then I realized my phone was downstairs somewhere. I'd left it down there after my call with Seph, then spent the rest of the evening riding Lucas's monster cock like I could fuck away all the potent emotions my sister had stirred up.

"He's got it handled," Cass assured me, grabbing a fluffy sponge and squirting a crapload of body wash onto it. "I might not be the biggest fan of Zayden De Rosa, but he's a fucking solid second."

I scoffed a laugh as he started running the soapy sponge over my skin. "Bullshit. You and Zed are quietly involved in a bromance, don't even try to deny it. All that mutual respect and shit." I tilted my head back, letting the water soak through my hair as Cass paid particular attention to washing my breasts. Especially my nipples. They seemed to need a whole lot of cleaning.

"Mmm," he replied, not agreeing but not *dis*agreeing.

"He'll kill you for breaking into his house, though." I swiped water from my face to give Cass a hard look. "How *did* you break in?"

The big tattooed bastard just smirked.

I rolled my eyes and reached out to pluck the saturated fabric of his shirt away from his washboard abs. "So, what are we doing in here, hmm? You've all but ghosted me for the whole week. I'm tempted to kick you out on your ass."

"You won't though," he murmured, dipping his head to kiss me slowly as his soapy sponge trailed lower down my body. His lips moved against mine, his tongue tangling in my mouth and making me temporarily forget my annoyance with him.

"Cass..." I breathed his name as he released my mouth. His sponge had made it between my legs, and I was about three seconds away from grinding against it like I was in heat. "What's going on?"

My hands slipped beneath his wet T-shirt to grip his smooth sides and pull him closer in to me. For all the answers I wanted about his behavior, I couldn't fight the physical magnetism between us.

"Right now, Red," he murmured, continuing to scrub every little inch of me with his sponge and totally ignoring his own state of dress, "I need to wash the smell of Lucas from your skin so that when I get you all sweaty and wrapped around my dick, I can pretend you're entirely mine."

Oh yup. Yeah, that was a quick way past my guard.

He dropped the sponge, backing me further into the water as his fingers took over the task of washing me. Or...getting me dirty again, depending on your perspective. His long digits slid inside my still aching pussy, stroking me as I shuddered in his arms.

"Jesus," I hissed when my cunt throbbed in response to his touch.

Cass let out a low, dark chuckle. "Nah, just a Saint."

"Oh my god," I groaned, pushing back from his grip to glare at him. "You did *not* just dad-joke me while fingering my pussy. Fucking hell, Cass."

His lopsided smirk was way too damn sexy in the low moonlight, and I tugged his wet shirt up. "This needs to come off," I informed him. "Right fucking now."

He quirked a brow at me but did as I asked, stripping the soaked fabric over his head and displaying his fully inked upper body. "Anything else while I'm letting you give the orders?"

I scoffed, reaching for the waistband of his black jeans. It took more effort than usual to unbutton them, given how saturated they were—not to mention the way his erection strained the seams.

"You really love tempting fate, huh? Take the rest off, and I'll *think* about letting you fuck me tonight." I tilted my chin back, my eyes meeting his with a clear challenge.

Cass gave a slow shake of his head, dragging his thumb slowly over my lower lip like he was giving me an opportunity to dial back the sass. He should have known better, though. I just took it as my chance to double down.

"Or maybe I won't. Maybe I'll just head back and wake Lucas up with my lips around his dick. Maybe I'll let him finish what you've started here...seeing as I'm so damn *wet.*"

Cass's eyes narrowed, and in a lightning-fast move he spun me around and slammed me into the shower wall hard enough to knock a little air from my lungs. His hot, hard body blanketed me, his lips against my ear and his hand around my throat.

"You're *mine* right now, Red," he growled, his jeans rough on the backs of my legs and his chest hot against my shoulders. That was all the warning he gave before he slammed his cock into me from behind, grunting as he slipped inside my wet, throbbing cunt.

The sudden intrusion made me gasp, but I arched my spine and pushed back into him, silently demanding more. My whole body still ached from my extended fuck session with Lucas, but that didn't stop me from melting under Cass's rough touch. He held me firm, one hand around my throat and one hand on my hip as he slammed into me a couple of times. Then he kicked my feet out further, spreading my legs wider as he increased his pace, fucking me until I was a moaning, panting mess against the shower wall.

He released my neck, his hand sliding down my front to play with a nipple as I shuddered and thrashed under his touch. I was so damn close to coming I could barely even form sounds, let alone words.

"Do you think about what I wrote in that letter, Red?" he asked me in a darkly seductive whisper, his short beard scraping over my shoulder as he kissed and bit my neck. "I do. All the time."

I moaned, bucking my hips when his fingers found my clit. "Yes," I panted.

245

His fingers stilled. As did his hips. *Fuck.*

"Yes, *what?*"

A low, frustrated and supremely aroused growl rumbled from my chest. "Yes, *sir,*" I corrected. "All the fucking time. The other night I woke up after a dirty dream about you, and I got myself off to the things you wrote."

There was a pause for a moment, then his lips moved on my shoulder in another kiss. "Next time you do that," he told me in a hoarse whisper, "send me a video."

My brows hitched, but shit, I was game. "Done."

Seeming satisfied, his hands smoothed over my wet hips, gripping my ass in a way that might leave fingerprints. Then he slapped one of my cheeks hard enough to sting.

I let out a small yelp, and he hissed through his teeth at the way my cunt contracted. It was too much fun.

"Shit, Red," he groaned, smoothing his palm over my warm-ass cheek, his cock still buried deep within me. "You have no idea how bad I wanna fuck your ass right now."

Even if I wanted to lie to him, my body betrayed me as my pussy throbbed and tightened with excitement. He let out a low laugh, sliding his hand over my skin until his thumb stroked my back door, teasing.

Shit. Cass was going to be the death of me.

"Now I'm getting all sorts of ideas," he murmured like he was just thinking out loud. His hips started moving slowly, fucking me in shallow thrusts and making me squirm.

I groaned and pushed back onto him, encouraging him to fuck me properly, and his fingers bit into my hip, holding me firm.

"So impatient," he commented, slicking his fingertip over my ass and applying a little more pressure this time. Shit. Now I was thinking about waking Lucas up again…and asking him to come join us. Not that Cass would *ever* go for that, but the mental image was *so nice.*

When he finally decided to quit playing with me, he pulled his dick almost entirely out of my pussy. Then slammed back in hard, along with his finger in my ass.

"Fuck," I yelped, then braced my hands harder against the wall and hung on for dear life as he worked me over into a panting, shuddering mess as I came in long, drawn-out waves.

He waited until I was nearly done before finishing himself in several bone-rattling thrusts that buried his dick so far inside me I could practically taste it.

For an extended amount of time, we just stayed like that, our bodies locked together and plastered to the shower wall as the water continued to fall. Both of us were breathing hard, and I seriously questioned my ability to stand up straight if Cass were to let go. But he had no intention of letting go.

Gently, with one arm around my waist, he eased us back into the shower spray and rinsed me off all over again. This time he kicked his sodden boots off and stripped his jeans down to leave him gloriously naked for my admiration.

"I'm gonna need a closer look at this," I murmured, running my fingers down the side of his tattooed dick. "A *much* closer look."

A sly smile touched his lips. "I thought I was on your shit list, Red. Don't you want me to make it up to you first?"

He had a good point. I released his dick, and he scooped me up in his arms.

"What—" I started to protest, then cut myself off. Fuck it. I didn't need to ask dumb questions when I already knew perfectly well what he was doing.

He bumped the shower off with his hip, then stepped out and placed me down on the edge of the vanity. No words were uttered as he spread my legs apart with firm fingers on my thighs. His mouth locked with mine, our tongues tangling in a violent kiss that made me feel like we shared the same breath, then I slid my hand up the back of his neck to grip his hair.

I gave it a sharp tug, pulling his face back enough that I could meet his eyes. Then I shoved him to his knees in front of me.

Cass gave a cluck of his tongue, like I was going to make up for that move later, but he didn't argue, just hooked his hands under my thighs and yanked me to the edge of the vanity as he dove face-first into my pussy.

His tongue found my clit with shocking accuracy, and I tipped my head backward as my legs draped over his broad shoulders. I still fully intended to get to the bottom of his mysterious absence before morning. But sue me if I wanted to reap the benefits before starting that conversation.

Besides, somehow I knew Cass wouldn't truly hide anything from me anymore. If I asked, he would tell me everything. Our secret-keeping days were done.

CHAPTER 31

When I eventually fell asleep once more, I dreamed of stupid, meaningless things—wandering through the vineyard at Demi's winery in Tuscany and being chased by faceless men...but they weren't anyone I was afraid of. In my dreams I was full of happiness and light, laughing uncontrollably when one of them tackled me to the grass and his huge hands burrowed under my long, loose skirt as he showed me what it meant to be caught.

I woke up with a gasp as a hot, hard cock slid inside me, filling me up and making me moan. My legs wrapped around a firm waist, pulling me closer before my eyes even opened to meet Cass's dark gaze.

He didn't speak, just locked eyes with me, barely even blinking as he pumped between my legs, every thrust bringing me closer and closer to the orgasm that had started in my dreams. The command was clear, and I forced myself to keep my eyes open as I came, letting him see every damn corner of my soul while I shattered to pieces under him.

Only when my shudders subsided did his fierce expression change, and a smirk touched his lips as he fucked me faster and filled me up with his cum.

"You better have been dreaming about me, Red," he told me in a rough, sleep-thickened voice after rolling to the side. He tucked his arm around my waist, pulling me back into his chest as he kissed my bare shoulder.

We'd fallen asleep sometime before dawn after spending hours talking. Actually talking. It'd started out with casual pillow talk and sexy banter, but somehow morphed into a shockingly intimate discussion about our gang lives.

The secrets we'd shared would be enough to decimate either of our empires, but I wasn't even the slightest bit worried. Something I'd learned over the course of our discussion was that I trusted Cass, really trusted him, the way I trusted Zed. Maybe more, considering I still didn't trust Zed with my heart. Not anymore.

I gave a small laugh, kissing his forearm where he had it banded over my chest, holding me to him like he thought I might disappear any second if he let me go.

"None of your fucking business, Saint," I replied before gently biting his arm.

My stomach gave a loud grumble before he could respond to that taunt, and I realized how starving I was. Groaning, I rolled over in his arms and cupped my hands behind his neck to kiss him long and hard.

"As much as I love waking up with you like this," I whispered, feathering kisses over his cheek where a tiny tattoo was inked near the corner of his eye, "I'm fucking starving for something more filling than your cock."

Cass gave a mock gasp. "You take that back, Red," he growled. "My cock is more than filling." He kissed me back deeply, then released me with a sigh when my stomach continued grumbling. "Fine. Zed's going to blow a gasket when he figures out I broke into his fortress and spent the night buried between his woman's thighs."

I shot him a sharp glare as I climbed out of bed. "Excuse me? I'm not—"

"Aw." Cass wrinkled his nose and stretched out one of his long arms to pat me on the head. "You're still in denial. It's adorable."

He escaped out of the bedroom door a fraction of a second before the pillow I threw had landed. Lucky. Fucking Cass and Lucas were as bad as each other when it came to Zed and me. Almost felt like they'd discussed it.

Shaking my head, I hunted out some clean clothes, then headed to the bathroom to clean up the evidence of my wake-up call. Nothing worse than messing up a fresh pair of panties with sticky cum. Okay, that wasn't true. It was a million times worse to sneeze an hour later and realize you hadn't cleaned up that well.

Ugh. Dudes were so gross. Pity I was so addicted to the dick.

When I got downstairs to the kitchen, I found Cass sitting at the counter in his clothes from the night before—dry now, thanks to me making him put them in the dryer at some stage between him eating me out in the bathroom and me choking on his dick back in my bedroom.

Lucas was pouring coffee for everyone, yawning and looking gorgeously sleep-rumpled, and Zed was at the stove flipping pancakes.

For a second I paused in the doorway, taken aback by the strangely domestic scene the three of them cut. Then I noticed the angry set to Zed's jaw and the forceful way he slapped his spatula on the pancake he'd just flipped.

Cass had a decidedly smug look on his face as Lucas handed him a coffee, not to mention the swelling in his lower lip where I'd bitten him a little hard last night. Good thing his tattoos covered the rest of the marks I'd left.

As for Lucas...

"Good morning, babe." He greeted me with a kiss and a cup of coffee. Then he kissed me again deeper, his hand grabbing a handful of my ass as he took his time. "I missed you when I woke up." He whispered this in my ear, and my cheeks flamed hot.

Zed dropped a fry pan onto the stove with a clatter and glared at me. "Can I have a word in private, Boss?"

Crap. I'd completely forgotten Cass saying he'd found one of our Wolves in possession of PCP last night.

"Yep," I replied with a nod, stepping away from Lucas's hold.

Zed stormed past us, leading the way through the house to his home office, which he rarely used. I reluctantly followed, knowing he was about to lay on a guilt trip that I rightfully deserved. I'd dropped my responsibilities last night in exchange for some dick. Seriously mind-blowingly good dick, mind you. But still unacceptable for someone in my position. People depended on my leadership. There was more at stake in the success of the Timberwolves than just money.

He slammed the office door shut after me, and I arched a brow at him. Yes, I deserved a bit of attitude for dropping the ball, but—

"We need to talk," Zed snapped.

"We do," I agreed. "Who was it?"

He jerked around to face me from where he'd started to pace. The expression on his face was complete confusion. "Who was what?"

I frowned back at him. "The kid caught with angel dust at Anarchy. Had he already been cleared by Alexi?"

Zed blinked at me a moment. Then shook his head. "That's not what I wanted to talk about."

"Oh." I rubbed the bridge of my nose, thrown off. "So, what do we need to talk about?"

The look he gave me said that he was actually questioning my intelligence for a hot second, but then he closed the gap between us in three strides and grabbed my waist with both hands, holding me close as his chest rose with an emotion-heavy breath.

"I want you to do me a favor, Dare," he said in a rough voice. "For thirty seconds, *thirty seconds only*, I want you to be perfectly honest with me. Will you do that? Will you give me just thirty seconds of raw honesty?"

There was so much vulnerability and desperation in his voice that there was no way I could even considering denying such a simple request. So I looped my arms around his neck, hugging him back as I nodded. "Of course, Zed. Whatever you want to know..." I shrugged. Whatever he wanted to know I was happy to tell him because it killed me when we hid things from each other anyway.

But instead of asking me a question, he carefully, deliberately, placed his lips against mine. I froze, confused as hell, then I finally understood what was going on. He didn't want my honesty in mere words that could be so easily twisted and misinterpreted. He wanted my truth in actions. He wanted to feel it in my kiss.

And I'd agreed. Because he was one of the few people on the planet who I truly loved, so I couldn't... There was no way I could deny his request. So I kissed him back.

As I responded, kissing him exactly the way I'd been quietly wanting to do for longer than I cared to admit, the tension noticeably dissolved out of his tightly wound frame. He melted into my touch, his arms sweeping around my waist as he pulled me closer and groaned when my teeth scraped his lower lip.

He'd asked me for thirty seconds of honesty, and that's what I gave him—or thereabouts. Then I pulled on my deepest well of strength and pushed him away, breaking our kiss.

"Did you get the answer you wanted?" I asked him in a hoarse whisper.

His eyes flashed with anger and frustration, and he jerked a nod. "And then some."

Fuck me, my nipples were hard to the point of painful as I stared back at him while mentally scolding my pussy for getting so wet over one kiss.

"Good." I licked my lips and folded my arms. "Then don't do it again."

Zed stared at me for a long moment, disbelief written all over his face. Then he gave a short, humorless laugh. "I never took you for a masochist, Dare."

He didn't mean it in the physical sense, but that was how I chose to interpret. "Well then, I guess you don't know me as well as you think." I quirked a brow, thinking about how good it felt when Cass smacked my ass or slammed me against a wall.

Zed shook his head, his eyes blazing with fury. "You can't keep pretending there's nothing more between us, Dare. This is too real."

I tilted my chin up, stubborn as fuck. "I can, Zed, and I will. I won't lose my best friend over this. I won't ruin what we've got by mixing sex into the equation."

He groaned, stepping closer again, and cupped my face in his hand. "It's already ruined, Dare." His voice was husky and raw. Honest. "I can't ignore the way I feel about you, and in case you missed the point here, let me spell it out. I don't just love you. I'm *in* love with you. No amount of hardheaded denial will change that. Neither will the added complications in the kitchen right now."

Panic chased through me, elevating my heart rate and making my palms sweat. I parted my lips, ready to disagree with everything he'd just said, but he was quicker.

"Don't even think about denying the truth of that statement either," he murmured, smoothing his thumb over my lower lip in a move that echoed all the way down to my pussy. "I know you feel the same way."

"Since when were we in a position to get everything we want, Zed?" I asked with an edge of bitterness. "And really? Right now? This is the moment you choose to confess your feelings for me after *all* the years we've had together? You wait until some fucking ghost of my ex is waging war on my empire and two other men are vying for my affections? And you thought... Shit, why not?"

He withdrew slightly, frowning his objection. "What? That

had nothing—" He cut himself off with a sigh and stepped away to run a hand over his short hair. "Yeah, actually, you know what? Yes. Now. Because without all those extenuating circumstances, nothing would have changed. It probably would have taken me years to confess how I felt because I knew that I had your heart. You may have been fucking other guys, but you didn't care about them. You didn't trust them. You didn't *love* any of them."

My brows shot up so high they almost flew off my face. "I don't love anyone else *now*."

He blinked at me. "Don't you?"

It wasn't a question, it was a challenge.

I scowled. "This is childish, Zed. Quit pushing me on this, or you'll push me away entirely."

His jaw tightened, and the muscles in his neck tensed. "Fine. Ball's in your court, Dare." I started to leave the office, but he stopped me when my hand was on the door handle. "But in the meantime I'd ask a courtesy from you. As my friend, of course."

My eyes narrowed as I turned back to face him. "Of course." I gritted the words out with heavy sarcasm. "What's the favor?"

He cocked one brow at me. "Don't fuck them in my house. If I have to spend one more morning lying in bed listening to you come on another man's dick..." He let his voice trail off with a short laugh, shaking his head in disbelief as he stepped closer once again.

Stubborn as ever, I met his gaze and raised my chin defiantly. "And if I do? What will you do about it, *friend*?"

A sly smile tweaked his lips as he braced his hands to either side of me on the door. Two months ago I'd have punched him for such a deliberately imposing move, and if anyone else had done it, I might have shot them. Yet now...now I was having a hard time convincing my pussy she wasn't about to meet any new friends today.

"The next time I hear you moaning and panting while you ride some other guy's dick?" He leaned in closer, his face right beside mine as he whispered his threat…or promise. "I'll have to come in and join you." He moved away again and shot me a knowing wink. "Food for thought…friend."

CHAPTER 32

After my little chat with Zed, I lost a good portion of my appetite. I mean, not enough that I pulled a dumb-girl move like skipping the meal entirely, but I was woman enough to admit the food didn't sit as comfortably as I'd have liked. Not with all the eyes on me making me squirm.

It made me seriously question what the actual fuck I'd been thinking by getting so intricately tangled up with *three* men at such a god-awful time for my personal and professional life. But then Lucas stretched and his shirt rose up to show off his deep V and chiseled abs and I nearly choked on my coffee.

Yeah. That'd do it.

My phone rang somewhere in the living room, so I made a speedy exit out of the kitchen to answer it. When I saw it was my new lawyer calling, I swallowed a groan of dread.

Still, I took the call and brought the phone to my ear. "Gen, what's new?"

"I'm at Pink Panther," she told me, naming one of my smaller clubs in Shadow Grove. It had formerly been a sports bar, and I hadn't done a whole lot to change it up. Hell, it wasn't even a Copper Wolf venue; it was just a Timberwolf bar and infrequently visited by anyone outside the Wolves.

It also wasn't open at this time of day. "Why?" I asked, anxiety twisting my stomach.

She breathed a sigh. "You'd better get down here," she told me. In the background I heard the distinctive sound of police sirens and I stiffened. "I tried to handle things as best I could, but…this is getting a bit beyond my abilities, Boss."

As new as Gen was to my company, she'd slotted in effortlessly, so much so that sometimes I forgot just how fresh she was.

"I'm on my way," I told her, rushing back through to the kitchen to wave a hand at Zed. "Give me the key points I need to know, Gen."

Zed gave me a nod of understanding, and I raced back upstairs to get dressed with Gen on speakerphone outlining how an "anonymous tip" to the SGPD had resulted in an early morning raid of the club. They hadn't found the guns and cocaine that the tip had promised, but there was a hefty package of PCP found stashed inside an empty beer keg.

"Fuck," I swore as I ended the call to Gen. I hurried my ass back downstairs, clipping on my gun holster on the way and holding my high heels in my fingers to put on in the car. I'd done the bare minimum on makeup, favoring speed over perfection but enough that I was fully put-together for anyone searching out cracks in my armor.

Cass was waiting in the foyer when I reached the ground floor, and I could see Zed's Ferrari already idling out the open front door.

"Need backup?" Cass asked, quirking that scarred brow I liked so much.

I flashed him a quick grin. "Nah. Only if I need an alibi for my whereabouts last night." I meant it as a joke, but then realized I might actually need it and grimaced.

Cass gave a short nod. "Understood. I'll take the Gumdrop to do something productive while you're gone."

I rose up on my toes to smack a kiss on his lips in thanks. He wasn't babysitting Lucas; he was taking a worry off my plate. And I doubted Lucas's safety was going to *not* be a worry for me anytime soon. Not with Chase, or Wenton, still gunning for me.

"You're the best, Saint."

He huffed. "Thank me later, Angel."

I hurried through the front door and found Lucas talking to Zed beside the open driver's door of the Ferrari. As I approached, Zed handed Lucas a Glock 19 and gave him some firm order that had Lucas glancing back up at Cass. No doubt Zed was instructing him to get lessons from my Grumpy Cat.

For all his macho bullshit in his office this morning, Zed didn't actually want Lucas to wind up dead. And I appreciated that.

"Stay safe, okay?" I told Lucas when he turned to me with a reassuring smile.

He nodded, holding the gun carefully at his side. "I'll be fine. *You* stay safe." He leaned down and kissed me quickly, then jogged back into the house where Cass was waiting for him.

Zed and I slid into the car, and he gunned it out of his driveway, only pausing for the front gates on their painfully slow motor.

"Where are we going?" he asked, not having heard my call with Gen. He'd jumped into action with just that one wave and look from me, not second-guessing me for even a moment.

"Pink Panther," I told him with a frustrated sigh. "Apparently a sizable package of PCP was found there this morning after an anonymous tip to the SGPD." He gave me an incredulous look, and I scoffed a humorless laugh. "My thoughts exactly. Gen was trying to handle it for us, but she's in over her head."

Zed jerked a nod of understanding. "Well, I have to say"—a smug grin pulled at his lips—"I'm pretty glad I went ahead and installed those surveillance cameras last month."

I rolled my eyes, biting back a grin. He'd suspected someone on the staff at Pink Panther had been smoking in the storeroom, which kept fucking with our fire sensors. So he'd installed hidden cameras to find the culprit, and I'd told him it was overkill because we had bigger problems on our plate.

The shithead was going to be so damn smug if those cameras found whoever had really planted the angel dust on my property. Then again, I'd rather deal with smug Zed than go to jail for an obvious setup like this.

This was unlikely to be the last attempt at framing me for shit, though, so we needed to tighten security on *all* of our properties, which was going to become a hell of a job for Dallas, seeing as I wasn't sure who the fuck else to trust these days. At least with him, I felt secure in the knowledge he was too intelligent to be manipulated by Chase—or Wenton. I'd already rescued him once from the Wraiths; he'd have to be a total idiot to double-cross me now, not with a baby and defenseless wife at home.

The vibe between Zed and me remained strictly business as we made our way across Shadow Grove to the Pink Panther. That we could switch back into Timberwolf mode so easily and leave the emotional crap at home gave me some small glimmer of hope.

When we arrived, several cop cars with their lights flashing sat in the parking lot, while a multitude of uniformed officers milled around the property. Gen was standing near her sensible white Lexus, her arms folded under her breasts and her toe tapping the concrete in irritation as she spoke to one of the officers. Her face brightened when she spotted Zed and me, though, and the cop turned to look at where she was nodding.

"Well, well, well, if it isn't Detective Douchebag," Zed crowed, rubbing his palms together as he approached the uniformed officer in a menacing way. "Why am I not surprised to find you harassing our newest team member?"

Officer Shane Randall—who was not a detective and clearly sour about that fact—scowled at Zed, then gave me a respectful nod. "Hades, we didn't expect you to show up in person."

Gen clucked her tongue in frustration. "I *told* you I'd called her. You simply didn't listen."

Officer Randall flicked an annoyed glare at Gen, then shifted his attention back to me. "Well, if your new employee has already filled you in, I'm sure you understand why we will need you to come in for questioning regarding the large supply of drugs found on your premises."

"I'll be doing nothing of the sort, Shane," I responded in a cool tone, kicking one brow up. "These sloppy frame jobs are starting to leave a sour taste in my mouth." I indicated for Zed to head inside. He could retrieve the camera footage from the closed-circuit recording, and I had no doubt he could handle anyone who wanted to try to stop him.

Officer Randall gave me a tight, humorless smile. "I don't know what you're talking about, Hades. This was on an anonymous tip, and—"

I cut him off with a scoff of laughter. "Your acting skills need some work too. Don't worry, we've got this one handled." I smiled wide, full of confidence because when Zed installed those cameras a month ago, the storeroom had been cleared entirely for a deep clean. Whoever placed the drugs *would* be on that recording, clearing us of culpability.

Officer Randall glared death back at me, hooking his thumbs into his gun belt, which was cute, considering how I could probably shoot him three times before he even pulled his weapon out.

"Gen, you can head home if you want," I offered my legal counsel. "We'll be done here shortly. Shane needs to try harder next time. His boss will be so displeased with this failure."

Zed came striding back across the parking lot, a satisfied smirk on his lips and a thumb drive between his fingers.

"Sorry that took a hot second," he said, reaching us and handing the USB drive to me.

"What were you—" Officer Randall started to ask, but Zed cut him off with a finger over his lips.

"Shush, Detective Douchebag. The adults are talking."

Shane smacked Zed's hand away from his face and glared pure venom at us both. "Touch me again and I'll—"

"You'll do *nothing*, Shane," I told him in a glacially cold voice. "The only reason you're still alive right now is because you serve a purpose. Don't test me, or you can join your brother in the underworld."

Officer Randall's face reddened with anger, but he wasn't smart enough to talk his way out of this situation. He used to be on the Wraiths' payroll and had close ties to Madison Kate's deranged stalker. We let him live because we knew how dirty he was. It was like a flashing neon sign screaming that a case or a crime scene was being meddled with by someone outside my organization.

"Gen, can I borrow your tablet?" Zed asked politely, and our lawyer quickly pulled the device from her handbag to hand over. When her fingers brushed Zed's on the handover, her eyes widened and a flirtatious smile touched her lips for a split second before she wiped it clear.

Shit. Gen was crushing on Zed.

Like a secure, well-adjusted adult, I shoved aside the niggle of territorial jealousy and focused on the current situation. Zed plugged his drive into the tablet and brought up the recording on the screen.

He must have already done a quick scan for our culprit while he was inside because he navigated the video to a precise point from just twenty-four hours earlier.

"Here we go," he announced, hitting the play button. The storeroom was brought up in color—as it'd been daytime when the recording took place—and showed stacks of liquor stock in cartons and a neat pile of beer kegs in the corner.

A moment after the recording started, the door opened and our regular delivery guy wheeled in a cart with three fresh kegs stacked up on it. He took them over to the side of the storeroom, unloaded them, then started loading the empty ones onto his cart.

Then someone else entered the room wearing a ball cap and carrying a sports bag over his shoulder. The newcomer went straight to the "official" security camera in the opposite corner to where Zed's extra camera was placed and switched it off before exchanging some words with the delivery guy.

Money changed hands, then the delivery dude left with only two of the three empty kegs. Alone, the second man quickly closed the storeroom door, then placed his bag down on the floor and unzipped it. From it, he pulled a large package that I could only assume to be the PCP in question. He unscrewed the top of one of the empty kegs, dropped the wrapped package inside, then closed it up again.

Just as he exited the room, he turned and gave Zed's extra camera a full view of his face. Which Zed paused the video on.

"Uh-oh," he murmured, sarcastic as fuck. "He looks familiar."

Officer Randall let out a string of curses, and I arched a questioning brow at Zed. He just shot me a secretive wink, and Shane bellowed across the parking lot, shouting for one of the officers on-site.

My brows rose in surprise, and I gave Zed a look. "Seriously? That's ballsy."

He smirked. "On my way in I spotted him looking sketchy as hell as he pretended to search through the bar stock. It was easy enough to guess the drugs would have been planted recently. They wouldn't risk them sitting there to be found by anyone else."

Gen gaped. "That was really smart thinking, Zayden."

I bit the inside of my cheek to keep from reacting. Zed was watching me for it, too, that prick. I bet he was already fully aware Gen had the hots for him, too. He was *always* aware of women's attention.

"Looks like someone isn't going quietly," I commented,

nodding at the entrance where an officer had just tried to make a break for it, only to be tackled by another of his colleagues. The quick-thinking officer knelt on the slimy bastard's back and cuffed him, his movements rough as he relieved the suspect of his gun belt and jerked him to his feet.

Officer Randall took over, pushing the drug carrier across the parking lot to one of the squad cars, then locking him inside. He stomped back over to where we stood watching, amused as hell, and his face was like pure thunder.

The other cop—the one who'd tackled our drug planter—was shouting commands for the other cops to clear out of my bar, and they were scurrying like rats.

"Look," Officer Randall snapped, coming back to stand in front of us with his hands tightly balled at his sides. "I've made mistakes in the past, and I'm well aware of that. But for what it's worth"—he dropped his tone lower, keeping the volume down so only we could hear—"I'm not as dirty as you think. This setup wasn't me."

I pursed my lips, giving him a long look. "Why do you feel the need to tell me this, Officer Randall?"

His face darkened like it was physically paining him to admit fault. "Because some bad shit is going down, and I'd rather be on your side. I'm *trying*."

I tipped my head to the squad car one of his own colleagues was currently locked up in and gave him a pointed look. "Seems to me like you could be trying harder, Shane."

The officer just grunted and held out his hand to Zed for the thumb drive. My second gave a laugh and shook his head, though.

"Sorry, Detective Douche, I think I'll hand-deliver this to your captain after I send myself and the commissioner some copies. Can't be too careful when it comes to the SGPD, now, can we?" Zed smirked and tucked the thumb drive into his pocket.

Officer Randall just gave an exasperated sound and stomped off back toward his squad car.

The uniformed officer who'd done the tackling strode over to us when most of the cop cars started departing my parking lot. He held his hand out for me to shake, his eye contact steady.

Curious, I shook his hand and gave him a mental check mark for not going limp-wristed when shaking hands with a woman.

"Hades," he greeted me in a gruff voice, "I apologize for meeting you under these circumstances. I'm Lieutenant Jeffries. We've spoken once by phone."

He was a bulky, middle-aged Black man with a face that seemed to be permanently creased into a frown, but based on the way he held eye contact, either he was the best actor I'd met to date or he had nothing to hide.

Dear lord. Had I just met SGPD's first totally uncorrupt cop? He was a recent transfer from out of state, so maybe it was possible.

Nah. Some things were too preposterous to suspend disbelief over.

"Lovely to meet you in person, Lieutenant Jeffries," I responded with an indifferent expression. "I'll send over an invoice for any damages your men caused here today. I trust that won't be an issue for you."

His eyes tightened, but he jerked a nod. "Understood," he muttered. "I look forward to a peaceful working relationship with your company in the future, Hades. Hopefully, this hasn't discolored that." He indicated the Pink Panther and the fact that an officer on his team had been the one to plant the drugs.

"We'll see," I replied, tilting my head to the side and holding his stare without blinking or smiling.

The lieutenant delivered a few polite greetings to Zed and Gen, then gracefully excused himself from our company.

He drove away with a small wave, and the three of us remained in the parking lot until he disappeared into the distance.

"Holy shit," Gen said on a long exhale. "I had no idea how I was going to get you out of that drug charge. Maybe I'm not experienced enough for this role after all."

"Nah," Zed replied before I could. "You're still new. You'll learn."

Gen gave him a bashful smile, and I tried really hard not to side-eye Zed. The shithead was trying to play me, and it wasn't going to work.

"Actually, while I have you both here..." Gen slid her tablet back into her bag and tucked the strap over her arm. "I heard a rumor about why Allied Insurance rejected your claim on 7th Circle. But it's just a rumor right now. I'm trying to gather hard supporting evidence of this."

"Spit it out," I ordered, my tone slightly harsher than it needed to be. Goddamn Zed flashed me a look, too, and I groaned inwardly. "We tend to find where there's smoke, there's fire," I explained, evening my tone out.

Gen nodded her agreement. "Well, apparently the FBI is looking into you as a person of interest. The fire investigation ruled it arson—of course—and someone's pointing the finger at you. Especially with your building being bombed, too. All the detonation points were on your parking level, you were identified at the scene..." She let her voice trail off with a shrug.

I quirked one brow. "I thought you handled that."

"I did," she responded quickly. "But this is some other department. Like I said, it's all just rumor for now. I'll keep my eye on things, but in the meantime, just...be careful."

I kept my expression neutral as I thanked her and walked back over to Zed's Ferrari, but internally I was rolling my eyes. No shit, Gen. All I'd ever done in my whole freaking life was be careful and cover my ass. I wasn't about to stop now, no matter what the distractions were like.

CHAPTER 33

My phone buzzed with a text message as Zed and I were leaving Pink Panther. A flash of panic jolted through me when I saw it was from Cass, and I held my breath as I opened it up.

Cass: Taking Gumdrop to the range at SS KJ-Fit.

I wrinkled my nose, trying to understand. Then it clicked that he meant the newly opened MMA gym on the south side of Shadow Grove. Kody had bought an old rifle range with a huge warehouse space and had converted it into his newest branch of KJ-Fit, complete with a parkour course and shooting range.

"Cass is taking Lucas to the southside KJ-Fit," I told Zed.

He gave a lopsided smirk. "Probably decided to teach him how to shoot. You want to head over there? Been a while since we've tested our marksmanship."

Oh man, I could never say no to a challenge like that. "You're on. I bet you're rusty as fuck. When's the last time you even needed to shoot someone?"

Zed scoffed. "Seriously? Last night. Trust me, if one of us is rusty, it ain't me."

"Bet me on it, then." I cocked my head and gave him a challenging grin. "If you're so confident, lay down some odds."

He gave me a sharp look, like he wasn't sure if I was being serious, then gave a soft laugh and shook his head. "All right, smart-ass. Hope you and your big-dick energy are ready to be taken down a notch."

"Cute. That won't be happening." I grinned because out of everyone... Yeah, Zed *could* beat me on this. He was an impeccable marksman, one of the best. And it had been a decently long time since I'd actually practiced at a range.

He shrugged. "Well then, you'll have nothing to worry about. Of course, if you lose..." He hummed as he thought up an appropriate punishment. "If you lose, then you have to learn a routine from Maxine and perform at Club 22 on a Friday night."

My brows shot right up into my hair. "What? No." Maxine was one of our senior dancers at Club 22. Senior in that she had been with us for the longest, not that she was old. Hell, she was probably younger than me. She was crazy popular, though, and headlined our Friday night shows, making them a packed crowd week after week.

"No?" Zed smirked. "Guess you're not so confident after all. Tell you what, if I lose, I'll do the same."

My lips parted in surprise. But...shit. That was too good to pass up, wasn't it? Beat Zed in a target-shooting competition and see him shake his ass onstage? Maybe Lucas could give him some tips.

"In Maxine's costume?" I taunted, pushing the bet even further.

Zed laughed. "Deal. Sequined nipple pasties and all."

I groaned. "Something tells me this is a bad idea...but you're on, De Rosa. I hope you've been paying attention to Lucas's moves because there's no way in hell I'm losing now."

He just grinned, his eyes on the road ahead of us. Smug fuck was *so* confident he could win. I might have to play dirty.

Leaning forward, I cranked up his stereo to eliminate any more talking. I wouldn't put it past Zed to try some psychological warfare to get into my head before we reached the range. I mean, I would have done the same, if not for the fact that right now it was likely to backfire on me.

We arrived at KJ-Fit half an hour later and parked beside Cass's bike. I squinted at it, then noted two helmets. Too. Freaking. Cute. I was actually devastated I'd missed seeing Lucas curled around Cass like that. Oh hell yeah, that was a mental image to file for later.

Zed gave me a knowing look, then led the way inside the warehouse, where we found a group of sweaty dudes standing around and EDM music booming from the speakers. It wasn't hard to spot what they were watching.

Above a thick crash pad in the gymnastics area, a shirtless Lucas hung from a wide bar, nine feet in the air, as he worked his way through a seriously impressive aerial routine, spinning, flipping, letting go, and catching himself over the horizontal bar like something out of the Olympics…which he had been training for. His muscles bunched and flexed as he smoothly transitioned through moves in time to the music, his face set with concentration and a ball cap somehow staying tucked backward on his head throughout.

I wanted to scold him for disobeying doctor's orders *yet again*, but at the same time I just wanted to stand there and gape at his skill—and his body—like the other spectators. So I just brushed past a couple of the guys who were calling out encouragement and glared up at him with my arms folded over my chest.

"Oh shit," Lucas muttered, locking eyes with me and knowing damn well he was in trouble. He swung around the bar a couple of times, then executed a flawless dismount onto the mat. "Hey, babe!"

Several of the guys watching had scurried back to their own workouts when they'd spotted Zed and me enter, but a couple were still standing around and gaped in shock at Lucas calling me *babe*.

Which he made worse by crossing the mat and stooping down

to kiss me straight on the lips. Yes, I probably could have avoided it. But I didn't want to. I loved Lucas's free and easy affections. He didn't give two shits what my reputation said about me because he *knew me*.

"You're in trouble, Wilder," I muttered when he released my lips. "Where's Cass?"

"He's over at the range talking to some dude from his gang. Hey, did you know I'm a natural at the whole shooting thing?" He grinned, clearly proud of himself, and I gave him a suspicious frown.

"Sure you are, Gumdrop," Zed replied, clapping Lucas on one sweaty shoulder. "Come on, Hades, we've got a bet to settle." He said that last part loud enough to draw the attention of literally *everyone* within earshot, and I glowered at his back. Prick was deliberately drawing a crowd to try to throw me off my game.

"What's your bet?" Lucas asked, walking beside me as I followed Zed through the massive gym to the far door leading to the shooting range.

I cast another look at him, taking in the backward cap, the low-slung black sweatpants with sneakers, the bare chest—albeit marked up with scars now. Goddamn, he was gorgeous. "Uh, Zed and I are just having a friendly wager on who has sharper targeting."

Lucas's eyes widened, and his smile hitched wider. "Well, shit. This will be entertaining. What's the bet?"

I groaned. "Just trust me when I say you want me to win this." Not that I was insecure with my body or my ability to learn Maxine's routine—I was a decent dancer and confident enough to strip on stage—but I *really* wanted to make Zed do it. Just the mental image of him in a sequined G-string and nipple covers had me giggling internally.

We found Cass just inside the range, chatting with a tatted-up older dude cleaning a series of handguns on the table in front of him.

"Saint," I snapped, my voice cracking through the space. His head jerked up, his eyes meeting mine instantly. "A word."

He inclined his head in acknowledgment, then excused himself from the conversation he'd been having. His strides were long and lazy as he closed the space between us, his gaze predatory.

"Hades," he politely greeted me, like we were nothing more than professional acquaintances. He tipped his head, indicating we head through the fire exit door so we could speak privately, seeing as we had plenty of eyes on us already after Damn Zed announcing to the whole damn gym that we had a bet.

I waved a hand, telling Cass to go first, and I followed him. When we stepped outside, I pulled the door shut behind us to cut us off from everyone inside.

"You okay?" he rumbled, closing the gap between us and sliding one of his huge hands into the back of my hair. "You look tense."

I glared up at him but slipped my hands under his shirt to grip his waist and pull him closer. "I *am* tense," I replied. "I just found Lucas showing off his gymnastic skills in the gym and potentially messing up his internal stitches. I thought you were teaching him how to shoot?"

A dark, sexy look flashed over Cass's face, and he tugged on my hair gently. "I was going to."

"So what happened?" I asked, tilting my chin up. Fuck, I wanted to kiss him. When did I become so obsessed with this huge, grumpy fuck? When did he start smiling more? It was totally intoxicating.

"What happened at your venue? Seemed serious when you left with Zed." He gripped my hair tighter, brushing his lips over mine teasingly and making my whole body quake.

"Cass," I breathed. "Are you going to kiss me or just tease?"

He huffed a short laugh, then quit messing around. His lips coaxed mine apart, his fingers in my hair controlling my head as his tongue lashed against mine and his huge frame crashed me against the door.

I arched my back, leaning in to him as he kissed me breathless, my short fingernails clawing at his muscular back as I lamented all the clothing between us.

"Christ, Red." He broke away from my lips with a groan. "You're the sweetest addiction, you know that?" He stroked his thumb down the side of my face, then dragged it across my lower lip. His dark gaze locked on my mouth, and I knew his thoughts were just as sordid as my own. The thick hardness between us spoke volumes, and I was so incredibly tempted to drop to my knees right there in the service road between warehouses.

"Rain check this," I told him, reaching between us to squeeze his dick. "What happened with Lucas?"

Cass grunted but didn't move away. He just braced his forearms on the door to either side of my head and held my gaze steadily. "Turns out he already knew how to shoot. He's no Zayden De Rosa, but he's sure as fuck no amateur. He knew exactly what he was doing—good stance, good grip, wasn't affected by recoil like anyone shooting for the first time should be—until I handed him an unloaded gun. Either he's a great actor or he's never loaded a magazine. Strange as fuck, Red."

I wrinkled my nose. "He never mentioned learning how to shoot."

Cass arched a brow. "He says he hasn't, just that he played a lot of video games as a kid."

"Speaking of Zayden De Rosa," I muttered, "I made a bet with him. Any chance I can get you to cause a distraction when he shoots? I'm quickly losing confidence that I can win this."

Cass pulled back a few inches, his eyes widening slightly. "Oh, this is going to be interesting." He ran a hand over his short beard, a touch of a smirk twisting his lips. "I'll see what I can do."

Flashing him a grin, I smacked a quick kiss against his lips. "You're the best, Saint."

He let out a low, primal growl and bit my neck slightly harder than teasing. "Don't you fucking forget it either, Angel."

Grinning, I pushed him away so I could open the door, and he took a second to adjust his pants to try to hide his boner before following me back inside the shooting range.

Zed was already chatting with one of the staff as he set up two targets for us, looking relaxed as all hell. Shit, he'd totally played me.

"Ready, Boss?" he asked with a confident grin.

I rolled my eyes. "Actually, I want to see Lucas shoot first. Our bet can wait a couple of minutes, right?"

"I'm not going anywhere," Zed replied, his voice loaded with meaning. "I'll wait as long as it takes...to win."

I scowled at him, letting him know I hadn't missed the double entendre, then waved Lucas closer.

"All right, Wild Child," I teased, "show me what you've got." I nodded to one of the fresh targets that had just been set up.

Cass handed Lucas the Glock that Zed had given him earlier in the day, and I watched Lucas carefully as he handled it comfortably. There was no awkwardness in his grip and no uncertainty in his posture as he stepped into position.

I shot Cass a look, and he just raised his brows as if to say *See what I mean?*

"Here," I said to Lucas, snagging a pair of earmuffs from a hook and slipping them over his ears. He gave me a smile of thanks, and I put a pair on myself before he took aim and started shooting.

As Lucas took his first shots, Zed's posture shifted, his spine stiffening and his attention becoming more focused. Lucas finished and placed his gun to the side, then pressed the button to return his target for assessment. I doubted Zed was any more surprised than me to see the accuracy of his shots on the paper target.

They weren't perfect by any means, but they were *good*. Far too good for a first-time shooter.

"Lucas..." I tugged my earmuffs off and frowned at the hole-filled paper.

"I have no idea," he told me before I could fully formulate my question. "I swear, I've never shot a real gun before. Like I told Cass earlier, I used to be crazy obsessed with this first-person shooter game my uncle gave me as a kid. It came with a pretty realistic gun controller, and I got decently good at it." He shrugged. "This just seems super similar, that's all."

Zed and I shared a look at Lucas's explanation, and Zed ran a hand over his head. "What was the game?" he asked.

Lucas shrugged. "It was something with a futuristic or sci-fi vibe. *Project X* or *Code Gray* or something like that. I dunno. Why? You wanna get it to improve your rusty marksmanship?"

Zed glowered, and I bit back a snicker of amusement.

"If you think of the name, I'd like to check it out," I told him with a hand on his still bare chest. "Now, could you pretty please put a shirt on so I can beat Zed in this dumb bet?"

Zed scoffed a laugh, swapping out Lucas's target for a fresh one. "Oh, now it's a dumb bet, huh?"

I scowled in his direction. "Shut up and shoot, De Rosa."

From the corner of my eye, I spotted Lucas talking to Cass as he pulled his T-shirt on and Cass's vaguely surprised gaze flicking over at me. What in the shit were they discussing?

"Ladies first," Zed said in a quiet purr, indicating to the fresh target back in place at the far end of the room. "Best of three? Otherwise this will be over way too quick."

I narrowed my eyes, searching his face for whatever fucking tricks he had up his sleeve. As always, though, he gave nothing away. So I gritted my teeth and stepped up to the same place Lucas had just shot from. I still wore my high heels but didn't bother taking them off. I actually had better aim while wearing them because that's what I was used to.

Planting my feet shoulder-width apart, I slid my earmuffs back on and drew my Desert Eagle from my underarm holster.

Before I raised it to aim, though, Lucas brushed up against my back as he reached past me to grab his earmuffs where he'd left them on the little hook. I tipped one of my ear covers off slightly and gave him a curious frown.

"Sorry, babe," he murmured. "Left these here." His arm brushed mine as he leaned in closer. "Also, you look so fucking sexy right now all I can think about is bending you over this little bench and fucking you from behind." He whispered the sexy confession right against my ear, and an instinctual shiver ran through me, ending right in my pussy, which throbbed in excitement. "Anyway, I'll let you get on with it," he said, brushing a kiss over my cheek. "Good luck, Hayden."

Crap. Hearing my name on his lips like that was such a fucking turn-on.

I swallowed heavily as I resituated my earmuffs and focused on the target ahead of me. There was no real need for fucking around with lining up my sight and shit; this was all second nature to me now, just a simple matter of raise my weapon, aim, fire. Over and over.

When I was done, I placed my gun down, pulled my earmuffs off, and hit the button to return my target to me.

"Not bad," Zed commented, standing all up in my personal space as the target whizzed back toward us. "I mean, you're definitely a bit rusty. But I think we all are. We haven't been practicing anywhere near as much as we used to."

The mocking in his tone was so thick I wanted to punch him in the mouth. I wasn't going to bite, though. There were countless eyes on us from the viewing window on the side that led to the main gym, and even here we needed to maintain our professional, united front.

"Shut up," I muttered. "Your turn."

I pulled my target sheet down as Zed stepped up to his own alley and started firing almost instantly, not even taking a few seconds to get in the zone.

Sure enough, he won that round. Not by much…but a win was a win. Mother*fucker*.

We reset both our targets, and I stepped up once more. This time, Cass positioned himself right in my peripheral vision, leaning on the bench a couple of alleys down from where I was shooting.

I could feel the intensity of his gaze, and when he cupped his junk—seemingly just to rearrange the crown jewels—I simmered with annoyance. Those bastards had ganged up against me. Somehow, probably while I was outside with Cass, Zed had swayed Lucas over to the side of evil. And Lucas had convinced Cass. Those fuckers were trying to throw my concentration, and it was working.

My glower in Cass's direction told him I was well aware of what he was doing, but he just shrugged and gave me one of his sly, sexy-as-hell smirks.

"You gonna shoot any time soon?" Zed teased from my other side. "Pretty sure the range is due to close any minute now."

Flipping him off, I set my feet, raised my gun, and squeezed off a series of shots that already felt better than my first round. Thank fuck Zed had suggested best of three.

He fired his rounds while my target returned to me so we could compare them simultaneously. When we determined that I'd won that round—by the most minuscule of margins—Zed shot an accusing glare in Cass's direction.

"Don't blame him," I scolded him. "You should be trying to win on your own merits, not trying to derail me."

Zed arched a brow, then inclined his head. "Fair enough. Last round." He extended his hand, indicating for me to shoot once more. Except this time as I brushed past him to take my place, he paused me with a hand on my waist. "I'm really looking forward to seeing you on that stage, *friend*. You can't imagine the number of times I've pictured you taking your clothes off for me."

His fingers stroked over my stomach, somehow finding a sliver of bare skin where my blouse had come untucked, and I needed to clench my jaw to hold back the hypersexed groan that wanted to escape in response to that touch.

Fuck. He had me this time.

I stepped up to my mark, but my focus was shot to hell. All I could picture was what it'd be like to strip for Zed. Would he sit back and watch or want to lay his hands all over me as I danced? I knew he had an exhibitionism kink, but would he also enjoy watching me with other guys? Would he get hard watching me grind on Lucas? On Cass?

Shit.

We shot off our last rounds simultaneously, and our targets whizzed back to us just a split second apart. I only needed one glance at Zed's smug fucking face to know he'd won.

"Fucking hell," Lucas commented, inspecting the six targets all lined up on the table. "You two are insane. Zed won this by less than a millimeter. That's scary-perfect precision."

Cass gave a huff of a laugh. "There's a reason Zayden De Rosa was offered a place in the Guild, Gumdrop, and it wasn't for that handsome face of his."

Lucas's brows shot up. "You were?"

Zed gave an easy shrug. "I wasn't interested." His sly smile flicked over me. "Shall I let Maxine know to set up lessons, or will you?"

I flipped him off, then shot a glare at both Cass and Lucas. "You're all on my shit list today. You know why."

CHAPTER 34

It was a couple of days later that I snapped. I'd been following through on my end of the dumb-as-fuck bet with Zed and was at a brutal dance lesson with Maxine when I got a call from Gen that I had been waiting on but dreading.

"They've denied your claims on all the cars," she informed me with regret in her voice. "The investigator is claiming you're the responsible party for bombing them all. The FBI has started looking into you as a suspect, and today they assigned an agent to tail you."

My fingers tightened on my phone, fury and frustration rippling through me. I'd already had Dallas try to pull any CCTV footage around the apartment that would clear me of the bombs, but everything had been wiped clean. Everything. Not even traffic cameras could support my innocence, and that in itself only seemed to incriminate me further. Especially with my neighbor as an eyewitness placing me outside the building at the time.

"Thank you for letting me know, Gen. Just be careful with your inquiries. The last thing I need is you getting dragged into this mess." My voice was underscored with clear anger, but I meant what I said. I loved that she was going above and beyond her job description—exactly as Demi had promised she would—but I didn't need to be responsible for her going to jail with me.

"Absolutely, Boss," she replied. "This info came from an, um, old friend of mine. He won't tell anyone that I know, and the intel is solid."

I grimaced. "You're the best."

Ending the call, I tried to draw a couple of calming breaths to center myself before turning back to Maxine. "We're going to have to push this off a week," I told her with a grimace. "I have a feeling my afternoon is about to get bloody."

She pursed her ruby-red lips at me but gave a short nod. "Not next week," she told me, tapping her long fingernail on her chin. "You have the main event fight at Anarchy. It'll have to be the week after."

I sighed. "So be it. I'll deal with my insufferable second over the bet."

Maxine smirked. "I'm sure he won't mind waiting. It'll give you more time to perfect that layback on the pole. You still look all stiff and awkward instead of effortless and sensual."

I gave her a hard look, and she just fluttered her lashes back at me. Having worked for me for close to three years, she was getting a good read on what lines she could safely push, and I respected her intelligence for paying that much attention.

"Careful, Maxine," I teased back. "I might get a taste for this and steal your headline slot."

She gave a mock wail and pouted. "Please don't. You're already set to triple my best tip night on a fucking bet performance." Her gaze ran down my body in my activewear. "With those tits, that ass, and your perfect, sexy killer face? Ugh, you'd have me unemployed in no time."

I snickered briefly. "Lucky the boss likes you, then. And this is a one-time show."

She shrugged. "Unless you go losing any more bets with Zed.

I have to admit I'm glad it was you who lost. I wouldn't be able to keep a straight face trying to show him how to do body rolls."

Well. There was a mental image I'd never known I needed and now couldn't get out of my brain.

Gathering up my things, I left the empty club and stepped out into the parking lot with my phone in hand, dialing Dallas. He didn't answer my call, so I sent a text as I slid into the Audi.

Hades: Check if Wenton Dibbs is back in the country. I have a feeling he is.

Because I seriously doubted these strings were being pulled from overseas right now. Nah, this was all a part of his grand sabotage plan, so he'd be on the ground here somewhere, watching and waiting. He was trying to push me into making a rash move, but he was underestimating my patience.

Dallas didn't reply until I was already back at Zed's house, and I paused halfway through changing my outfit to read what he'd sent.

Dallas: Done. You're right. Landed late last night at a private airstrip outside Cloudcroft.
Dallas: Got a positive ID off the airstrip security camera. It's Wenton Dibbs.

Surprise rippled through me, and I stood for several moments staring down at his text before replying to him.

Hades: How positive?
Dallas: There's always a margin for error, but three different programs gave a positive match to Wenton Dibbs. I'll send the image over.

I held my breath, waiting for the freeze-frame image to come through on the message, and Lucas appeared in my doorway.

"Is everything okay, Hayden?" he asked, his face filled with concern. He'd been to see his mom while I was at my dance lesson, and his eyes were tight with exhaustion.

"Yeah," I replied, nodding. "Yeah, just... Dallas managed to finally get a CCTV image of Wenton."

Lucas's brows rose, and he came farther into the room. "He did? That's good news, right?"

I blew out a breath, tapping my phone on my palm. "Yeah, I guess so. I just..." I let my words trail off, not wanting to voice my vulnerable thoughts out loud.

He wrapped his arms around my waist, holding me in the safe circle of his arms and letting me rest my face on his chest. But then I remembered the dark, healing scar of his brand was right in front of my nose—hidden by just a thin layer of T-shirt fabric—and it lit me up with confusion all over again.

"I don't get it, Lucas," I muttered, wrapping my own arms around his waist and holding him tighter. Guilt washed through me again as I thought about how close I'd come to losing him before I'd even realized how much I cared. "Why would Wenton be on a vendetta like this? Why impersonate Chase to fuck with my head?"

Lucas didn't answer immediately, then gave a sigh. "I can't even start to speculate." He pulled back slightly and cupped my face with his hand. "The human mind is a fucked-up thing, babe."

There was an edge of distress in his gaze and a bitterness to his voice that made me frown. "Hey, what happened with your mom? You seem upset."

He gave a small headshake. "It's not important. She was just having a bad day, I think. The MS is messing with her memory and making her think I'm my uncle. He was her older brother, and I think they were pretty close when they were kids."

I reached up and stroked my fingers through his hair, wanting to comfort him but knowing full fucking well that didn't come naturally to me. "What does she say when she thinks you're him?"

Lucas gave a headshake. "Just…nonsense. Shit that makes zero sense at all. I keep trying to ask her about Jack being in the Guild, but it never goes well. She just…yells accusations at me—him— that she won't let him anywhere near her babies anymore." He gave a frustrated sigh. "I don't know. It sounds totally insane…but if I was an outsider listening in? It sounds like my uncle Jack did something to hurt me when I was a kid."

I bit my lip, my heart hurting for him. That was a *lot* like what it sounded. I was almost positive Sandra knew her brother was in the Guild, too.

"But then she was going on about hurting her *babies*. Plural. And I am an only child, so…I have no idea. Maybe there's something else going on with her. The clinic asked if they could run some more tests and make sure they didn't miss anything in her original diagnosis." He sounded so resigned to it all. And so guilt-ridden.

"Lucas, you can't accept responsibility for your mom's medical condition," I told him gently. "Life just dealt her a crappy hand. That's not on you."

My phone buzzed and I pulled back from Lucas's embrace with an apologetic look. "Sorry, it's…" I clicked into the message and opened the still image Dallas had sent. "It's…Wenton." It really was, too. Dallas had also included some files he'd managed to dig up on Wenton Dibbs, and I clicked into those as I sank down onto the edge of the bed.

"What is it?" Lucas asked, sitting down beside me and keeping one hand on my waist like a physical sign of support. "Medical records?"

"Yeah," I replied, scanning over the documents. "How the fuck Dallas accessed these I have no idea. But it explains a lot…I think? It sounds like Wenton suffered some serious abuse as a kid—no real shock, knowing the Lockharts—but since then has been in and out of psychiatric care with delusions that he was actually his dead cousin, Chase Lockhart."

"Shit," Lucas breathed. "That's…intense. Zed's downstairs. Want me to grab him?"

I stood up, my mind whirling as I tossed my phone onto the bed. I was only half-dressed in my yoga pants and bra, and if I was going to go kill a ghost from my past, I needed to look the part.

Without answering Lucas—because my attention was already a million miles away—I went over to my closet and started hunting for the right outfit to confront my tormentor in. To deal with the man who had taken on Chase's identity and grudges and made them his own. Whatever psychological trauma had caused Wenton to follow this path, he'd done the damage. It was on me now to end it and exact retribution for the offenses he'd committed.

Lucas said something else but I wasn't listening, and a moment later he left my room.

I dressed carefully, selecting a pair of second-skin leather pants and a bra top that consisted of two dozen straps and buckles. My hair went into a tight braid, and my makeup was heavy on the eyeliner and scarlet lips.

Zed stomped into my room as I sat on the end of the bed to lace up my thigh-high boots and jerked to a stop when he locked eyes with me. Then his gaze ran over me with so much intensity I could almost feel it as a physical caress.

"You look like you're dressed for murder tonight, Boss," he commented, keeping his tone casual as he watched me meticulously lace up my second boot. I needed them tight because I hated the feeling of thigh-high boots slipping down and scrunching.

"You know me so well, Zed," I replied, calm as the eye of a storm. "I take it Lucas filled you in."

Zed jerked a nod. "He did. Wenton Dibbs."

"Wenton Dibbs," I repeated back. I didn't want to dwell on what this meant for me…for my memory. Because now I was starting to second-guess a lot of things I'd classified as fact. If Chase

283

could make Wenton's death feel so real, what else had he fooled me on?

"I'm coming with you," Zed announced. "Don't fucking leave without me."

I finished my boot and stood up. "No, I need you here."

He froze in the doorway. "Excuse me?"

"You heard me. I'm going alone, and you're staying here with Lucas in case Wenton sees me coming and tries to grab him again." I jerked my chin up, my gaze hard as I dared him to disobey me. This wasn't about us though. This was business, and Wenton had fucked with my business one too many times. Or...that's what I was trying to convince myself.

Zed stared at me for a long moment, neither of us blinking. Then he closed the space between us and grabbed my face with a rough grip. "Stop it," he snapped. "Just fucking *stop*. After everything we've been through together, you seriously think I'm going to sit on the sidelines and babysit your fucking boy toy while you put your life on the line again? No. Hell no. Don't even think about pushing this issue, Dare, or I swear I'll knock you out and handcuff you to my bed until you wake the fuck up and see that you're not alone. You've never been alone."

I held his intense gaze, my expression hard and unyielding despite the way he gripped my face like a rough lover. I eventually blinked and gave a small nod. "Good. I hoped you'd say that. Go arm up. I want this fucker dead before close of business."

The tension radiating through Zed flooded out, his shoulders dropping and his fingers releasing my chin. "Thank *fuck*." Then he grabbed my braid and crushed his lips to mine for one of the hottest goddamn kisses of my life. "Don't test me like that again, Dare. I won't hold back next time."

He kissed me again, making my heart pound against my ribs and my breath catch, then released me to race out of the room.

In his absence, I raised a shaking hand to my lips, tasting his kiss still there.

"Get Lucas a vest and a gun!" I shouted, my voice full of steel that my body wasn't sharing in that moment. "We're not taking chances."

This ended now. Wenton Dibbs was a dead man.

CHAPTER 35

Cold determination coursed through my veins as I stalked through the front entrance of Locked Heart Enterprises. The metal detectors screamed, and a security guard tried to stand in our way. His hand had barely even brushed the Taser on his belt when Zed disarmed him. By the time the elevator doors slid open, the guard was handcuffed to a chair with his own cuffs and had a gag over his mouth.

Lucas stuck close to my side as I stepped into the elevator and stabbed at the button for the thirty-second floor.

"Cass is on his way," Lucas told me, checking his phone as I stood there watching the display tick off each floor level. "He wanted us to wait for him."

"Not our fault he wasn't around when we left Shadow Grove," Zed commented as he checked his gun and tightened a strap on the knife holster strapped to his thigh.

"This is nothing we can't handle without him," I murmured, my eyes locked on the floor display. We were almost there. "I don't care how many delusions of grandeur Wenton has had in recent years, he's still no match for us."

Of that I was confident. If it were Chase himself, it'd be a very different matter. But Wenton…nah. It explained why he'd been taking potshots at me from a distance; he knew he wouldn't stand a fucking chance if he came at me head on.

The elevator dinged a cheery sound to announce we'd arrived, and I drew a deep breath as the doors opened and I raised my gun. But there was no one in the reception area for Locked Heart Enterprises. The lights were off and the desk sat totally vacant; not even a computer was set up.

Unease rippled through me as I cautiously made my way to the main office floor, only to find it equally as empty. It was midafternoon on a Friday; there was no way this office should be empty. Hell, the desks didn't even look like they'd ever been used. Blank, lifeless monitors were set up on each one with identical swivel chairs neatly in place, but otherwise there was absolutely no evidence that this office was in use.

"What the fuck?" Lucas whispered, his eyes darting all around and his gun at his side.

"Stay alert, Gumdrop," Zed snapped. "This could be a trap."

"It *is* a trap," I murmured back. But I didn't turn and run. This wasn't the sort of trap that would end in my death. Wenton had put too much effort into playing with me to end it so soon. I wasn't anywhere near scared enough yet to die.

I continued further into the vacant office, but Lucas grabbed my arm to stop me before I could get far.

"Hayden, if it's a trap, then we should go." His eyes radiated concern, and even Zed hitched his brows like he wanted to agree with Lucas.

Fuck that. I didn't come this far to tuck tail and run at the first sign of danger. Reckless? Yes. But what a boring fucking life I'd be leading if I always took the safe path. Besides, I was no amateur with delusions of heroism. I knew my skills and my limitations. I wouldn't have come this far if I weren't confident I could handle whatever nasty tricks Wenton had up his sleeve for me.

I shot Lucas a reassuring wink. "Just stay alert, Wilder. We got this."

He reluctantly released my arm but didn't try to argue anymore as I led the way through the empty office, gun at the ready. A short corridor gave access to some closed offices, but the one at the end was my focus. It was the only office with the door open, and from where I stood, I could already see someone sitting at the desk, just the top of a head above the high-backed chair. I trained my gun on that swatch of hair.

After stepping through the door, I swiftly moved aside so Zed could sweep for any potential threats. But there were none. No armed thugs hiding behind the door, ready to shoot us on sight. No trip wires rigged to explosives either. That I could see, anyway.

"Sorry I didn't make an appointment," I said aloud, returning my gun to the bit of Wenton's head that I could see. "I figured you'd be expecting me sooner or later."

He gave a low, amused laugh that sent a ripple of dread rolling through my body. As he laughed, he spun his chair around, and my heart shuddered to a complete stop inside my chest.

"You always knew me so well, Darling," he replied with a sly grin, linking his fingers on the desktop as he sat forward. "We really are so evenly matched."

My gun waivered as my palms turned slick with sweat, and a tiny quiver shook my knees. "Chase," I croaked.

His smile pulled wider. "In the flesh, Darling girl. You should have double-tapped, then followed up with a chest shot." He clucked his tongue in reprimand, pointing a finger at his scarred forehead and the leather eye patch covering his left eye.

He was right. I knew better than to fire one shot and expect it to have done the job. We'd always been taught to fire at *least* three bullets to ensure our target was dead, not just badly injured.

The tense silence hanging between us was abruptly broken as several ceiling panels dropped with a crash and a half-dozen heavily armed men surrounded us in a flash. But their guns weren't on me. They were on Zed and Lucas. Not even Zed could shoot his way out when he was *that* outgunned in such a small space.

"Gentlemen, please escort my fiancée's friends back downstairs. I'd like to speak with her alone." Chase delivered his order with all the casual nonchalance of ordering a turkey club sandwich for lunch.

I already sensed Zed coiled, ready to fight to the death, so I wrenched my gaze away from Chase to nod at my second. "Go," I told him, flicking my eyes over Lucas to include him in my order. "Now."

Zed's lips parted, the defiance clear on his face, and I hardened my glare to silently communicate just how badly he was *not* to undermine me right now. He got the message—he always did. But that didn't mean he liked it.

His nostrils flared with anger and his jaw twitched with tension, but he jerked a short nod. "Understood, Boss." His furious gaze shifted past me to the supposedly dead man at the desk.

"That's it, Zeddy," Chase taunted, "be a good lapdog and do what your mistress says. Some things never change, do they?"

Zed was so close to throwing his life away and shooting Chase where he sat that I could feel it. Hell, I was tempted too. But the second one of us fired our weapon, all three of us would be dead. And that wasn't the outcome I was still hoping for tonight.

"Zed," I warned him, my tone low. "Take Lucas and go."

"Yeah, Zed," Chase repeated. "Oh, Stripper Boy, I almost didn't recognize you without all the blood covering your pretty face."

"Just go," I snapped, giving Lucas just as hard of a look. He was angry and scared, but this wasn't his fight.

Zed put his gun away and stuck his hands up to show his escorts he was unarmed—sort of—then turned both hands around to flip Chase off. One of Chase's men slammed the butt of his rifle into Zed's stomach, making him double over, and I kept my spine straight, refusing to react.

Neither Zed nor Lucas protested any further as they left, and I steadied my arm as I kept my gun trained on Chase. We didn't speak. We just stared at each other, and that creepy, cold smile sat on his lips like he was thoroughly enjoying himself.

A few moments later the elevator dinged, echoing through the empty office floor, and Chase let out a sigh.

"You can drop the act now, Sweetness. We're alone." He sat back in his chair, relaxed as all hell, and nodded to my gun. "We both know you're not going to shoot me, so just put it away. Or better yet, hand it over. It's *mine* after all."

My mouth went dry. It had been...once. Then I'd grabbed it from him in our fight and shot him in the face with it, and it'd been my closest companion ever since.

"How?" I asked, my voice hoarse. "How did you survive?"

He cocked his head to the side, his one eye trained on me like a laser sight. "You'd have known if you'd taken the time to finish me off properly, Darling." He tapped his forehead. "I never did tell you that I was born with a section of my skull missing. Doctors fixed it with a titanium plate. Luckily for *me*, your bullet hit that plate and ricocheted. Took my eye, of course." He waved at the eye patch. "But kept my brain from turning into scrambled eggs. How's that for good karma, huh?"

My stomach flipped like I was going to vomit. "Nothing you've ever done in this life would earn you good karma, Chase," I told him with disgust. "Why didn't you burn in the fire?"

He sat forward again, totally ignoring my gun and drumming his fingertips on the desk. "The fire that killed my whole family, you mean?"

I narrowed my eyes. "If it helps, your parents were already dead. Too quickly, now that I think back on it."

"My little sisters weren't," he commented, holding my gaze.

I steeled my spine, freezing my expression to hide my lingering guilt and regret over the younger Locharts' entirely accidental deaths. I should have done things differently, should have somehow gotten them out, gotten them safe, before going after Chase. But in the heat of the moment...

"I should just finish the job now," I commented, looking down the barrel of my gun at my ex-fiancé. At my worst nightmare and my first love.

He shrugged. "You could. Of course, the FBI agents that have been tailing you all day will probably arrest you before you leave the building. I was organized enough to let them know you'd be stopping by here today and that we have *history*. That combined with my company underwriting the insurance claims that were just denied..." He let out a low whistle. "That'd be a slam-dunk guilty verdict, don't you think? And now correct me if I'm wrong, but I don't *think* the infamous Hades has managed to strong-arm the entire state's justice system."

I gave a cold smile in reply. "Yet."

His answering smile was a hell of a lot more amused than mine. "Yet. Well, in the meantime I think I'll keep taking advantage of the situation."

Fury coursed through my veins like lava, but the cold chill of fear had pooled in my stomach and stiffened my joints. I would probably miss if I tried to shoot him; I was that tense. So with a brittle smile, I tucked my gun away in its holster where it was safely away from Chase's reach. No way in hell was I giving it back to him. He could pry it from my cold dead hands.

"What the fuck do you want, Chase?" I asked in a bored tone. I'd be damned if I'd let him see how terrified I was of him...of everything he reminded me of. I wasn't her anymore. I was Hades, and no ghost would shake me. Not visibly, anyway.

He pushed back from his desk, stood, and sauntered around to close the distance between us. I drew a silent breath, letting the air fill my lungs and ground me as he got closer with every step. Chase and Zed were the same height, six foot three, and I needed to tip my head back to maintain eye contact, even with the advantage of my high-heeled boots.

"You're a smart girl, Darling," he told me, condescension dripping from every word. "What do you think I want?"

He lifted a hand to stroke a finger over my cheekbone, trailed it down my neck, over my collarbone, then followed the straps of my bra-style top all the way down to my exposed midriff. A deep shudder ran through me at his touch, and I bit the inside of my cheek hard enough to bleed so I could maintain my calm, indifferent facial expression.

"Who knows with you, Chase," I replied in a hollow voice. "I take it those medical records were all a work of fiction, along with that CCTV image of Wenton."

He gave a low chuckle. I used to love that laugh. It used to light me up inside and make me crave more. Now, though, it just turned my stomach.

"Wenton," he murmured. "Poor, stupid Wenton. I'm shocked you even fell for that red herring, Darling. You *saw* me shoot him." His smile was pure evil. How in the hell I'd ever loved this man, when the very devil himself resided within his skin, I'd never know. "But you didn't know what to believe, did you? Someone suggested Wenton was still alive, and suddenly you were second-guessing everything you knew." The glee in his voice was sickening.

"What do you *want*, Chase?" I asked again. "These silly games, blowing up my property, leaving cryptic notes…those are just an amusement for you. So excuse the turn of phrase, but cut to the chase. What do you want? Revenge? Believe me when I tell you I'm a hell of a lot harder to kill now than I was then. I won't forget to finish you off this time around."

He crowded my space, leaning in like he wanted to kiss me, and I stubbornly refused to step back from him. My days of being

292

intimidated by Chase Lockhart were long gone, never to be repeated.

Goddamn, I wished that were true.

"You think I want revenge, Darling?" he asked, his voice thoughtful and slightly hurt. "You think I want to do what you did to me? Kill everyone you love, then come after you?"

I clucked my tongue, sending a malicious smile right back at him. "I didn't kill *everyone* you loved, Chase. Suicide was never in the plan for me."

His one good eye hardened with anger, but he managed the emotion with ease, not letting it out and giving me the satisfaction of seeing him lose his cool. Instead, he splayed out his hand on my bare side, gripping my flesh with a rough hold, and pulled my body against his.

"I don't want *revenge*, Darling. How utterly pedestrian and cliché of you to assume I want you dead." His hold on me shifted as the whole length of him crushed against me, and his excitement at our confrontation was growing all too evident between us. "I don't want to kill you, Hayden. I simply want to take back what was mine all along." He paused for dramatic effect, but I already knew what he was going to say before the word left his painfully perfect lips. "You."

Swallowing the heavy lump of fear and disgust in my throat, I tugged a short blade free from my thigh sheath and stabbed it into his leg right beside his groin. Chase didn't even make a noise, the sick fuck, nor did he take his hands off me.

"Put your hands on me again, Chase, and my knife will be a quarter inch to the left. You've bitten off more than you can chew this time, and I *will* finish what I started five years ago." My voice was practically glacial, my gaze hard and unflinching. He wouldn't get even a whiff of fear from me. Never again.

His lips curled in a smirk. "Not today, you won't."

He gave a small grunt of pain when I jerked my knife out,

releasing him from the threat of slicing through his femoral artery. Unblinking, I wiped my knife on his shirt, then tucked it back into my sheath.

I gave a casual shrug. "I'm patient. Watch your six, babe. I'll be coming for you."

Spinning on my heel, I stalked out of his fake office with my head high and spine stiff. Yet the sound of his maniacal laughter followed me all the way down to the foyer and would probably stick in my brain forever.

For all my bravado, I was a trembling mess inside. I was in way, *way* over my head.

CHAPTER 36

Stepping out onto the sidewalk, I spotted Zed and Lucas hovering beside the car, waiting for me. Several of Chase's men lurked in the lobby, their weapons still in hand, keeping the threat present to stop my guys from storming back into the building to rescue me.

Frowning, I paused there on the sidewalk, turning back around to give each of Chase's guys a closer look through the glass doors. It wouldn't hurt to commit those faces to memory for later. He'd recruited them from *somewhere*...

One of them, standing just outside the foyer entrance with his shoulder propped casually against the glass, met my gaze and gave a small inclination of his head.

"Have a good evening, Hades," he murmured.

I tilted my head to the side, studying him more closely but not recognizing him at all. How curious.

The roar of a motorcycle coming down the street pulled my attention away from the strangely polite personal security, and I looked up to find Cass flying toward us. He pulled up with a screech of rubber, his dark eyes fierce on my face until they locked onto my bloody hand.

I shook my head. "Not mine."

He huffed. "Get on."

Looking past him to Zed and Lucas, I gave them a nod to tell them to follow, then swung my leg over Cass's bike. As he revved the engine, Chase's man gave me a small salute, and I filed his face away for later. There was something odd going on there.

Lucas and Zed slid back into the car as we peeled out of the street, and within a few minutes they'd caught up to us on the highway back to Zed's house. It was a long drive, but the roar of the motorcycle meant I could just cling onto Cass's broad, leather-covered back and work through everything in my mind. I could deal with my damage the way I'd always done—alone and silent.

By the time we got home, I was calm and collected, fully back in control.

I climbed off Cass's bike with legs stiff from a three-hour drive, but he didn't give me a chance to stretch it out, just grabbed me by the waist and hauled me against him, his mouth crashing into mine with the sort of desperate, possessive kiss that spoke volumes about how wound up he was.

"You pull a stunt like that again—" he started to threaten, and I cut him off with another deep kiss, letting him fully consume me and turn my whole damn body to jelly in his arms.

I'd sorted my shit out internally. I'd stuffed all the messy, ugly emotions and memories back in their boxes and locked that shit up tight. But my body had yet to get the message until Cass held me like I was the missing piece to his soul, reminding me that I wasn't doing this alone. Not this time.

A sharp realization jolted through me, and I broke away from his kiss, my eyes locking with Zed's as he climbed out of his Mercedes.

"I need to talk with Zed," I told Cass in a husky voice. "Then I want to get stupid stoned and pretend everything is okay."

Cass dropped a kiss against my collarbone, his rough beard tickling my skin. "Done." He climbed off his bike and gave a shrill whistle to Lucas. "C'mon, Wilder. I'll teach you how to roll a joint."

Lucas scowled at Cass's back as Cass sauntered up Zed's front steps to let himself into the house. "I'm not a fucking puppy, asshole," he snapped when Grumpy Cat was out of earshot, then paused to give me a troubled look. "Are you okay, Hayden? Did he—"

"I'm fine," I assured him in a soft voice. The fact that he was concerned for me after facing the man who'd tortured and nearly killed him? That spoke volumes about his selflessness.

Lucas gave a small nod, but his frown didn't ease. He just headed inside, and I knew I would need to talk things out with him soon. I kept forgetting how innocent he was. He didn't grow up with danger and violence like the rest of us.

Zed came over to stand in front of me, his eyes heavy with pain and guilt, but he said nothing. For all my determination to speak with him honestly, the words all just evaporated off my tongue. Instead, I reached out and wrapped my arms around his waist, hugging him tight and tucking my face against his chest.

He only hesitated a fraction of a second before hugging me back. His strong arms banded around me, and his face rested against my hair like he was inhaling the scent of my shampoo.

"What happened after I left?" he asked eventually, his voice rough with emotion.

I swallowed heavily and lifted my face away from his chest to meet his eyes. "Fuck-all. Just...Chase playing out his lifelong fantasy of becoming a Bond villain. How dramatic was that whole reveal?" I rolled my eyes, trying to lighten the mood.

Zed gave a watery smile, then pulled my arms away from his waist and held my bloody right hand up between us. "His?"

"Of course," I murmured, curling my fingers around his. "He wasn't walking away from that unscathed. Not a goddamn chance."

This time Zed's smile held more warmth. "Good."

He brought my hand to his lips and kissed the side of it gently. His eyes were locked on mine, heated and intense, and it was on the tip of my tongue to confess my reciprocal feelings. But something held me back, as always. Maybe it was just that I didn't want Chase overshadowing that pivotal moment for us. Maybe I was just a coward, scared that I'd end up losing my best friend when it inevitably went sour.

"Zed," I whispered. "Thank you." I meant that thanks more than any I'd ever given in my life. There was *so much* loaded into those two words as well, way more than I could even start to unpack, but he understood. He always did.

A small head nod, and he tugged me inside the house. We were good again. The tension between us could wait for another day because it sure as fuck wasn't going anywhere. But goddamn, it felt good to know that our friendship remained solid underneath it all. So far, anyway.

"This seems like a really bad idea," Lucas was saying to Cass as we made our way through to the courtyard where they'd lit the firepit. "Shouldn't we be laying booby traps or, like, cleaning our guns or making a plan or something? Getting fucked up feels like a stupid move. What if that psychopath attacks while we're all stoned out of our minds?"

Cass shot him a look with a tiny smile on his lips, then ran his tongue along the edge of the joint he was rolling to stick the paper down. "Damn, Gumdrop. You watch too many movies."

Lucas gave an exasperated sound, threw his hands up, and looked to me to talk some sense into everyone.

I just grinned and swiped one of the bottles of beer from the table to take a sip. "Cass has a point," I said with a shrug. "Besides, Chase isn't going to attack us tonight. Not here. He's made his point, and now he'll lull us into a false sense of complacency before he strikes again. It's...it's his pattern. Just trust us."

Zed eyed the cold beers that Cass and Lucas had brought out, then murmured something about needing stronger booze. His hand brushed the bare skin of my lower back as he moved past me, and I couldn't help the delicious shiver of arousal that rippled through my body.

He was right. The damage was already done. Our friendship was never going to go back to what it was, and I was strangely okay with that.

"Nope," Cass said, plucking the beer bottle out of Lucas's fingers before it reached his lips. Lucas looked ready to argue, but Cass handed him the freshly rolled joint instead. "Smoke first, then drink, or you'll end up cross-faded as fuck."

I snorted a laugh, stepping over Cass's legs to drop my butt down on the lounge between them. "He's right, Wild. You're not used to it, and you don't want to end up sick."

Lucas pouted but lit the joint anyway. He inhaled, holding my gaze with hooded eyes, then blew it out in a long exhale. "Is this what it'd be like dating a girl with older brothers?"

I grinned at the analogy, and Cass draped his arm around my shoulders, kissing my neck.

"Sure, if we're talking non-blood-related stepbrothers who get to fuck your girl whenever they want. It'd be just like that." His fingers trailed down my bare arm, making my skin tingle and my thighs tighten.

I gave a small sound of disagreement, though. "Whenever *you* want? Think again, Saint." I shoved his hand off my shoulders just to keep the power balance in check and leaned over to kiss Lucas right after he'd taken another deep drag on the joint.

Inhaling the smoke directly from his lips, I gave a small groan and leaned in to kiss him harder. Yeah, that was exactly what the doctor had ordered after staring down my worst nightmare back from the grave. Drinks, weed…and sex. Hopefully. I hadn't forgotten Zed's threat if he heard me riding dick again in his house, but I could be so quiet if I needed to be.

"Fucking hell," Cass muttered, reminding me that Lucas and I weren't actually alone. "Never thought I'd be down for this poly shit."

I sat back against the cushions where his long arm was still draped, giving him a curious side-eye. "And now?"

He held my gaze as he took a long swallow from his beer, then licked his lips. "Jury is still fucking out," he rumbled.

I snorted a laugh, taking the joint from Lucas's fingers as Zed returned carrying a bottle of scotch and a couple of glasses with ice cubes. He sat down across the fire from us and poured triple shots into each of the glasses before handing one over to me. I swapped him for the joint, and he took a drag before passing it across to Cass.

"So what happens now?" Lucas asked, slouching into the corner of the outdoor lounge.

I took a huge mouthful of my liquor and let it warm a fiery path down to my belly before I answered him. "I have no idea," I admitted softly. "This isn't something I could have prepared for. He's ten steps ahead, and I—I have no clue what to do."

Cass curled his arm around me again, pulling me into his side and dropping a kiss to the top of my head. "We'll kill him." He said it as casually as if he were talking about washing his car.

Zed scoffed. "Obviously." He shifted his gaze to me. "We're not solving anything tonight, though. So let's stick a pin in it until tomorrow and just chill."

I took another gulp of my scotch and winced at the burn. "Fine by me," I agreed, snagging the joint from Cass's lips.

"Gumdrop, why don't you tell me more about that video game your uncle gave you," Zed suggested, refilling his drink, then standing up to fill mine as well.

Lucas scowled. "Are you guys going to stop calling me that anytime soon?"

Cass huffed a husky laugh. "Unlikely."

He and Zed shared a smirk, and I shook my head at them both.

"Fucking save me if you two become friends," I muttered with a groan. "But I am interested if you have anything more to tell us, Lucas."

He shrugged, taking the joint when I offered it. Zed jerked his head to Cass, and Cass tossed him the little leather pouch he kept his weed and rolling papers in.

"It was just a pretty normal first-person shooter," Lucas told us, "like *Call of Duty*, but with hyper-realistic graphics. The only real difference was that cool game controller that legit simulated a real gun, but I think that was some prototype thing that Uncle Jack's best friend was developing. He worked for some big tech company, if I remember right."

My brows hitched, but the weed and liquor were hazing my brain already and my reaction was dulled by that. Still…it was lighting up my curiosity something wicked. Knowing now that Lucas's uncle was in the Guild, I had to wonder if that "game" wasn't actually some experimental training simulation.

"You think my uncle was grooming me to become a mercenary?" Lucas asked, reading my mind perfectly.

Zed sat back in his seat, kicking his boots up on the edge of the table. "That's what it sounds like."

"Who got you into gymnastics?" Cass asked, his fingers stroking a teasing pattern over my upper arm.

Lucas frowned, his eyelids heavy. "I don't remember. I would have assumed my mom, but now you're making me wonder if Uncle Jack had something to do with it."

I locked eyes with Zed across the fire and sensed he was on the same thought path I was. "Maybe we could reach out to the Guild?"

He grimaced. "We need to tell them about the gun haul anyway. No way am I game to steal Guild property."

"Agreed," I murmured. "Remind me tomorrow."

He nodded, pulling his phone from his pocket and probably setting himself a reminder.

Lucas gave a long yawn, sliding down the lounge further until his head rested on the low back and his legs sprawled out in front of him. "I guess I'm not such an unsullied marshmallow after all, huh?" He cracked one eye at me, a smile sitting on his lips.

I grinned back at him. "You're full of surprises, Lucas Wildeboer, that's for fucking sure."

CHAPTER 37

For a while, Cass, Zed, and I just chatted idly about the Guild, cars, guns…our preferred methods of torturing someone for information. All our shared interests. Lucas's hand had found my ankle at some point, and he'd fallen asleep with his fingers wrapped around my leg, as if touching me made him feel safe enough to rest.

"Jesus," Zed muttered, eyeing Lucas. "He's making my neck hurt just looking at him. That can't be comfortable."

I peered over at Lucas, smiling at how peaceful and relaxed his face was. But Zed was right; the angle of his neck and back was going to leave him aching in the morning if we left him like that.

"I should wake him up," I murmured, my own voice thick with scotch and weed.

Zed groaned and stood up with a slight wobble. He leaned over Lucas and shook his shoulder to try to wake him up. No response.

Cass gave a low chuckle. "Good luck. That kid sleeps like the fucking dead."

He'd know. A surge of arousal rippled through me on remembering how he'd stolen me straight out of Lucas's bed the other night.

Zed gave a heavy sigh and grabbed Lucas by the arms. "Help me carry his heavy ass inside," he told Cass.

"Nah," Cass replied, finishing the last drag on another joint. "You got this."

Zed glared but hauled Lucas's deadweight over his shoulder in a fireman carry. "Good point," he grunted. "Wouldn't want you to break a hip, old man."

I laughed out loud at that dig, then clapped a hand over my mouth to try to stifle the sound. Then I laughed harder at the fact that I'd laughed in the first place.

Zed just smirked his victory and carried Lucas inside, leaving Cass and me alone by the fire.

"You little shit," Cass growled when I continued to laugh. His fingers wound around my braid, and he tugged my head back to look up at him. Whatever else he was going to say he discarded in favor of kissing the crap out of me instead.

He devoured me with his lips, his tongue, his touch, and I squirmed in his arms, aching for more. He released me just long enough to haul me into his lap, my legs straddling him, and his hard length crushed against my throbbing pussy. Suddenly I was regretting my choice of pants over a skirt in tonight's outfit because, holy shit, I wanted Cass's hands on me more than I wanted air.

But a sobering thought flashed through my mind, and I groaned, pulling back from his lips. "We can't," I muttered with heartfelt regret. "I promised Zed..." Ugh, I was really questioning my sanity for agreeing to that fucking stupid request of his. But I had, and I couldn't just break my word. Could I?

Cass arched his scarred brow. "Zed made you promise not to fuck me?"

I winced. "Or Lucas. Not here, anyway." I indicated the fact that we were in Zed's home, and yeah, that did mean I had to pay him *some* respect.

Cass stared into my eyes for a long moment, his palms splayed across my ass and holding me tight against him. "Or what?" he murmured, a glint of evil touching his dark gaze.

I frowned, stoned enough that I wasn't following his train of thought. "Huh?"

"Zed…I know how he operates. I bet he gave you an ultimatum. What'd he threaten to do if you *do* fuck one of us in his house?"

My eyes widened, and I licked my suddenly dry lips. "He said he'd have to join in."

Cass tipped his head back as an easy laugh rolled through him. "Predictable bastard." He shifted his grip on my ass and ground his erection against my core, watching with heated eyes when I moaned. "So let him."

I blinked a couple of times in confusion. "What?"

Cass's lips found my neck, sucking at my flesh and making me shiver and arch into him. "Let him," he murmured against my skin. "Or if you want to turn the tables, you can let him watch but not touch."

A small gasp passed my lips at that suggestion, and I was willing to bet my leather pants would need to be dry-cleaned before they could be worn again, I was that wet.

Cass lifted me with strong hands and laid me down on the lounge where Lucas had just been sleeping. "Either way, I'm gonna make you come for me, Red."

I groaned, stretching my arms over my head and lifting my hips as he peeled my pants down. I'd taken my boots off earlier while we were chatting and drinking, so it was only a matter of seconds before he hitched my legs over his shoulders and slammed his face into my pussy.

"Oh *fuck*," I hissed, my whole body quaking as his tongue found my clit and his beard scraped the soft skin of my thigh.

"*Seriously*, Dare?" Zed barked, storming out of the house toward us with a conflicted expression on his face.

I moaned at what Cass was doing between my legs, then threw Zed a smug smile. "Dead serious, Zayden. You know weed makes me horny."

He glowered. "Breathing seems to make you horny these days."

I gave a throaty laugh, then gasped as Cass pushed his fingers inside me and his tongue lashed my clit. Zed's eyes widened as he watched, seemingly frozen in place as I squirmed and bucked on Cass's face.

"Dare..." he groaned. "I told you—"

"You told me not to ride dick in your house," I cut him off, my breath short as Cass worked me into a frenzy. "And I'm not."

Zed glared, appearing outraged at how literally I was taking his threat. But he should know how to word his deals more carefully.

"Semantics," he growled, moving around the fire toward us.

I gave another laugh, followed by a lust-filled moan, but held my hand up at him. "Touch me without consent and I'll castrate you, Zed. Sit the fuck down and watch."

He stared at me like he couldn't decide if I was serious or not. Cass gave my inner thigh a bite, pulling my attention down to him and the wicked grin on his face. I understood perfectly what he was thinking, too—that I loved it when he took liberties without explicit consent. Zed didn't know that, though. And I wanted to punish him for trying to manipulate me.

Zed's eyes narrowed like he'd decided I wasn't kidding, and he gave a slow shake of his head. "You're playing with fire, Dare."

I licked my lips. "Am I?"

He gave a short laugh, swiping his hand over his hair, then retreated back to his original seat opposite us. "Go on then, Saint. Show me how it's done."

Cass leaned up to look over at Zed and spread my legs farther apart. His fingers thrust in and out of my soaking cunt, lazy and unhurried as he shifted us to give my best friend a prime view.

"You've had your fair share of watchers in the past, De Rosa," he commented, dragging my own arousal down my perineum to tease my ass. "How does it feel being on the other side?"

Zed didn't answer, just flipped Cass off and hitched his ankle up on his knee. There was no hiding how hard he was, but he made no move to get his dick out. Apparently he was taking literally that I'd told him to watch.

Cass chuckled, pushing his pinkie finger into my tight hole and making my breath catch in a sharp gasp. His index and middle fingers slid back into my pussy, and he fucked me like that for a couple of moments while Zed stared. Then Cass's mouth returned to my clit, blocking Zed's view, and my best friend's eyes locked with mine across the fire.

I held that eye contact as Cass fucked me with his hand, two fingers in my pussy and one in my ass, and tortured me with his skillful tongue all over my clit. Every time I wanted to turn my face or close my eyes, I forced my gaze to remain locked on Zed's face. This was punishing me just as much as him, but damn if I wasn't getting off on it.

When I finally came, I couldn't stop my lids from fluttering closed as my spine arched and my toes curled. Zed muttered a curse under his breath and swiped his hand over his face in frustration, then stood up abruptly.

"I need a fucking shower," he announced, his voice rough with arousal and anger. "The rules still stand, Dare." His gaze was hard, practically begging me to test him over that threat, and I just gave him a lazy, blissed-out smile in return.

He shot a glare at Cass, who was casually kissing my inner thigh, then stomped his horny ass back inside the house.

"You know he's gone to jerk off," Cass commented when he was gone.

I snickered an intoxicated laugh. "I'd be offended if he wasn't."

Forcing my limbs to obey me, I sat up, then slid to my knees in front of Cass. "He told me not to *ride* dick," I murmured, unbuckling his belt and palming his hot, hard dick. "Never said anything about choking on it."

A sly grin pulled at Cass's lips as his hand went to the back of my head, his fingers weaving into my braid. "That's my girl."

Eagerly, I took him into my mouth, running my tongue around his crown and tasting the saltiness of his arousal before taking him deeper into my throat. Cass grunted, lifting his hips to meet me as his hand forced my head lower, pushing his dick deeper still until I could barely breathe, then releasing me momentarily before repeating.

He fucked my face with rough, demanding thrusts that left me wet and shaking all over again. By the time he came, hot cum filling my mouth and dripping down my throat, I was seriously considering calling Zed's bluff.

Cass must have known it too. He gave a soft laugh and pulled me to my feet as he stood up. "Come on, Angel. I'll give you a hand in the shower."

I grinned as he scooped me up in his arms to carry me inside, but couldn't help noticing the light on in Zed's bedroom over-looking the courtyard. Or the silhouette of someone standing at the window.

CHAPTER 38

Nightmares of Chase woke me far too early the next morning. Despite all we'd done the night before to push those memories aside, to dilute their power, the second I'd fallen asleep those dark thoughts, the soul-aching terror of memories, had come back with a vengeance.

Cass seemed to sleep more deeply with the help of a solid high, and instead of waking him with my thrashing and screams, I dressed and went to the gym. Sleep wasn't an option for me, apparently, so I may as well beat the ever-loving crap out of a sandbag while picturing my psychopathic, abusive ex.

It almost seemed laughable that even with his scarred face and eye patch he was still as handsome as ever. But then, loads of serial killers were attractive people. It helped them lure their victims so much easier, and Chase was a master of that.

When I'd hit the bag so many times my arms were shaking and weak, I tossed my gloves aside and went for a shower. I still had no clue how to deal with him. I couldn't just shoot him and feed his body to my shark in the Club 22 aquarium, not if he was in communication with the FBI and had already cast suspicion my way. His death, or even disappearance, would just add to their mounting case against me.

I was no closer to a solution when I went in search of coffee and found Zed sitting at the dining table with his laptop open in front of him.

"Morning," I muttered, not totally sure how we were going to handle everything that had happened last night. Being high as fuck had definitely contributed to my lack of inhibitions, but I regretted nothing.

Zed reached out as I passed him, grabbed my wrist, and tugged me off-balance, causing me to land in his lap with a sharp exhale.

"Zed—" I started to say, but I clamped my lips shut when he tapped his ear, showing me the Bluetooth headset.

"Yes, absolutely," he said to whoever he was speaking to. "I understand."

I raised a brow. He nodded to his phone on the table beside his laptop, and I peered at the screen to see who was on the call. The number was a random one, but the call location was Edinburgh, Scotland, also known as the birthplace of the Guild.

"We've had the site sealed for the time being," Zed continued, his hands resting on my hips as he shifted me in his lap, getting comfortable like we were high school sweethearts or some shit. "But the owner wants to move back in. We'd prefer if you collected your property as soon as possible."

I tried not to think about the heat of his hands on my body or the way my ass was pressed to his crotch, so I tapped his laptop screen to see what he'd been looking at. A dozen browser tabs were open, and I flipped through them one by one while Zed finished his call to the mercenary guild.

When the call ended, he placed his earpiece on the table beside his phone. "You're awake early," he commented, reaching past me to grab his mouse and click into one of the tabs I hadn't gotten to yet.

"Couldn't sleep," I replied, shocking myself at how hollow and haunted my voice was.

Zed just gave a hum of understanding, and his hands returned to my waist, sliding around to my stomach in a loose hold. "Read that," he told me.

I double-clicked to zoom the scanned document on his screen and ran my eyes over the details. A huge portion of the file had been redacted, but there were two clues that hadn't been concealed: the patient's name—because it was a medical record—and the doctor's name below the signature line.

Turning slightly, I gave Zed a curious look, but he just took the mouse from me and clicked into another tab, one where he'd already pulled up that doctor's photograph and bio.

As I read through the description of the doctor, Zed brushed a light kiss over my shoulder that made me shiver.

"Lucas has a sibling," I said out loud when I finished reading the doctor's bio. The medical record had been for his mother, and the treating physician was a specialist in IVF. Sure, the details of her treatment had been redacted, but if it walked like a duck and quacked like a duck...

"That was my conclusion, too," he agreed. "Roughly ten years older than him, if Lucas is turning nineteen next week."

"Next week?" I repeated, swiveling my head to look at him. "Lucas's birthday is next week?"

Zed grinned. "You didn't know that?" He clucked his tongue. "Worst girlfriend ever. His birthday is next Saturday."

I cringed. That really did seem like a detail I should know. I needed to think of something special to do for him.

"Okay, back to this," I redirected, indicating to the laptop. "Maybe we're jumping to conclusions. Just because Sandra visited an IVF clinic doesn't mean it was successful. Maybe it took her that long to get pregnant with Lucas?"

Zed winced. "I doubt it was anything so innocent. She would have only been sixteen when that redacted file was written."

I clicked back to the medical file to double-check Sandra's date

311

of birth and grimaced. "Jesus Christ," I muttered. "That poor girl." Because not even a single part of me thought she was visiting an IVF doctor at age sixteen—with heavy redaction on her file—of her own free will. That had nefarious intent written all over it.

"What poor girl?" Lucas asked, coming into the room looking all sleepy and sexy and totally clueless.

I stiffened in Zed's lap, and my second caught my eye before I turned to look over at Lucas.

"Uh, no one we know," I lied, "just reading the news." I closed the lid of Zed's laptop, making him cringe, then stood up out of his lap.

"How'd you sleep, Gumdrop?" Zed asked, also standing and brushing a hand over my hip as he moved past me toward the kitchen. Apparently he'd decided to wage war by casual physical contact, and it was goddamn working for him.

Lucas yawned, ruffling his fingers through his hair, then draped his arms around me in a warm hug. "Like the dead," he replied, his voice still thick. "How'd I get into bed, though?"

Zed rolled his eyes but didn't reply as he headed for the coffee machine. Lucas pulled back to give me a curious look, and I grinned. "Zed carried you upstairs and tucked you in."

Lucas's brows hitched, and he released me to turn toward Zed. "Aw, big brother, you *do* love me after all!" The teasing in his voice was thick, and I vaguely feared for his life when he wrapped Zed in a bear hug.

Zed just grunted, though, and shoved Lucas off him. "You're lucky you're so skinny. You barely weigh more than Dare when she's passed-out drunk." He nodded to Lucas's insanely ripped torso—because apparently T-shirts weren't needed around the house. "Better start working on some muscle, Gumdrop, or we'll have to call you Marshmallow."

It was a joke, obviously. Even after the surgery and his recovery time, Lucas was still cut like a fitness model. He was so far from becoming a marshmallow it was laughable.

"Mm-hmm," Lucas replied to Zed with a smug grin. "Green is such a good color on you, big bro."

I snorted a laugh when Zed frowned and peered down at his gray T-shirt. It took a second, but he figured it out and glared at Lucas like he was thinking about punching him.

"Are you going to see your mom today?" I asked, redirecting the conversation. As cute as it was that they were comfortable enough to joke, I really didn't need another dick-measuring competition so soon. The tension from last night was already thick between Zed and me, even if neither of us had mentioned it.

Lucas nodded. "Yeah, I'd like to. If that's okay?"

We'd all been taking turns driving him to see her because I didn't want him alone. Ever. Not after Chase had already nearly killed him and especially not now. Chase said he wanted *me* back... which meant Lucas and Cass would be targets. Not to mention Zed... Shit. Zed needed to be more careful than ever. The swipe Chase had taken at him, calling him my lapdog, told me he wasn't interested in making amends with his childhood best friend.

"I'll take you," Zed offered, meeting my gaze. "Hades has business to take care of with Dallas. Besides, I'm curious to meet the woman who produced such an *interesting* child." He said it with a smile, but it was the sort of smile a crocodile might offer before dragging its victim into the water to drown.

Lucas gave a confused frown but shrugged. "Sure, cool. Thanks. Is everything okay, though?" He turned back to me with concern on his face.

I nodded. "Fine. Just tightening up security at the clubs."

Zed handed me a mug of coffee, his fingers brushing mine as I took it and his stare way too damn intense for this time of morning.

Lucas noticed it too. His gaze bounced between the two of us a couple of times before a small smile tugged his lips. He grabbed a coffee mug out of the cupboard and helped himself to the fresh pot before turning back to face us both.

"Everything okay with you guys? You both seem…tense." The smirk on his lips said he knew perfectly fucking well what was causing that tension, even if he hadn't witnessed the show I gave Zed last night.

Zed leaned back against the cabinets, cool as a cucumber as he sipped his coffee. "I'm fine. How about you, Dare?"

My answering smile was brittle and severely lacking in sincerity. "Better than fine."

Lucas snorted a laugh and shook his head. "You guys need to fuck so bad it's painful."

Zed choked on the sip of coffee he'd just taken, and my eyes bugged out as I glared at Lucas.

"What?" He shrugged. "It's pretty obvious."

"I'm going to get changed," I announced, making a speedy exit from the kitchen, despite the fact that I'd literally *just* showered and changed after my workout. I wasn't fast enough, though, and I heard Zed's response to Lucas.

"You're officially the most secure teenager I've ever fucking met, Wilder. Or are you just not concerned about losing your woman to another man?"

I paused, wanting to hear Lucas's reply.

He didn't disappoint either. In fact, he laughed. "I won't *lose* her to you, Zed. She already loves you and has since before I met her, so there's nothing to be insecure about. Hayden has room in her heart for both of us and for the grumpy old man snoring upstairs. Either get on board or get out, but I'm locked in for the whole damn ride."

A rush of warmth flooded my chest hearing that, and I hurried upstairs before he caught me listening outside the kitchen. Lucas was delivering on everything he'd promised me and more. He really was my lighthouse in the raging storm of my bloody, violent, fucked-up life.

It was about damn time I reciprocated, and I knew how I could start: by working out what the hell was going on with his mom and the riddle wrapped in the mystery of her past.

CHAPTER 39

The week passed in a blur as I buried myself in strengthening our security around Zed's house and all the Copper Wolf businesses. I needed to change insurance companies for everything and thoroughly investigate all our external contracts to find anywhere else Chase might have wiggled his way in.

Cass spent most of his time either doing Reaper business or training for his fight, so it was a pleasant surprise when he showed up at my office on Friday afternoon.

"Grumpy Cat," I greeted him with a grin, sitting back in my chair. "This is unexpected. Don't you have somewhere to be?"

He gave an easy shrug. "Not for a few hours. Thought I'd come pick you up."

Zed had driven me to Copper Wolf earlier in the day, seeing as we both had shit to do here. But he'd left to sort out final details for the fight night tonight, so I did need a ride back.

"That's very thoughtful of you," I commented, my eyes narrowed with suspicion.

"I'm a thoughtful guy," he replied, coming around my desk and leaning down into my personal space. "Besides, I wanted to give you something."

I grinned, my gaze flicking to the glass door of my office and the employees at their desks on the other side. "Here? It's probably not the most professional move. How about in the bathroom?"

Cass gave an exasperated headshake. "Not what I was talking about, Red." Then he paused, looking thoughtful. "But now that you mention it..."

"No, now I want to know what you came to give me if you weren't talking about a quick afternoon orgasm." I tilted my face back, smiling up at him. Fuck me, I was so into Cassiel Saint that it was sickening.

He glanced up at the door like he was checking for anyone watching, then ducked his head down to kiss me deeply.

"Come on, it's downstairs." His gruff voice was next-level sexy after kissing me like that, and I was sorely tempted to fuck him in the elevator. "You done here?"

I nodded. "Yep, sure am."

He straightened up, waiting by the door as I logged off my computer and shut it down. I grabbed my tailored blazer from the back of my chair and threaded my arms in while Cass watched me with hungry eyes, then slung my purse over my shoulder.

"Let's go," I told him, and he held the door open for me.

"Have a great weekend, Boss!" Hannah called out from her desk across from Macy's. Her smile was wide as she gazed up at Cass and me. "Good luck at your fight tonight, Mr. Saint."

Cass just grunted a noise because his talkativeness didn't extend to anyone outside my little crew. So I gave her a nod in response, making up for his lack of manners.

"Are you coming to the fight, Hannah?"

She shook her head and gave a small laugh. "No, I'm not a fan. Johnny and I have history, and I'd rather stay well clear."

I tilted my head, curious, but didn't push for the story. Hopefully, one day she'd feel comfortable enough to volunteer it and let me deal with Johnny Rock should he need it. "Fair enough." I flashed a smile at Macy too. "Don't work too late."

She just arched a brow at me as if to say *Don't tell me what to do* and continued with her work.

I started toward the elevators but paused when I realized Cass wasn't following me. He was frowning down at Hannah, who looked like a startled animal staring up at him.

"Bad history?" he asked in a low, dangerous rumble.

She jerked a nod and licked her lips. "You could call it that. I have a restraining order against him."

I wasn't shocked. The flicker of anxiety when she'd mentioned *history* had hinted enough. Cass just grunted another sound, then ran a hand over his beard.

"Noted." That was it. Then he stalked across the carpet to where I waited and pressed the elevator call button.

I kept my mouth shut until we were alone in the elevator, then turned to him with narrowed eyes. "What was that all about?"

He quirked his scarred brow. "What?"

I rolled my eyes. "Nothing." I had a feeling I already knew what he was planning anyway. "Parking level, huh?" I indicated to the level he'd selected, and he shot me a dark, mischievous look back.

"I can't decide," he muttered, his gaze burning a hot path over my body as he inspected me from top to toe, "if I prefer you in skirts or pants."

I was wearing a pair of tight black jeans with my replacement Louboutins that I knew made my legs and ass look incredible. But I still gave him a short laugh and propped a hand on my hip. "I'd think that was an easy decision, Saint. Only skirts give you quick access."

He hooked his thumb through my belt loop and tugged me closer so he could palm my ass through the jeans. "That's true," he agreed, kissing my neck and making my breath quicken. The elevator dinged to announce we'd reached the parking floor, and the doors slid open behind me. "But pants mean you can ride a motorcycle without flashing your sexy ass to the whole world."

He gave me a nudge, pushing me out into the parking garage, and I stopped short when I spotted the second bike parked beside his Harley.

My eyes shifted to him, and he dangled a familiar Ducati key from his finger. "I told you it was yours, Red. 'Bout damn time I got around to giving it to you."

I couldn't fight the smile on my face as I took a closer look at the bike and ran my hand over the smooth leather seat and glossy red paintwork.

"This is a Superleggera V4," I murmured, caressing the handlebar, then flicking my attention back to Cass. "They only made five hundred of these."

He gave a shrug. "Yeah, but the red matches the soles of your shoes. And it goes fucking fast."

I snickered at his clueless act. He knew more about bikes than I did, and I knew *a lot*. This wasn't the most expensive Ducati in the world, but it would have been goddamn hard to get his hands on. And he was right, it was *fast*.

"This is more than thoughtful, Saint," I commented, still touching the bike. It was a thing of beauty; I could hardly believe I'd told him to shove this gift up his ass a few weeks earlier.

He came closer, holding out the key—which wasn't an actual key so much as an electronic fob—for me to take. "Does that mean you'll keep it? It's not really my style."

I looked over at his black-and-chrome Harley Davidson and was inclined to agree. "I guess it'd be rude not to," I murmured, snagging the key from his finger. Then I launched myself into his arms and wrapped my legs around his waist as I kissed him half to death.

"I'll take that as a thank-you," he growled when I pulled back, breathless and hot with arousal. His huge hands gripped my ass, holding me against him effortlessly, and I wanted nothing more than to strip my jeans off and show him just how thankful I was feeling.

Instead, I raised a brow and wriggled out of his grip. "For the record, Saint, I could have bought this for myself."

As I turned away, he gripped my hips, pressing his hot body against my back, and teasingly bit the side of my neck. "That's not how a gift works, Red. Besides, I bought the only one available for sale, so no. You couldn't." He stepped back, then smacked me on the ass. Hard. "Now get on. I wanna get the whole visual."

I grinned, tucking the key into my pocket. I pulled the strap on my handbag loose to loop over my body, then unhooked the helmet from the handlebar. "Yes, sir."

Tugging the helmet on over my loose hair, I swung my leg over the sleek machine and situated my ass in place with a wiggle.

Cass let out a pained groan, biting his knuckle as he watched me get comfortable, then scrubbed his hand over his face. "Shit. I'm gonna walk into the fight with a raging hard-on now."

I laughed under my full-face helmet and pressed the ignition button. As the bike roared to life between my legs, I shivered with excitement. Oh hell yes. I was keeping this baby for sure.

"Race me home, and I'll take care of that for you," I told him, then peeled out of the parking garage before he could even get on his own bike.

I was just teasing, though, and waited at the top of the ramp for him to catch up. After all, it was no fun racing him if I had such a sizable advantage in the first place. I wanted *all* the glory when I whipped his ass, and that meant giving him a fair start.

He caught up a few seconds later, and we gunned our engines at the same time, tearing out into the street and dodging traffic to get to the highway.

Unsurprisingly, my new baby left Cass way in her dust when we hit the open roads heading back to Shadow Grove. I made it back to Zed's house with enough time to park, strip out of my clothes, and put my shoes back on before Cass rolled in on his Harley.

When he found me waiting with my butt propped against the seat of my bike and not a stitch of clothing covering my flesh, he almost dropped his whole damn motorcycle. He recovered it well, though, hopping off and tossing his helmet aside as he advanced on me like a wild animal.

Then he proceeded to fuck me like said wild animal over the seat of my bike with my matching red-soled shoes still on my feet. In fairness, it gave me the extra height needed so he could fuck me standing up, his fingers curled around my hip bones and his pants around his knees.

It was goddamn delicious.

I came with little to no effort, my pussy already throbbing and wet from the exhilaration of the race, and Cass joined me in climax only a few moments later.

"I guess you like the bike, then?" he commented with a husky laugh as he pulled his jeans back up and I gathered up my hastily tossed-aside clothes.

Rising up on my toes, I kissed him deeply and smiled. "I love it. But if you're late to your fight, I will castrate you. Go. I'll meet you there when I've cleaned up."

He looked indecisive as hell, but I hardened my stare and he reluctantly made his way back to his bike. "Fine," he growled. "But Zed can take his stupid rule and jump off a damn cliff tonight. When I win this, I'm fucking you until you can't walk. Clear?"

A deep shiver of excitement ran through me, and my nipples hardened. "Clear," I replied. "I'm all yours, *sir*." Then I smirked, unable to keep from teasing him. "If you win, of course."

He scowled at me but roared back out of the garage again a moment later.

I checked the time on my phone in the bundle of clothes and

weapons in my arms and muttered a curse at how late it already was. Knowing how many eyes would be on me tonight—big fights always pulled a mixed bag of criminals and shady individuals—I needed to ensure my Hades mask was firmly in place, a task that was proving to be harder every damn day.

I gave myself a long mental pep talk in the shower, and when I got out, I looked in the mirror and groaned. All I saw staring back at me was a well-fucked woman with rosy cheeks, puffy lips, and bruised bite marks on her throat. All I saw...was happiness.

That wouldn't do at all. Luckily, I knew exactly what would put my head back in the right gear.

I quickly dressed in a simple but elegant black evening gown, then added a thigh sheath full of knives, which would be on full display with the split in my dress, and opted to leave my Desert Eagle at home for the first time in five years.

The lack of weapons sent more of a message than if I were armed to the teeth because it showed that I wasn't afraid of anyone in attendance tonight. The knives? Well, they were just sexy as hell.

When I was satisfied with my appearance, the only thing left was to regain that hardness in my eyes and in my posture. I needed to shrug off the warm, fuzzy, sexed-up glow of Cass's and Lucas's affections and coat myself in cool metal once more.

So as I made my way down to Zed's garage, heading for the Audi thanks to my dress, I pulled my phone out and pressed the *contact us* button on the Locked Heart Enterprises website.

The phone rang twice, then clicked and redirected, just as I'd predicted.

A moment later, he answered.

"Darling, how unexpected." His voice was a low purr, so fucking familiar, and it set my skin crawling. Perfect.

"Chase, sweetheart," I drawled back. He'd caught me off guard last time, but I was prepared now. I knew who I was dealing with, and he wouldn't get to me so easily again. My acting skills had improved dramatically since his "death" five years before. "I take it you received the good news today?"

He gave a soft cluck of his tongue, and smug triumph rolled through me. I'd spent the week overturning his shell company's decision on my insurance claims and eventually managed to get a judge in the state court to rule in my favor. It was really his own fault; if he hadn't helpfully informed the FBI that we had personal history, I'd have never been able to prove bias in the claim rejection. Gen had seriously earned herself the bonus I'd wired through to her Cayman account this afternoon.

"You're quite proud of yourself, aren't you, Darling?" he replied, sounding almost impressed. "This is more fun than I anticipated."

I gave a soft laugh, letting him hear how unbothered I was by his creepy-ass bullshit. "You're out of your league, Chase. Slink back into the shadows where you belong."

He chuckled back at me. "Nah, I've only just gotten started. We're soulmates, Darling. And if I can't have you, no one will." He paused, then gave me exactly what I'd wanted when I placed this call. "Oh, how is Stephanie doing, by the way? I bet she grew up so pretty."

Cold hatred settled into my bones, and the shift in my personality snapped into place with an almost physical jolt. I ended the call without another word, having achieved what I set out to get. Focus. Determination. Bloodlust.

Hades was back.

CHAPTER 40

Zed and Lucas were already at our reserved area directly beside the octagon when I arrived. Some smaller, lower-billed fights had been scheduled before the main event of the night, but I was here for one fight only.

"Holy shit, Hayden," Lucas exclaimed when I joined them, his jaw dropping. The high-profile events at Anarchy were always formal dress for VIP guests—because why the fuck not? So Lucas and Zed were both sharply dressed in suits and Lucas's hair was slicked back with gel, making him look easily in his twenties. The scruff of stubble that he wore on his jaw definitely helped in that department.

I let a small smile touch my lips in response, but Zed put a hand on Lucas's arm to stop him from reaching out for me.

"Not here, Wilder," he muttered, the noise of the crowd covering his voice. "Not while she's like that." He nodded toward me, and I met his gaze with cool eyes. He knew where my head was at and he knew that Lucas's affection would make it impossible to keep my mask in place, so he was intervening. And for that I could fucking kiss him.

Keeping my chin high and my shoulders relaxed, I accepted a

glass of champagne from an Anarchy VIP waitress and took a sip. One of the fighters in the octagon got knocked out as blood splattered out of the cage and spotted the floor at my feet, but I didn't react. Instead, I just swept my gaze toward the far side of the room.

Chase Lockhart, looking devastatingly handsome with his designer suit and black leather eye patch, met my gaze as he casually sauntered his way down the aisle to where Johnny Rock's supporters had a reserved area.

He took a glass of champagne from a server, too, and raised it toward me in a silent toast. The smile on his lips said he thought he'd surprised me, but I just smiled and raised my glass back.

"Did you know he was going to be here?" Zed muttered, coming to stand at my side slightly behind my right elbow.

I took another sip of my drink, still locked in a stare-down with my psychopathic, unstable ex. "Yep," I replied. "He might be six steps ahead, but goddamn, he's predictable."

Zed huffed a quiet laugh as the commentator announced the winner of the fight that had just ended. Someone walked in front of me, breaking my eye contact with Chase, so I took the opportunity to sit down in my reserved seat between Zed and Lucas.

"Hayden, are you okay?" Lucas whispered, barely even moving his lips as he leaned forward and pretended to be super interested in what the commentator was saying about the fight.

I shifted slightly, biting the inside of my cheek to keep from reacting. "Sorry, Lucas," I breathed in reply. "I should have told you he'd be here."

It couldn't be easy for him to see the guy who'd branded him, who'd stabbed him, and not march straight over there to deck him. I was beyond impressed at his self-composure.

He turned his face slightly, flashing me a brief but blinding smile. "I'm not worried. I just wanna be there when you cut his heart out and stomp on it in those killer heels of yours."

I brought my glass back to my lips, hiding my laugh with

another slow sip of champagne. Chase watched me across the crowd, the intensity of his stare making my skin crawl, but I didn't pay him any more attention.

Instead, I used the time before Cass's fight to speak briefly with the key players I'd known would be in attendance. Vega was significantly less ballsy in his approach with me this time, and Maurice had clearly heard about what'd happened because for the first time in a long time he treated me with the respect I deserved.

When the commentator announced that the main event was about to commence, the crowd went wild.

Johnny Rock came out first, jumping around and beating on his chest, playing up for the crowd and generally making me want to nut-punch the arrogant son of a bitch. How in the hell did Hannah have history with this complete clown?

Chase was on his feet with his lackeys, clapping for Johnny, and I spotted the Locked Heart Enterprises logo printed on the fighter's shorts when he shrugged his hoodie off.

This wasn't an official fight, not by a long shot, but we adhered to all the usual safety standards so we could avoid lawsuits, now that Anarchy was operating as a Copper Wolf venue. So it took a few minutes before the referee allowed Johnny into the octagon.

He wasted no time playing up for the crowd, doing flips and shit that made me want to roll my eyes something awful. The cocky little shit even had the audacity to pause in front of our seats and leer at me like I was some Johnny Rock fangirl begging to suck his dick.

I simply shifted in my seat to cross my legs, letting the deep split of my dress fall open and display the deadly sharp blades strapped to my thigh. Then I held his gaze without blinking and let a whole tsunami of violence and death roll through my mind.

He saw it. There was no way he couldn't have. His tanned face paled slightly, and he was quick to move on.

"Fucking idiot," Lucas muttered with a laugh. "Probably thought Zed was Hades."

"Undoubtedly," Zed replied, reclining in his chair and letting one of his arms rest on the back of my seat. "It happens a lot."

The commentator announced Cass next, and he came stomping out of his locker room without any fanfare. No jumping around or fist pumps for the crowd, and the music—I was willing to bet—had been chosen by someone else. I could practically hear Cass saying he didn't give a fuck what song they played.

"Did he give you the Ducati?" Zed asked casually, his fingers trailing over my bare back where no one but Lucas would be able to see the touch. Sneaky shit.

I looked at him from the side of my eye as Cass ran through the safety checks with our referee and climbed into the octagon.

"Yeah, he did."

Zed's light touch brushed down my arm on Lucas's side, and Lucas arched a curious look at the two of us.

"Zed," I murmured, "what do you think you're doing?"

He sat up straighter with a deep inhale, his hand moving to grip the back of my chair as he turned toward me. "Chase's been playing with you, Dare. He's been deliberately sending you messages that remind you of the past, trying to scare you and throw you off your game." His eyes narrowed in determination. "Don't you think it's time we struck back?"

My brows rose slightly, but I didn't offer any more of a reaction than that. Chase was still watching us; I could see him from the corner of my eye.

"I'm with Zed on this," Lucas offered from my other side. "You guys have a shared history, so he's not the only one who can play that game."

I shifted my attention back to Zed. "What did you have in mind, De Rosa?"

His lips hitched in a sly grin. "This."

I should have known. Or rather, I *did* know, but I was so distracted by keeping Chase in my peripheral and maintaining my stone-cold facade and desperately wishing I could lean in to Lucas and show that I was there with him…that I let Zed catch me off guard.

Zed's lips met mine as his hand found the back of my neck, pulling me in toward him as he coaxed my mouth open and teased at my tongue. He didn't kiss me with all the domineering, possessive desire that I could feel pent up in his tense grip, because he knew, like I did, that there were more people watching us than just Chase. And I still had a reputation to maintain.

So I took control, winding his tie around my fist and jerking him to me as I kissed him back, ravaging his mouth and not even remotely faking it.

When I released him a few moments later, our breathing was rough and my usually smudge-proof lipstick was smeared across his lips.

"Last time Chase saw you kissing me," Zed said in a rough voice, "it triggered the beginning of the end for him and his revolting family. I hope this reminds him of that and of everything you're capable of when pushed."

He brushed my cheek with his thumb like he didn't want to stop kissing me despite our point having been made. Then the crowd roared, and a spray of blood from the octagon splattered the side of Zed's face.

I released his tie, jerking my attention up to the fighters in the ring. Cass had Johnny Rock shoved into the cage, blood pouring from the younger fighter's face as Cass landed blow after blow with his eyes locked on mine.

"Shit, Zed," I hissed, "that maybe wasn't the best timing."

Zed snickered, wiping the blood off his face with a fabric handkerchief and cleaning up his lips while he was at it. "Or was it perfect timing? Look how determined he is to murder that little prick now."

Stifling an eye roll, I snatched the handkerchief from him and did my best to clean up my own lipstick smears using one of my knives as a mirror.

Zed leaned in again as I was doing it, brushing his lips over my ear. "Besides, you forgot the new security system in the garage. What did I tell you about riding dick in my house, Dare?"

I froze. Fuck. I *had* forgotten the new security system that I'd personally fucking overseen. I hadn't turned it off after I parked my bike—I'd been in a hurry—and it would have sent camera footage straight to Zed's phone.

Whoops.

Johnny Rock struggled, and Cass released him. The crowd roared and booed, clearly wanting him to end it then and there. But it was only the first round, and I'd politely requested he put on a good show. So now he was playing with his victim, and it was amusing the hell out of me.

Cass had been holding back in his practice sessions with Zed and Alexi. Big time. Johnny Rock wasn't even close to a serious contender against the lethal machine that was Cassiel Saint. I found myself drawn in, totally unable to tear my eyes from the swift, powerful, and damaging strikes Cass delivered to his opponent, and I jittered with excitement through the one-minute breaks between rounds.

After the third round—of five—the referee came over and crouched down in front of us, his fingers holding the cage as he grimaced. "You want me to call an end to this mess, Boss? It's a clear win for the Reaper."

I shook my head, a cruel smile playing across my lips. "No. Let it play out. They're giving a good show." If by *good show* I really meant *violent bloodbath*, then that was the truth.

The referee inclined his head in understanding, then stood back up to call the start of the fourth round. Johnny Rock could barely stand, weaving on his feet as he tried to keep Cass in his sight despite puffy swelling already closing one eye and blood dripping in the other. He was so used to winning that all his arrogance must be taking a worse beating than his face.

"Sending a message?" Lucas asked quietly, and I gave him a small smile.

"You know it," I murmured back. "Chase made it so clear he was sponsoring Johnny... Well, he brought this on himself."

"Can I ask a question?" Lucas whispered, his eyes on the fight like he wasn't even paying attention to me.

I bit back a smile. "You just did." He flicked a sideways glance at me, and I sipped my fresh drink. "Sorry, go ahead." My spine was still straight, my legs crossed and my posture perfect, but I was violently aware of the men on either side of me. It was a whole new form of torture.

"How come it's okay to kiss Zed in public but not me?" He asked the question quietly, not letting anyone overhear, and I didn't sense any real hurt behind his words. He was just genuinely curious about the intricacies of my power dynamic.

I caught Zed's look but didn't acknowledge him as I drew a breath to answer Lucas honestly. "Because you soften me, Lucas. You make me human, and I can't afford to be soft or human right now. Not here, not with Chase watching."

He gave a small nod of understanding and seemed content with that response as he sat back in his seat.

Zed brushed my hair over my shoulder and stroked his fingertip down the back of my neck, teasing. I was going to have to junk punch him when we were alone.

"I don't soften you too?" he murmured.

I snorted a laugh before I could catch myself, then covered it up with a sip of my drink. "You fucking know you don't, asshole." I gave him a long look from the side of my eye. "You strengthen me."

The last round started in the fight ring, and I gave Cass a nod of thanks for dragging it out. The longer a fight lasted, the more money changed hands. It was just smart business.

Cass pounded on the poor fool a while longer, then took him down in a flawless arm bar. Johnny Rock tried to tap out, but the ref hesitated, looking over at me for approval before calling the fight.

I gave a nod, but not before Cass broke Johnny's arm. As the younger fighter howled in pain, I watched Cass lean down, and it wasn't hard to read his lips when he delivered the punch line to the whole painful show.

"That was for Hannah, you piece of shit."

I didn't think it was possible, but somehow I fell even harder for Cass in that moment.

CHAPTER 41

After the fight commentator did his thing announcing the winner—which was entirely unnecessary but protocol, nonetheless—I stood up with the guys to clap politely, joining in on the crowd's deafening screams and cheers. Cass hadn't lied about his popularity in the cage-fight scene; he had a whole lot of fans in attendance. Or hell, maybe he'd just won them over with that brutal, bloody display of violence.

"Hayden," Lucas muttered, touching a hand lightly to the small of my back to get my attention. "Something's going down at Club 22 right now."

I turned to face him with a confused frown. "What do you mean?"

He gave a tiny, subtle nod toward Chase and the Johnny Rock supporters' area. "They're talking about Club 22 right now. I think Chase has something planned while everyone is distracted here."

I didn't question him, just spun to look at Zed, but he was already one step ahead of me with his phone pressed to his ear. Leaving him to contact the manager of Club 22, I searched the crowd for Alexi and jerked my head at him when he caught my eye.

He hurried over with Rixby at his side, and I deliberately

turned my back on Chase as I barked my orders. "Take a team and get over to Club 22 *right now.*"

The two of them nodded, and Alexi frowned. "What are we looking for, Boss?"

"We're not sure yet," I admitted. "We'll call when we know more, but for now just get over there and be ready for anything."

Alexi didn't need to hear any more than that and took off with Rixby in tow as they rounded up a crew.

I turned to Zed with a raised brow, and he gave me a shrug as he spoke to Rodney, the bar manager.

"Let's get over there," I said to Lucas.

He gave a curt nod, then waved over one of the Anarchy waiters. "Hey, man, we need you to go tell Cassiel Saint that the after-party is at Club 22. Can you do that for us?"

The waiter's eyes flicked to me, and then he bobbed his head and headed off in the direction of the lockers.

"Smart thinking," I murmured, and Lucas flashed me a wide smile.

The three of us made our way toward the exit but didn't rush. Whatever Chase was planning, we didn't want to give him any indication that we were on to him. Complacency was key.

"Leaving already, Darling?" he called out as we passed near the Johnny Rock seating area.

I flashed him a dazzling smile. "You know how much a good bloodbath turns me on, sweetheart. I simply can't wait to get Zed home."

Zed played it up right on cue, wrapping his arm around my waist and kissing my cheek—and totally ignoring Chase—as we continued oh-so-casually departing the fight arena.

The second we made it outside, though, we were all business once more and increased our pace to get out to the parking lot as quickly as possible without actually running.

I'd driven Zed's Audi over, so the three of us slid into that to drive over to Club 22. We were about five minutes away when Zed's phone rang again.

He flicked it onto Speaker, and Rodney's voice filled the car.

"Boss, you were right. One of the VIP girls just killed herself in front of a customer." His tone was gruff and haunted. "He reported she was acting real weird beforehand, too, screaming and talking to herself and shit."

"Hallucinating?" Zed asked, his voice tight with anger.

"Sounds like it," Rodney replied. "Then she grabbed a knife from somewhere and stabbed herself in the throat while she was riding her customer. It's a hell of a mess."

"Alexi should be arriving any second," I snapped. "Get his guys on cleanup."

"Understood, sir," Rodney replied.

I gave a frustrated grimace. "Tell him to be *fast*. This is a setup. I'm guessing you've already shut the club down and are clearing out patrons?"

"Yes, sir," he replied. "Want me to send the staff home too?"

"No," Zed replied for me, "keep them. Start running a thorough search for drugs on the venue too. Dispose of anything you find, no matter how small."

"Got it," Rodney acknowledged.

Zed ended the call, then shifted in his seat to frown at Lucas. "How'd you know?"

Lucas just shrugged, meeting my eyes in the rearview mirror when I glanced up. "I can lip-read."

I arched a brow. Somehow I got the feeling he didn't just mean occasionally make out short phrases someone was saying when you already had a good idea of the subject, like I'd just done with Cass at the end of his fight. Lucas meant he could actually lip-read, and I was willing to bet his uncle had been the one to teach him.

"Of course you can," Zed muttered, shaking his head. He turned back to his phone and dialed Alexi.

"Just arrived," Alexi said on answering.

"Body cleanup," Zed replied. "Rodney's waiting for you."

"Understood," Alexi replied, ending the call.

I glanced at Lucas in the mirror again, briefly though, given how fast I was driving. "Did you pick up anything else?"

Lucas shook his head. "Not really. I hadn't been paying attention, but then I caught 'Club 22.' The guy who sat beside Chase said that the job was underway. Then Chase replied, saying to wait for confirmation before calling in a tip."

Zed ran a hand over his face. "All right, we might have time."

Just in case, though, I pressed my foot closer to the floor and got us to Club 22 just a few minutes later.

To my relief, there were no flashing lights of cop cars in the parking lot, and the three of us hurried inside to figure out what was what. I was pleased to find all the patrons already cleared out, leaving just staff, who sat in a group on the side of the stage while Alexi's team and the Club 22 security guards swept the venue for hidden drugs.

"All okay here?" I asked Maxine when I spotted her sitting with the other staff.

She gave me a sharp nod, but her face was pale and drawn. "Yes, Boss. Rodney is upstairs with Alexi and..." Her voice cracked and broke, but she swallowed and composed herself quickly. "And Jessie."

Jessie must have been the girl who'd killed herself.

"Thanks, Maxine. This is Lucas," I told her, indicating for him to step forward. "He's recently joined upper management." And by that, I meant Zed and me. We were "upper management" when gang terminology wasn't appropriate. Which was often.

"Nice to meet you, Maxine," Lucas said, offering his hand for her to shake.

"Maxine, I want you to tell Lucas everything that happened just now, okay? Literally everything you can think of, including if

anyone saw Jessie acting strange tonight. Can you do that for me?"
I gave her a tight smile, trying to be reassuring, and she jerked a
nod back.

"Yes, Boss," she replied in a small voice. "I can do that."

I touched my hand to Lucas's arm, and he gave me a confident
look in return. His people skills were off-the-charts good, so if
anyone could get the shaken strippers to open up about what they'd
seen, it'd be him. With a small sigh, I left Lucas there and headed
upstairs to where Zed had already disappeared.

A couple of guys from Alexi's team passed me on the stairs,
giving polite greetings but not slowing down as they carried large
plastic tubs out—no doubt the remains of Jessie. Fucking hell.

Zed and Rodney were at the far end of the VIP corridor, where
the brothel operated, and a bound-and-gagged man in boxer shorts
crouched on the floor at their feet. Inside the room nearest to them,
Alexi's team was hard at work ripping out bloodstained carpets and
scrubbing splatter from the wall with peroxide. The bedsheets had
already been stripped, and thanks to the waterproof mattress pro-
tectors we used in our VIP rooms, the bed itself was pristine.

"Good work, Alexi," I commented, running my eyes over the
surfaces, then checking the time on my phone. "Get the evidence
well away from here."

"On it, Boss," he replied, hefting a roll of ruined carpet over
his shoulder and leaving the room.

"Where do you want this guy?" Rodney asked, nudging the
near-naked man with his toe. Blood coated a large portion of his
upper body and face, and he looked like he was about three seconds
from pissing himself.

"Basement," I decided. "Secure him there until we can deal
with this, then we can find out what he knows." Even if he had
nothing to do with Jessie being drugged, he didn't stop fucking her
when she was screaming and hallucinating, so he deserved what
he had coming.

Zed hauled the guy up and dragged him along to a staff staircase at the back of the corridor while I turned to Rodney with a sigh.

"We anticipate cops here any second," I told him. "Head back downstairs and give your staff a quick briefing. Let them know that if anyone utters a word about this, they'll be answering to me. Personally."

"Understood," he responded and departed to do what I'd ordered.

I turned back to the cleaning crew in the bedroom and watched them work for a couple of moments. "Get some sheets back on that bed and set the room up as normal," I told them as they packed up their supplies. "Then get out of here."

They silently did as they were told, and I tapped out a quick text to all the gang leaders under my rule. Given so many of them had been at the fight, it shouldn't be a hard task to call them into an emergency meeting tonight. Ezekiel might not be able to attend, and Archer definitely couldn't, but I could conference call both of them in.

Alexi's team finished up and pulled out of the parking lot all of three seconds before two SGPD cop cars pulled in with lights and sirens on and an unmarked car behind them. FBI, I'd be willing to bet. The agent they'd had tailing me all week was laughably incompetent, and I'd ditched him earlier in the day. But at a glance through the club's window, it looked like his car.

I passed Alexi on my way down to the main floor and told him to wait for me in the basement and keep our guest quiet until the cops had gone.

He gave me a grim smile in return. "Yes, sir."

When the cops entered my club, I bit my cheek to keep my expression cool and neutral. It was Lieutenant Jeffries again with a couple of less familiar faces, and he looked like he wanted to be anywhere but here.

"Hades." He greeted me with a grimace. "This is a surprise. We heard you had a big event over at Anarchy tonight."

I pursed my lips, my arms loosely linked under my breasts and my index finger tapping my forearm. "I just bet you did. I found the need to visit some of my other venues tonight. What can I do for you?"

He cleared his throat. "We've had another anonymous tip."

I said nothing, letting the stupidity of that sentence hang in the air between us, and watched Lieutenant Jeffries sweat on it.

"I have to do my job, Hades," he told me with an edge of frustration.

I raised one brow. "And what does your job require you to do this evening, Jeffries? I seriously doubt you have the required paperwork to conduct another drug search of my club." I was playing dumb because I'd be an idiot to do anything else.

"We've had a report of a murder here," he told me, his expression tight. "Eyewitness says one of your, ah, dancers was stabbed to death."

"Eyewitness, huh?" My sarcasm was heavy. "Same witness who tipped you off about planted drugs at Pink Panther, I'd bet." But I stepped aside, inviting him further into the club nonetheless. "You're welcome to come in anyway. You'll see for yourself that there are no dead strippers here."

One of the other cops sneered in my direction. "You've probably already cleaned the scene."

Lieutenant Jeffries cringed like he was imagining throttling his officer, but I just gave a polite smile in return. "That would be awfully proactive of me. When did this tip come through?"

"Ten minutes ago," Jeffries replied, shooting a death glare at his officer. "I don't think even Hades can clean a stabbing murder in ten minutes, Dickson."

I quirked a brow at *Dickson* and filed his face in my brain for later. That was a dirty cop if I'd ever seen one and on Chase's payroll

I'd bet. And Jeffries was entirely right, ten minutes would have been a pinch. Fifteen, though? With a solid head start prior to the crime? Yeah, that was doable. Just.

"We've got nothing to hide, Jeffries. See for yourself. But we are in the middle of a staff meeting so I'd ask you to be quick."

The lieutenant assured me they'd be quick, and his cops scattered through the venue, searching for a murdered girl who was currently on her way to be dissolved in acid well away from Timberwolf territory.

It only took them ten minutes before an embarrassed-looking Lieutenant Jeffries returned to me with his hat in hand. "Hades, I apologize for the intrusion. Again. I hope you understand I—"

"Need to do your job. Yes, I understand. As do I." I kept my expression neutral and let him draw his own conclusions from that.

The cops cleared out, and I gave Rodney the go-ahead to send his staff home. I had a meeting to conduct, and none of my legit staff needed to get mixed up in that crowd.

"I'll stay on," Rodney offered. "You look like you could use a drink."

That was an understatement. In the wake of the cops departing, and with the FBI douche still parked outside with his crappy little binoculars, I was ready to collapse from stress.

But falling to pieces was a luxury I couldn't afford, so I accepted his offer of a drink and ordered one for Lucas and Zed while I was at it.

Cass arrived not long after the staff had left, his jaw tight and his eyes blazing with anger as he looked around the empty club.

"What fucking happened?" he demanded.

Zed gave him a sharp headshake, and I slid off my barstool. "Cass, follow me. We can speak privately."

I trusted Rodney, to a point. But as Chase had proven time and time again, he was awfully good at flipping loyalties, and I wasn't going to take chances. So I led the way out of the main bar and through to a private lap-dance room down a short corridor. Cass followed me inside, and I jerked the heavy velvet curtain shut before falling into his arms.

He grabbed on to me, understanding what I needed without being told. His mouth found mine, his lips caressing me and easing the heavy tension on my mind as his arms banded tight around me and took my feet off the floor.

Eventually, though, he lowered me back to the carpet and released my lips with a heavy sigh. "I could have fucking murdered Zed for that kiss during my fight," he growled, anger and frustration shining bright in his eyes.

I smiled. "I'm pretty sure that's the reaction he wanted." I wrinkled my nose. "I forgot to turn the security system off in the garage earlier."

Cass's scarred brow twitched, then his lips curled in a smug smile. "Good."

I rolled my eyes. Cass and Zed were giving me whiplash with how fast they switched from bromance to petty jealousy. "Whatever. We have bigger issues tonight."

Cass's expression sobered. "I saw the meeting invitation."

I gave a sigh. "Yep. It needs to happen. Chase tried to frame someone for a murder here tonight. Sounds like one of the girls was overdosing on PCP and stabbed herself to death while fucking a client. I'd be willing to bet that, somehow, the knife has the fingerprints of one of our staff on it and that the customer would have conveniently disappeared after leaving here."

Cass grimaced. "Creative."

I rubbed my eyes. "It's starting to give me a migraine."

"Boss," Zed called from outside the curtain, "Vega just arrived. I'll take him downstairs."

"Thanks," I called back, then gave Cass a pained look. "I guess it's time for business. You got Roach coming?"

He jerked a nod. "Yeah, he should be here soon."

339

I reached for the curtain, but he stopped me with a hand on my wrist. With a deep frown, he pulled me back into his embrace and tilted my chin up so our eyes could meet.

"Before we leave this room, I need to be perfectly fucking clear with you about something." His voice was low and rough, barely above a whisper. "I said it in my letter, but I need to say it again, aloud, to make sure you believe it." His rough hand cupped my face, and his nose brushed mine. "I love you, Red."

My heart raced, my pulse fluttering uncomfortably fast, and I swallowed heavily. "Don't give me that end-of-the-world crap, Saint. I've got this shit handled."

But I still closed the gap between us, kissing him with all the emotion I was too stubborn and too broken to convey in words. Then I peeled myself out of his grip and jerked the curtain open. I had a meeting to conduct and yet another message to send to Chase *fucking* Lockhart.

Cass shadowed me out to the main bar, then murmured something about waiting for Roach while I headed for the basement.

"Lucas," I called out. "You coming?"

He looked over at me from where he'd been waiting at the bar. "Am I allowed to come?"

I gave him a small smile. "You're upper management now. We can sort out your Timberwolf tattoo another day." I flashed a quick wink at Cass, seeing as he was the best tattoo artist in Shadow Grove.

Lucas grinned way too hard at that and hurried to catch up with me as I headed down to the basement level. Zed was already down there, his shirtsleeves rolled up to the elbows, his tie gone, and extra guns on display. Vega and his new second, Diego, were at the long banquet table in the wine cellar, and someone had already set up a Zoom call with both Ezekiel and Archer.

I entered the room and gave a tight smile to everyone. "Gentlemen, thanks for joining me this evening. We're just waiting on the Reapers and Vipers, and then we'll get down to business. I'll keep it quick. I know you all have better things to be doing tonight."

I looked around for Alexi, then waved at him to join us at the table as well. "Alexi, sit in on this."

"Who's your new friend, Hades?" Ezekiel asked, staring at Lucas with far too much interest.

Zed answered for me, though. "Shut the fuck up, Ezekiel," he barked. "If Hades wanted to introduce him, she'd have done it."

Amusement rippled through me, and I turned a cold smile to the laptop camera. "He's mine, Zeke. That's all you need to know."

Goddamn Lucas and his gorgeous face were going to give me gray hairs if he kept attracting attention from dangerous parties because I could and *would* slaughter the next person who laid unwanted hands on him. He was mine, and I was more than capable of defending that claim.

"Understood, sir," Ezekiel replied, holding his hands up defensively. "No offense intended."

Archer, on the other side of the screen, just shook his head in disgust.

A moment later Cass entered the room with his second, Roach. He took a seat across the table from me, and a minute later Maurice arrived with his own second in tow.

"Excellent fight tonight, Cass," Maurice commented as he sat down at the table. "You won me some pretty money."

Cass just glared in response, and I sensed Lucas fighting a laugh.

I let silence build the tension for a moment, then drew a breath. "Thank you all for attending on short notice. We've had an incident here tonight that I feel needs to be addressed. First and foremost, I think it's pertinent to inform you who is responsible for the recent disruptions to our business." I paused, letting my gaze trail over each and every man in attendance. "Chase Lockhart is back from the dead and waging a twisted little war on me. You're all pawns on the board, so sharpen up or you'll be knocked over."

Stunned silence met my announcement, so I continued.

"As I think most of you are aware, angel dust was the Lockhart family trade, and that's what he's been using to make his presence known within the Timberwolf territory. I understand from speaking to several of you in the last week that you've been having more incidents of PCP on your streets and in your communities. Has anyone traced the supply chain for me yet?"

More silence. Archer—calling in from Demi's house in Italy—looked shell-shocked at my news, and Cass was a goddamn statue across from me, his gaze locked on the wood grain of the tabletop.

"No one?" I prompted, looking at Vega and Maurice, even sparing a glance at Ezekiel, despite him being so far removed from Shadow Grove. "No one can tell me how the drugs are being distributed in our zones?"

Footsteps echoed down the stairs, and then an uninvited party entered the wine cellar. "Oh, pick me," Chase suggested, his grin wide and smug. "I know."

Fury burned through me. The temptation to shoot him was so high, but he'd more than proven he wouldn't make it so easy. He survived the first time I'd thought I killed him, and he'd have put considerably more contingencies in place to royally fuck me over if I tried again now.

A muttered curse came from the laptop screen, and Chase ducked down to peer at the display. "Oh, hello, Baby D'Ath. Zeke. It's been too long, don't you think?"

"Chase," I said with an irritated sigh. "This is a closed meeting. You weren't invited."

He shrugged. "Whoops. I might have let myself in by shooting your guard upstairs. My bad." He gave another unhinged grin. "But don't you want to know who's been peddling my dirty drugs in your streets, Darling? You know I couldn't possibly have set up that much of a network under your nose. You know I had to have help from someone in this very room, especially since you wiped out the Wraiths." He clucked his tongue, mocking me.

I ground my teeth together, biting back all the violent curses sitting on the tip of my tongue. Then the words dried up entirely with Chase's next confession.

"Good thing the Reapers stepped up to the plate, huh? Where would I be without your help, Cassiel Saint?"

My whole body stiffened, ice forming down my spine, and my chest ached like I'd just been stabbed. Cass slowly raised his eyes from the table, meeting mine with pain and guilt etched across his features.

"Bullshit," Archer scoffed from the video call. "Cass would never—"

"Actually, sir," Alexi spoke up, "the douche from upstairs started talking already. He said it was a guy with a Reaper tat that gave him the drugs Jessie took."

Chase's grin was so wide it was practically climbing off his face. "Uh-oh. Do I smell trouble in paradise, Darling? You and Saint were fucking recently, weren't you?" He gave a low chuckle, his one-eyed gaze darting between Cass and me with glee. "Well, this is awkward."

I drew a couple of deep breaths, desperately searching for my strength, frantically clinging to my steel walls and neutral expression, but I could feel it slipping.

"Cass," I started, then stopped myself when I heard how raw my voice was. Shit. *Shit.*

His eyes were dark as he stared back at me, his frown drawn deep, and his hands balled into fists on the table. Instead of denying the accusation, he just shook his head.

"I'm sorry, Red," he croaked, resigned to his fate.

No one else in the room spoke. They all knew what happened when someone crossed me. They'd seen it before.

My mouth was bone dry, but I needed to swallow the lump of emotion choking my throat. I could scarcely breathe for fear of losing my shit all over the place, so I just closed my eyes in a drawn-out blink, blocking Cass's tortured face from my gaze.

I extended my hand to Zed, silently asking for his gun, but he didn't give it to me.

"Zed," I snapped, glaring at him.

He just shook his head. "Don't do this," he told me in a quiet voice. "Chase is lying. He's *always* lying. At least investigate this first."

"He's not," Cass spoke up, his rough voice full of regret.

Roach's eyes bugged out, staring at his leader in horror and silently shaking his head with denial. I noted that and ground my teeth together. I had to handle this just like I'd handle any other betrayal of this scale.

"Roach," I barked, "you've got one chance and one chance only to tell me the truth."

The young gangster gaped at me like a fish for a moment, then frantically shook his head. "I had no idea, Hades, sir. None. I swear to you—"

"He wasn't involved," Cass interrupted. "This was all me."

I turned my attention back to Zed, ignoring Chase still standing in the doorway like a kid waiting for Christmas. He'd get what was coming to him, sooner or later, but tonight he had the upper hand.

"Give me your gun, Zed," I ordered, hardening myself against the pleading in his eyes.

When he didn't move to hand it over, I reached down and pulled one directly from the holster at his hip. He didn't stop me, but he turned his gaze away in clear disgust.

"Hayden, don't," Lucas muttered beside me. "Don't do this. You'll regret it forever."

But that's where he was wrong. I never regretted killing those who betrayed me. So I raised the gun, aimed it straight at Cass across the table from me, and fired three shots as he mouthed the words *I love you*.

His body jerked backward, tumbling out of the chair and smashing several bottles of wine behind where he'd sat. For a long moment, no one moved. No one spoke. I didn't even breathe. Then Chase started clapping and laughing.

"Get out!" I roared, slamming the gun down on the table. "All of you. *Out.*"

The stunned gang leaders all did as they were told, murmuring polite thanks as they hurried out of the wine cellar. Vega and Diego needed to step over Cass's body and the mess of blood and wine all over the floor.

Eventually, it was just Zed and Lucas left with me. And Chase. The sick fuck sauntered over to Cass's body and crouched down to dip his fingers in the spilled wine mixed with blood.

"Well, this was entertaining," he commented, wiping his bloody fingers on his shirt as he straightened up once more. "One down, two to go."

CASS'S LETTER

Red,

You told me tonight to write you a love letter. I'm at least eighty percent sure you were joking, but whatever. Here it fucking is. I'm not great with words. You already know this though. So, I dunno. This might take me a while to write. Hopefully you won't shoot me in frustration before I even finish, but with you...who knows?

I like that about you, though. How fierce you are, and how you don't put up with anyone's bullshit. Fucking no one scares you and that impresses the hell outta me. I'm gonna be honest with you, Red. I don't have the first fucking clue how to write a woman a love letter. Let alone a woman like you. So I hope you'll excuse the lack of structure and prose and see this for what it is. Everything I wanna say out loud, but can't. Everything that rattles around in my brain when I look at you, but can't seem to make the words leave my mouth.

Fuck, you're beautiful. It's almost painful to look at you and not touch you, not grab you and—

7th Circle exploded today, and for a heartbeat, I thought you were dead. And I thought my whole world was crumbling around me, like my soul had been ripped clean out of my body. Then I remembered who the fuck you are. You're Hades, for fuck's sake. No one can kill you so easily. You're one step away from inhuman, at least in my eyes.

Roses are bloody, I've been blue, you're a goddess and I want to fuck you.

Just two kisses and you've left a permanent stain on my soul, Angel.

I love when you challenge me. We harmonize, like a filthy symphony.

Sometimes, I swear to fuck, Red, sometimes I want to throttle you. You're infuriating! The guilt you're carrying tonight after finding Lucas in such a state made me want to bundle you up in my arms and just let you fucking break for five goddamn seconds. But we're not in a good place yet. You'd never let me offer that sort of support. More to the point, you'd never let yourself break. Not with me, not even with Zed, I'd bet. You're carrying too damn much, though, and sooner or later it's going to crush you if you don't accept help from those who care about you.

I hope you know that I'm one of those people. I want to be the one you turn to when it all gets to be too much. I want to shoulder that weight and offer you a fucking break. You've already dealt with so much.

You made a flippant comment tonight at the hospital about me writing this letter, and it almost made me laugh. You really didn't think I'd do it, and that tells me you've got no idea how obsessed I am with you. Everything about you. You've consumed my thoughts for five fucking years, Red. Since the moment I met you, no woman has been able to compare. They were all simply placeholders for the real thing. You.

Here's the thing, though. I never thought we would ever get to this point. I figured that picturing you in my mind while I fucked some random faceless chicks with red hair would be the best I could ever get.

Words can't express how glad I am to be wrong. I feel like I owe you an explanation, though, for why I pushed you away when you made your move.

In short, you shocked the crap outta me. I don't know why I was so surprised. You aren't exactly the type of woman to sit around and wait for a man to sweep her off her feet. But...is it selfish to wish that I had done that for you?

So, yeah, I handled it badly. I pushed you away because I panicked. You're the woman I've literally dreamed about, and suddenly you were within reach. Problem was I knew—still know— that I'm bad for you. And you deserve better, so I tried to push you away. Look how that turned out, huh? I was totally kidding myself. You're the brightest flame on earth and I'm nothing more than a moth.

I'm bad for you, Red. So fucking bad. I'm damaged, emotionally unavailable, cruel, reckless, and selfish. You deserve so much fucking better. You deserve that fucking stripper. Lucas. He's everything I'm not, and everything that would be good for you. And yet, I can't seem to stay away. So here I am, writing a fucking love letter like a lovesick teen.

Love. Fucking hell. Pretty safe to say that's not an emotion I'd ever thought to feel again. I thought that part of my soul had curled up and died a long damn time ago. I thought all I felt for you was obsession, infatuation...lust. But I was wrong. It took these last few weeks for me to see that. It wasn't until you so rightfully rejected my apology at Anarchy to make it finally sink in.

I love you, Red. And if it takes me another five years to make you see that, for you to forgive my insane behavior, then so be it. I'm not going anywhere, and I'm not giving up.

Almost every damn night, you're in my dreams. I can't wait to get my hands on you properly. Those few kisses have only made me desperate for more, made my fantasies about you so much more graphic and real.

I dream about all the ways I want to fuck you. How tight and hot your cunt will be around my cock, how sweet your moans will be in my ears, and the salty taste of your sweat on my tongue as I bite your neck.

You know what you're getting into with me. I can see it in your eyes. You want it rough, and that's exactly how it'll be. I've thought long and hard about wrapping that gorgeous red hair around my fist, holding you captive as I fuck your ass. Every time you wet your lips, I picture them wrapped around my cock as you swallow me deep, choking on my cum as that sinful eye makeup stains your cheeks. I want to taste your pussy, and make you scream my name as you come all over my face. I want your thighs to grab my head so tight I suffocate in your sweet cunt and drown in your juices.

Red, I want to make you scream until you're hoarse, I want your legs to shake so bad you can't walk, and I want to see those perfect tits heaving as you struggle to catch your breath.

There are so many things I want to do to you, with you, for you…but instead of writing it all down, I'd much rather play it all out in person.

Zed just called and asked me to come over to his place. You must be in pain if he's turning to me for help. Yet somehow I can't help but feel glad. Because even though you're hurting, it's giving me an excuse to get closer—and trust me, Angel, I won't back down again. I'll give you this letter tonight and hopefully you'll give me another chance.

If not, I'll just write another. And another. And another. One day, maybe you'll believe me when I say how much I love you and will always love you.

So, fuck it. When you dream of me, make it rough. I can't wait to make it a reality, then hold you afterwards. Hold you forever.

—Cass

349

READ ON FOR A SNEAK PEEK OF THE NEXT BOOK IN THE HADES SERIES

CHAPTER 1
CASS

Two Months Ago...

Irritation rippled through me as I glanced down at my watch. I'd been lurking around the bar for way too long already, yet she still hadn't emerged from her office. *Was she okay in there?*

As soon as the thought crossed my mind, I shook it away. Of course she was okay. She was *Hades*, more than fucking capable of handling herself if a bunch of mouthy upstarts wanted to test her dominance.

I glanced at my watch again. Shit. Not even a minute since the last time I checked it.

"Can I get you another drink, Cass?" the pretty young bartender, Sara, asked me with a heavy bat of her false lashes. She knew she wasn't my type, but that didn't stop her flirting.

I shook my head, declining, then finished the last mouthful of my beer. I'd hung around long enough that I was starting to draw attention, and that sure as fuck wasn't going to do me any favors. And for what? To feed my sick obsession with seeing a woman too guarded, too beautiful, and too damn untouchable to ever be mine.

With a self-disgusted grunt, I slid off my barstool with every intention of leaving the club. Yet, as if on autopilot, my feet carried me toward the narrow staircase that would lead up to the mezzanine level where I knew Hades kept her office. Where I'd caught a flash of her blazing red hair disappear hours ago with a handful of Timberwolf enforcers trailing behind like naughty puppies.

"Boss is in a meeting," the stern-faced, muscle-bound Timberwolf bouncer announced as he stepped in front of me before I reached the first step. "Doesn't wanna be disturbed."

I narrowed my eyes, picturing my fist slamming into this steroid-pumped fucker's face. Vividly imagining the way his cartilage would crunch under my knuckles and the hot, wet spray of blood from his nose. But shit, he was just doing his job. So I rubbed a hand over my jaw, thinking, then gave a small nod of understanding.

"I'll swing back later, then." Even though I really shouldn't. I had no good reason to request a face-to-face with Hades. None. Except that I just wanted to *see* her. It felt like I hadn't seen her in weeks, even though we'd interacted in a professional capacity plenty. It was different under the eyes of rivals, though. I couldn't just *watch* her like I'd grown so addicted to doing—not with that punk-ass bitch Skate watching my every move.

Reluctantly, I forced myself to turn away, but the bouncer called out again.

"Hold up, Reaper." His gruff voice made me pause and tilt my head back toward him. His finger was to his ear, holding his radio earpiece in place as he listened to something. Then he raised the microphone attached to the wire and muttered a few words into it before flicking his gaze up to mine. "Boss said to send you up. She just finished her meeting."

This was undoubtedly a bad idea, but I just brushed past him and started up the stairs, nonetheless. Fuck me, I needed to turn around, walk out of the damn club, and call up a sure thing to fuck away all this godforsaken tension. But no. No, I just had to torture myself further.

The Timberwolf enforcers passed me in the short corridor that housed the administration offices, and none of their gazes were friendly. Hell, they were downright hostile, but it didn't faze me in the least. There was only one person in the state who intimidated me, and it was none of these testosterone-soaked bastards.

A second after I passed them, they were gone from my mind as I spotted the door to Hades's office slightly ajar. Goddamn if my pulse didn't kick up a gear.

Still, I kept my expression neutral and my posture relaxed. No matter how badly I wanted to do filthy things to the woman in that office, she was still a threat. I'd seen what she was capable of when pushed and knew better than to underestimate her. So I paused and tapped politely at her door to announce myself.

Her eyes swept up slowly, clearly having already known I was there before I knocked, and her gaze was as unreadable as ever when it met mine.

"Cass," she said in that hard-edged voice of hers. I ached to hear her speak to me without the carefully built fortress guarding her every fucking thought. "I didn't know we had a meeting planned."

Neither did I, and yet here I am.

I just gave a casual shrug and took a few more steps into the office, glancing around for her shadow. "Where's Zed at?"

Her brow twitched with something faintly resembling irritation. "Did you come here to see me or him? My time is money, Cassiel, and you're wasting it."

Not exactly the response I'd quietly been hoping for, given I'd just sat at the fucking bar amidst a crowd of Gatsby-styled drinkers, desperate to get my fix of my worst obsession. But also not unexpected. I folded my arms over my chest, wishing like hell she'd check me out like her bartender had been a few minutes ago.

"I was in the area taking care of business," I lied. "Figured I'd stop by and tell you the boys at Rex's are expecting Seph's car tomorrow. They'll get it fixed up and dropped back to you before school on Monday morning."

Yes, I could have told her this by text message. But then I wouldn't have a fresh image of her in my mind while cramming my dick down some random gang whore's throat later. I knew how fucked up that was, but so what? I never claimed to be a fucking choirboy.

"Is that all?" she asked, her eyes narrowing with suspicion. I liked to lie to myself and pretend she was too young for me, but it was the weakest of lies. It only took one look into her eyes to see she'd dealt with more in her twenty-three years than most seasoned mob bosses would see in their entire lives. She'd dived headfirst into the gauntlet of fire and come out harder than titanium.

I searched my brain for another excuse for why I was there, *any* excuse, but came up blank. *Fuck.* Now she was staring at me even harder, and it was making sweat form on my spine. How? How could she have that effect on me?

"Yeah," I muttered, still with nothing to fucking say but bluffing like a poker champ, "some prick tried to slash the tires on Zed's Ferrari on my way in. I scared him off, but he had that Wraith look about him." I gave a shrug. "Maybe look into it. Skate's been acting shadier than usual."

Hades continued to stare at me for a long moment, her eyes still totally unreadable as her fingernails tapped a rhythm on the side of her crystal tumbler. I hadn't even noticed when I'd walked in, but there was barely a mouthful left in her glass and the bottle sitting on her desk was less than half-full. Was she drunk?

"Cass, why do I get the feeling those *aren't* the reasons you came in here tonight?" she asked, tilting her head to the side. A faint smile touched her scarlet lips, and my chest tightened. She wasn't drunk—her gaze was far too steady and clear—but shit, she was probably on her way.

Desperate not to let my thoughts play out over my expression, I swiped a hand over my face and broke eye contact with her. This had been a bad fucking idea. But she almost always had Zed lurking somewhere nearby, unknowingly keeping me in check and reminding me that she already *had* someone. Someone with a hell of a lot less damage than me. I hadn't realized how fucking *tempting* it would be to make a move when we were alone.

"I should head out," I muttered, not answering her question. But I didn't leave.

She pushed her chair back from the desk and stood, making me freeze to the spot. Fucking hell, she was gorgeous. Her tight jeans hugged her legs in a way that made me envious of the goddamn denim. I was jealous of *fabric*. Christ, I needed an intervention.

A couple of steps carried her around the desk, and I needed to swallow heavily at the picture she painted in those sexy-as-fuck heels and the huge gun strapped under her arm right beside her breast.

"What are you doing tonight, Cass?" she asked, stepping right into my personal space so I needed to look down to meet her eyes. Fuck, she was short, even in those heels. My hands *itched* to grab her by the waist and shove her against the wall while I impaled her sweet cunt on my dick. If I thought for a second she wouldn't put a bullet in me for that, I'd have done it by now.

I gave a small frown in response. "Uh, Reaper shit," I grunted. "Why?"

Her left shoulder rose and fell in a slight shrug. "I've had a crappy day and could use some company tonight."

What...the fuck? Is she hitting on me?

Dumbstruck, I just blinked at her in confusion. Then she bit her lower lip and her usually hard gaze heated and I was a fucking dead man. My dick strained against my jeans, and my pulse raced like I was a prepubescent boy about to be kissed for the first time.

"Hades..." I murmured, trying and failing to keep the ache of longing out of my voice. But *shit*. Was I on a trip? Nah, not possible. I hadn't even smoked tonight, and unless someone had drugged my beer, there was no way I was imagining this. Was there?

She drew a noticeable breath, then reached up to place a hand on the back of my neck. The shock of her fingers against my skin was like a lightning strike, and I could barely breathe when she leaned in closer.

Fate was never so kind to me, though. The second I made the decision to kiss her, the false wall panel behind her slid silently open, and Zed met my eyes with a threatening glare, his hand resting casually on the butt of his rifle. A split second before Hades's lips met mine, I turned away, and her kiss seared a hot brand against my cheek instead.

"Sorry," I grunted as my stained soul screamed in agony. "I've got shit to do."

Anger and embarrassment flashed across her beautiful face as she stepped back, but it was gone in an instant as her signature hardness returned. "I guess I misread the way you were just eye-fucking my mouth then, huh?"

I swallowed heavily, hating myself already. But Zed's presence was the last nail in this coffin. She deserved better than my broken bullshit. Better to squash the spark now before it burned either one of us.

"Yeah," I muttered. "You did. I don't fuck children."

It was a phrase I used so damn often when Shadow Grove's college girls came sniffing around, searching for a taste of the dark side, so it just fell from my lips before I could even consider the consequences. But I *instantly* regretted it when her eyes widened and her body flinched like I'd physically struck her.

Fuck. *Fuck.* What had I just done?

Too late now, though. So I jerked my head to Zed in acknowledgment and stomped my moody shit out of the office, out of the bar, and straight across to my bike. I needed to get the fuck out of there before I finally broke and begged for forgiveness at her feet. What a fucking mess.

I didn't look back once as I kicked my engine over and roared out of the parking lot, but I had to stop at a traffic light two blocks away. A sleek black Ferrari pulled up beside me as I waited for the light to change, and fury rippled through my whole damn body.

"Fuck off, De Rosa," I snarled, barely even glancing over at the driver, who'd rolled his window down.

Still, I could see enough of him to know he was smirking at me in *victory*. Son of a motherfucking whore. If I wasn't afraid of the backlash from Hades, I'd have kicked his head in by now.

"She's out of your league, Saint," he replied, but his voice lacked the mockery I was expecting. It made me turn to inspect him closer, and I found nothing but bitter regret on his face.

I huffed. "No shit. Yours too."

Zed didn't argue. He just jerked a nod. "I know."

The light changed to green, and we both peeled out in opposite directions without another word. Zed seemed to be heading toward 7th Circle, and I was on a mission to get fucked up and fucked. Anything to make me forget the monumental mistake I'd just made with the one woman who haunted my dreams day and night.

Shit. I really was a fuckup.

AUTHOR'S NOTE

Just two days after writing the ending of this book, I found out that the model who originally inspired Cass, Chris Kash, has died very unexpectedly. In a touching message from his family, we know that on his death, he donated his organs and ultimately saved three lives in doing so.

His loss is a huge blow to the people who knew him, but also to the book world as he was such a prolific and recognizable face on so many romance covers. His final act of kindness in saving those three lives with his organ donation is unquestionably true to Cass's character, so I couldn't be more proud and grateful to have Chris on the original cover for *Club 22*. In my mind, he will always be Cassiel Saint.

My heart goes out to his family and his beautiful wife. I simply can't imagine the pain they're going through.

ABOUT THE AUTHOR

Tate James is a *USA Today* bestselling author of contemporary romance and romantic suspense, with occasional forays into fantasy, paranormal romance, and urban fantasy. She was born and raised in Aotearoa (New Zealand) but now lives in Australia with her husband and their adorable crotchfruit.

She is a lover of books, booze, cats, and coffee, and is most definitely not a morning person. Tate is a bit too sarcastic, swears far too much for polite society, and definitely tells too many dirty jokes.

Website: tatejamesauthor.com
Facebook: tatejamesauthor
Instagram: @tatejamesauthor
TikTok: @tatejamesauthor
Pinterest: @tatejamesauthor
Mailing list: eepurl.com/dfFR5v